UGLIES
Cutters

ALSO BY SCOTT WESTERFELD

Uglies
Pretties
Specials
Extras
Bogus to Bubbly: An Insider's Guide to the World of Uglies

UGLIES
Cutters

Created by
SCOTT WESTERFELD

Written by
SCOTT WESTERFELD and DEVIN GRAYSON

Illustrations by
STEVEN CUMMINGS

Ballantine Books DEL REY New York

Uglies: Cutters is a work of fiction. Names, characters, places, and incidents are the products of the author's imagination or are used fictitiously. Any resemblance to actual events, locales, or persons, living or dead, is entirely coincidental.

A Del Rey Trade Paperback Original

Copyright © 2012 by Scott Westerfeld

Published in the United States by Del Rey,
an imprint of The Random House Publishing Group,
a division of Random House, Inc., New York.

Del Rey is a registered trademark and the Del Rey colophon is
a trademark of Random House, Inc.

ISBN 978-0-345-52723-3
eBook ISBN 978-0-345-53530-6

Printed in the United States of America

www.delreybooks.com

2 4 6 8 9 7 5 3 1

Toning and lettering: Yishan Li
Coloring assistant, front-cover artwork: Espen Grundetjern

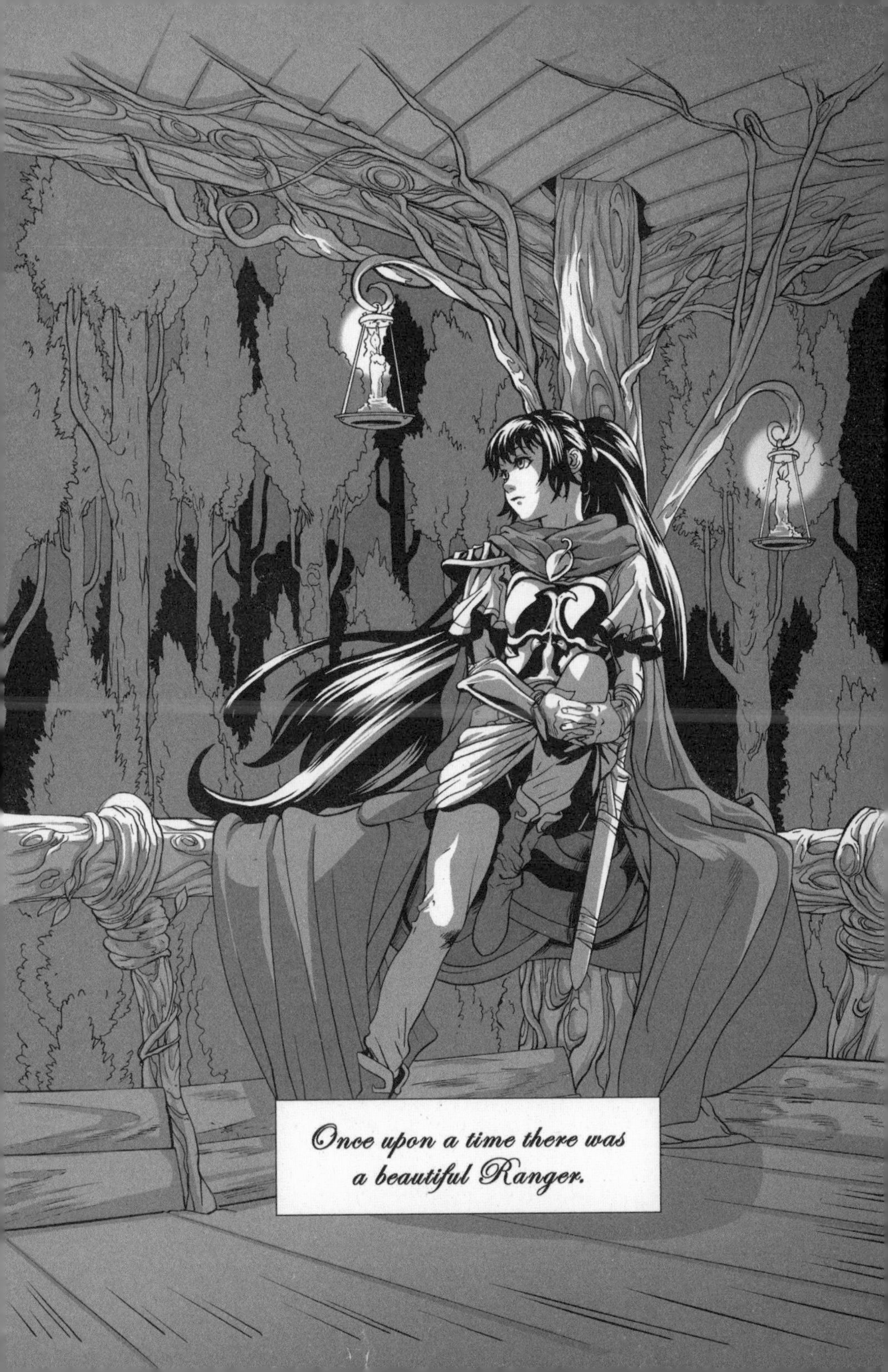
Once upon a time there was
a beautiful Ranger.

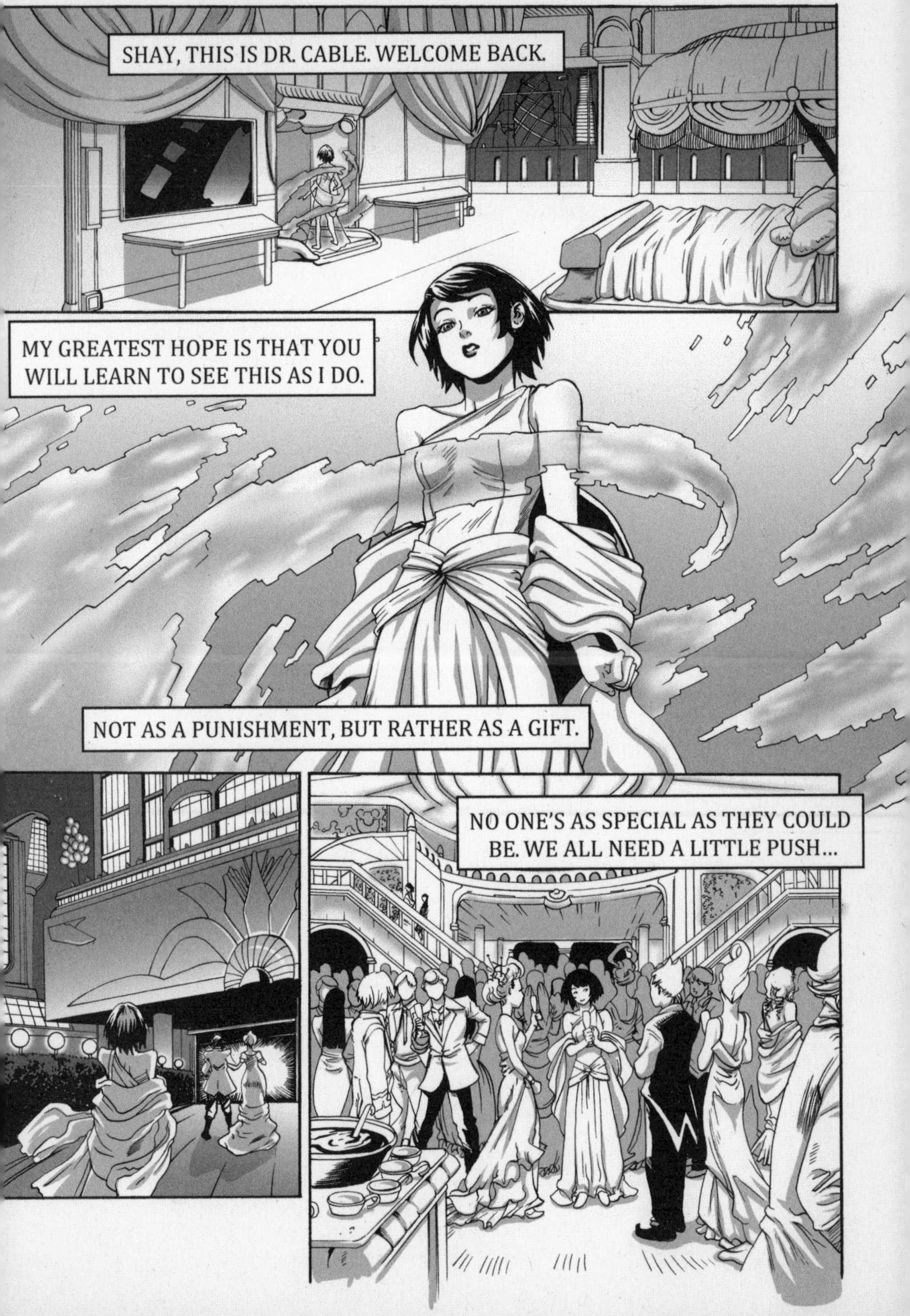
SHAY, THIS IS DR. CABLE. WELCOME BACK.
MY GREATEST HOPE IS THAT YOU WILL LEARN TO SEE THIS AS I DO.
NOT AS A PUNISHMENT, BUT RATHER AS A GIFT.
NO ONE'S AS SPECIAL AS THEY COULD BE. WE ALL NEED A LITTLE PUSH...

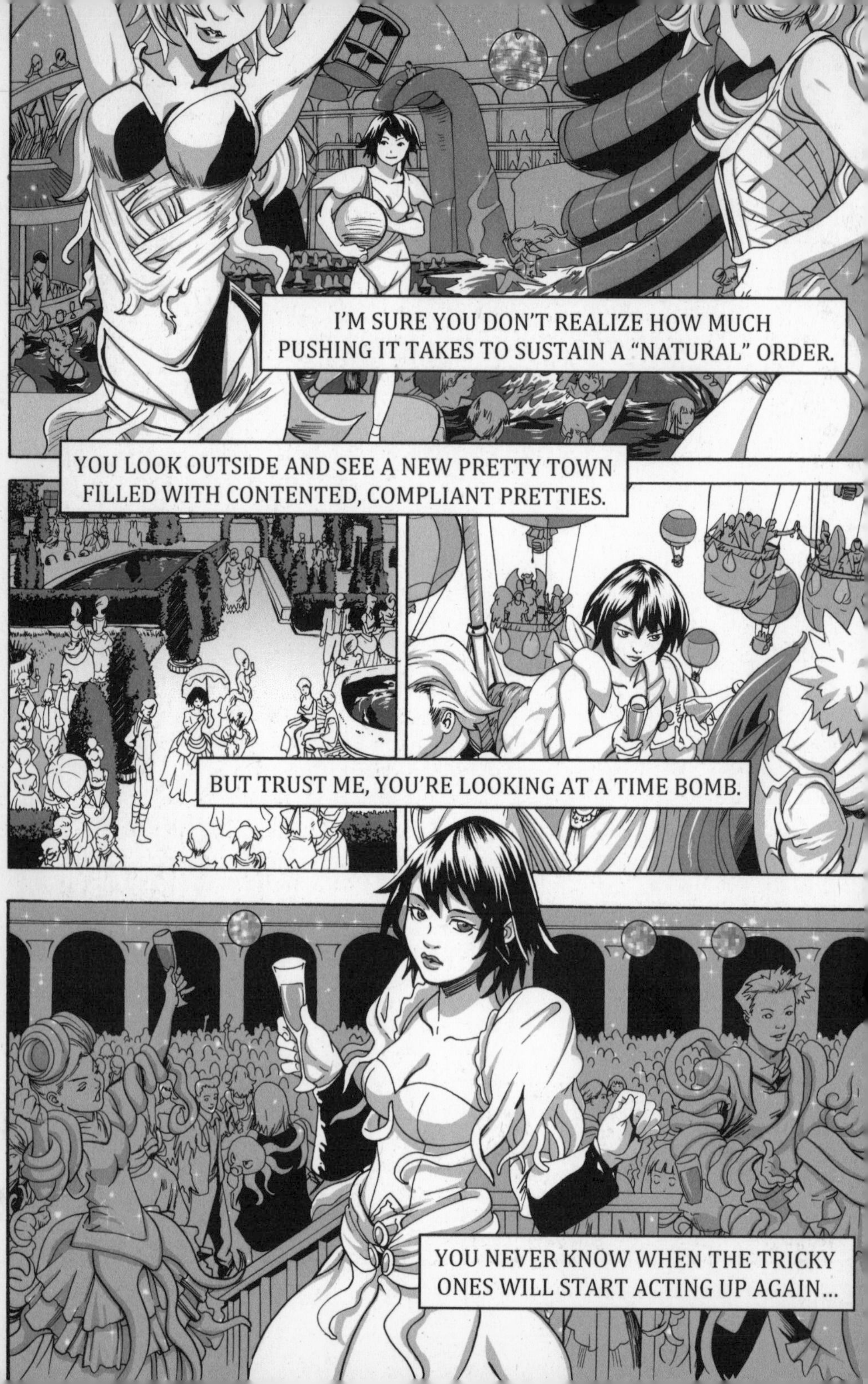
I'M SURE YOU DON'T REALIZE HOW MUCH PUSHING IT TAKES TO SUSTAIN A "NATURAL" ORDER.
YOU LOOK OUTSIDE AND SEE A NEW PRETTY TOWN FILLED WITH CONTENTED, COMPLIANT PRETTIES.
BUT TRUST ME, YOU'RE LOOKING AT A TIME BOMB.
YOU NEVER KNOW WHEN THE TRICKY ONES WILL START ACTING UP AGAIN...

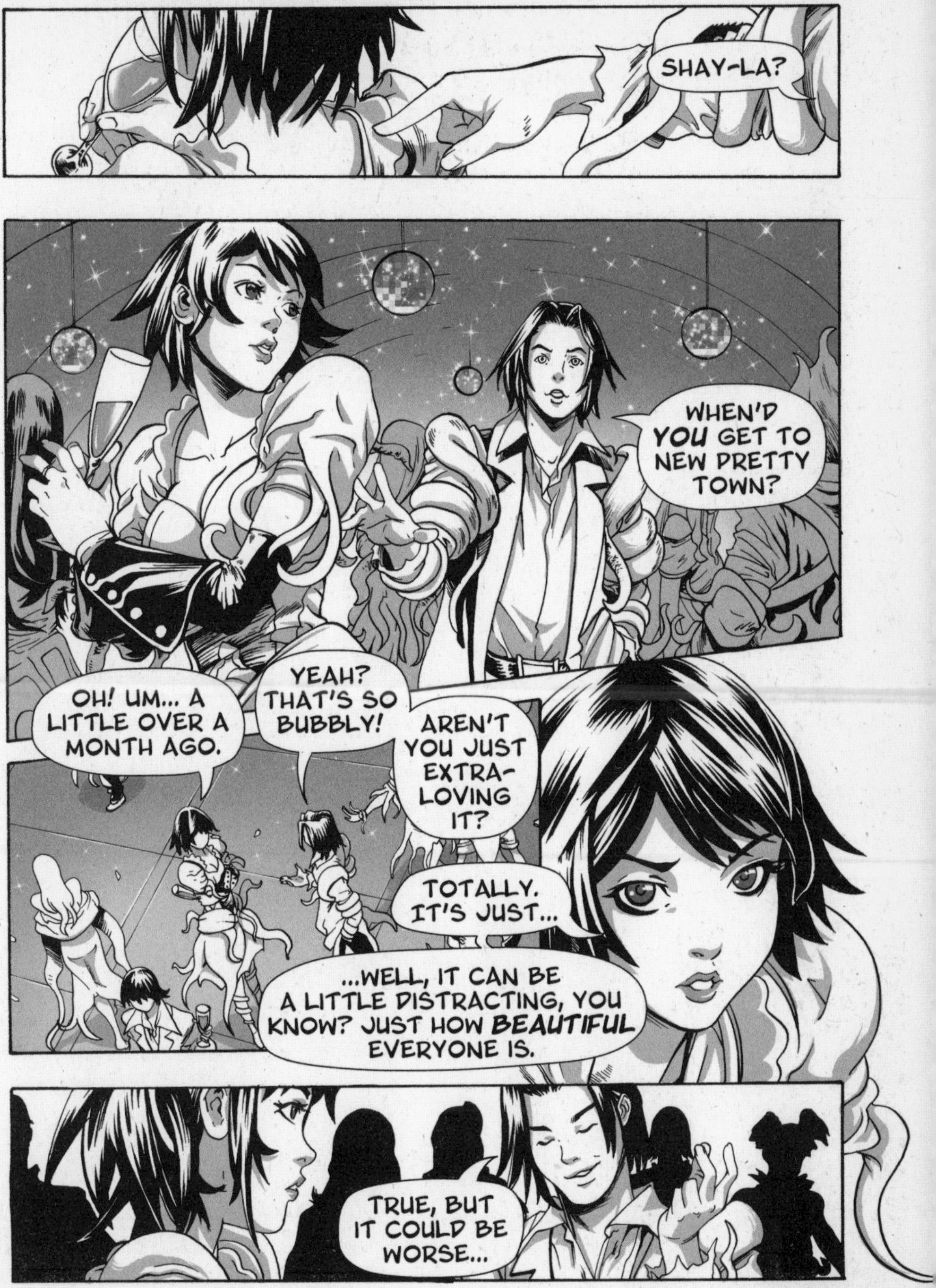
SHAY-LA?
WHEN'D YOU GET TO NEW PRETTY TOWN?
OH! UM... A LITTLE OVER A MONTH AGO.
YEAH? THAT'S SO BUBBLY!
AREN'T YOU JUST EXTRA-LOVING IT?
TOTALLY. IT'S JUST...
...WELL, IT CAN BE A LITTLE DISTRACTING, YOU KNOW? JUST HOW BEAUTIFUL EVERYONE IS.
TRUE, BUT IT COULD BE WORSE...

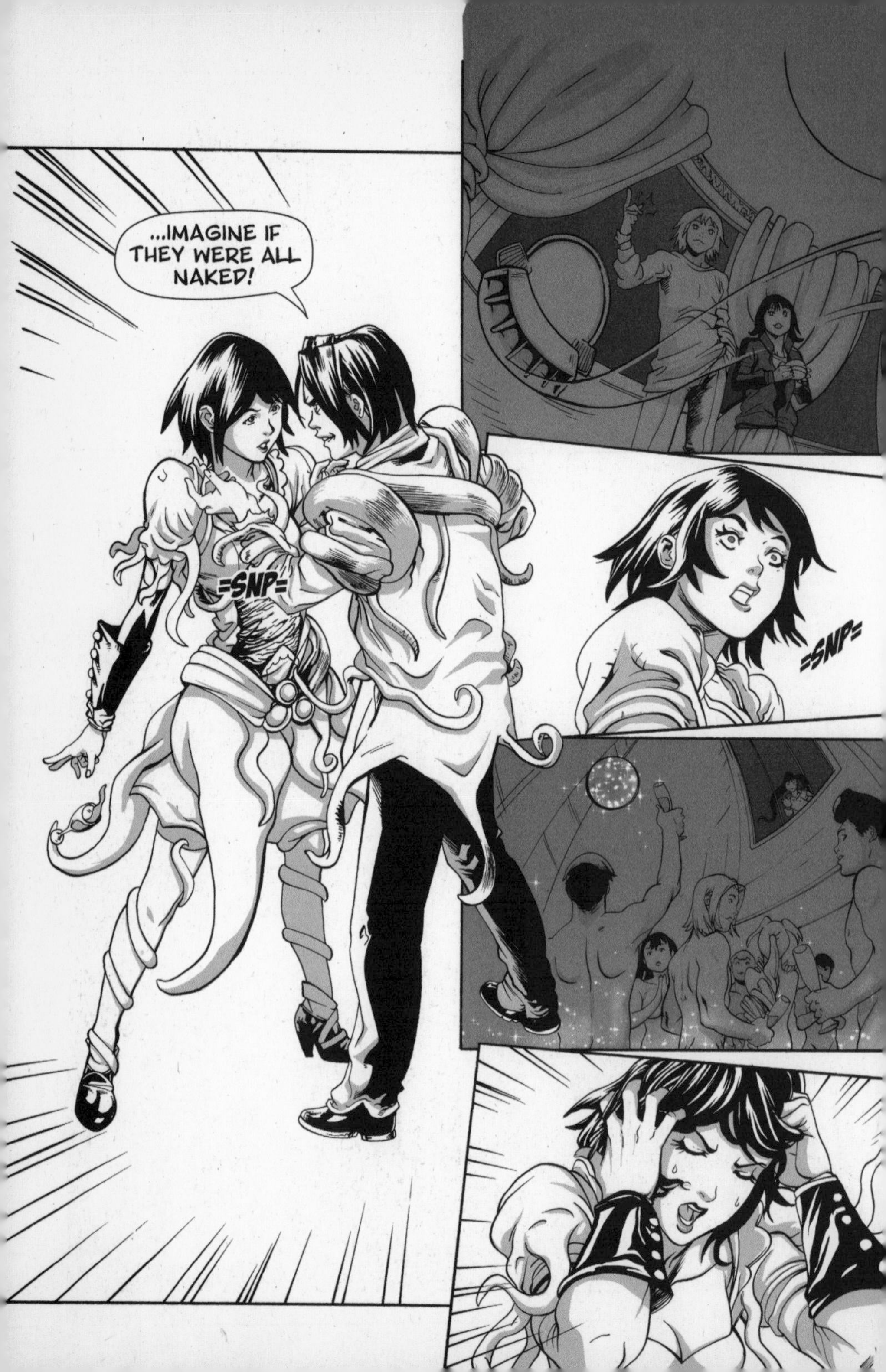
...IMAGINE IF THEY WERE ALL NAKED!
=SNP=
=SNP=

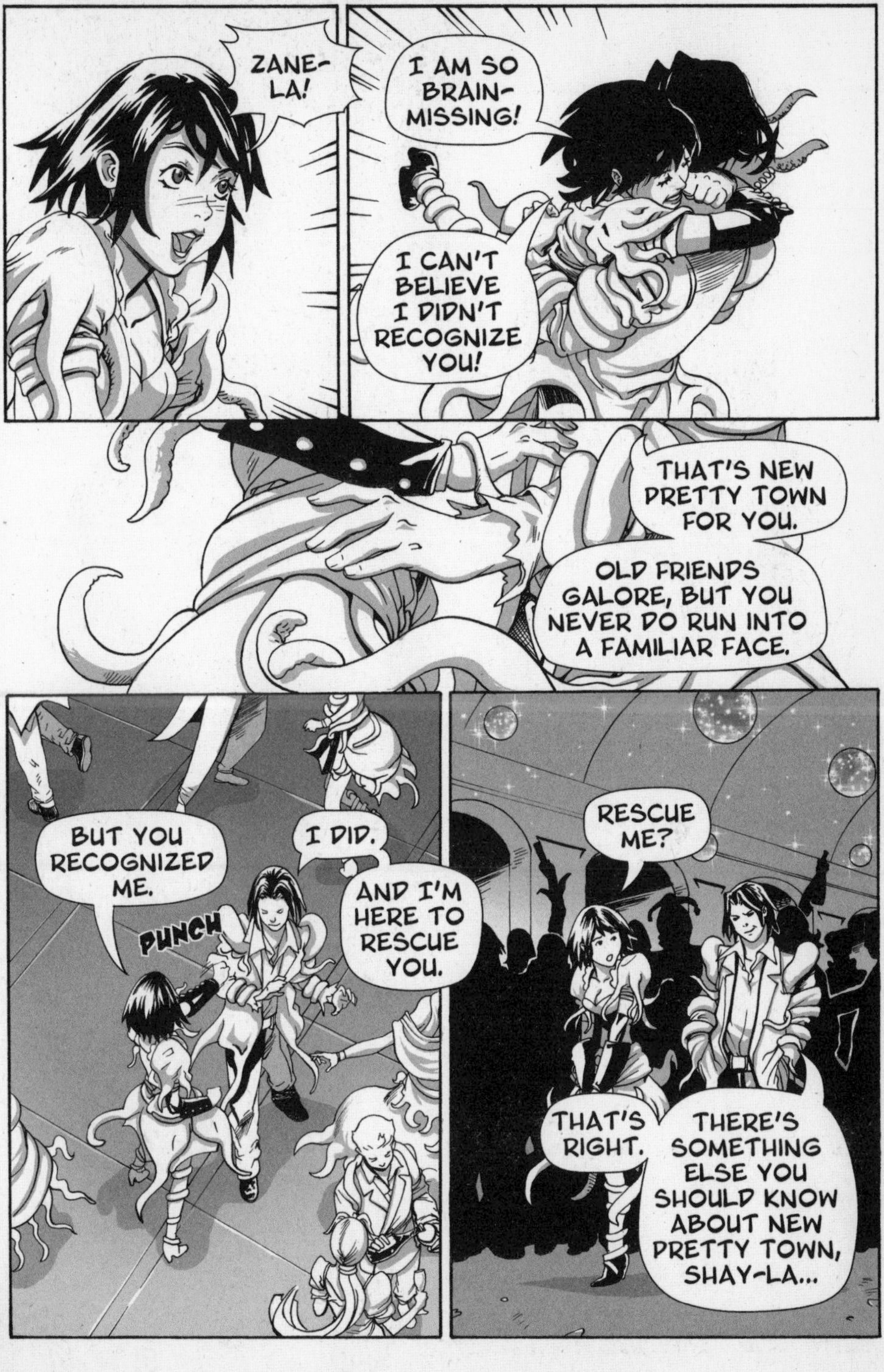
ZANE-LA!
I AM SO BRAIN-MISSING!
I CAN'T BELIEVE I DIDN'T RECOGNIZE YOU!
THAT'S NEW PRETTY TOWN FOR YOU.
OLD FRIENDS GALORE, BUT YOU NEVER DO RUN INTO A FAMILIAR FACE.
BUT YOU RECOGNIZED ME.
I DID.
AND I'M HERE TO RESCUE YOU.
PUNCH
RESCUE ME?
THAT'S RIGHT.
THERE'S SOMETHING ELSE YOU SHOULD KNOW ABOUT NEW PRETTY TOWN, SHAY-LA...

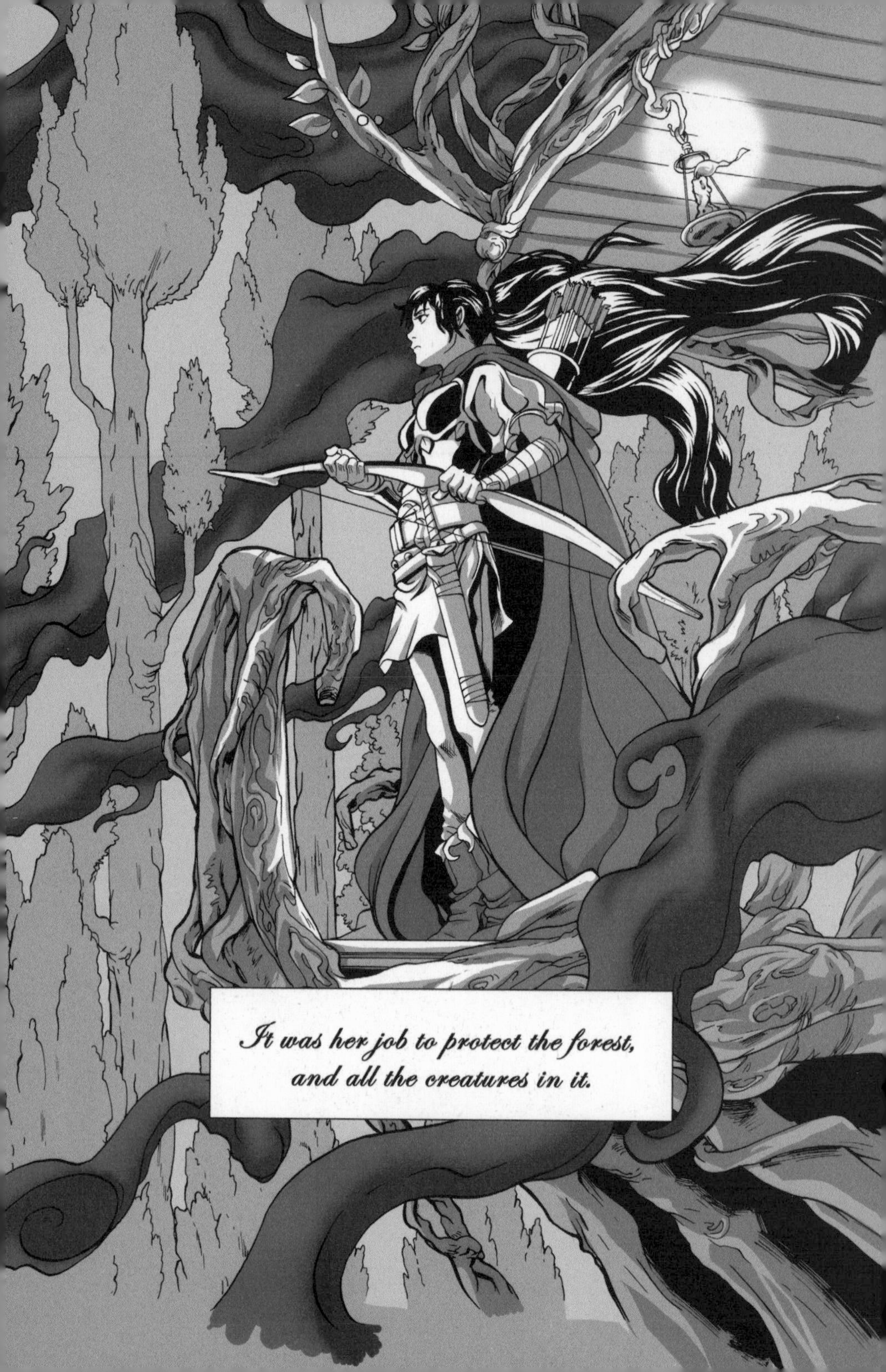
It was her job to protect the forest, and all the creatures in it.

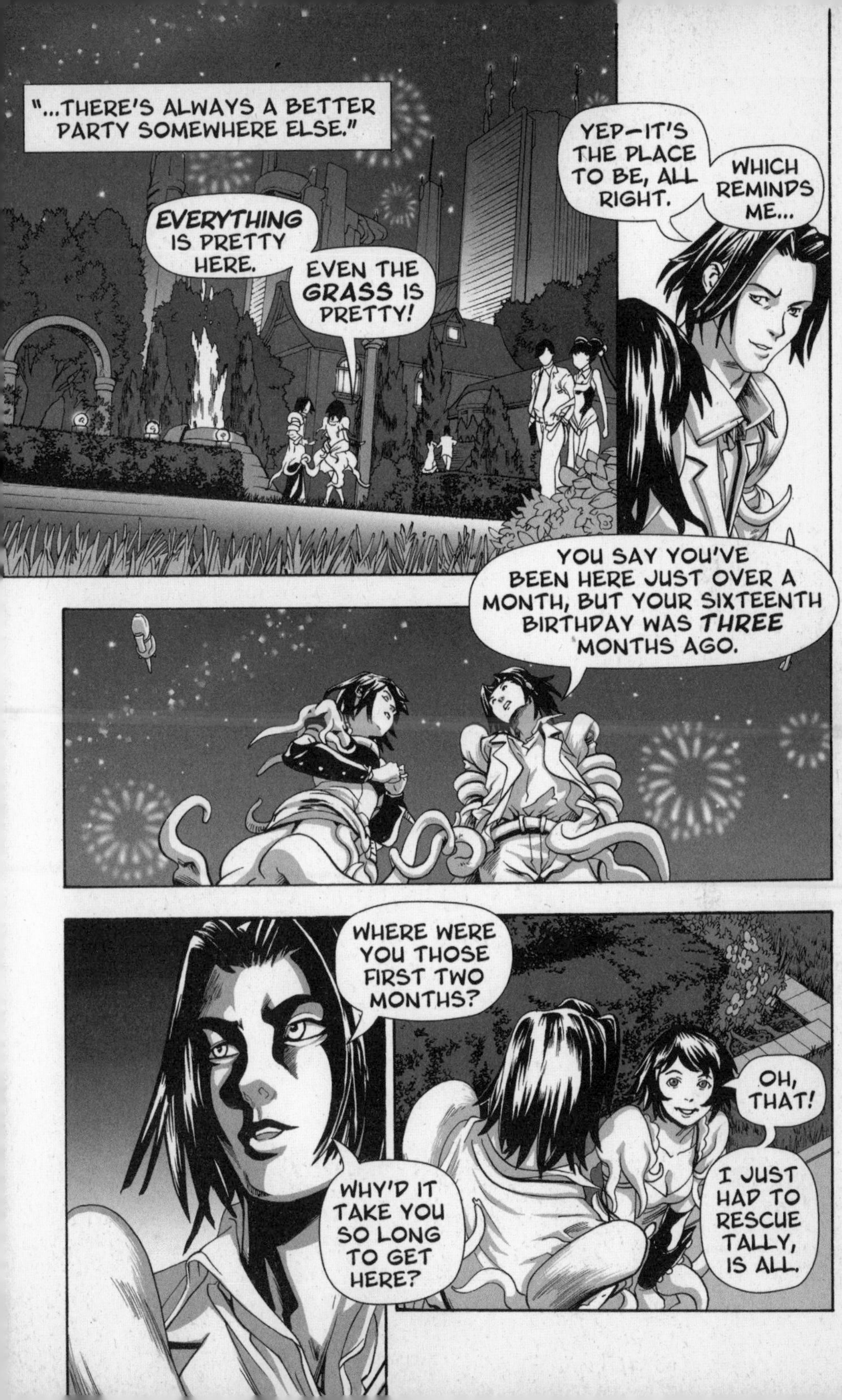
"...THERE'S ALWAYS A BETTER PARTY SOMEWHERE ELSE."
EVERYTHING IS PRETTY HERE.
EVEN THE GRASS IS PRETTY!
YEP—IT'S THE PLACE TO BE, ALL RIGHT.
WHICH REMINDS ME...
YOU SAY YOU'VE BEEN HERE JUST OVER A MONTH, BUT YOUR SIXTEENTH BIRTHDAY WAS THREE MONTHS AGO.
WHERE WERE YOU THOSE FIRST TWO MONTHS?
WHY'D IT TAKE YOU SO LONG TO GET HERE?
OH, THAT!
I JUST HAD TO RESCUE TALLY, IS ALL.

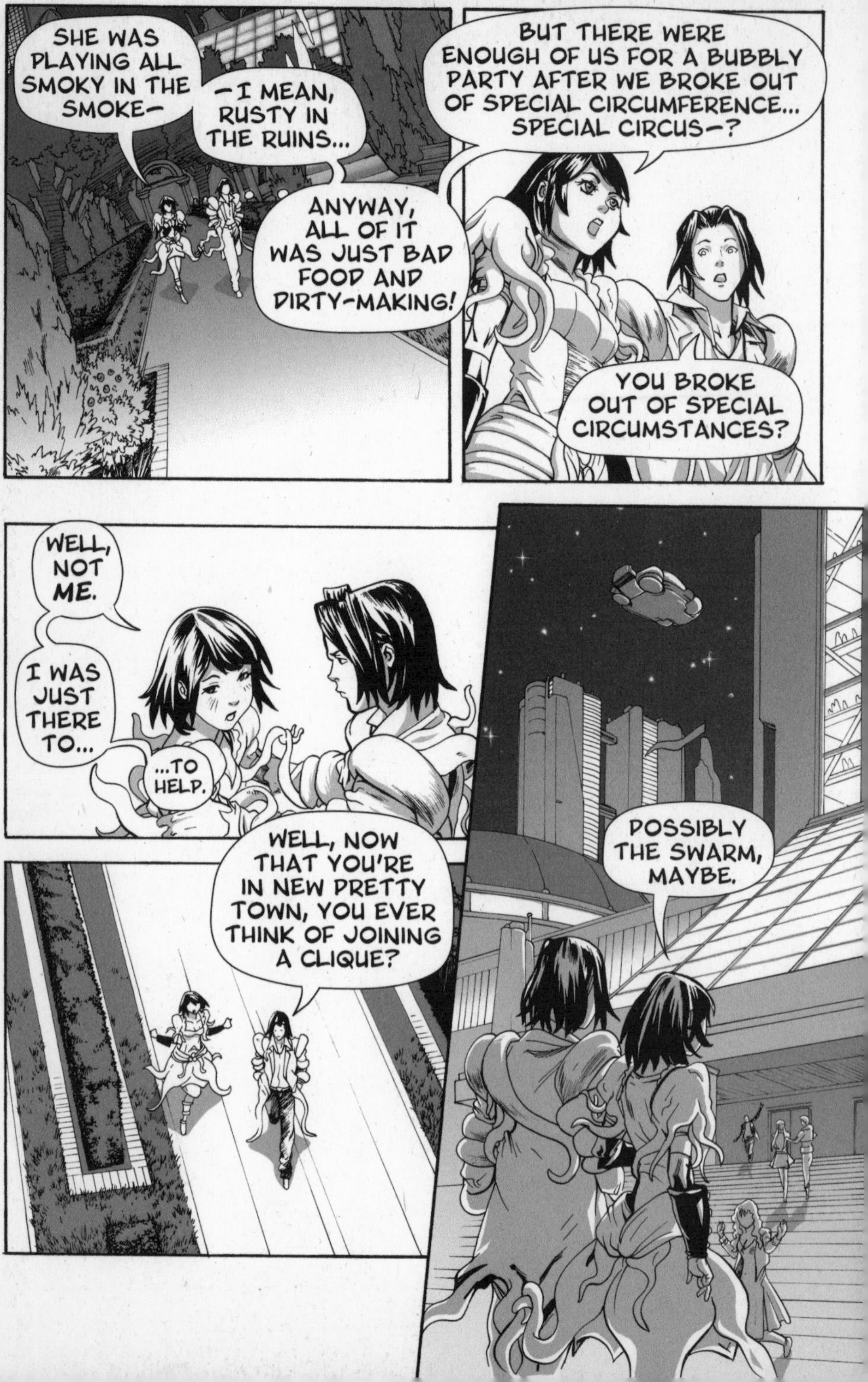

SHE WAS PLAYING ALL SMOKY IN THE SMOKE—
—I MEAN, RUSTY IN THE RUINS...
ANYWAY, ALL OF IT WAS JUST BAD FOOD AND DIRTY-MAKING!
BUT THERE WERE ENOUGH OF US FOR A BUBBLY PARTY AFTER WE BROKE OUT OF SPECIAL CIRCUMFERENCE... SPECIAL CIRCUS—?
YOU BROKE OUT OF SPECIAL CIRCUMSTANCES?
WELL, NOT ME.
I WAS JUST THERE TO...
...TO HELP.
WELL, NOW THAT YOU'RE IN NEW PRETTY TOWN, YOU EVER THINK OF JOINING A CLIQUE?
POSSIBLY THE SWARM, MAYBE.

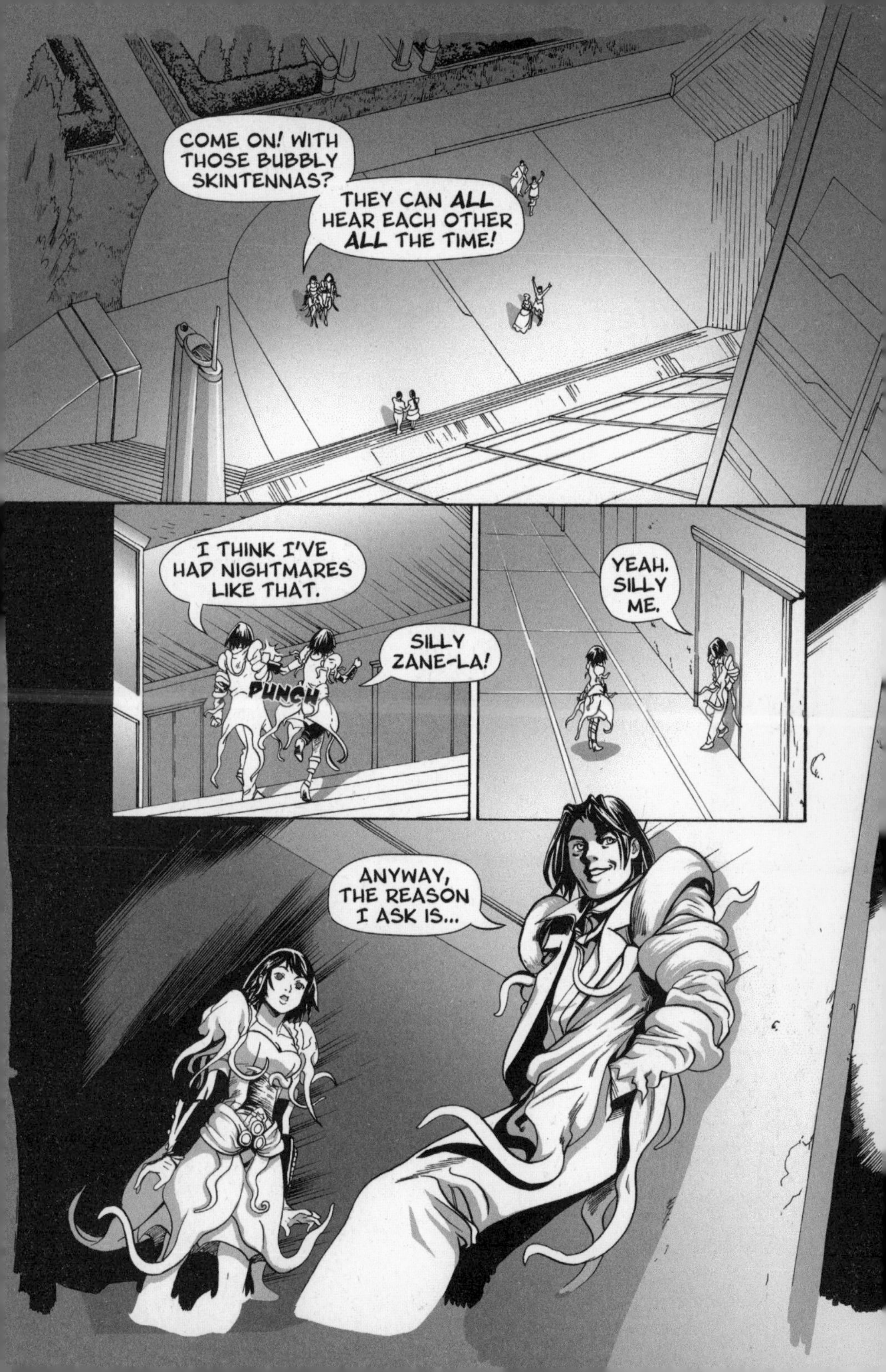
COME ON! WITH THOSE BUBBLY SKINTENNAS?
THEY CAN ALL HEAR EACH OTHER ALL THE TIME!
I THINK I'VE HAD NIGHTMARES LIKE THAT.
PUNCH
SILLY ZANE-LA!
YEAH. SILLY ME.
ANYWAY, THE REASON I ASK IS...

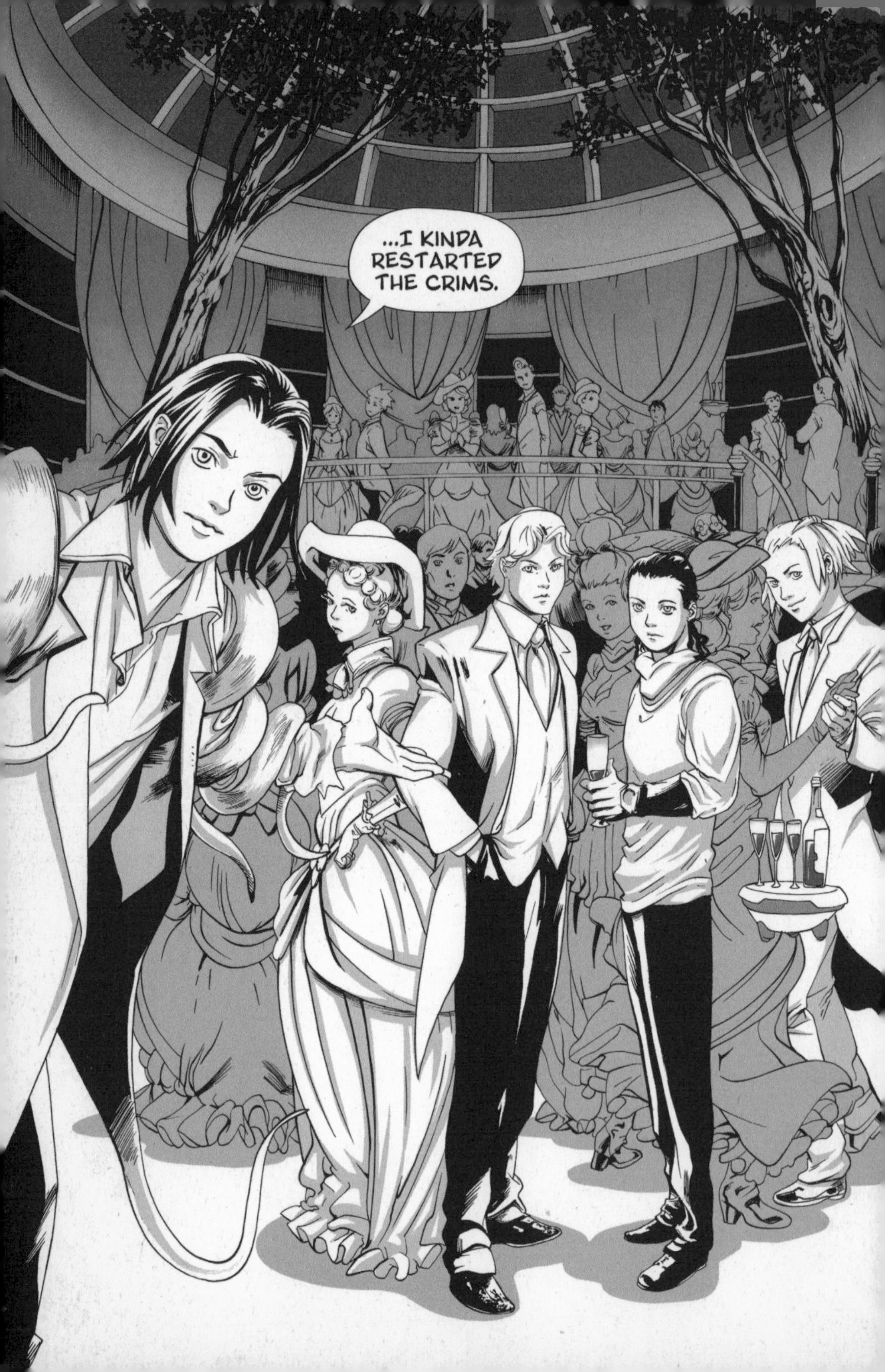
...I KINDA RESTARTED THE CRIMS.

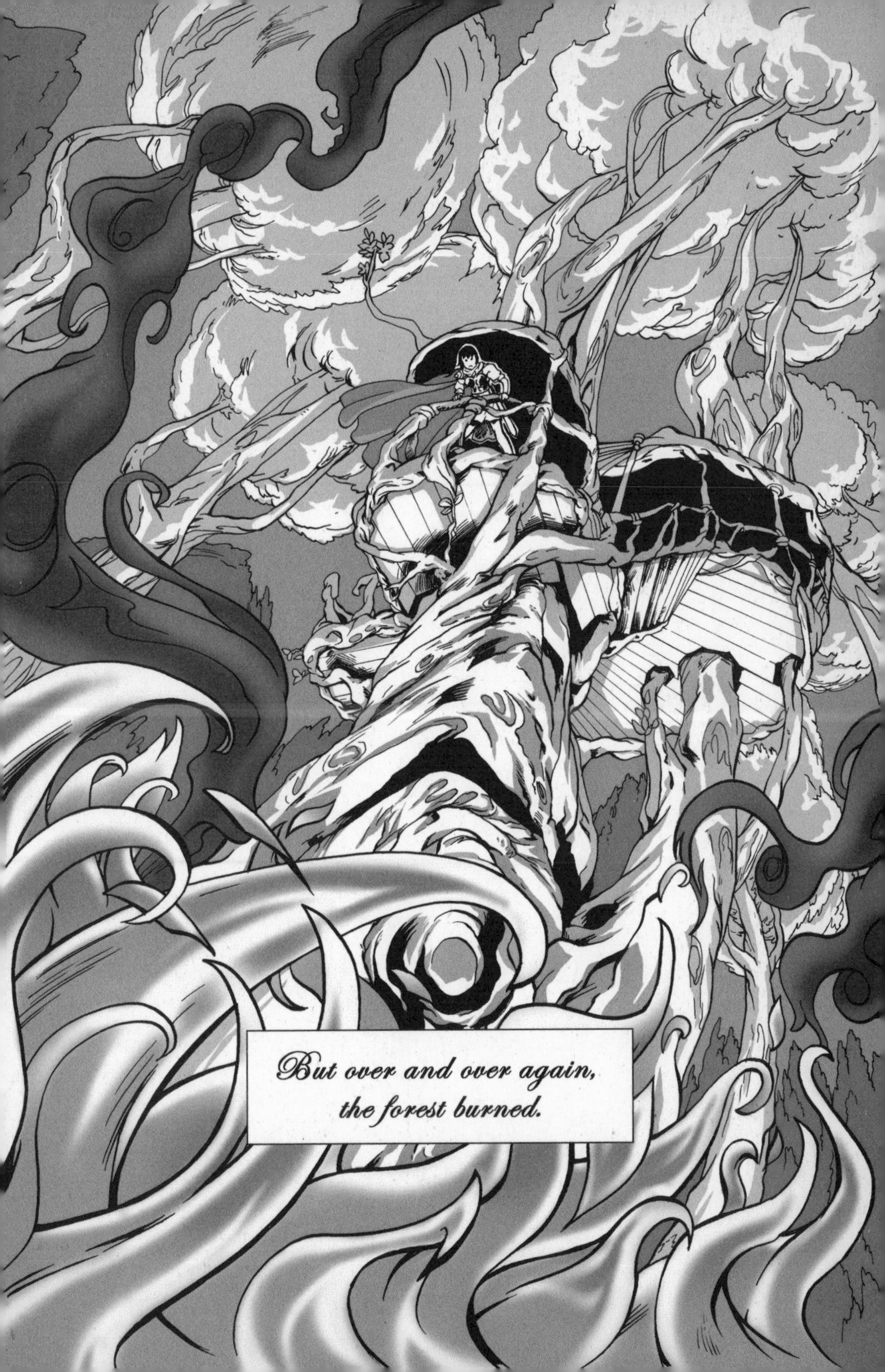
But over and over again,
the forest burned.

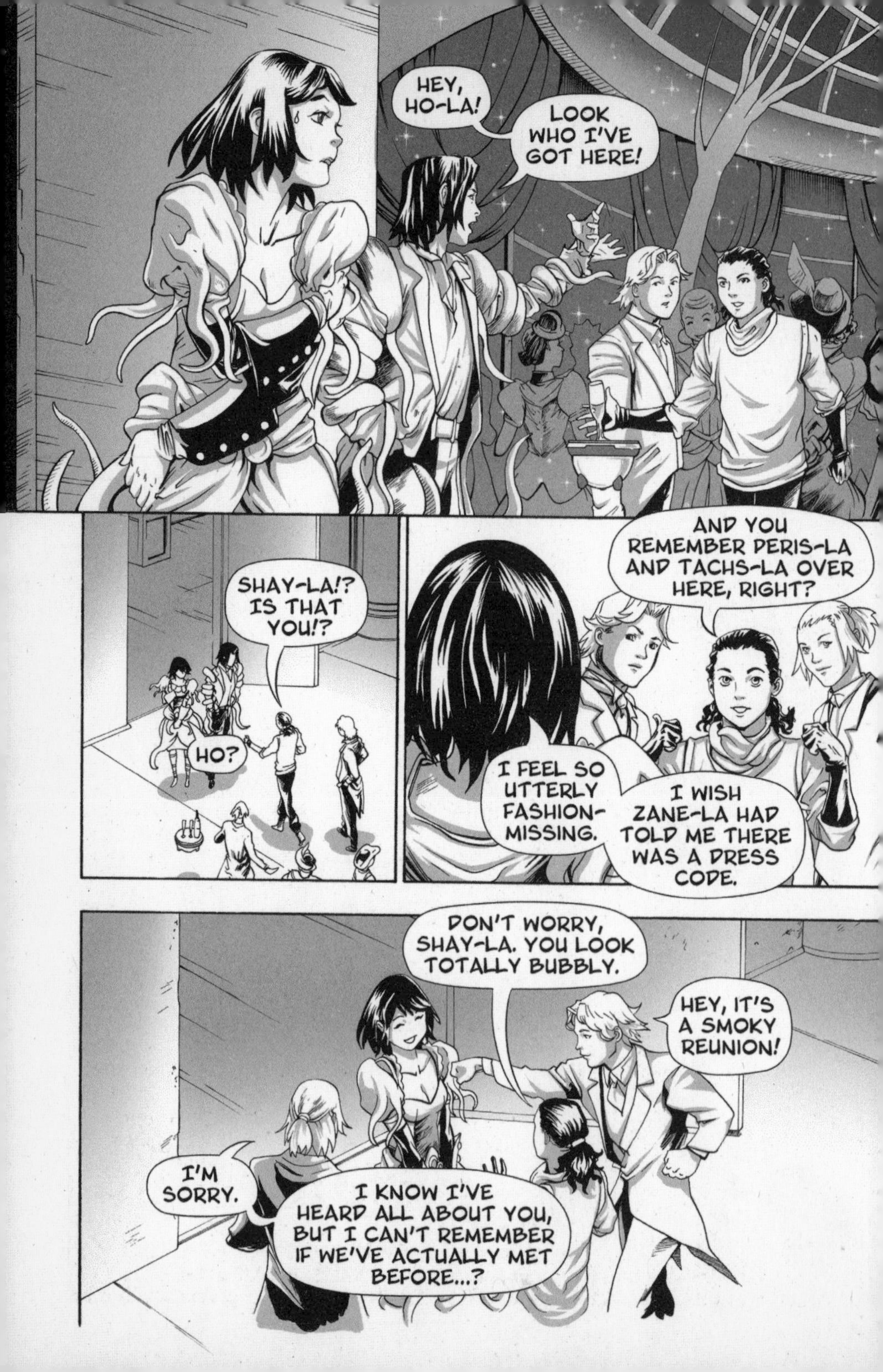
HEY, HO-LA!
LOOK WHO I'VE GOT HERE!
SHAY-LA!? IS THAT YOU!?
HO?
AND YOU REMEMBER PERIS-LA AND TACHS-LA OVER HERE, RIGHT?
I FEEL SO UTTERLY FASHION-MISSING.
I WISH ZANE-LA HAD TOLD ME THERE WAS A DRESS CODE.
DON'T WORRY, SHAY-LA. YOU LOOK TOTALLY BUBBLY.
HEY, IT'S A SMOKY REUNION!
I'M SORRY.
I KNOW I'VE HEARD ALL ABOUT YOU, BUT I CAN'T REMEMBER IF WE'VE ACTUALLY MET BEFORE...?

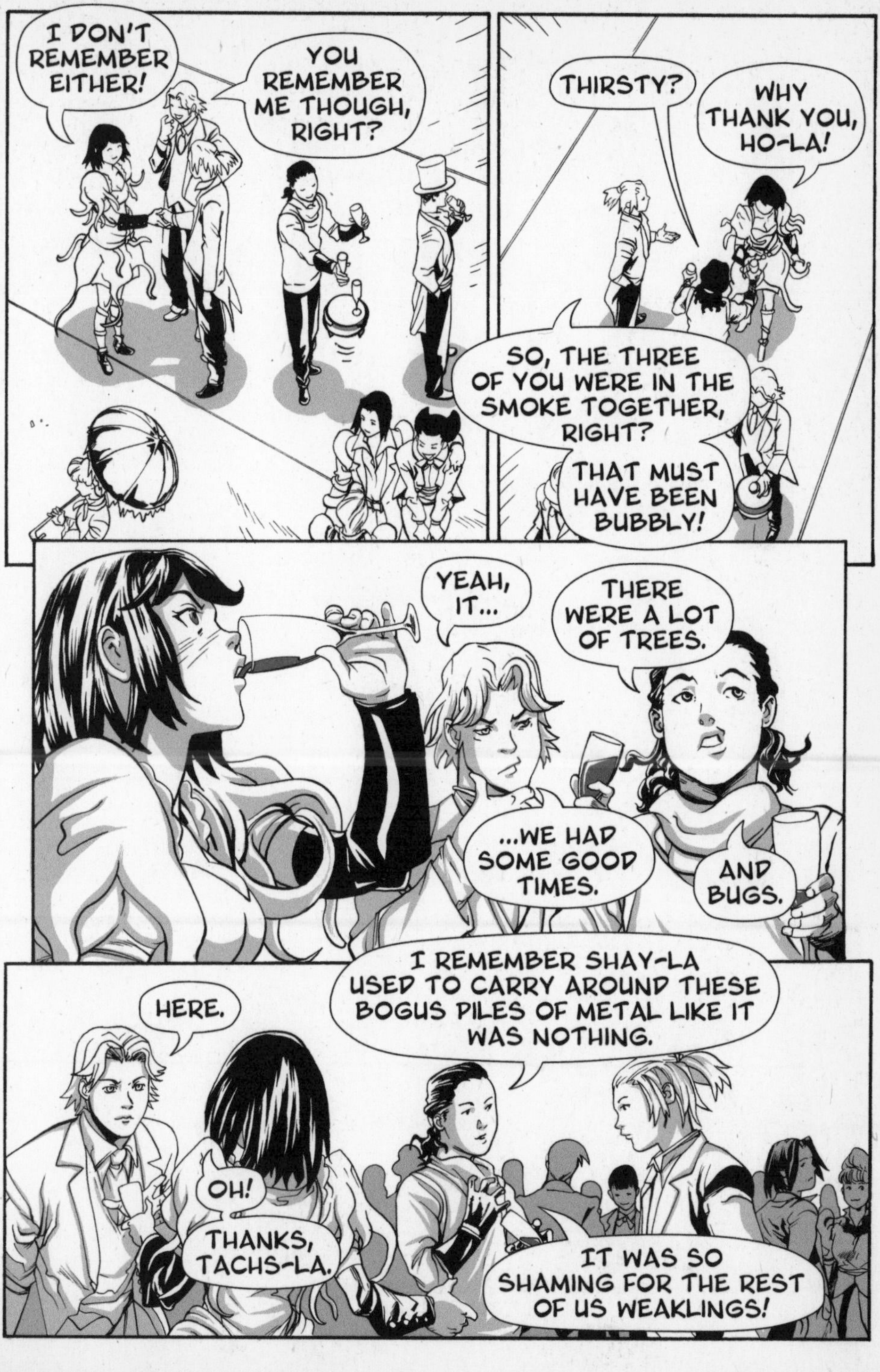
I DON'T REMEMBER EITHER!
YOU REMEMBER ME THOUGH, RIGHT?
THIRSTY?
WHY THANK YOU, HO-LA!
SO, THE THREE OF YOU WERE IN THE SMOKE TOGETHER, RIGHT?
THAT MUST HAVE BEEN BUBBLY!
YEAH, IT...
THERE WERE A LOT OF TREES.
...WE HAD SOME GOOD TIMES.
AND BUGS.
HERE.
I REMEMBER SHAY-LA USED TO CARRY AROUND THESE BOGUS PILES OF METAL LIKE IT WAS NOTHING.
OH!
THANKS, TACHS-LA.
IT WAS SO SHAMING FOR THE REST OF US WEAKLINGS!

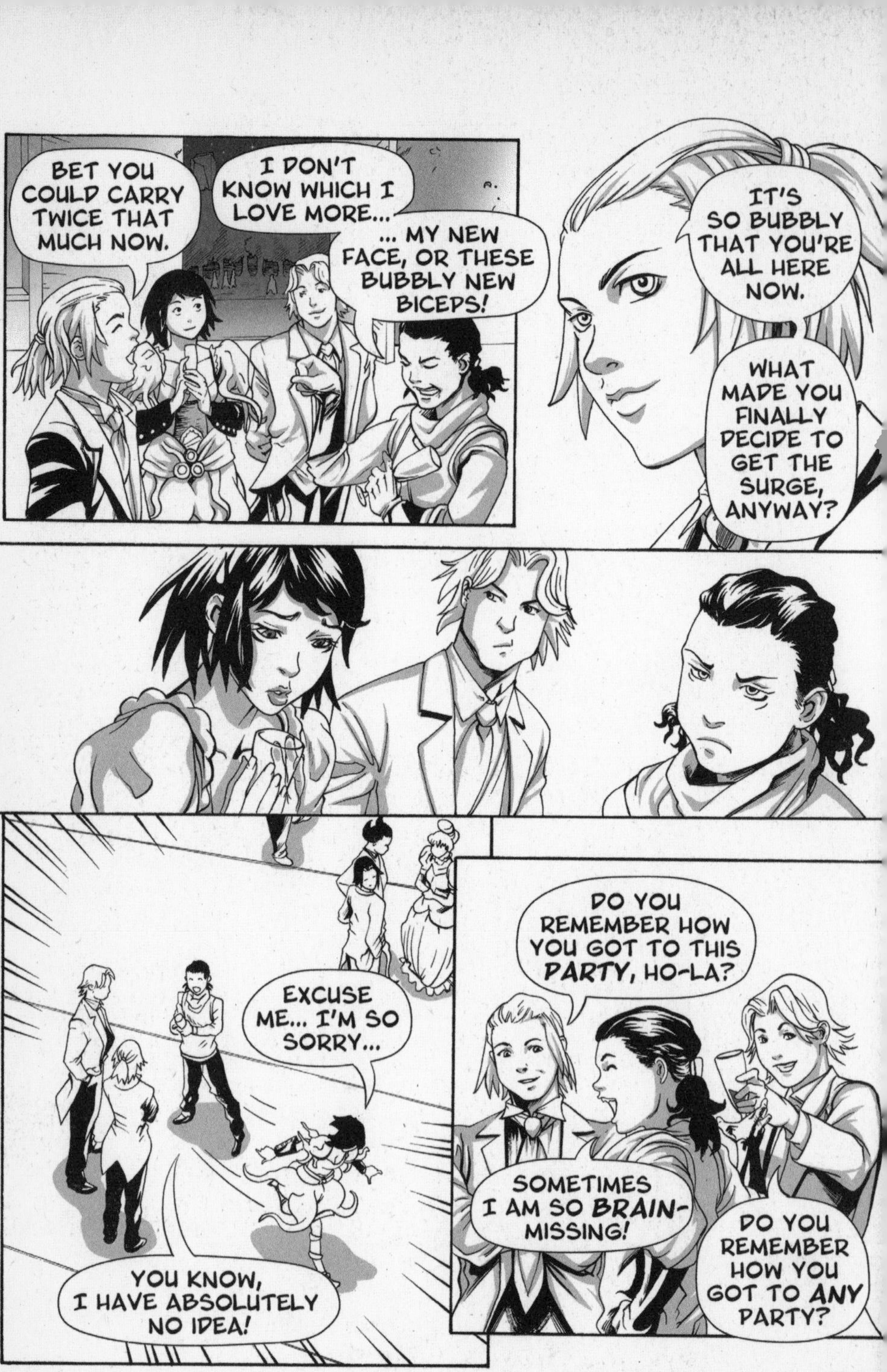
BET YOU COULD CARRY TWICE THAT MUCH NOW.
I DON'T KNOW WHICH I LOVE MORE...
... MY NEW FACE, OR THESE BUBBLY NEW BICEPS!
IT'S SO BUBBLY THAT YOU'RE ALL HERE NOW.
WHAT MADE YOU FINALLY DECIDE TO GET THE SURGE, ANYWAY?
EXCUSE ME... I'M SO SORRY...
YOU KNOW, I HAVE ABSOLUTELY NO IDEA!
DO YOU REMEMBER HOW YOU GOT TO THIS PARTY, HO-LA?
SOMETIMES I AM SO BRAIN-MISSING!
DO YOU REMEMBER HOW YOU GOT TO ANY PARTY?

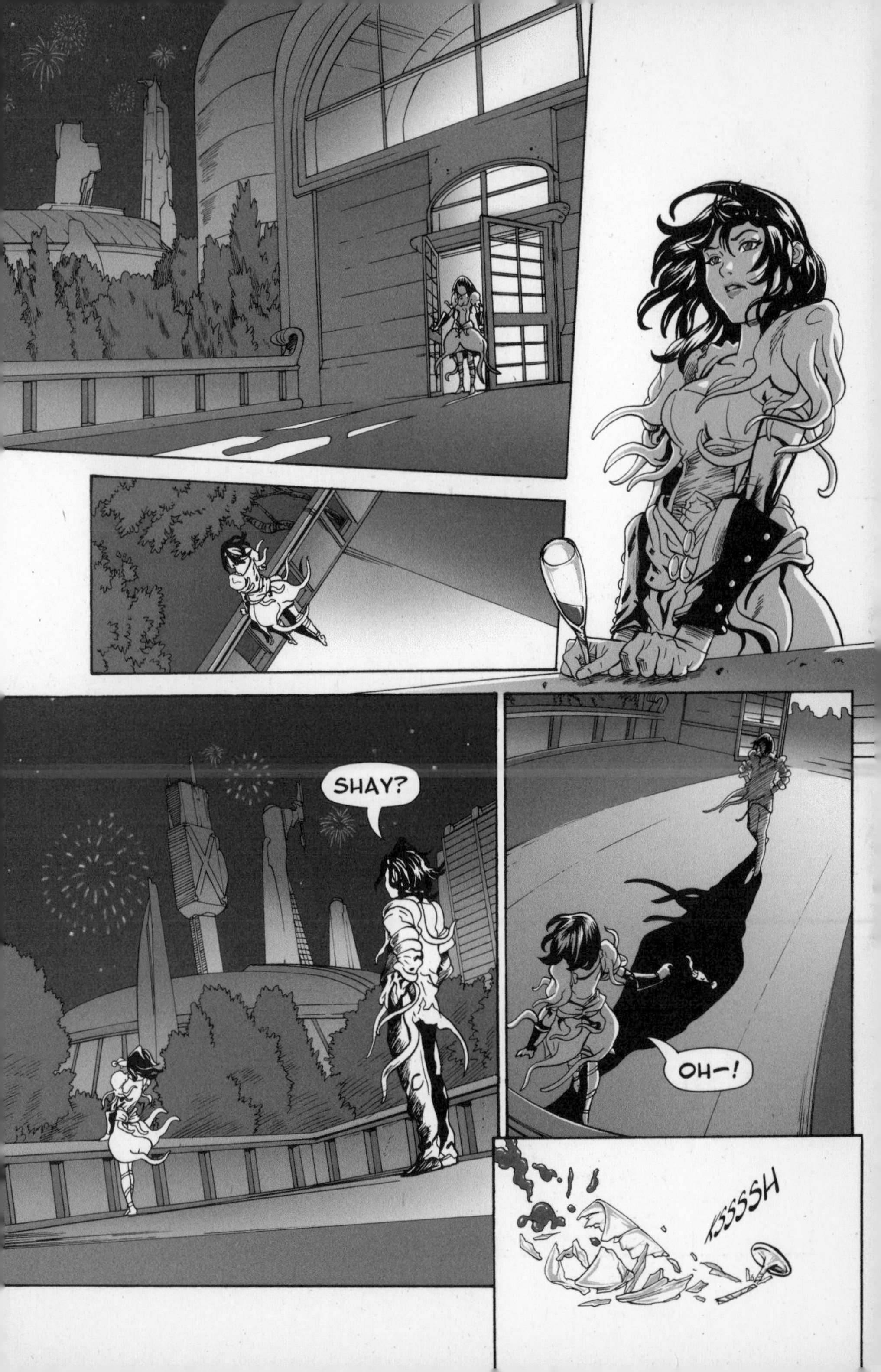
SHAY?
OH-!
KSSSSH

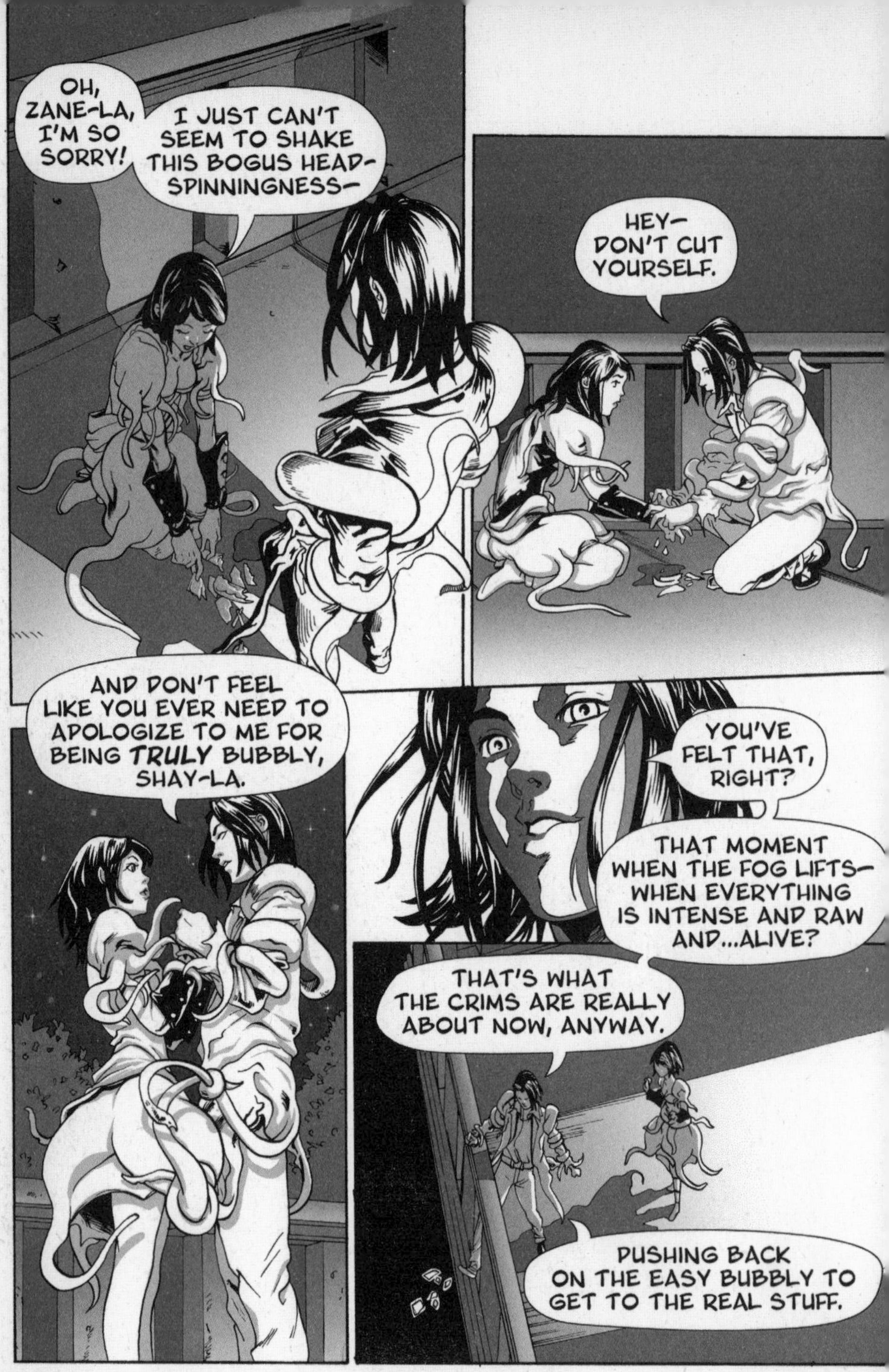
OH, ZANE-LA, I'M SO SORRY!
I JUST CAN'T SEEM TO SHAKE THIS BOGUS HEAD-SPINNINGNESS—
HEY— DON'T CUT YOURSELF.
AND DON'T FEEL LIKE YOU EVER NEED TO APOLOGIZE TO ME FOR BEING *TRULY* BUBBLY, SHAY-LA.
YOU'VE FELT THAT, RIGHT?
THAT MOMENT WHEN THE FOG LIFTS— WHEN EVERYTHING IS INTENSE AND RAW AND...ALIVE?
THAT'S WHAT THE CRIMS ARE REALLY ABOUT NOW, ANYWAY.
PUSHING BACK ON THE EASY BUBBLY TO GET TO THE REAL STUFF.

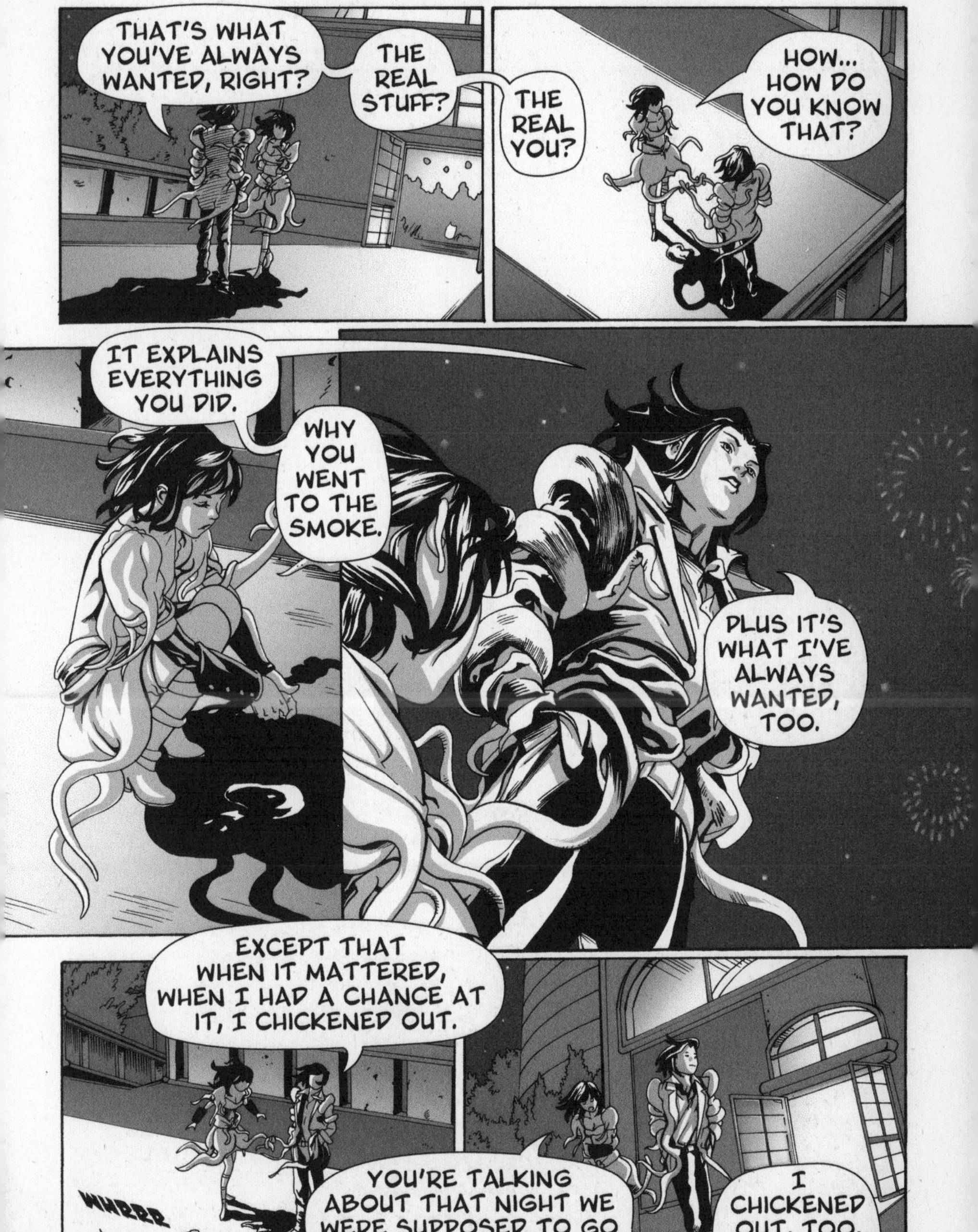
THAT'S WHAT YOU'VE ALWAYS WANTED, RIGHT?
THE REAL STUFF?
THE REAL YOU?
HOW... HOW DO YOU KNOW THAT?
IT EXPLAINS EVERYTHING YOU DID.
WHY YOU WENT TO THE SMOKE.
PLUS IT'S WHAT I'VE ALWAYS WANTED, TOO.
EXCEPT THAT WHEN IT MATTERED, WHEN I HAD A CHANCE AT IT, I CHICKENED OUT.
WHRRR
YOU'RE TALKING ABOUT THAT NIGHT WE WERE SUPPOSED TO GO TO THE SMOKE.
I CHICKENED OUT, TOO, REMEMBER?
BEEP

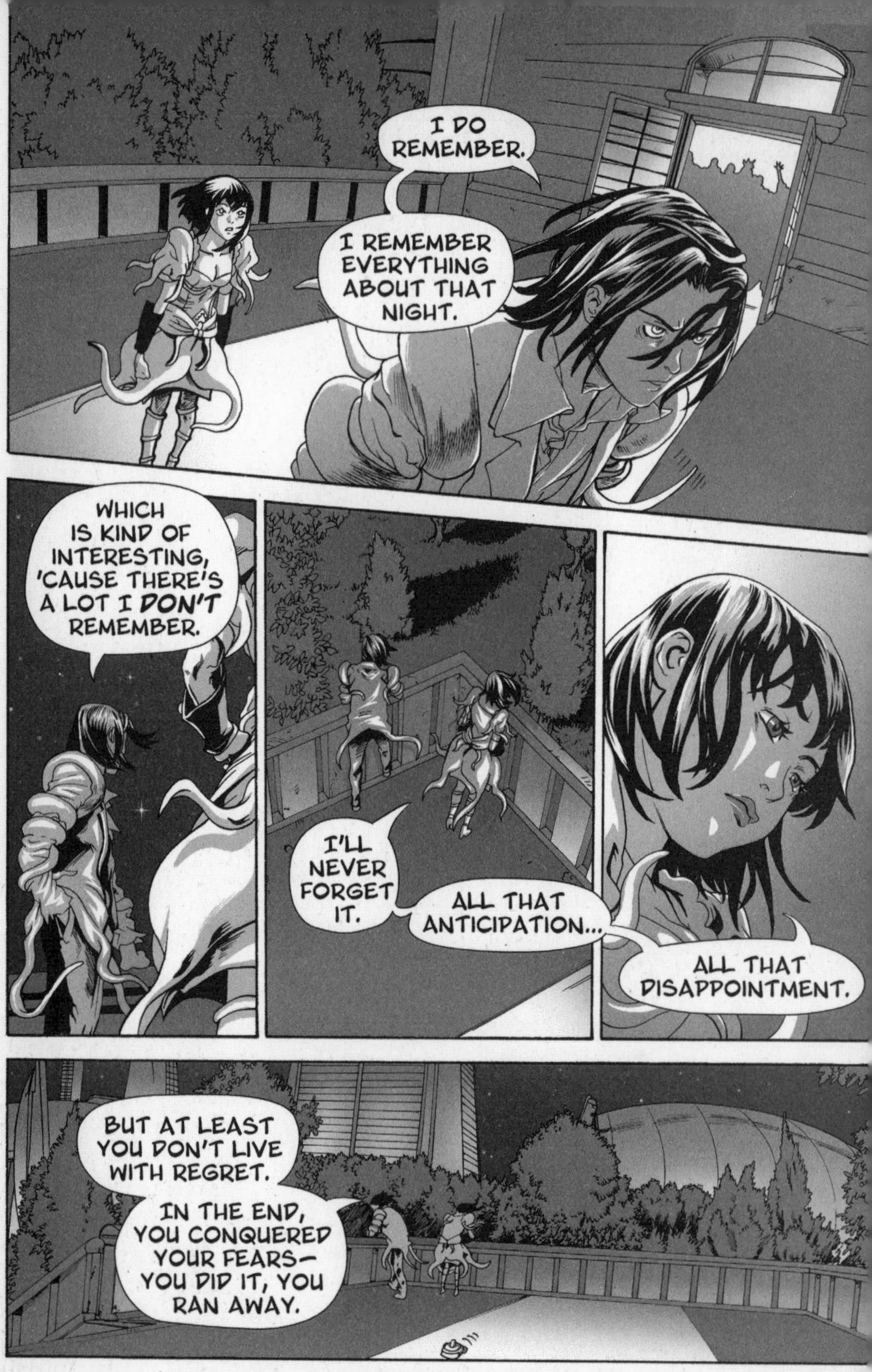
I DO REMEMBER.
I REMEMBER EVERYTHING ABOUT THAT NIGHT.
WHICH IS KIND OF INTERESTING, 'CAUSE THERE'S A LOT I *DON'T* REMEMBER.
I'LL NEVER FORGET IT.
ALL THAT ANTICIPATION...
ALL THAT DISAPPOINTMENT.
BUT AT LEAST YOU DON'T LIVE WITH REGRET.
IN THE END, YOU CONQUERED YOUR FEARS—YOU DID IT, YOU RAN AWAY.

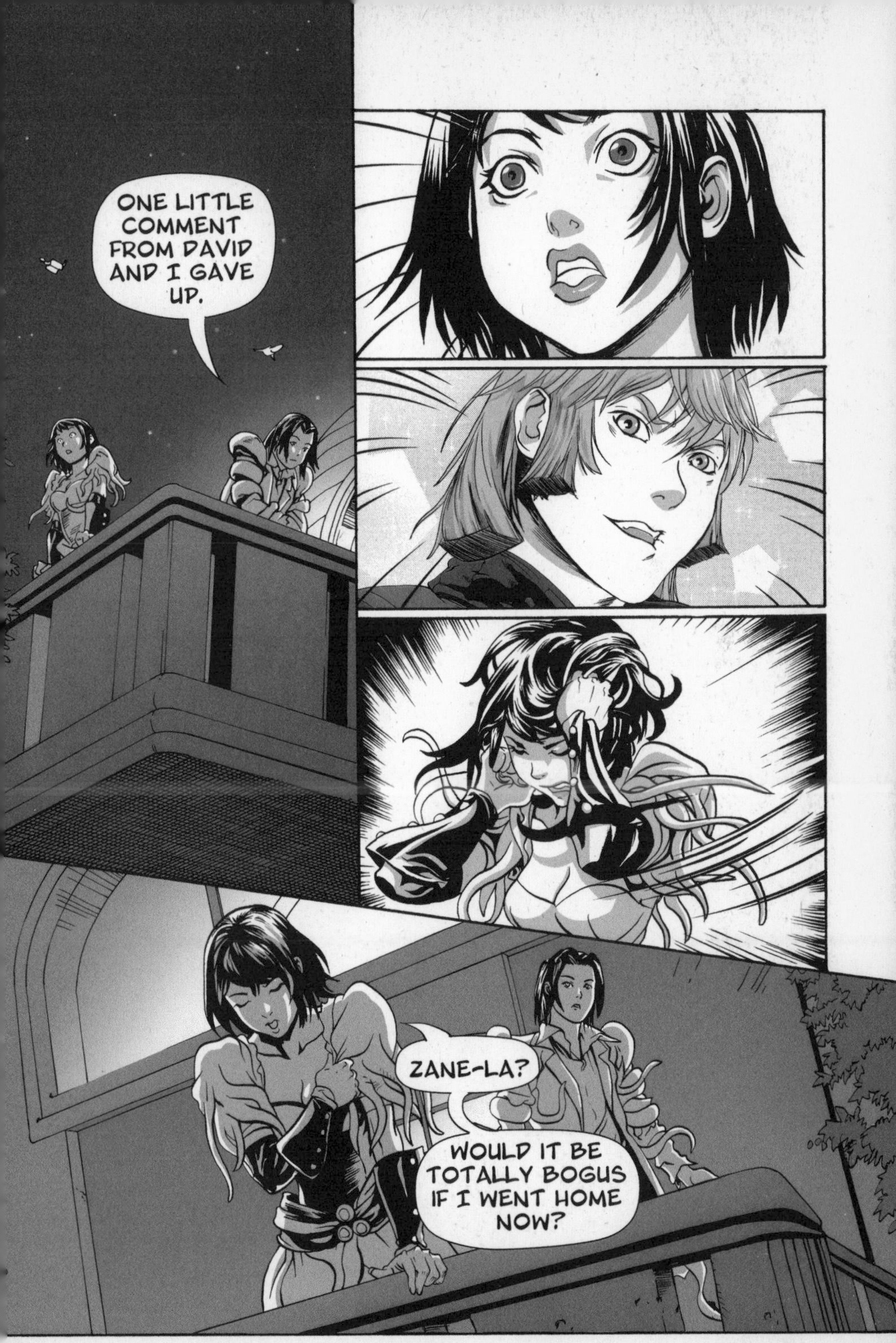
ONE LITTLE COMMENT FROM DAVID AND I GAVE UP.
ZANE-LA?
WOULD IT BE TOTALLY BOGUS IF I WENT HOME NOW?

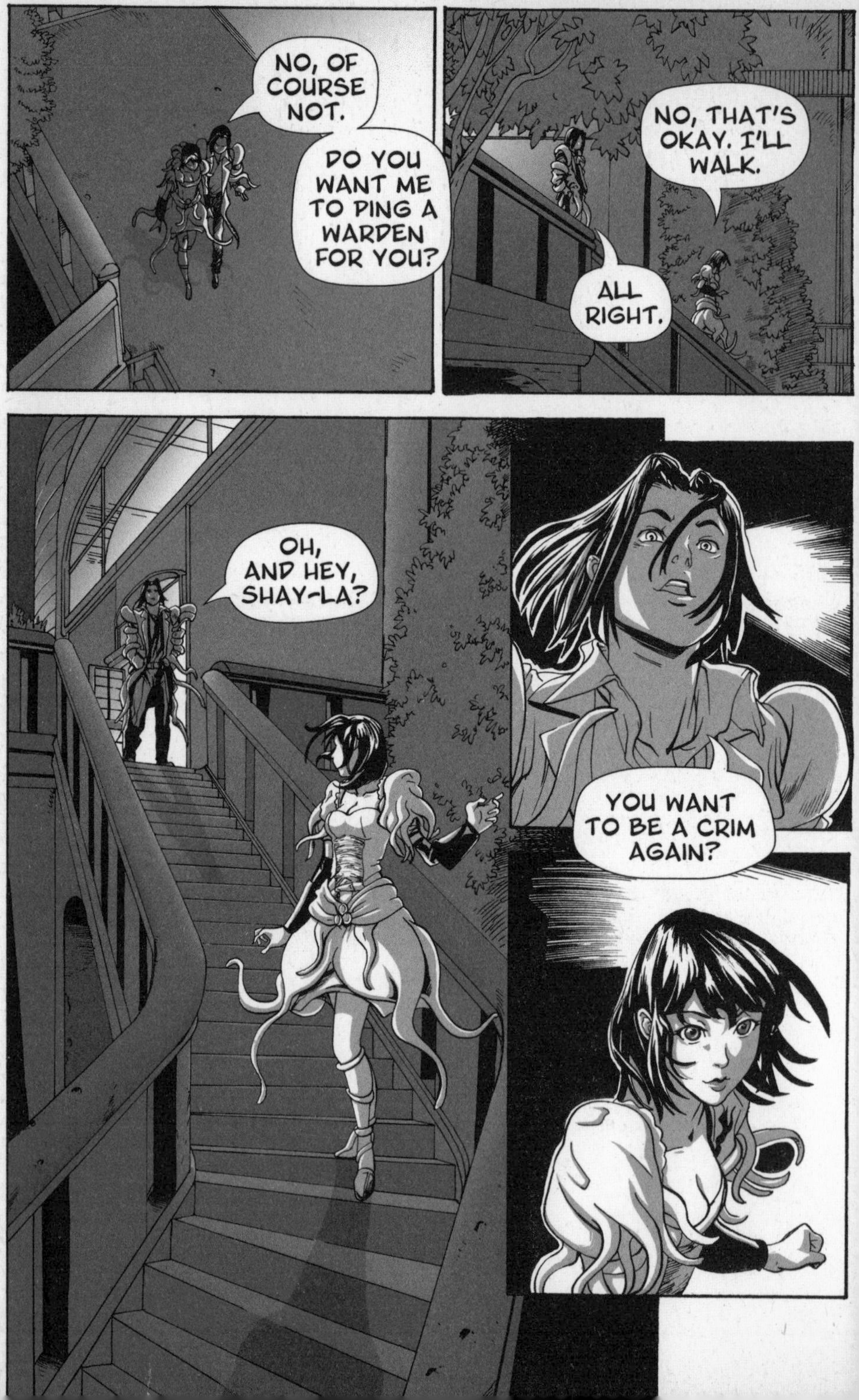
NO, OF COURSE NOT.
DO YOU WANT ME TO PING A WARDEN FOR YOU?
NO, THAT'S OKAY. I'LL WALK.
ALL RIGHT.
OH, AND HEY, SHAY-LA?
YOU WANT TO BE A CRIM AGAIN?

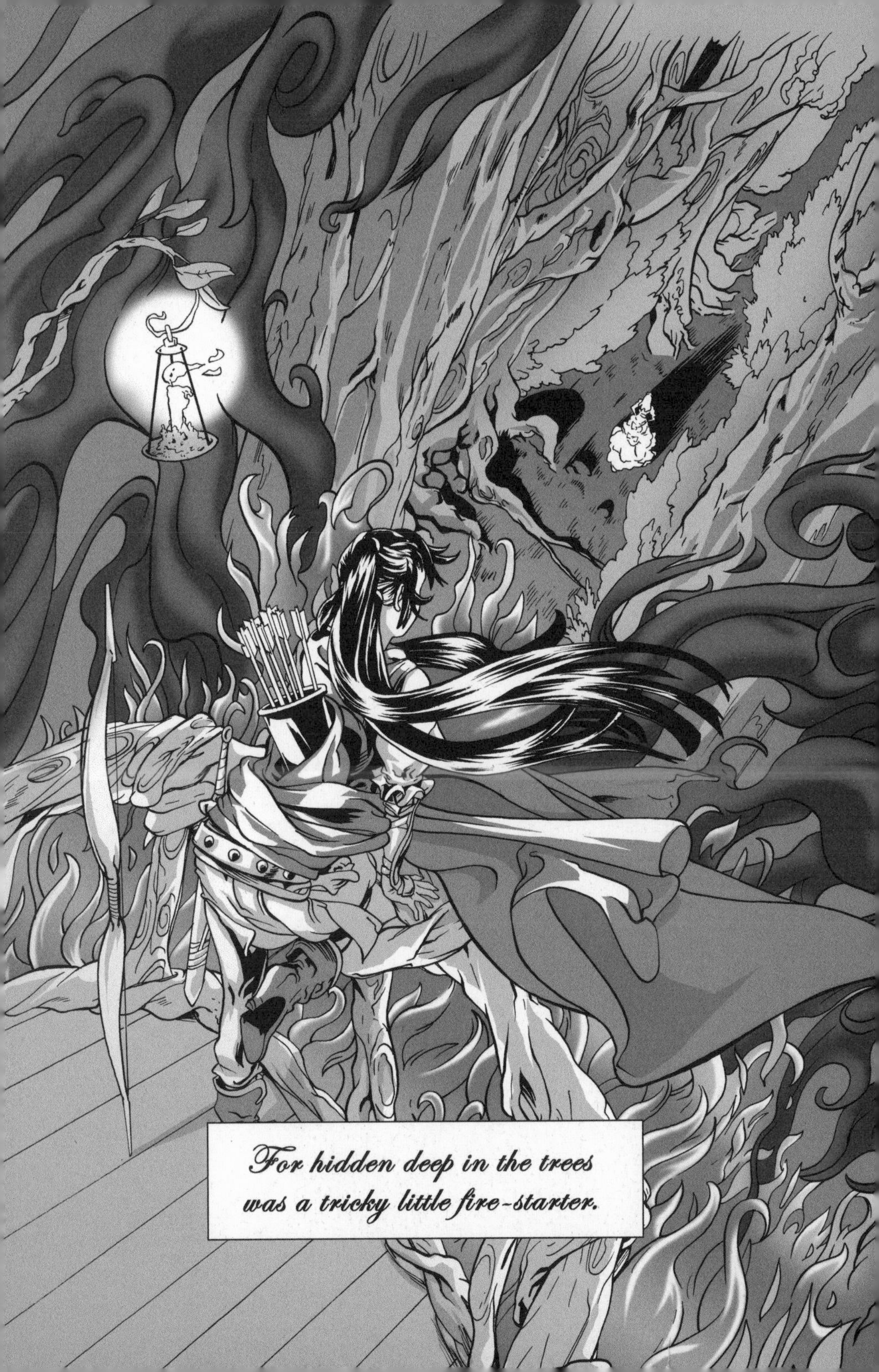
For hidden deep in the trees
was a tricky little fire-starter.

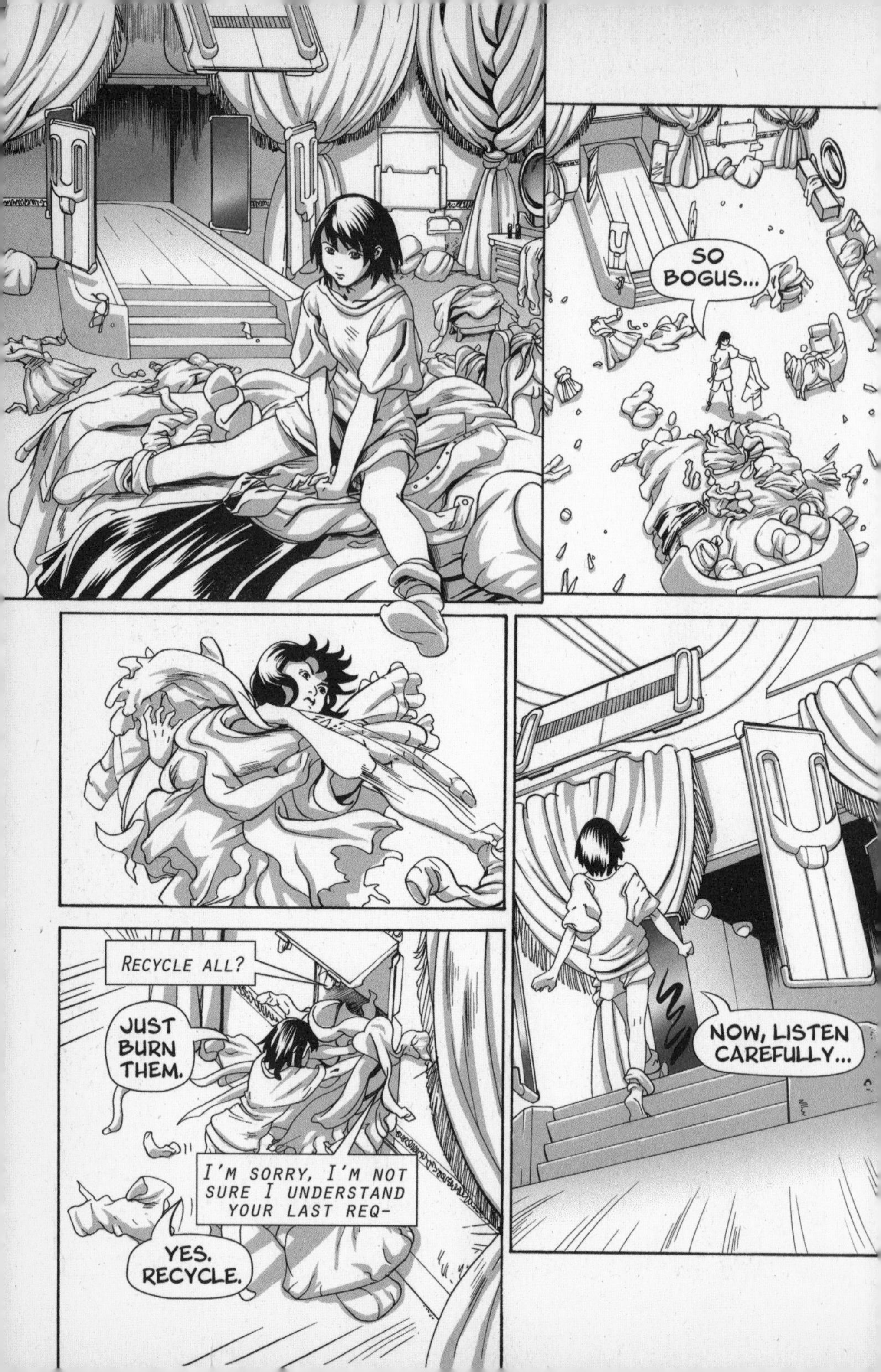
SO BOGUS...
RECYCLE ALL?
JUST BURN THEM.
I'M SORRY, I'M NOT SURE I UNDERSTAND YOUR LAST REQ-
YES. RECYCLE.
NOW, LISTEN CAREFULLY...

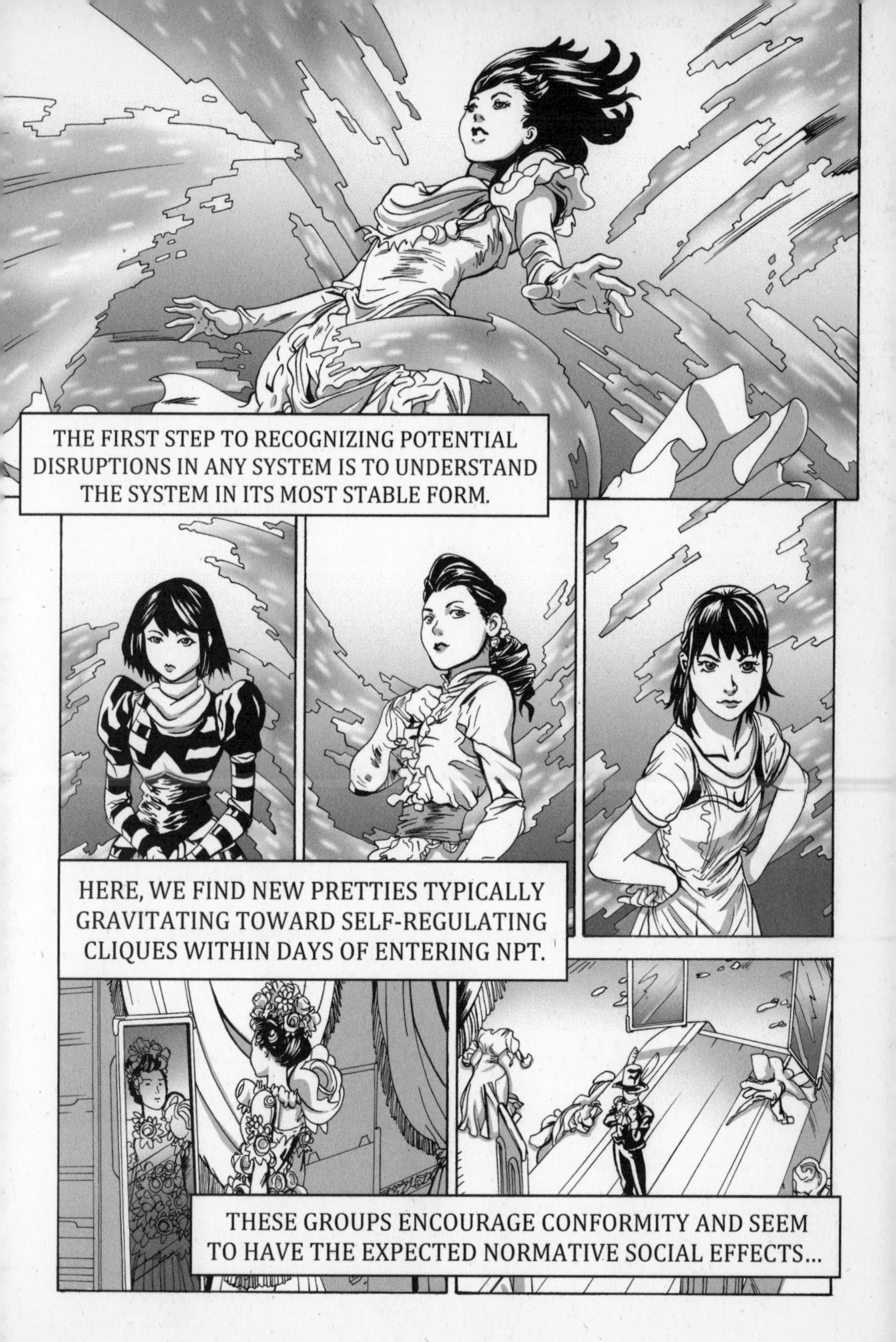
THE FIRST STEP TO RECOGNIZING POTENTIAL DISRUPTIONS IN ANY SYSTEM IS TO UNDERSTAND THE SYSTEM IN ITS MOST STABLE FORM.
HERE, WE FIND NEW PRETTIES TYPICALLY GRAVITATING TOWARD SELF-REGULATING CLIQUES WITHIN DAYS OF ENTERING NPT.
THESE GROUPS ENCOURAGE CONFORMITY AND SEEM TO HAVE THE EXPECTED NORMATIVE SOCIAL EFFECTS...

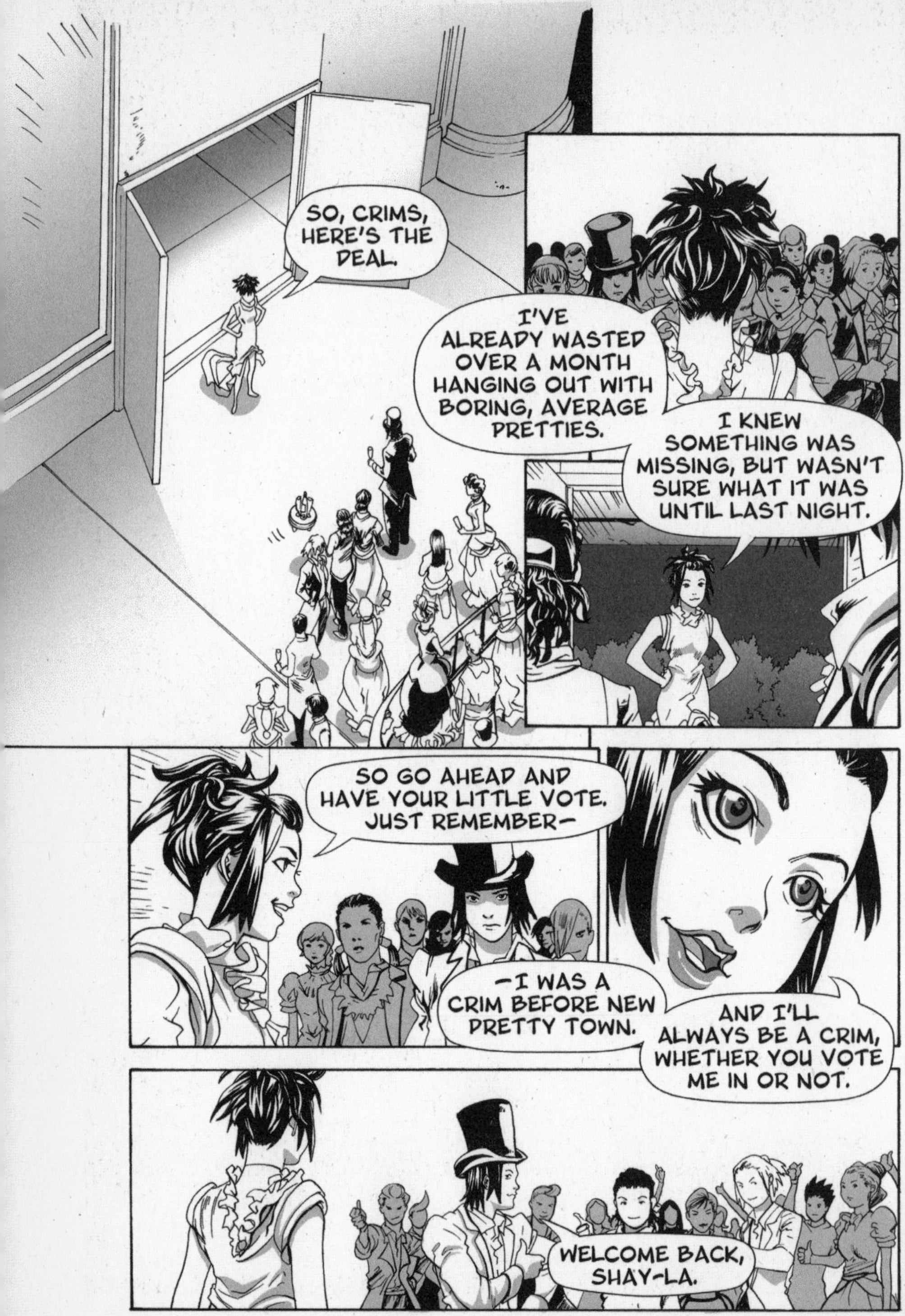
SO, CRIMS, HERE'S THE DEAL.
I'VE ALREADY WASTED OVER A MONTH HANGING OUT WITH BORING, AVERAGE PRETTIES.
I KNEW SOMETHING WAS MISSING, BUT WASN'T SURE WHAT IT WAS UNTIL LAST NIGHT.
SO GO AHEAD AND HAVE YOUR LITTLE VOTE. JUST REMEMBER—
—I WAS A CRIM BEFORE NEW PRETTY TOWN.
AND I'LL ALWAYS BE A CRIM, WHETHER YOU VOTE ME IN OR NOT.
WELCOME BACK, SHAY-LA.

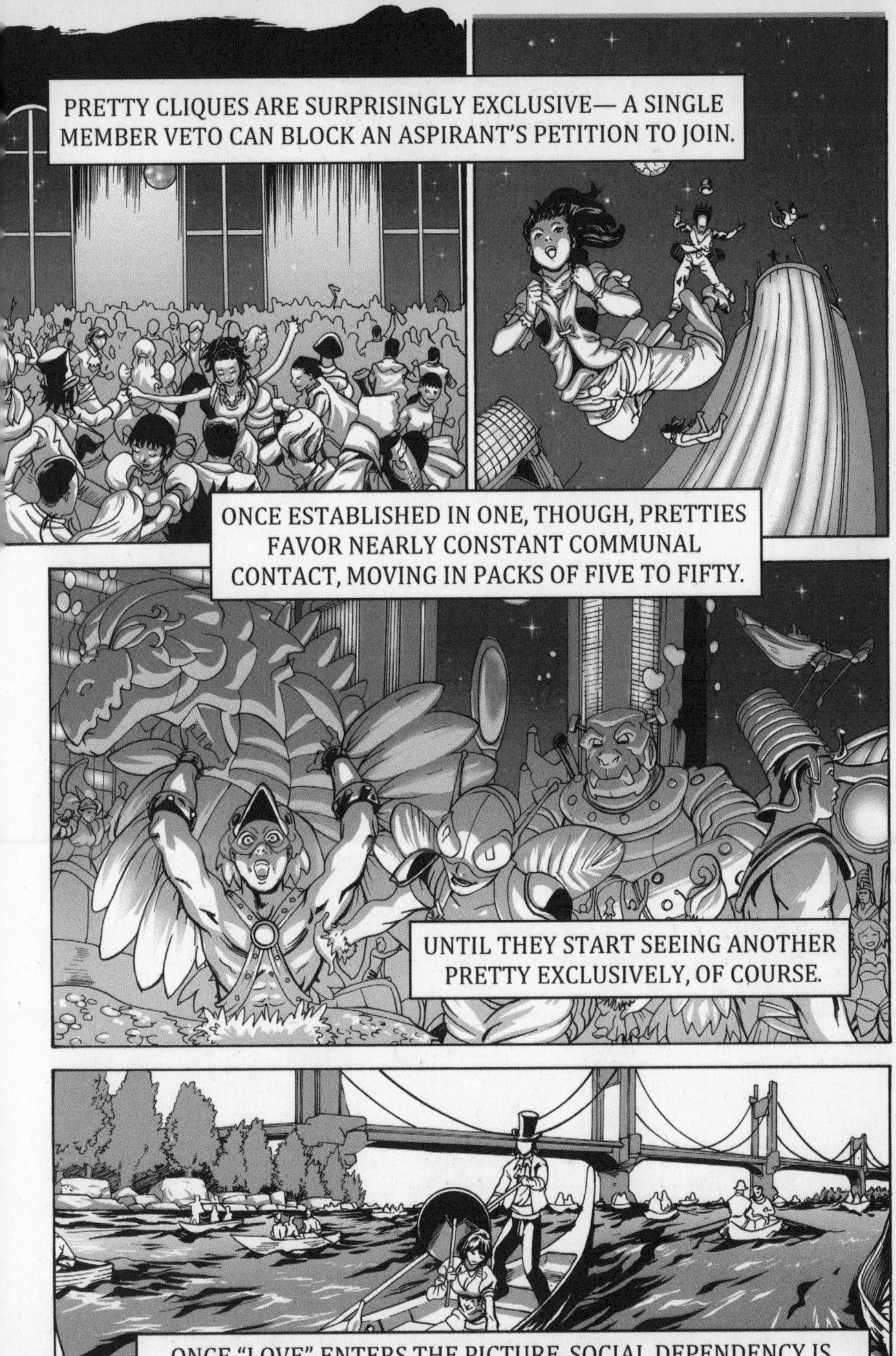
PRETTY CLIQUES ARE SURPRISINGLY EXCLUSIVE— A SINGLE MEMBER VETO CAN BLOCK AN ASPIRANT'S PETITION TO JOIN.
ONCE ESTABLISHED IN ONE, THOUGH, PRETTIES FAVOR NEARLY CONSTANT COMMUNAL CONTACT, MOVING IN PACKS OF FIVE TO FIFTY.
UNTIL THEY START SEEING ANOTHER PRETTY EXCLUSIVELY, OF COURSE.
ONCE "LOVE" ENTERS THE PICTURE, SOCIAL DEPENDENCY IS TRANSFERRED FROM THE GROUP TO THE SELECTED INDIVIDUAL.

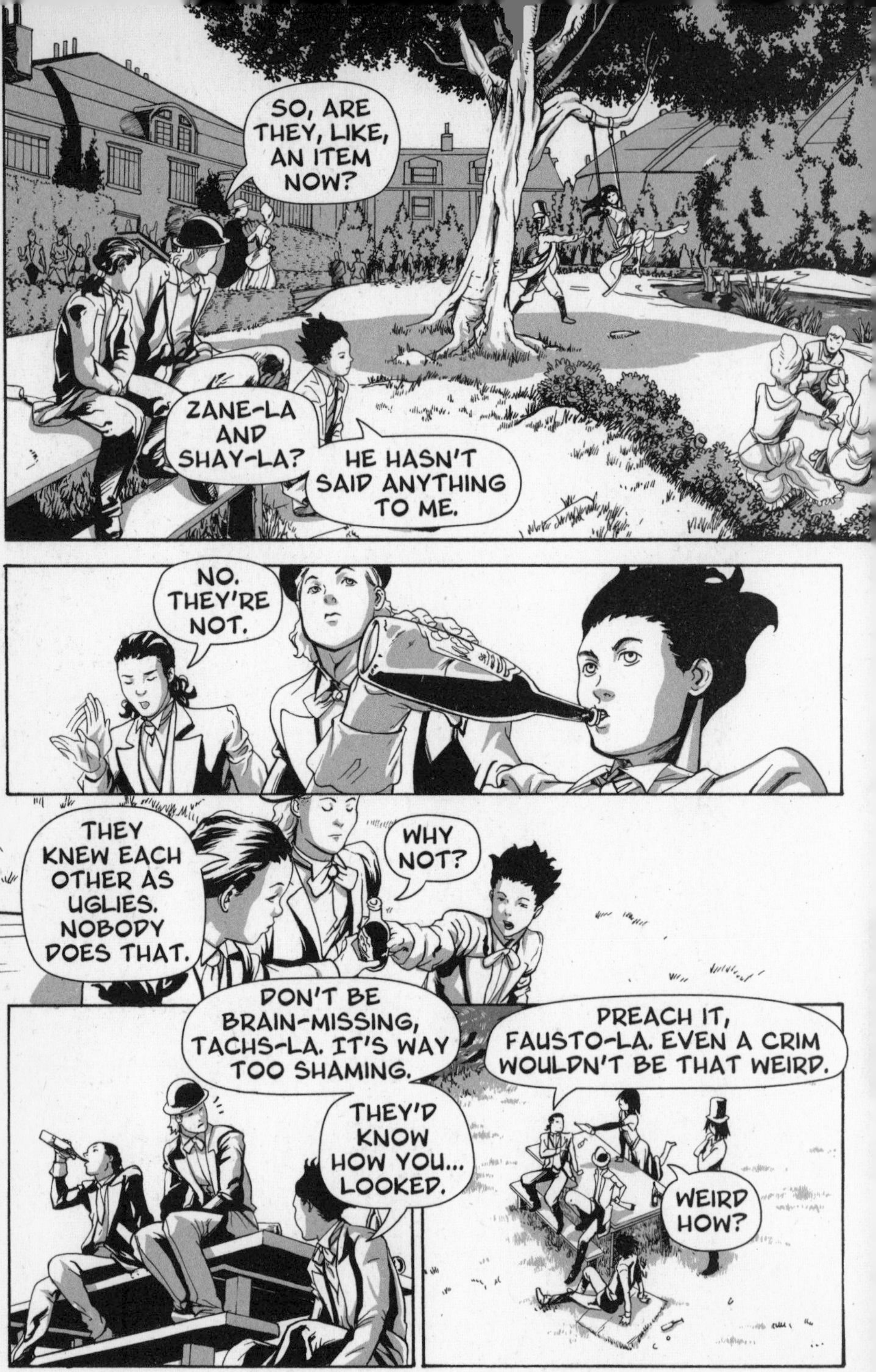
SO, ARE THEY, LIKE, AN ITEM NOW?
ZANE-LA AND SHAY-LA?
HE HASN'T SAID ANYTHING TO ME.
NO. THEY'RE NOT.
THEY KNEW EACH OTHER AS UGLIES. NOBODY DOES THAT.
WHY NOT?
DON'T BE BRAIN-MISSING, TACHS-LA. IT'S WAY TOO SHAMING.
THEY'D KNOW HOW YOU... LOOKED.
PREACH IT, FAUSTO-LA. EVEN A CRIM WOULDN'T BE THAT WEIRD.
WEIRD HOW?

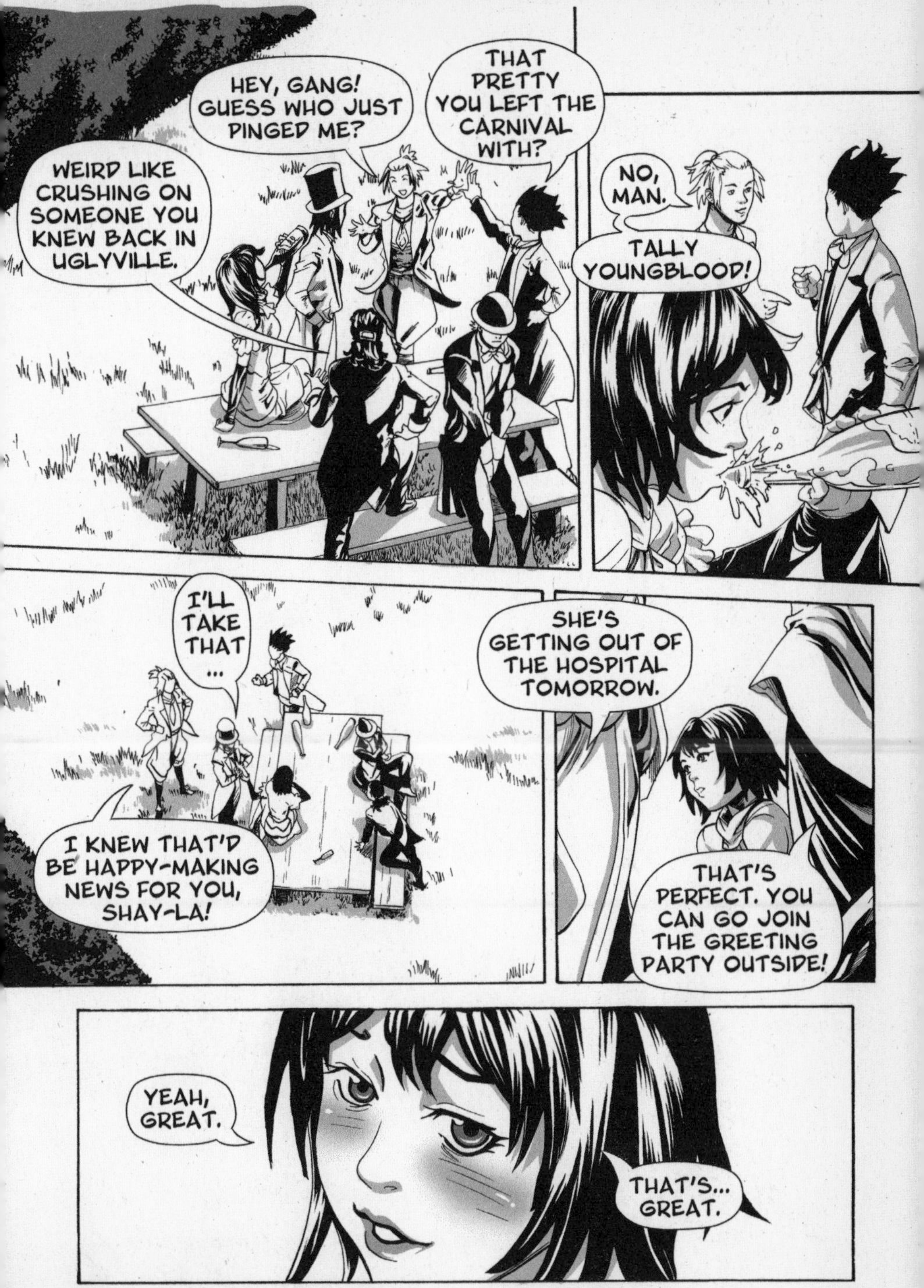
HEY, GANG! GUESS WHO JUST PINGED ME?
THAT PRETTY YOU LEFT THE CARNIVAL WITH?
WEIRD LIKE CRUSHING ON SOMEONE YOU KNEW BACK IN UGLYVILLE.
NO, MAN.
TALLY YOUNGBLOOD!
I'LL TAKE THAT ...
I KNEW THAT'D BE HAPPY-MAKING NEWS FOR YOU, SHAY-LA!
SHE'S GETTING OUT OF THE HOSPITAL TOMORROW.
THAT'S PERFECT. YOU CAN GO JOIN THE GREETING PARTY OUTSIDE!
YEAH, GREAT.
THAT'S... GREAT.

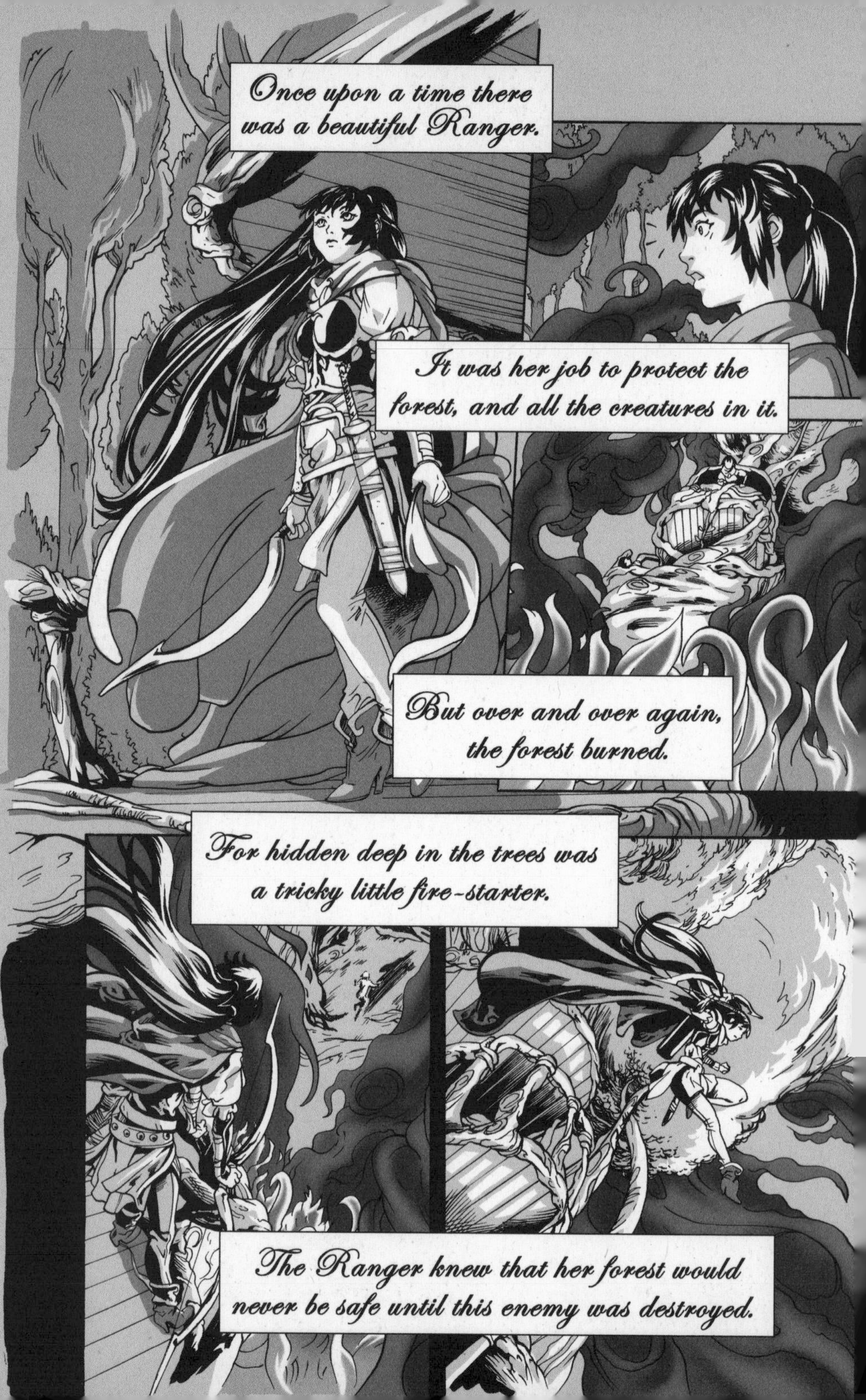
Once upon a time there was a beautiful Ranger.
It was her job to protect the forest, and all the creatures in it.
But over and over again, the forest burned.
For hidden deep in the trees was a tricky little fire-starter.
The Ranger knew that her forest would never be safe until this enemy was destroyed.

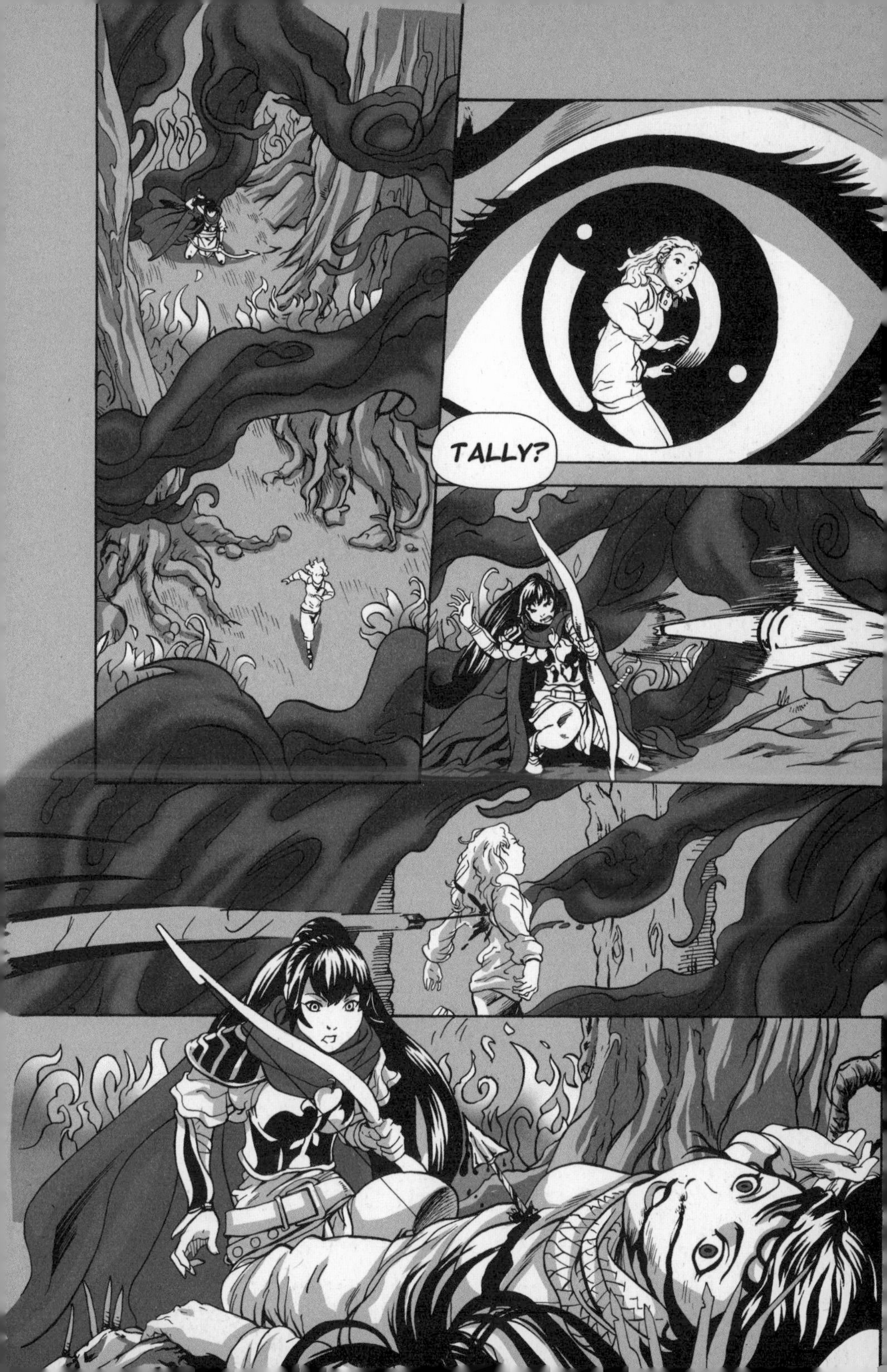
TALLY?

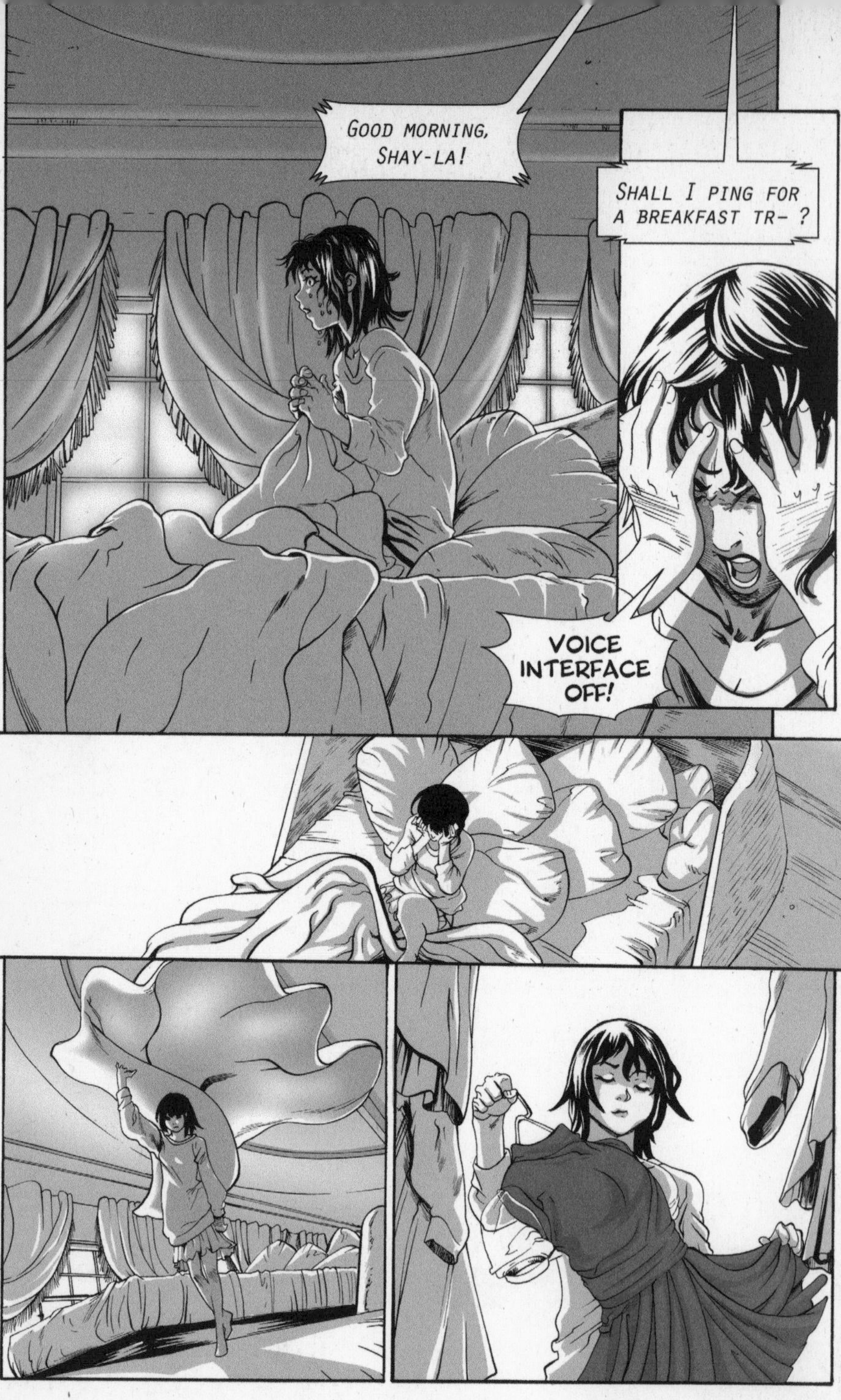
GOOD MORNING, SHAY-LA!
SHALL I PING FOR A BREAKFAST TR- ?
VOICE INTERFACE OFF!

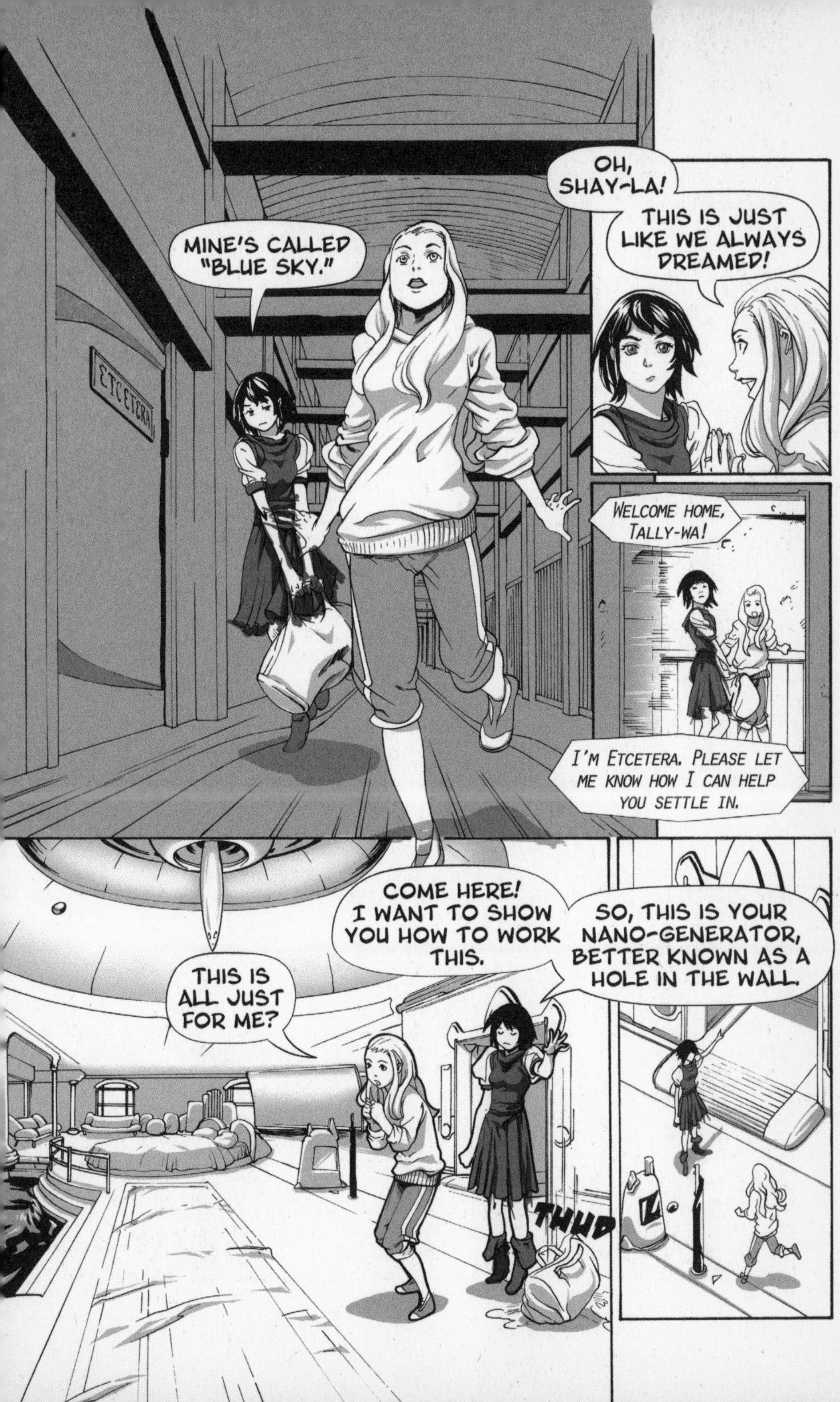
ETCETERA
MINE'S CALLED "BLUE SKY."
OH, SHAY-LA!
THIS IS JUST LIKE WE ALWAYS DREAMED!
WELCOME HOME, TALLY-WA!
I'M ETCETERA. PLEASE LET ME KNOW HOW I CAN HELP YOU SETTLE IN.
COME HERE! I WANT TO SHOW YOU HOW TO WORK THIS.
THIS IS ALL JUST FOR ME?
THUD
SO, THIS IS YOUR NANO-GENERATOR, BETTER KNOWN AS A HOLE IN THE WALL.

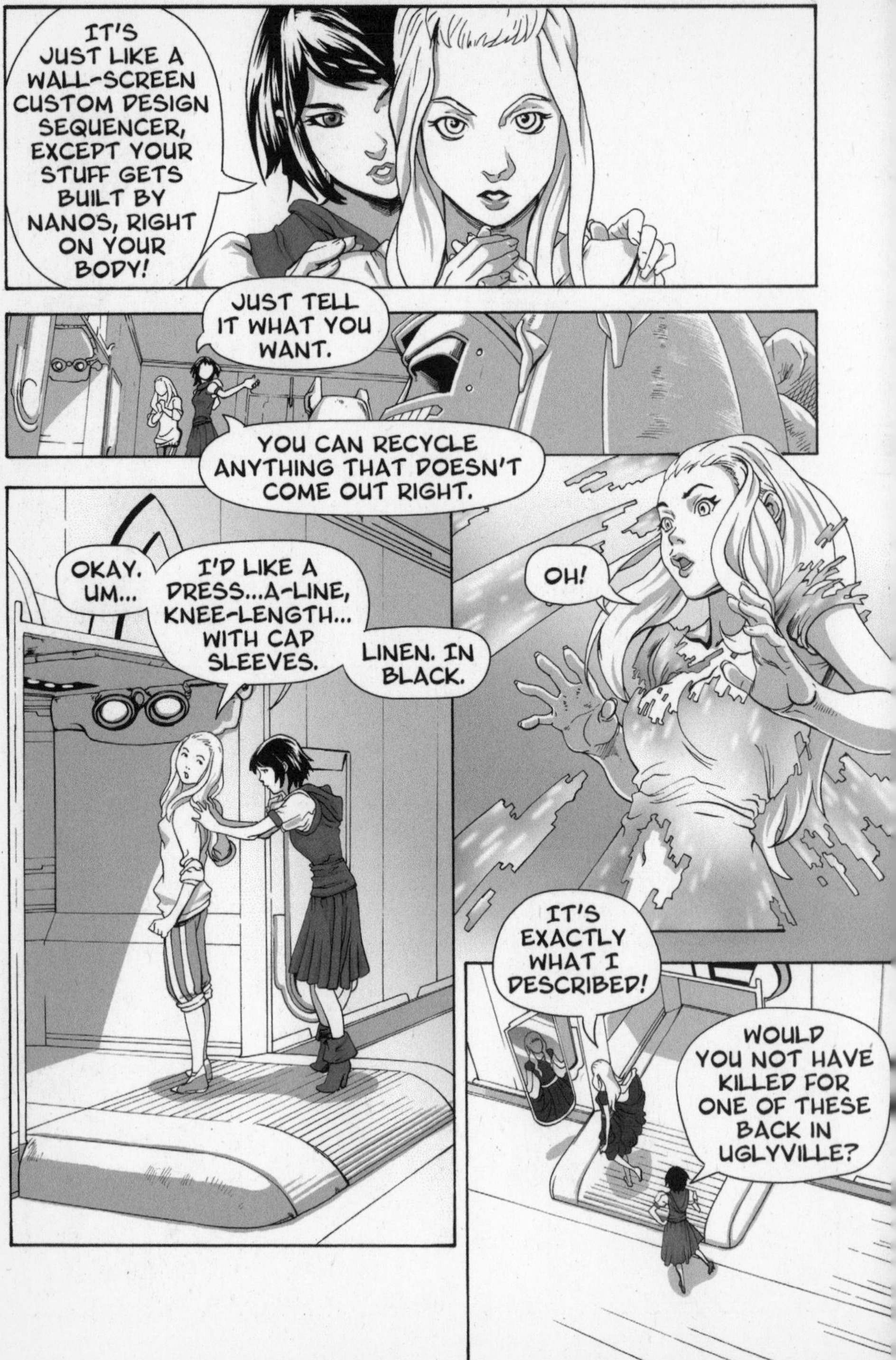
IT'S JUST LIKE A WALL-SCREEN CUSTOM DESIGN SEQUENCER, EXCEPT YOUR STUFF GETS BUILT BY NANOS, RIGHT ON YOUR BODY!
JUST TELL IT WHAT YOU WANT.
YOU CAN RECYCLE ANYTHING THAT DOESN'T COME OUT RIGHT.
OKAY. UM...
I'D LIKE A DRESS...A-LINE, KNEE-LENGTH... WITH CAP SLEEVES.
LINEN. IN BLACK.
OH!
IT'S EXACTLY WHAT I DESCRIBED!
WOULD YOU NOT HAVE KILLED FOR ONE OF THESE BACK IN UGLYVILLE?

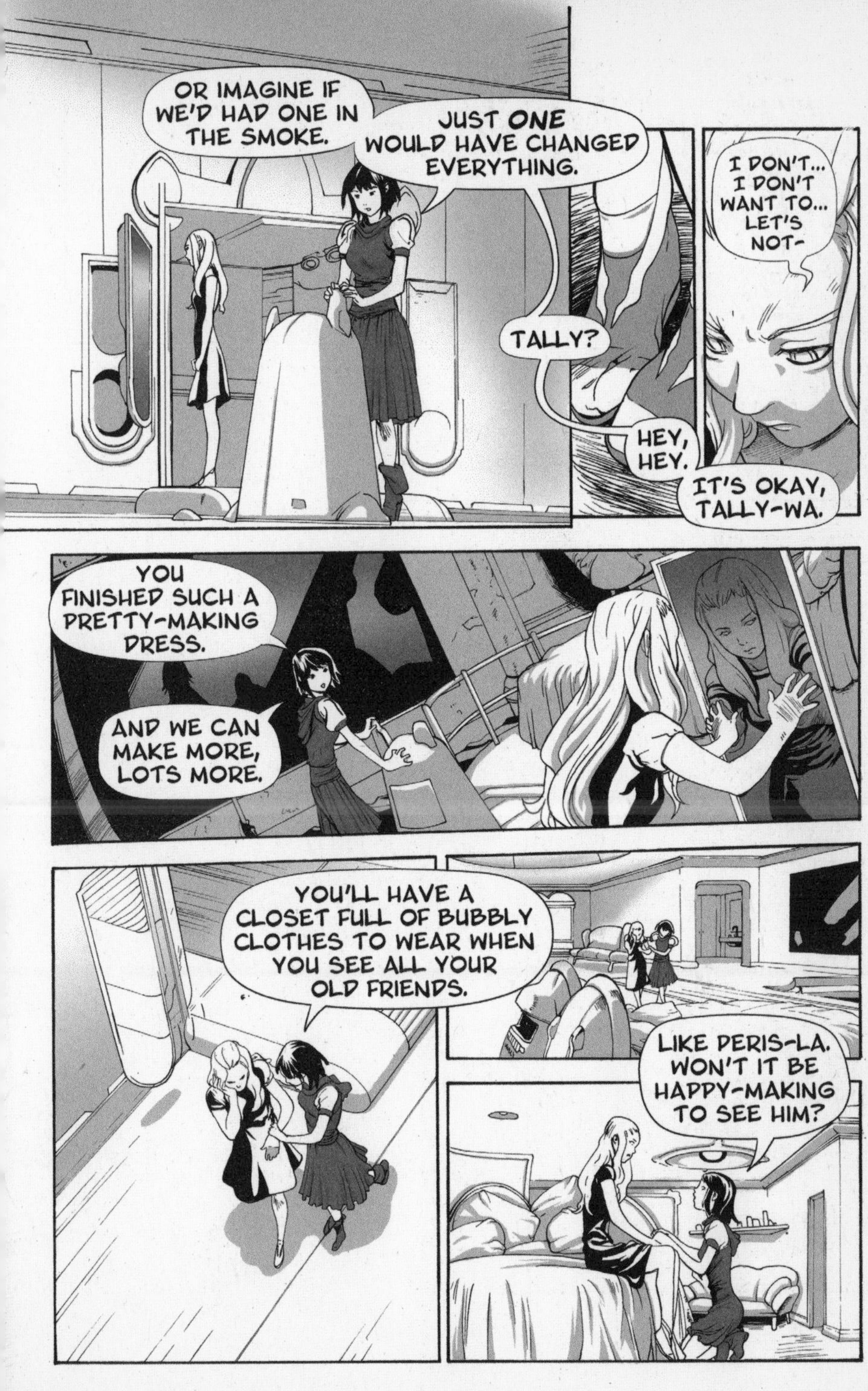
OR IMAGINE IF WE'D HAD ONE IN THE SMOKE.
JUST ONE WOULD HAVE CHANGED EVERYTHING.
I DON'T... I DON'T WANT TO... LET'S NOT-
TALLY?
HEY, HEY.
IT'S OKAY, TALLY-WA.
YOU FINISHED SUCH A PRETTY-MAKING DRESS.
AND WE CAN MAKE MORE, LOTS MORE.
YOU'LL HAVE A CLOSET FULL OF BUBBLY CLOTHES TO WEAR WHEN YOU SEE ALL YOUR OLD FRIENDS.
LIKE PERIS-LA. WON'T IT BE HAPPY-MAKING TO SEE HIM?

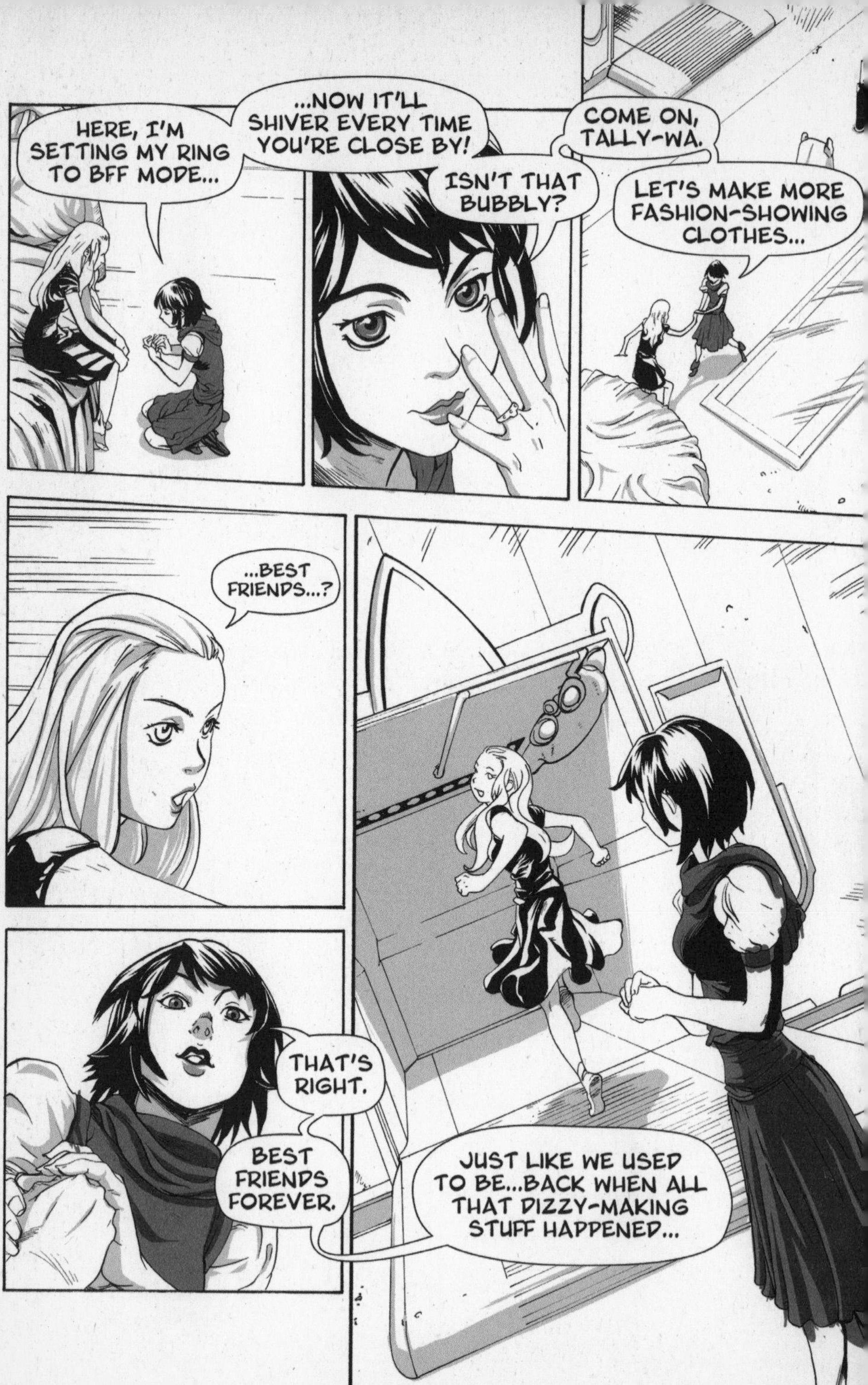
HERE, I'M SETTING MY RING TO BFF MODE...
...NOW IT'LL SHIVER EVERY TIME YOU'RE CLOSE BY!
ISN'T THAT BUBBLY?
COME ON, TALLY-WA.
LET'S MAKE MORE FASHION-SHOWING CLOTHES...
...BEST FRIENDS...?
THAT'S RIGHT.
BEST FRIENDS FOREVER.
JUST LIKE WE USED TO BE...BACK WHEN ALL THAT DIZZY-MAKING STUFF HAPPENED...

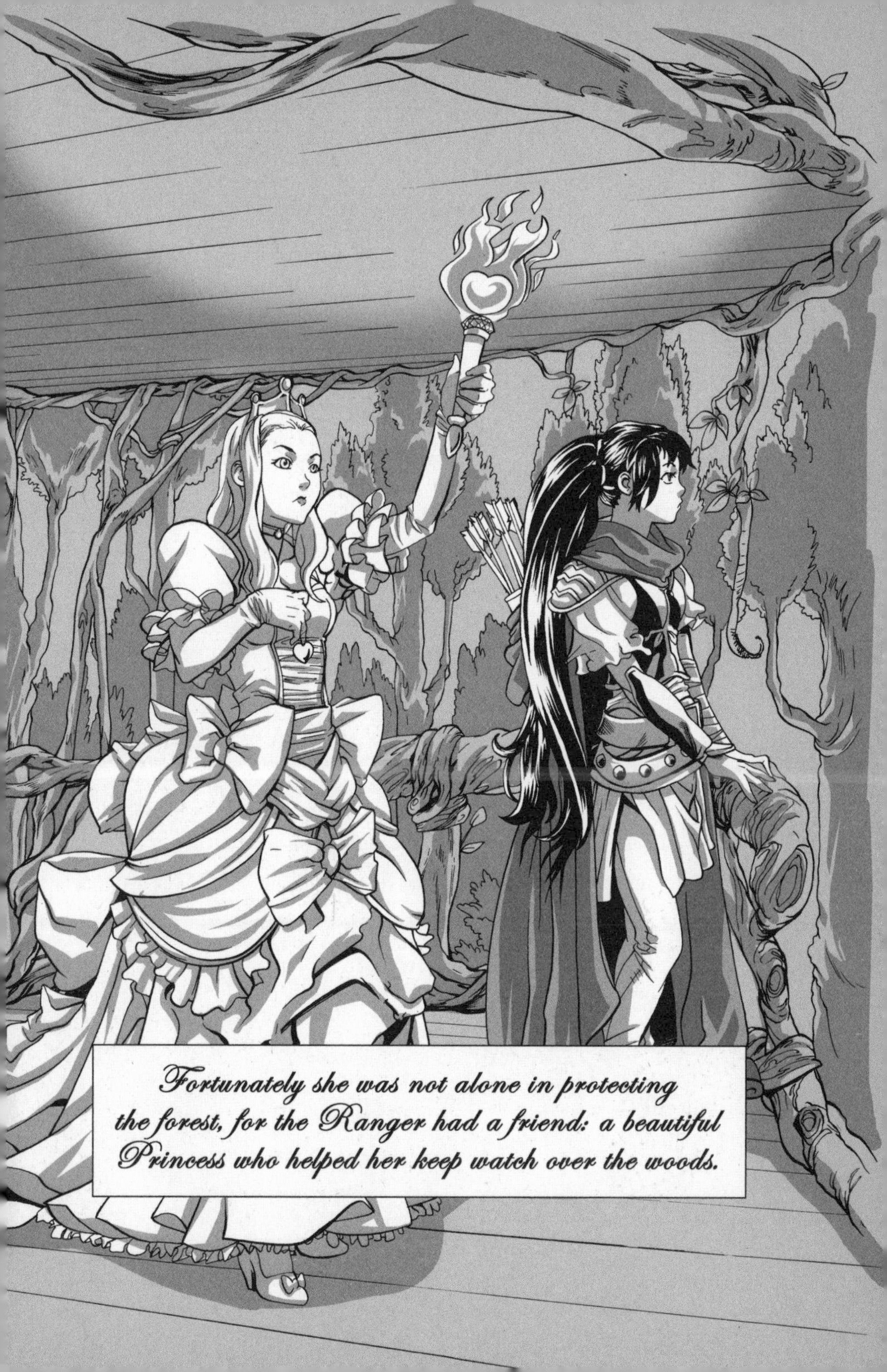
Fortunately she was not alone in protecting the forest, for the Ranger had a friend: a beautiful Princess who helped her keep watch over the woods.

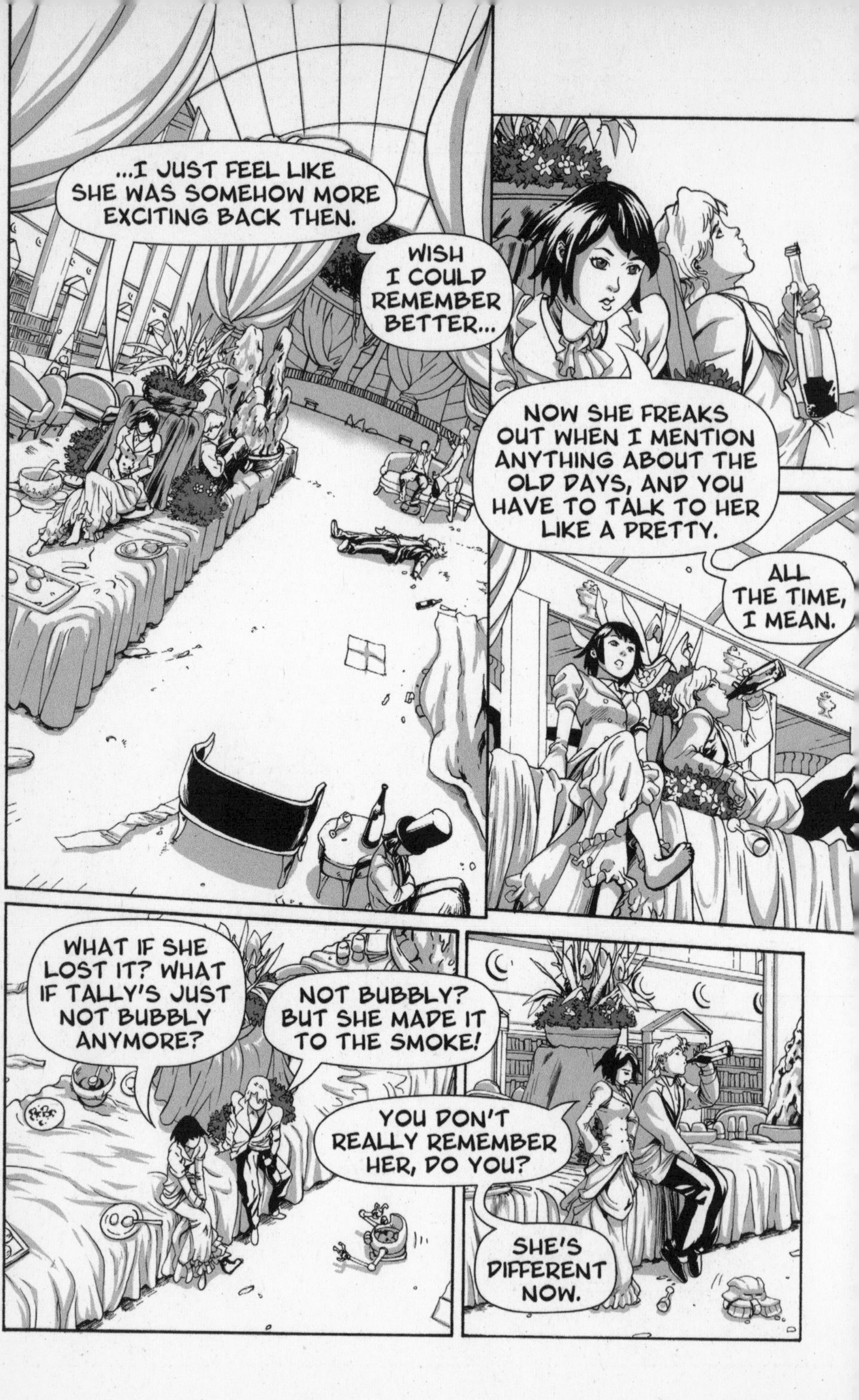
...I JUST FEEL LIKE SHE WAS SOMEHOW MORE EXCITING BACK THEN.
WISH I COULD REMEMBER BETTER...
NOW SHE FREAKS OUT WHEN I MENTION ANYTHING ABOUT THE OLD DAYS, AND YOU HAVE TO TALK TO HER LIKE A PRETTY.
ALL THE TIME, I MEAN.
WHAT IF SHE LOST IT? WHAT IF TALLY'S JUST NOT BUBBLY ANYMORE?
NOT BUBBLY? BUT SHE MADE IT TO THE SMOKE!
YOU DON'T REALLY REMEMBER HER, DO YOU?
SHE'S DIFFERENT NOW.

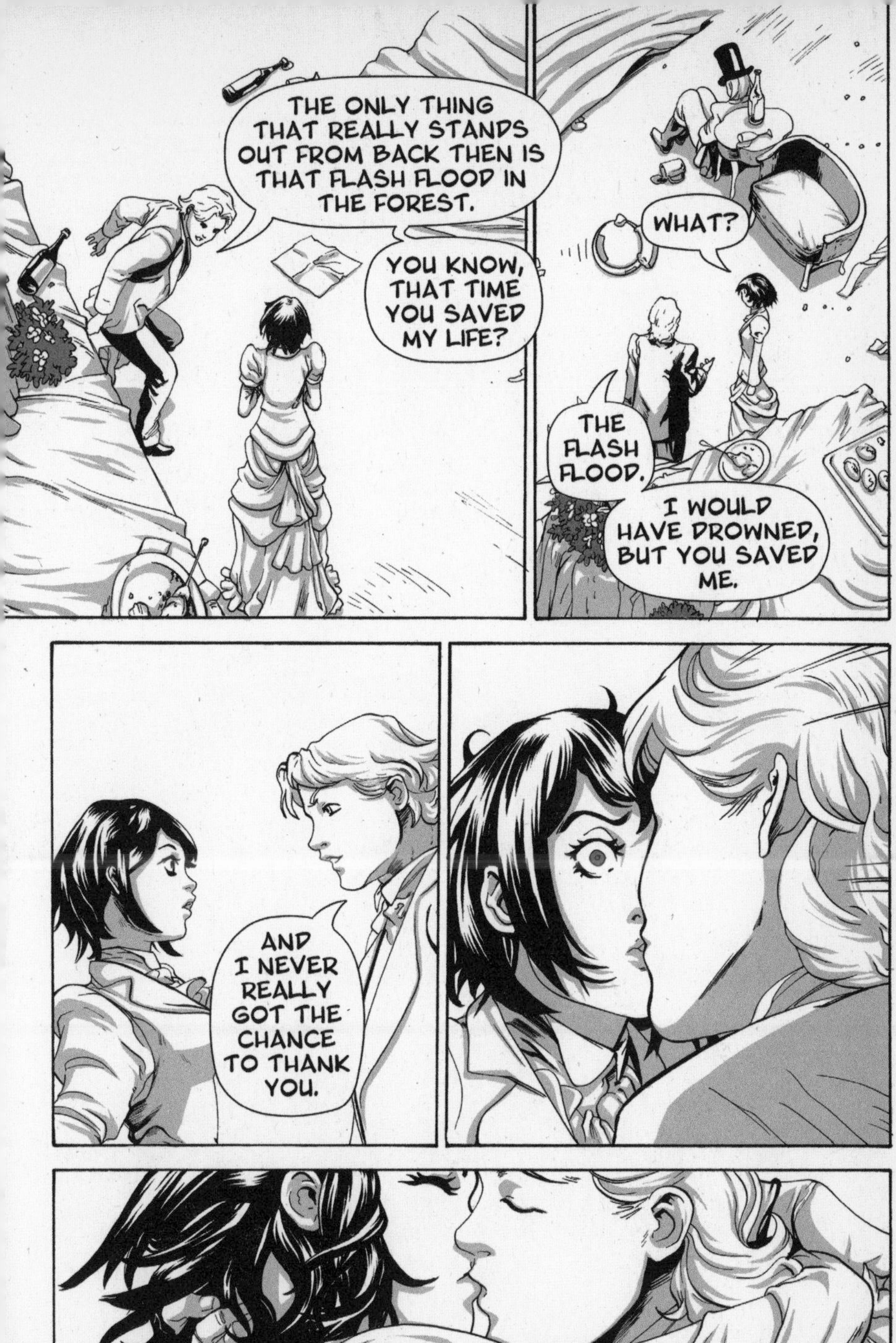
THE ONLY THING THAT REALLY STANDS OUT FROM BACK THEN IS THAT FLASH FLOOD IN THE FOREST.
YOU KNOW, THAT TIME YOU SAVED MY LIFE?
WHAT?
THE FLASH FLOOD.
I WOULD HAVE DROWNED, BUT YOU SAVED ME.
AND I NEVER REALLY GOT THE CHANCE TO THANK YOU.

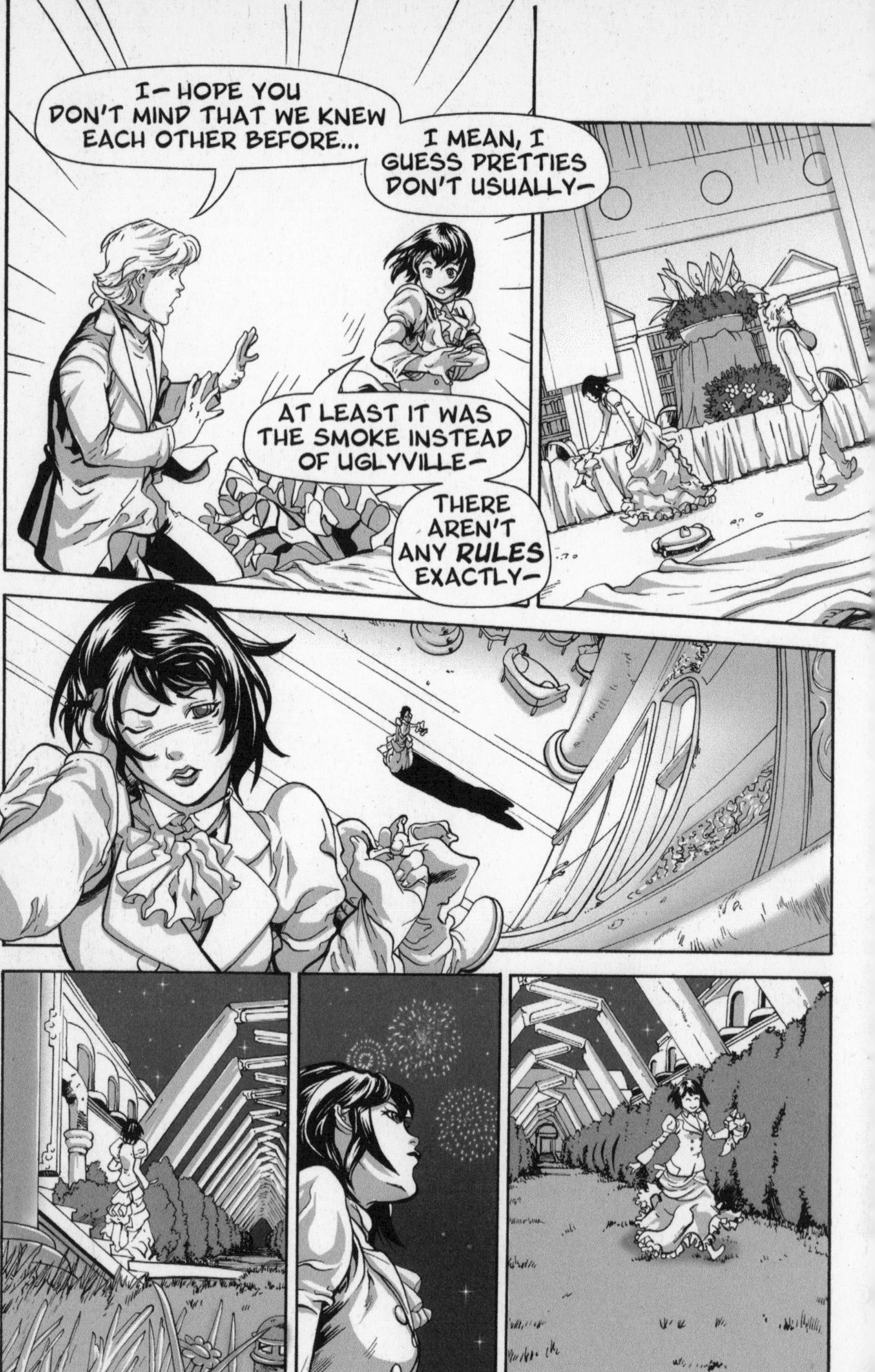
I— HOPE YOU DON'T MIND THAT WE KNEW EACH OTHER BEFORE...
I MEAN, I GUESS PRETTIES DON'T USUALLY—
AT LEAST IT WAS THE SMOKE INSTEAD OF UGLYVILLE—
THERE AREN'T ANY *RULES* EXACTLY—

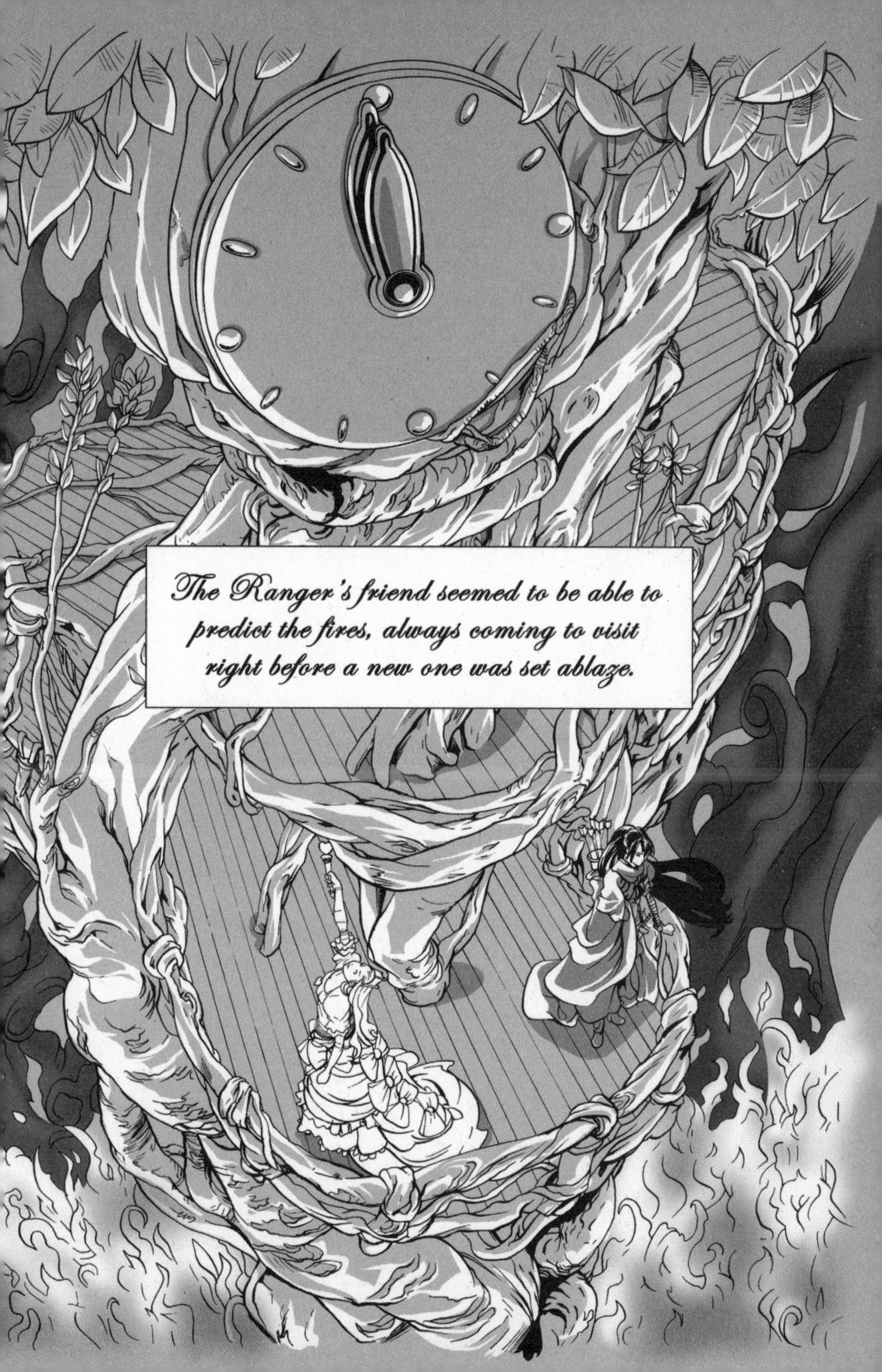
The Ranger's friend seemed to be able to predict the fires, always coming to visit right before a new one was set ablaze.

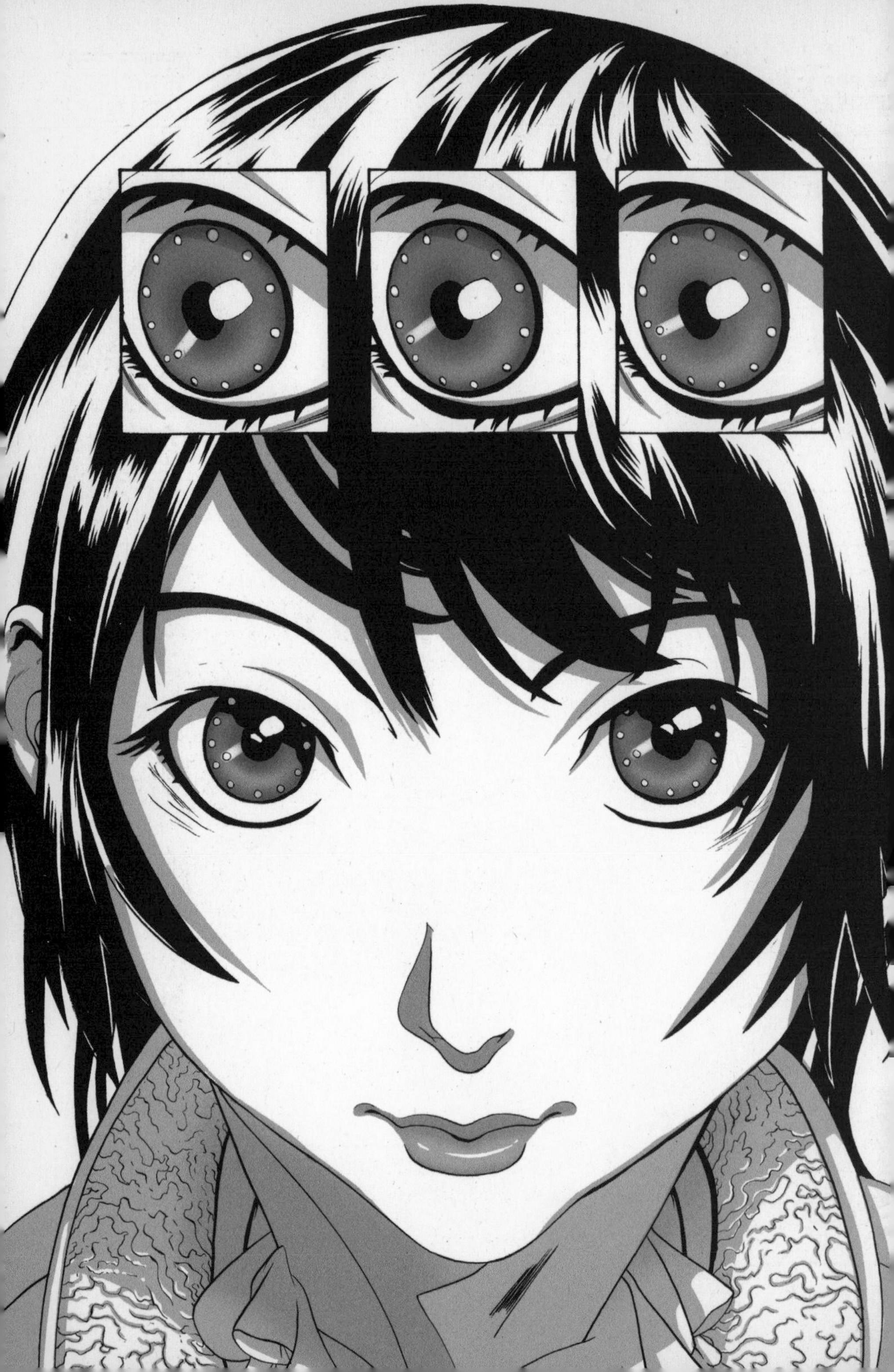

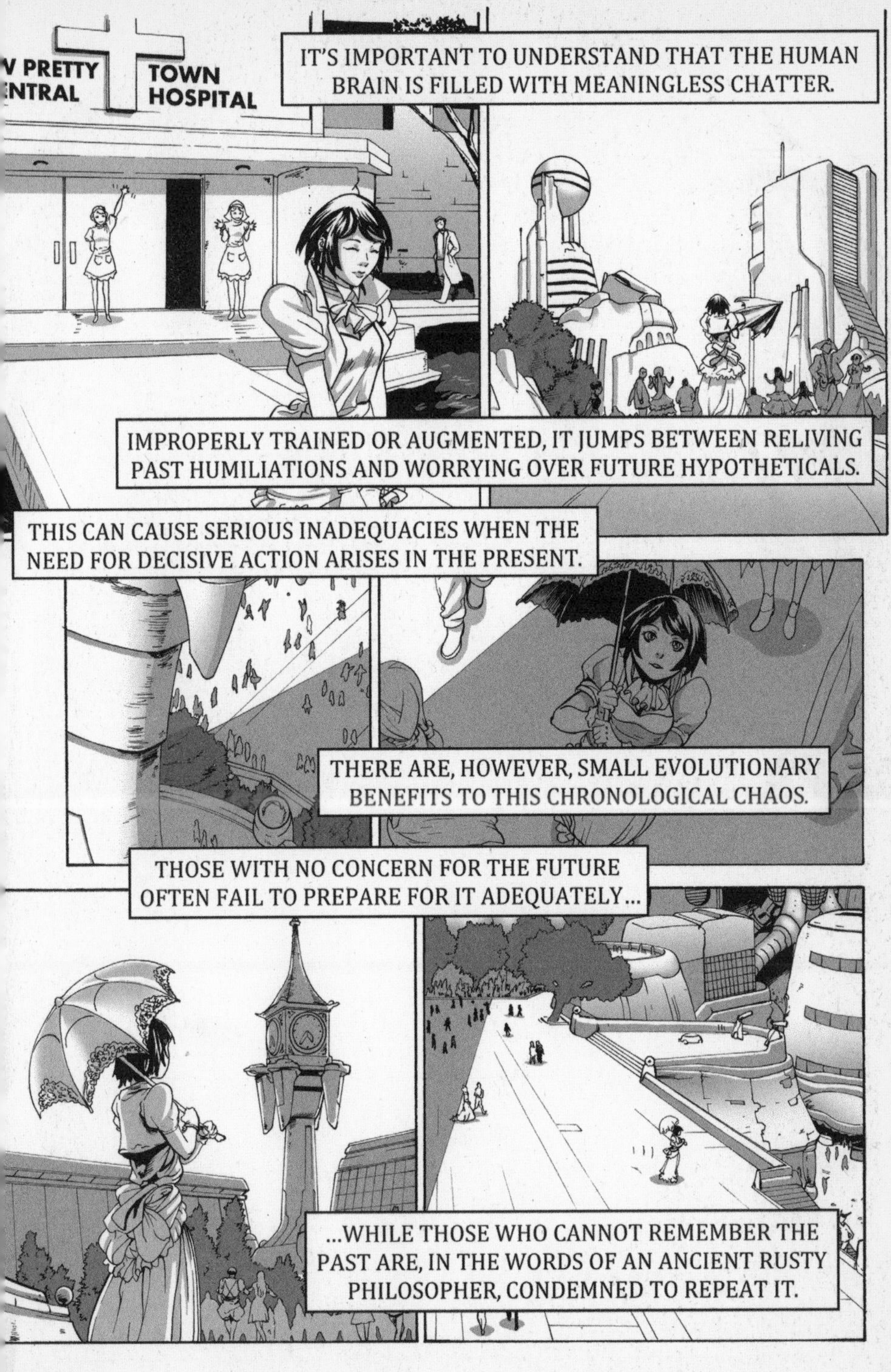
V PRETTY TOWN
NTRAL HOSPITAL
IT'S IMPORTANT TO UNDERSTAND THAT THE HUMAN BRAIN IS FILLED WITH MEANINGLESS CHATTER.
IMPROPERLY TRAINED OR AUGMENTED, IT JUMPS BETWEEN RELIVING PAST HUMILIATIONS AND WORRYING OVER FUTURE HYPOTHETICALS.
THIS CAN CAUSE SERIOUS INADEQUACIES WHEN THE NEED FOR DECISIVE ACTION ARISES IN THE PRESENT.
THERE ARE, HOWEVER, SMALL EVOLUTIONARY BENEFITS TO THIS CHRONOLOGICAL CHAOS.
THOSE WITH NO CONCERN FOR THE FUTURE OFTEN FAIL TO PREPARE FOR IT ADEQUATELY...
...WHILE THOSE WHO CANNOT REMEMBER THE PAST ARE, IN THE WORDS OF AN ANCIENT RUSTY PHILOSOPHER, CONDEMNED TO REPEAT IT.

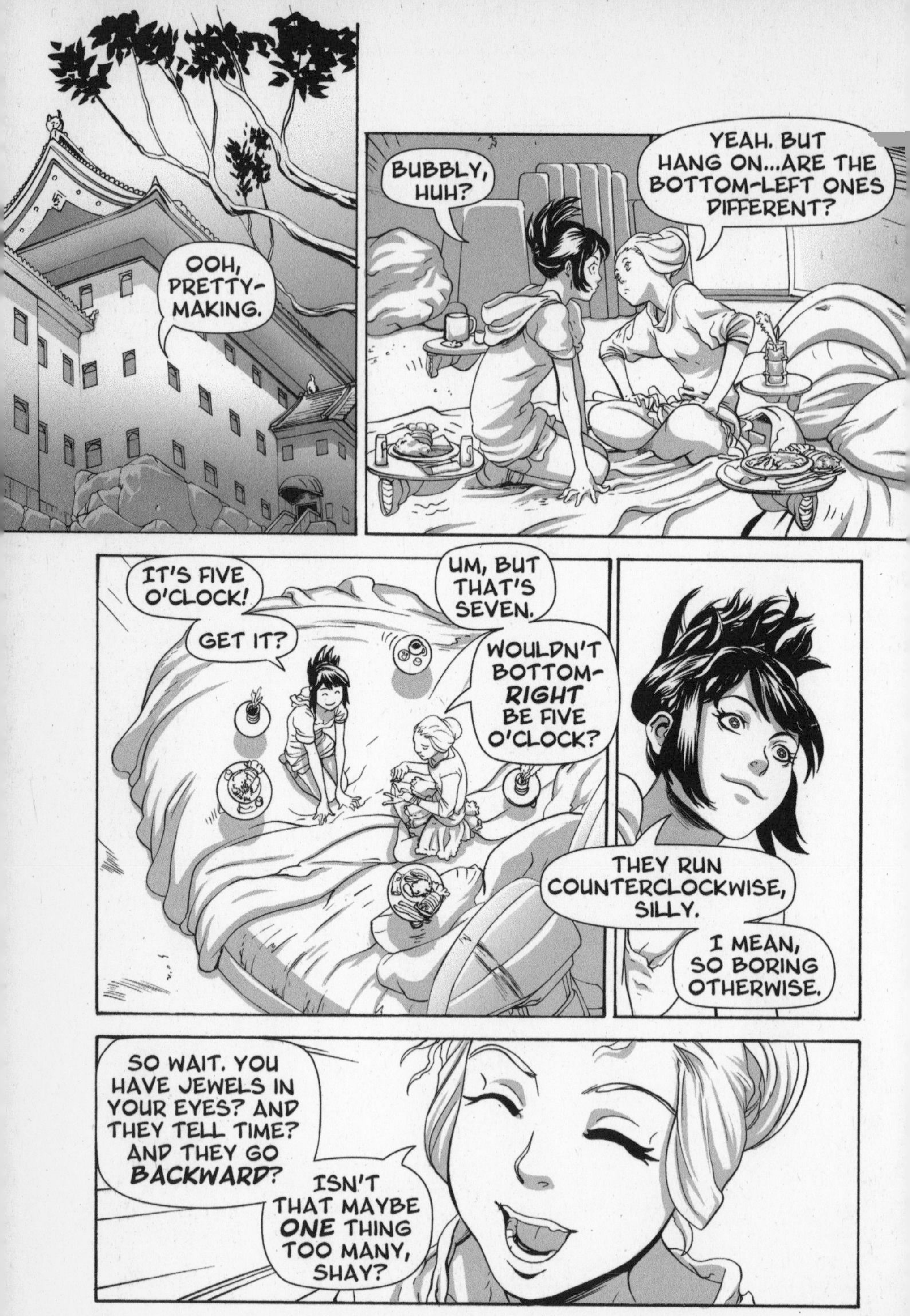
OOH, PRETTY-MAKING.
BUBBLY, HUH?
YEAH. BUT HANG ON...ARE THE BOTTOM-LEFT ONES DIFFERENT?
IT'S FIVE O'CLOCK!
GET IT?
UM, BUT THAT'S SEVEN.
WOULDN'T BOTTOM-*RIGHT* BE FIVE O'CLOCK?
THEY RUN COUNTERCLOCKWISE, SILLY.
I MEAN, SO BORING OTHERWISE.
SO WAIT. YOU HAVE JEWELS IN YOUR EYES? AND THEY TELL TIME? AND THEY GO **BACKWARD**?
ISN'T THAT MAYBE **ONE** THING TOO MANY, SHAY?

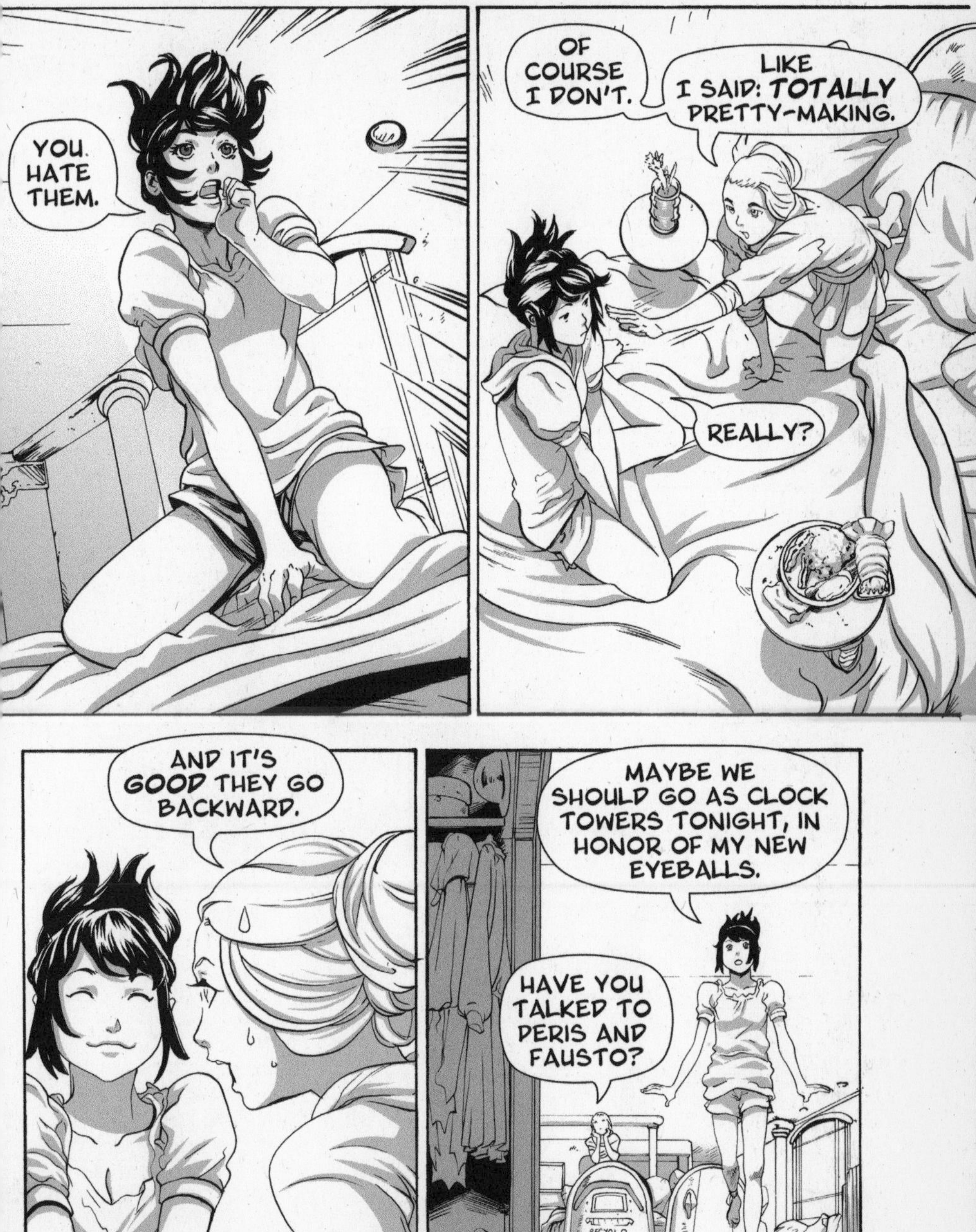
YOU. HATE THEM.
OF COURSE I DON'T.
LIKE I SAID: TOTALLY PRETTY-MAKING.
REALLY?
AND IT'S GOOD THEY GO BACKWARD.
MAYBE WE SHOULD GO AS CLOCK TOWERS TONIGHT, IN HONOR OF MY NEW EYEBALLS.
HAVE YOU TALKED TO PERIS AND FAUSTO?
RECYCLE

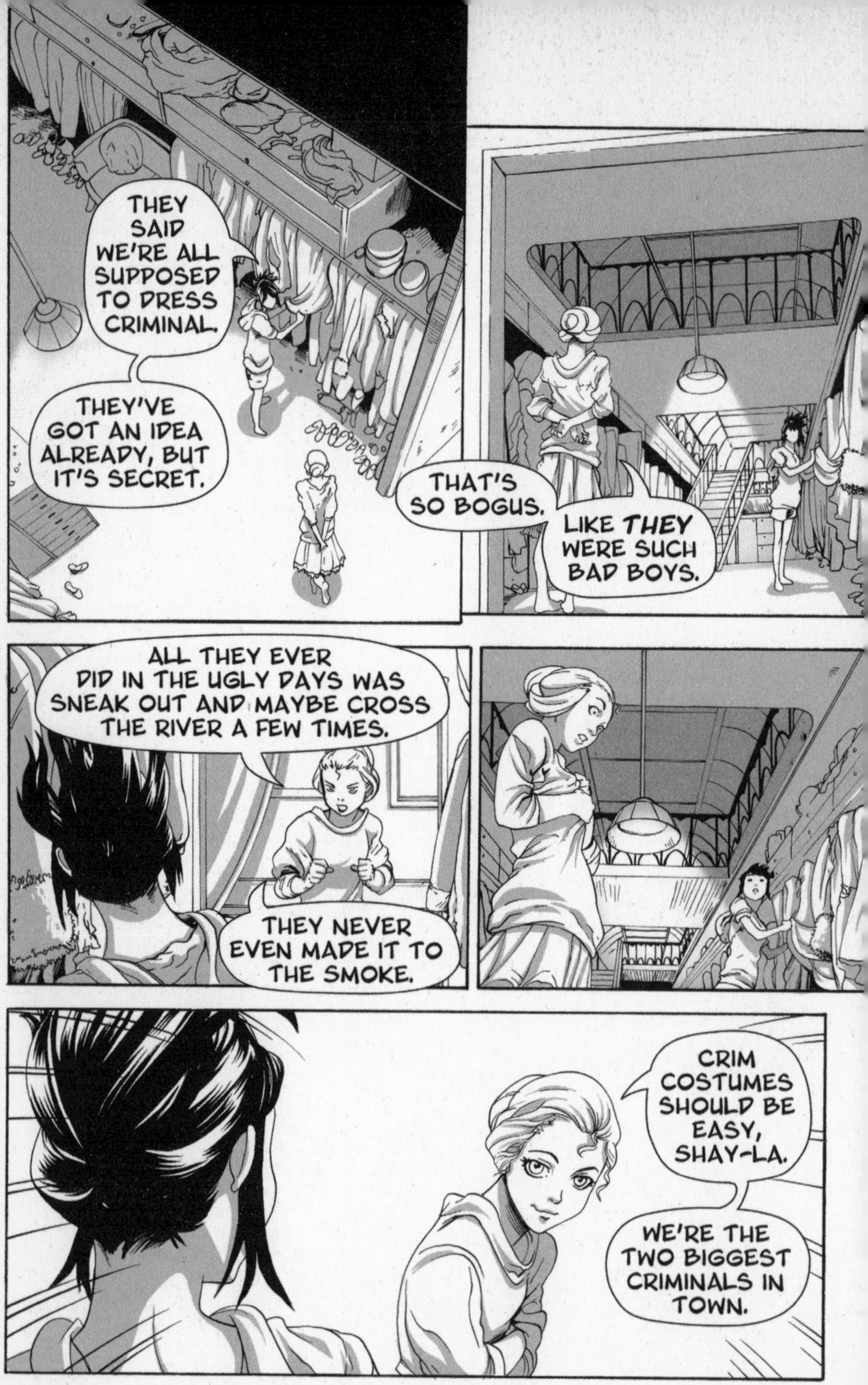
THEY SAID WE'RE ALL SUPPOSED TO DRESS CRIMINAL.
THEY'VE GOT AN IDEA ALREADY, BUT IT'S SECRET.
THAT'S SO BOGUS.
LIKE *THEY* WERE SUCH BAD BOYS.
ALL THEY EVER DID IN THE UGLY DAYS WAS SNEAK OUT AND MAYBE CROSS THE RIVER A FEW TIMES.
THEY NEVER EVEN MADE IT TO THE SMOKE.
CRIM COSTUMES SHOULD BE EASY, SHAY-LA.
WE'RE THE TWO BIGGEST CRIMINALS IN TOWN.

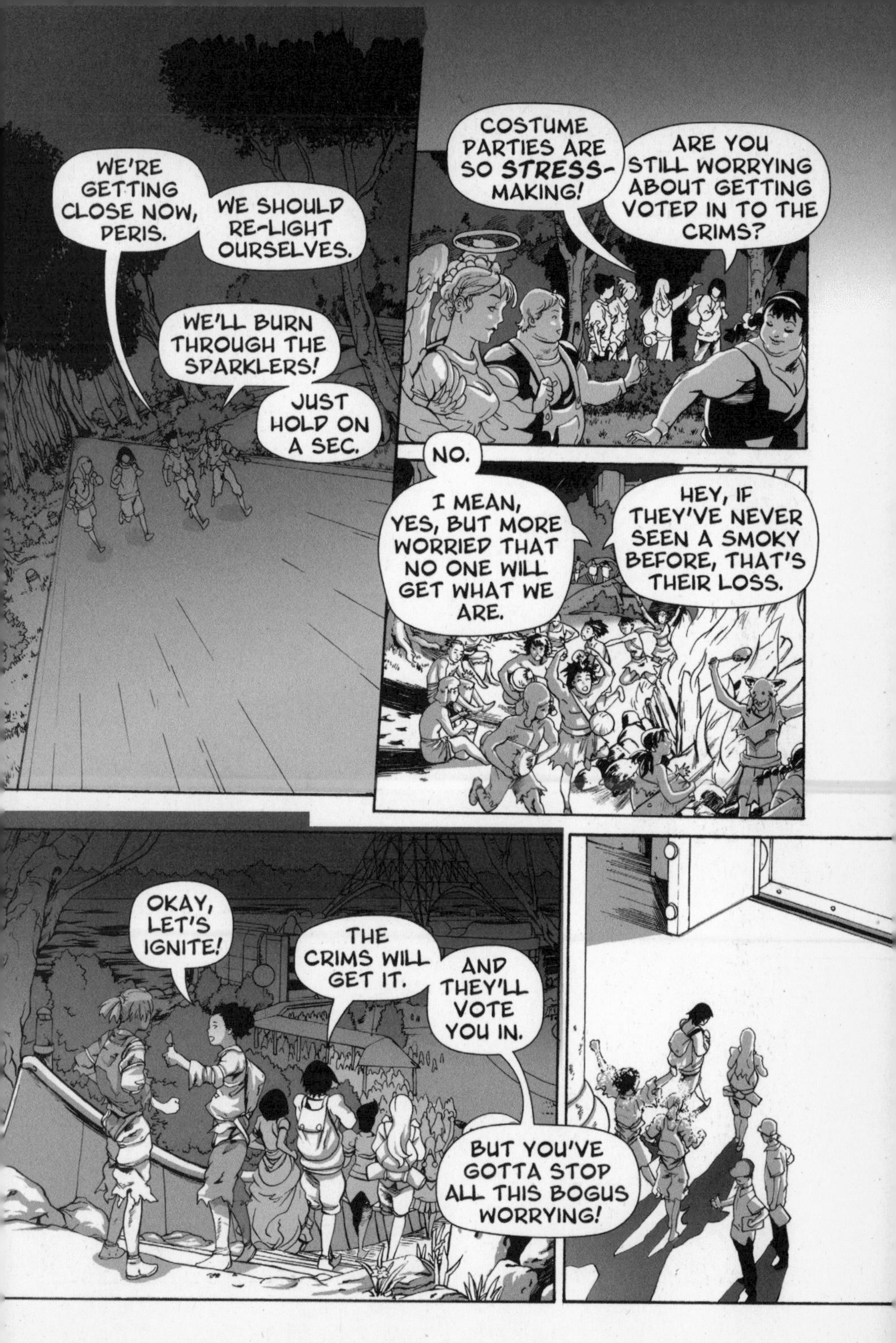

WE'RE GETTING CLOSE NOW, PERIS.
WE SHOULD RE-LIGHT OURSELVES.
WE'LL BURN THROUGH THE SPARKLERS!
JUST HOLD ON A SEC.
COSTUME PARTIES ARE SO **STRESS**-MAKING!
ARE YOU STILL WORRYING ABOUT GETTING VOTED IN TO THE CRIMS?
NO.
I MEAN, YES, BUT MORE WORRIED THAT NO ONE WILL GET WHAT WE ARE.
HEY, IF THEY'VE NEVER SEEN A SMOKY BEFORE, THAT'S THEIR LOSS.
OKAY, LET'S IGNITE!
THE CRIMS WILL GET IT.
AND THEY'LL VOTE YOU IN.
BUT YOU'VE GOTTA STOP ALL THIS BOGUS WORRYING!

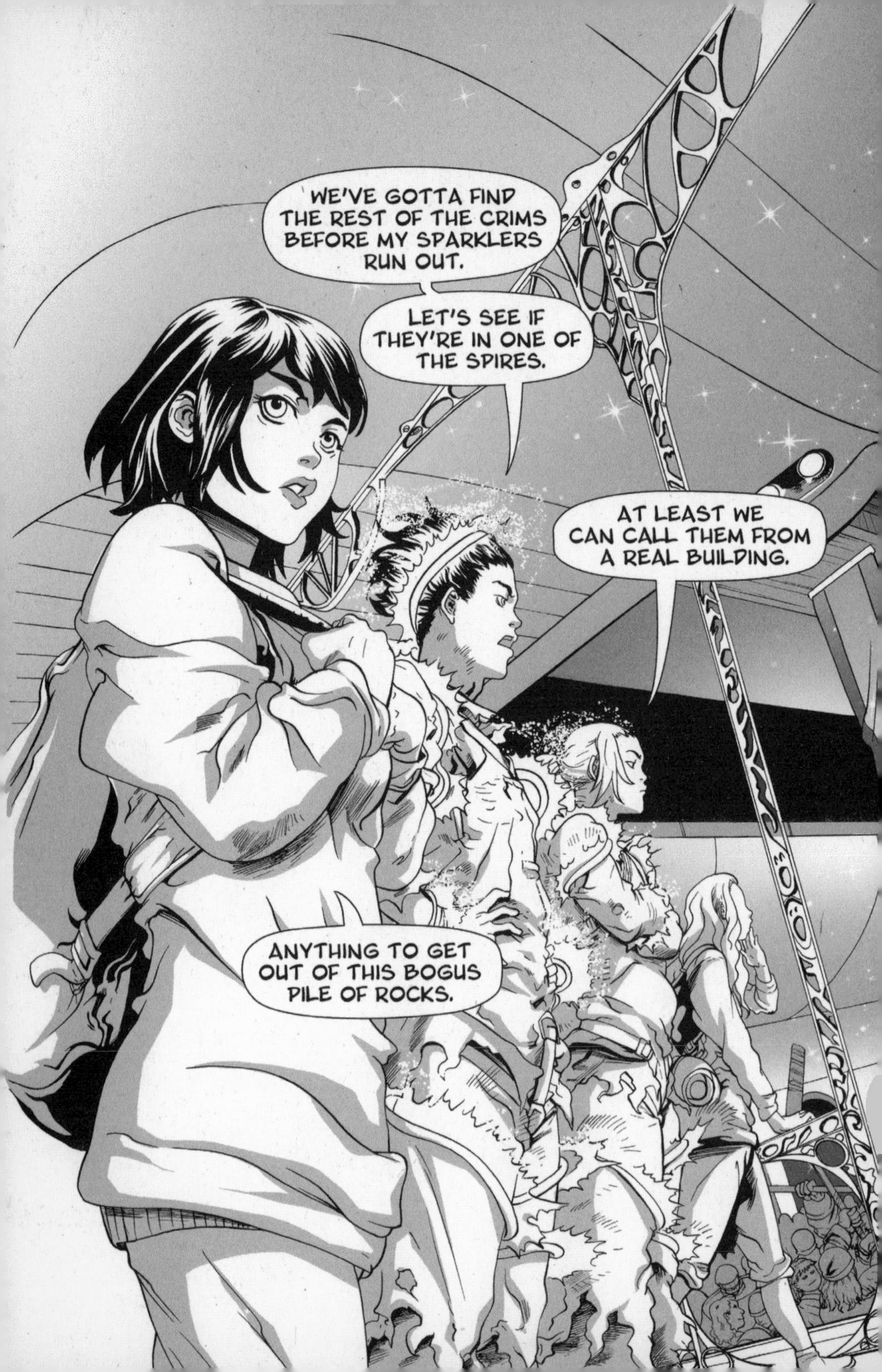
WE'VE GOTTA FIND THE REST OF THE CRIMS BEFORE MY SPARKLERS RUN OUT.
LET'S SEE IF THEY'RE IN ONE OF THE SPIRES.
AT LEAST WE CAN CALL THEM FROM A REAL BUILDING.
ANYTHING TO GET OUT OF THIS BOGUS PILE OF ROCKS.

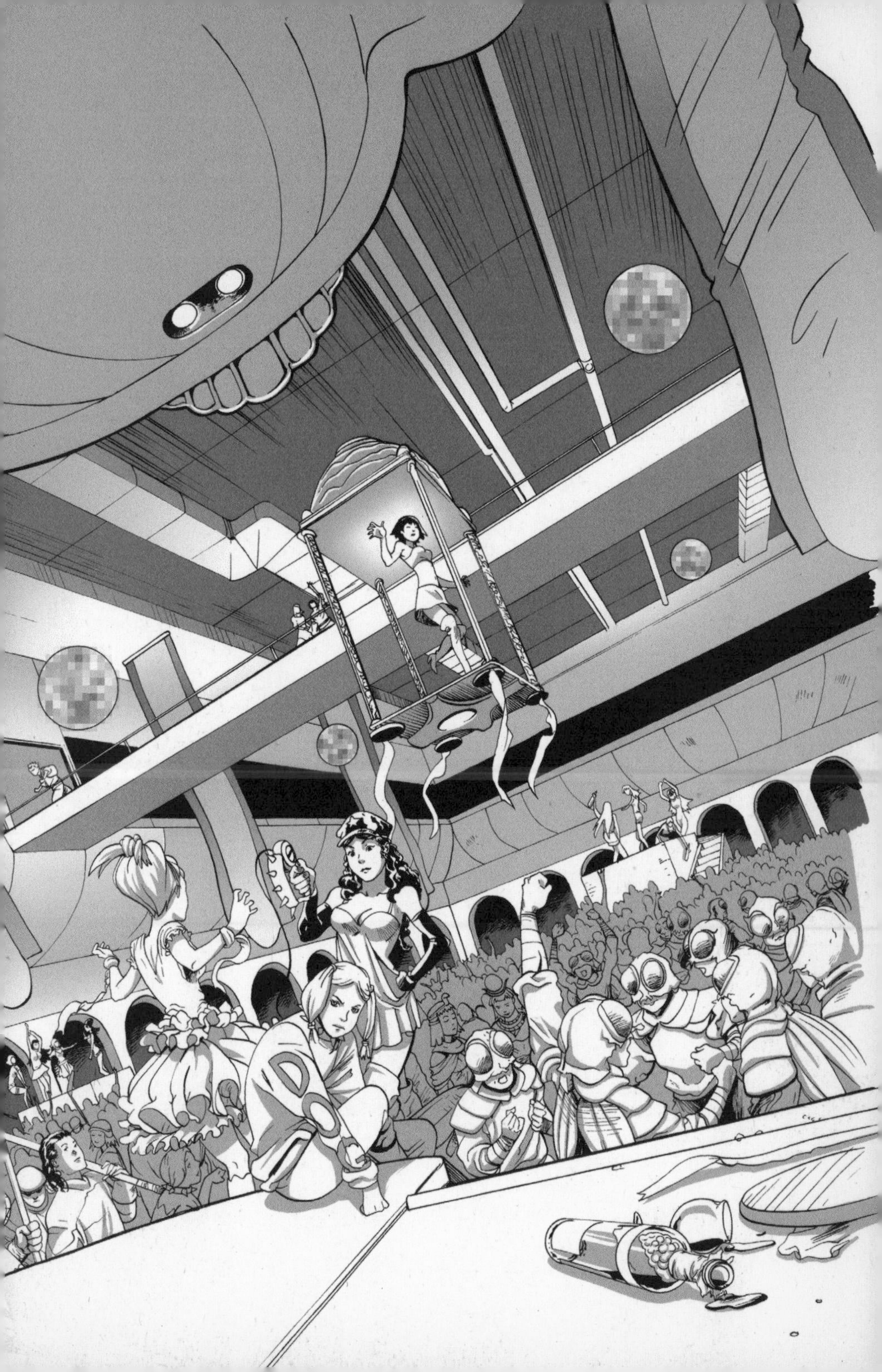

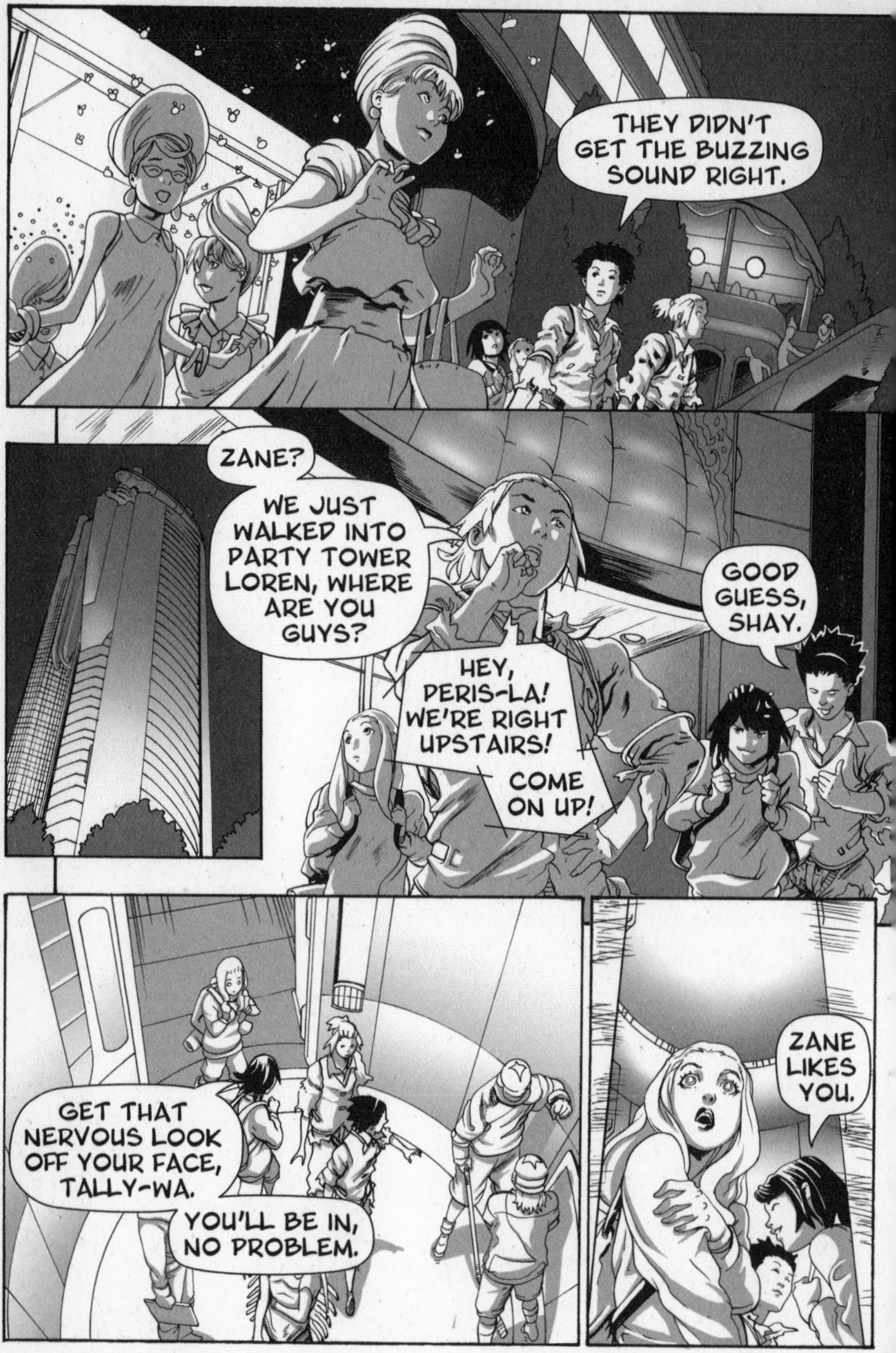
THEY DIDN'T GET THE BUZZING SOUND RIGHT.
ZANE?
WE JUST WALKED INTO PARTY TOWER LOREN, WHERE ARE YOU GUYS?
HEY, PERIS-LA! WE'RE RIGHT UPSTAIRS!
COME ON UP!
GOOD GUESS, SHAY.
GET THAT NERVOUS LOOK OFF YOUR FACE, TALLY-WA.
YOU'LL BE IN, NO PROBLEM.
ZANE LIKES YOU.

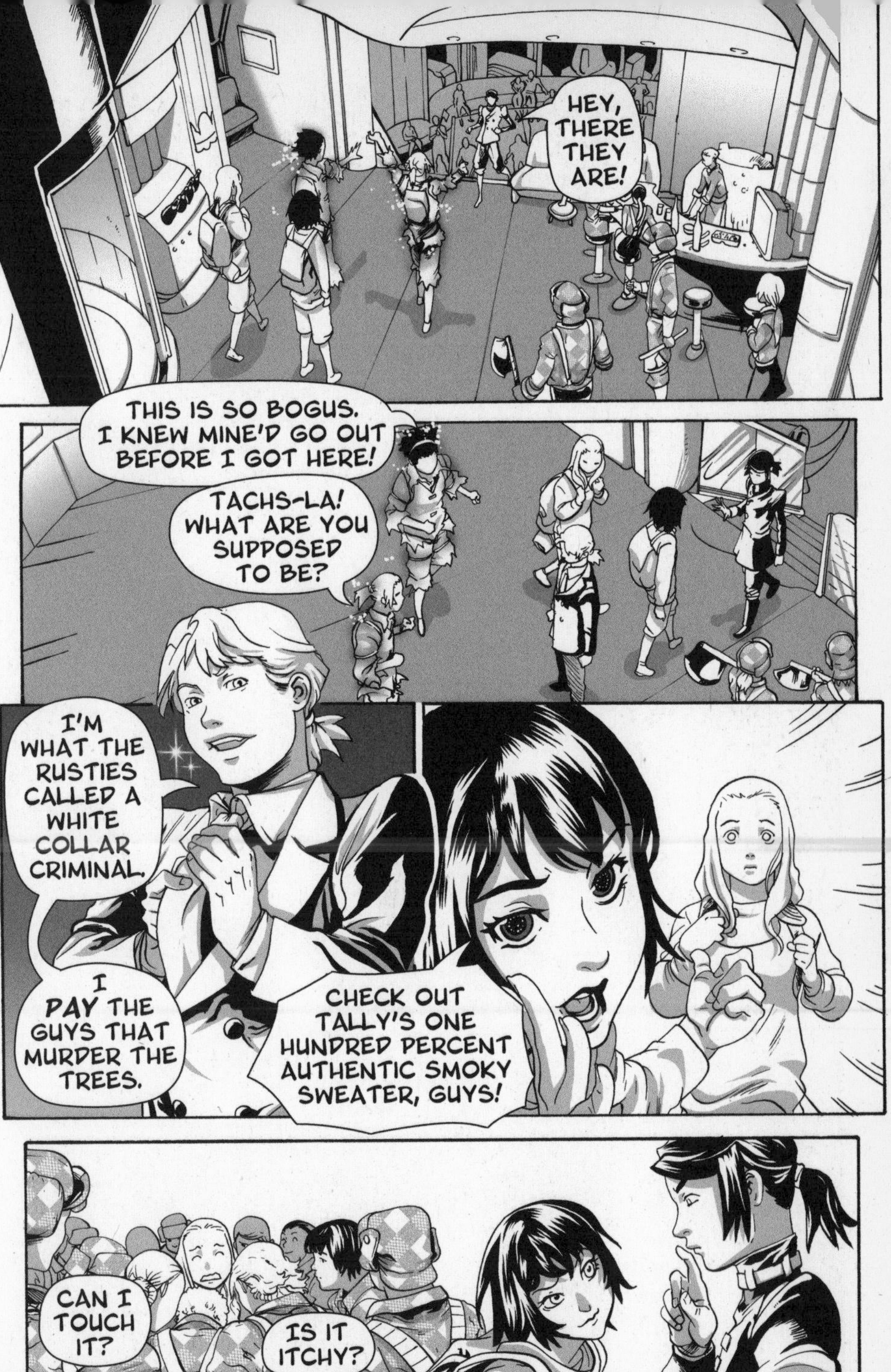
HEY, THERE THEY ARE!
THIS IS SO BOGUS. I KNEW MINE'D GO OUT BEFORE I GOT HERE!
TACHS-LA! WHAT ARE YOU SUPPOSED TO BE?
I'M WHAT THE RUSTIES CALLED A WHITE COLLAR CRIMINAL.
I PAY THE GUYS THAT MURDER THE TREES.
CHECK OUT TALLY'S ONE HUNDRED PERCENT AUTHENTIC SMOKY SWEATER, GUYS!
CAN I TOUCH IT?
IS IT ITCHY?

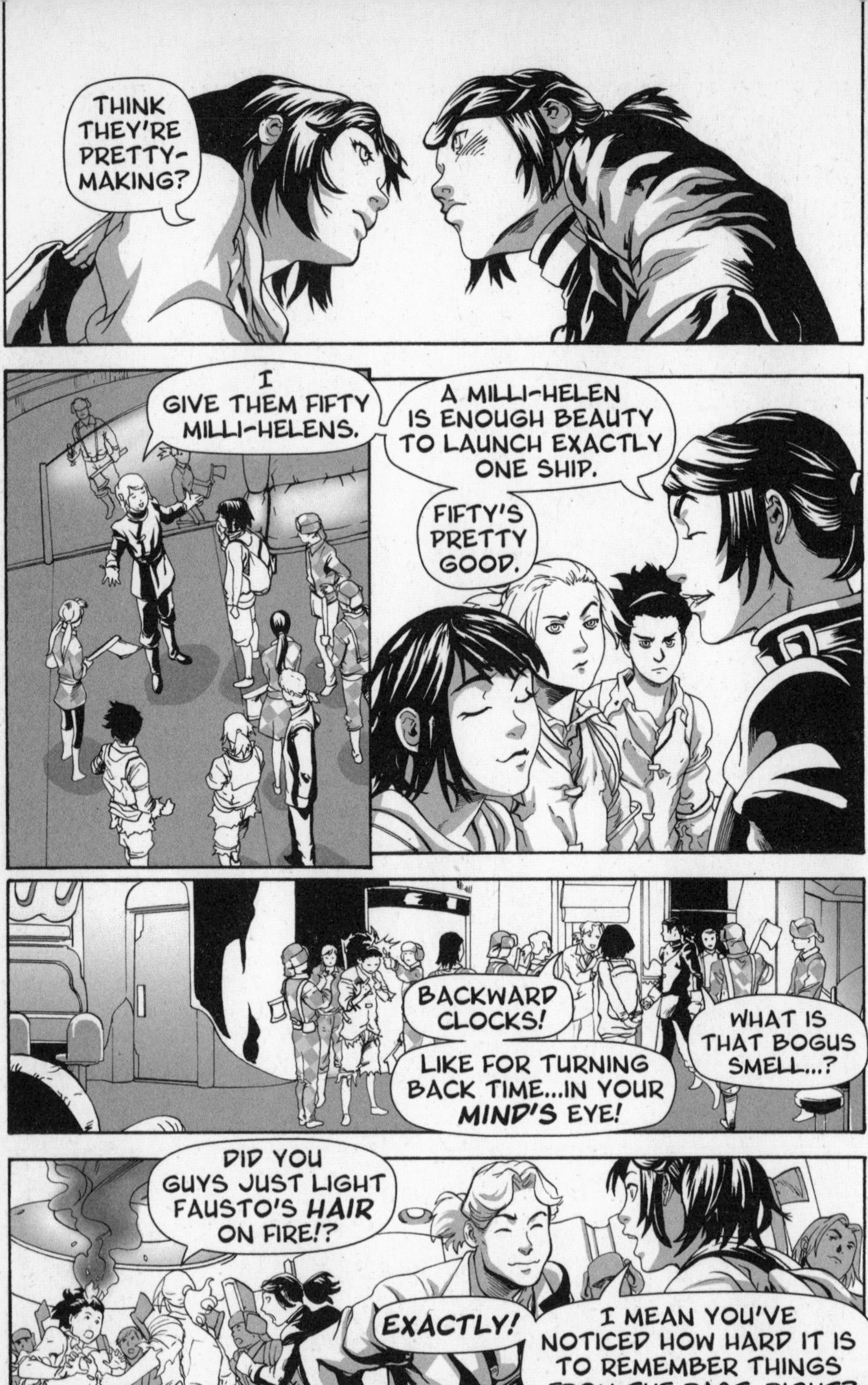
THINK THEY'RE PRETTY-MAKING?
I GIVE THEM FIFTY MILLI-HELENS.
A MILLI-HELEN IS ENOUGH BEAUTY TO LAUNCH EXACTLY ONE SHIP.
FIFTY'S PRETTY GOOD.
BACKWARD CLOCKS!
LIKE FOR TURNING BACK TIME...IN YOUR MIND'S EYE!
WHAT IS THAT BOGUS SMELL...?
DID YOU GUYS JUST LIGHT FAUSTO'S HAIR ON FIRE!?
EXACTLY!
I MEAN YOU'VE NOTICED HOW HARD IT IS TO REMEMBER THINGS FROM THE PAST, RIGHT?

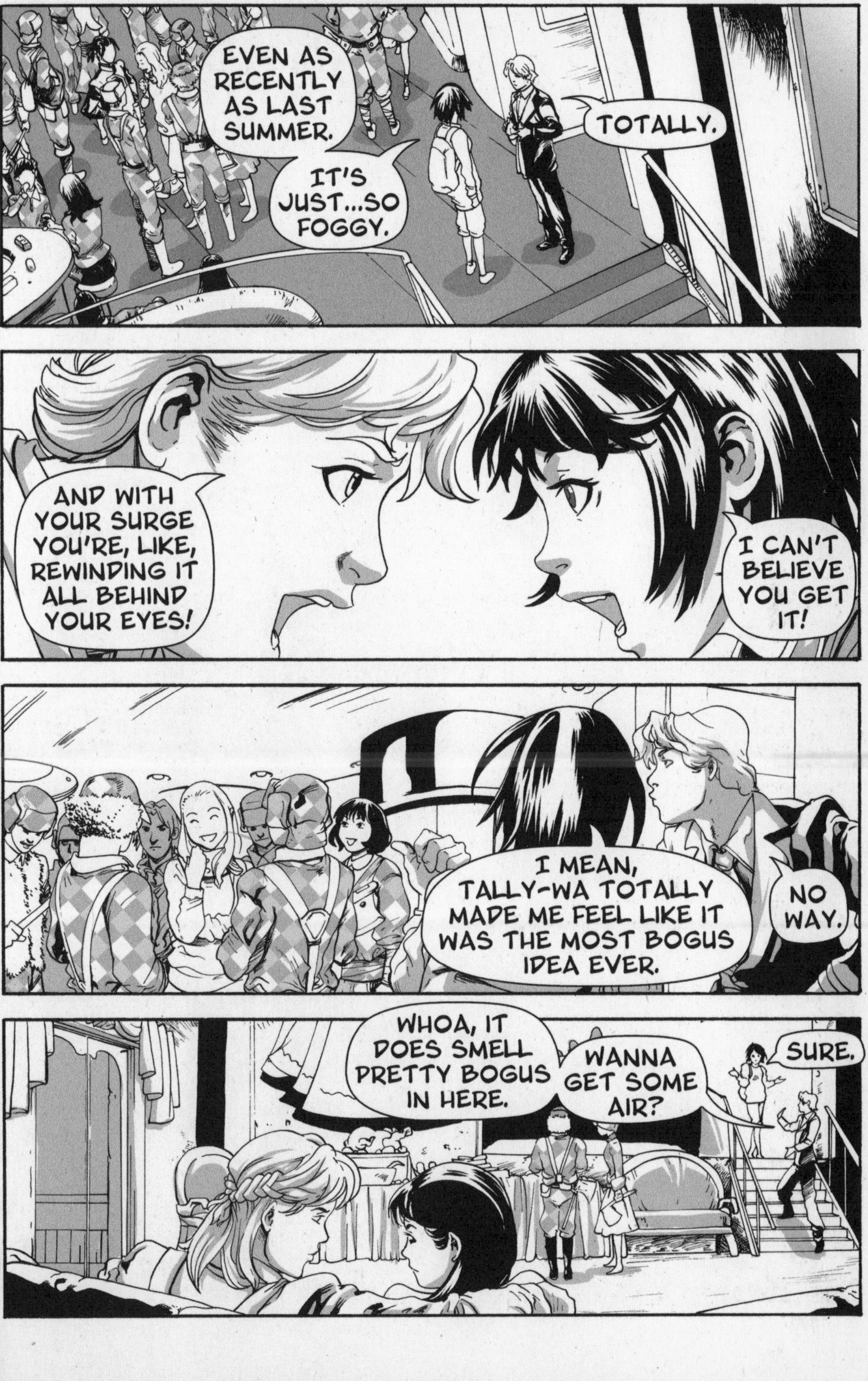
EVEN AS RECENTLY AS LAST SUMMER.
IT'S JUST...SO FOGGY.
TOTALLY.
AND WITH YOUR SURGE YOU'RE, LIKE, REWINDING IT ALL BEHIND YOUR EYES!
I CAN'T BELIEVE YOU GET IT!
I MEAN, TALLY-WA TOTALLY MADE ME FEEL LIKE IT WAS THE MOST BOGUS IDEA EVER.
NO WAY.
WHOA, IT DOES SMELL PRETTY BOGUS IN HERE.
WANNA GET SOME AIR?
SURE.

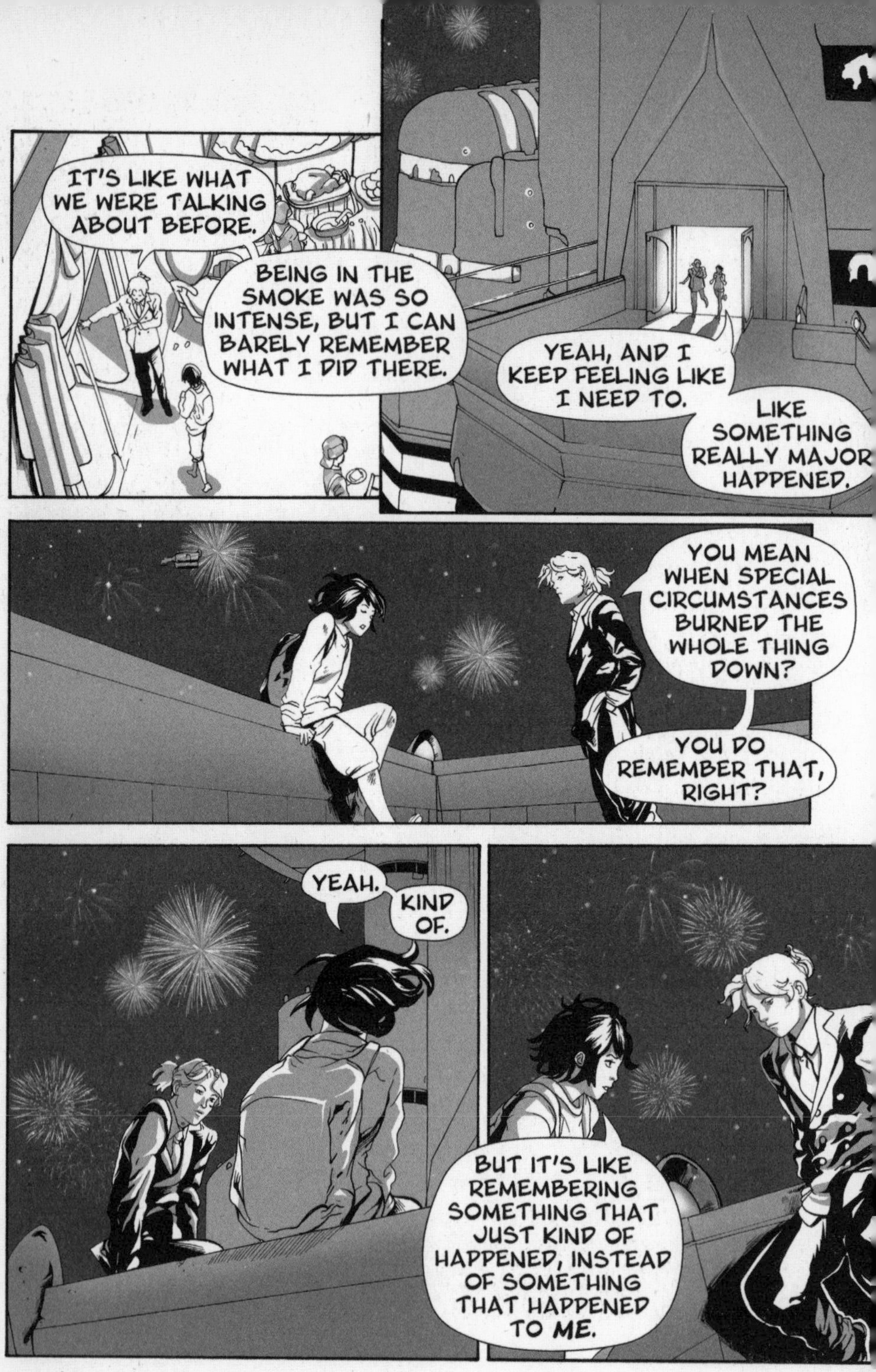
IT'S LIKE WHAT WE WERE TALKING ABOUT BEFORE.
BEING IN THE SMOKE WAS SO INTENSE, BUT I CAN BARELY REMEMBER WHAT I DID THERE.
YEAH, AND I KEEP FEELING LIKE I NEED TO.
LIKE SOMETHING REALLY MAJOR HAPPENED.
YOU MEAN WHEN SPECIAL CIRCUMSTANCES BURNED THE WHOLE THING DOWN?
YOU DO REMEMBER THAT, RIGHT?
YEAH.
KIND OF.
BUT IT'S LIKE REMEMBERING SOMETHING THAT JUST KIND OF HAPPENED, INSTEAD OF SOMETHING THAT HAPPENED TO ME.

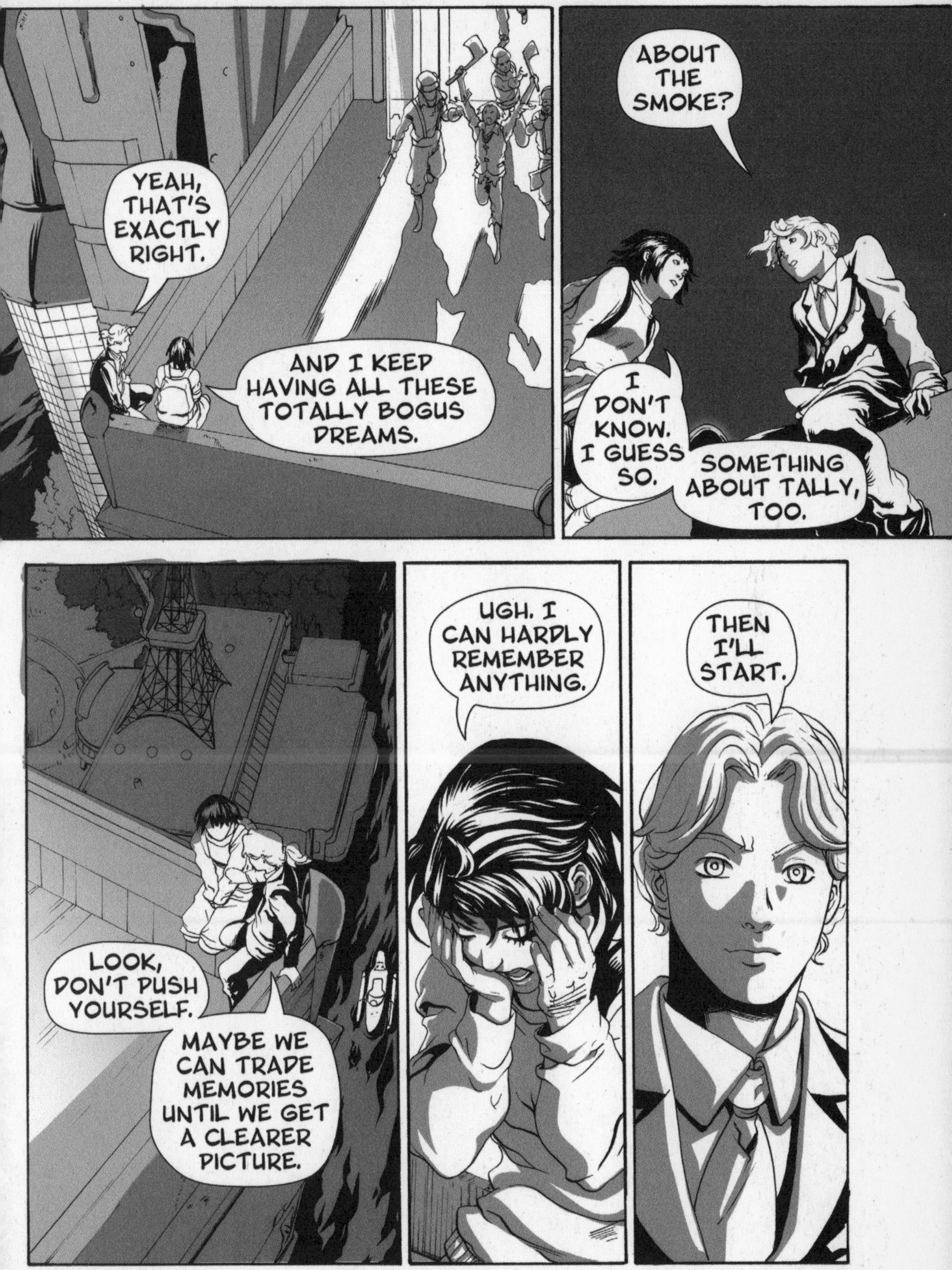
YEAH, THAT'S EXACTLY RIGHT.
AND I KEEP HAVING ALL THESE TOTALLY BOGUS DREAMS.
ABOUT THE SMOKE?
I DON'T KNOW. I GUESS SO.
SOMETHING ABOUT TALLY, TOO.
LOOK, DON'T PUSH YOURSELF.
MAYBE WE CAN TRADE MEMORIES UNTIL WE GET A CLEARER PICTURE.
UGH. I CAN HARDLY REMEMBER ANYTHING.
THEN I'LL START.

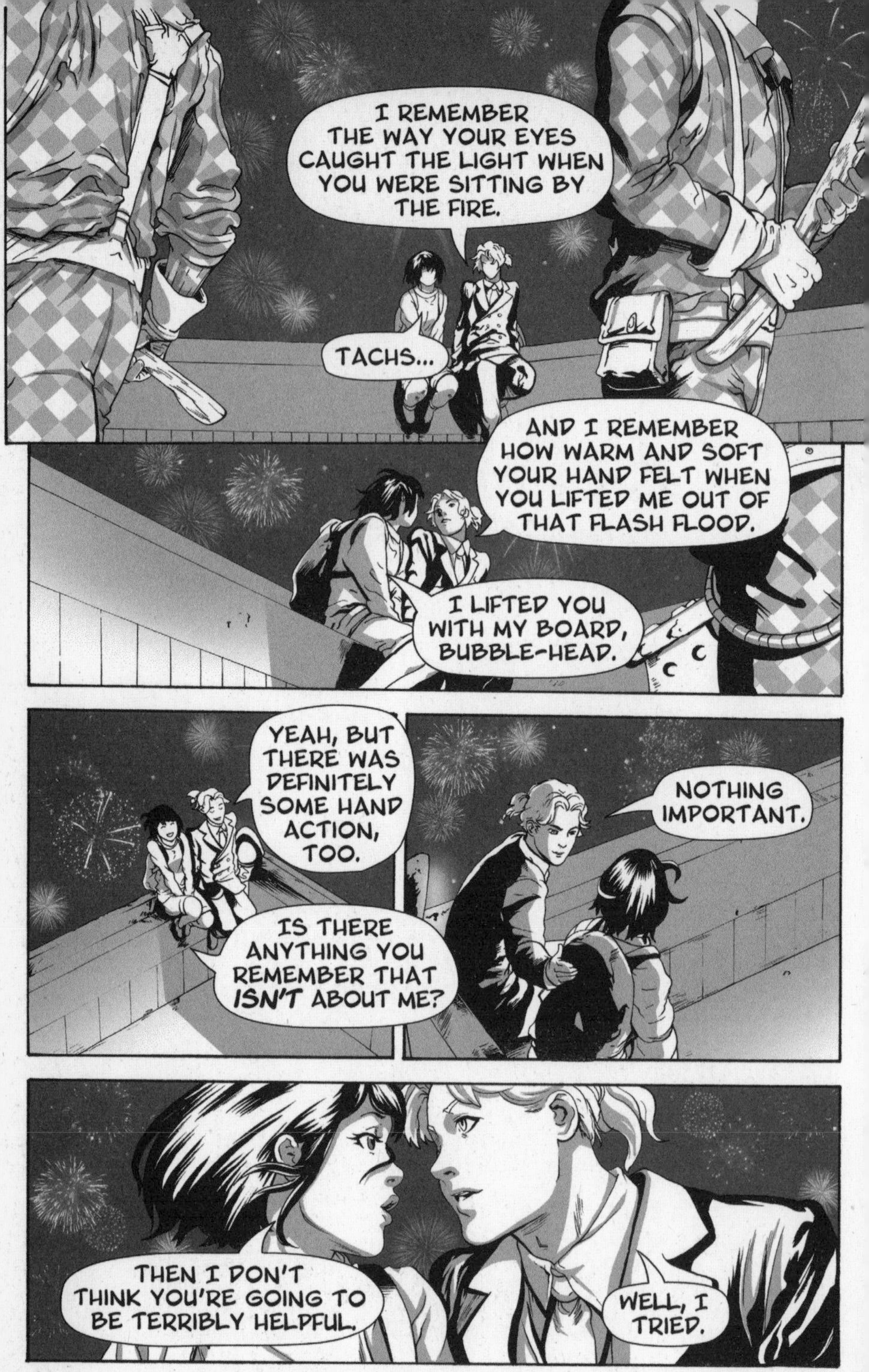
I REMEMBER THE WAY YOUR EYES CAUGHT THE LIGHT WHEN YOU WERE SITTING BY THE FIRE.
TACHS...
AND I REMEMBER HOW WARM AND SOFT YOUR HAND FELT WHEN YOU LIFTED ME OUT OF THAT FLASH FLOOD.
I LIFTED YOU WITH MY BOARD, BUBBLE-HEAD.
YEAH, BUT THERE WAS DEFINITELY SOME HAND ACTION, TOO.
IS THERE ANYTHING YOU REMEMBER THAT ISN'T ABOUT ME?
NOTHING IMPORTANT.
THEN I DON'T THINK YOU'RE GOING TO BE TERRIBLY HELPFUL.
WELL, I TRIED.

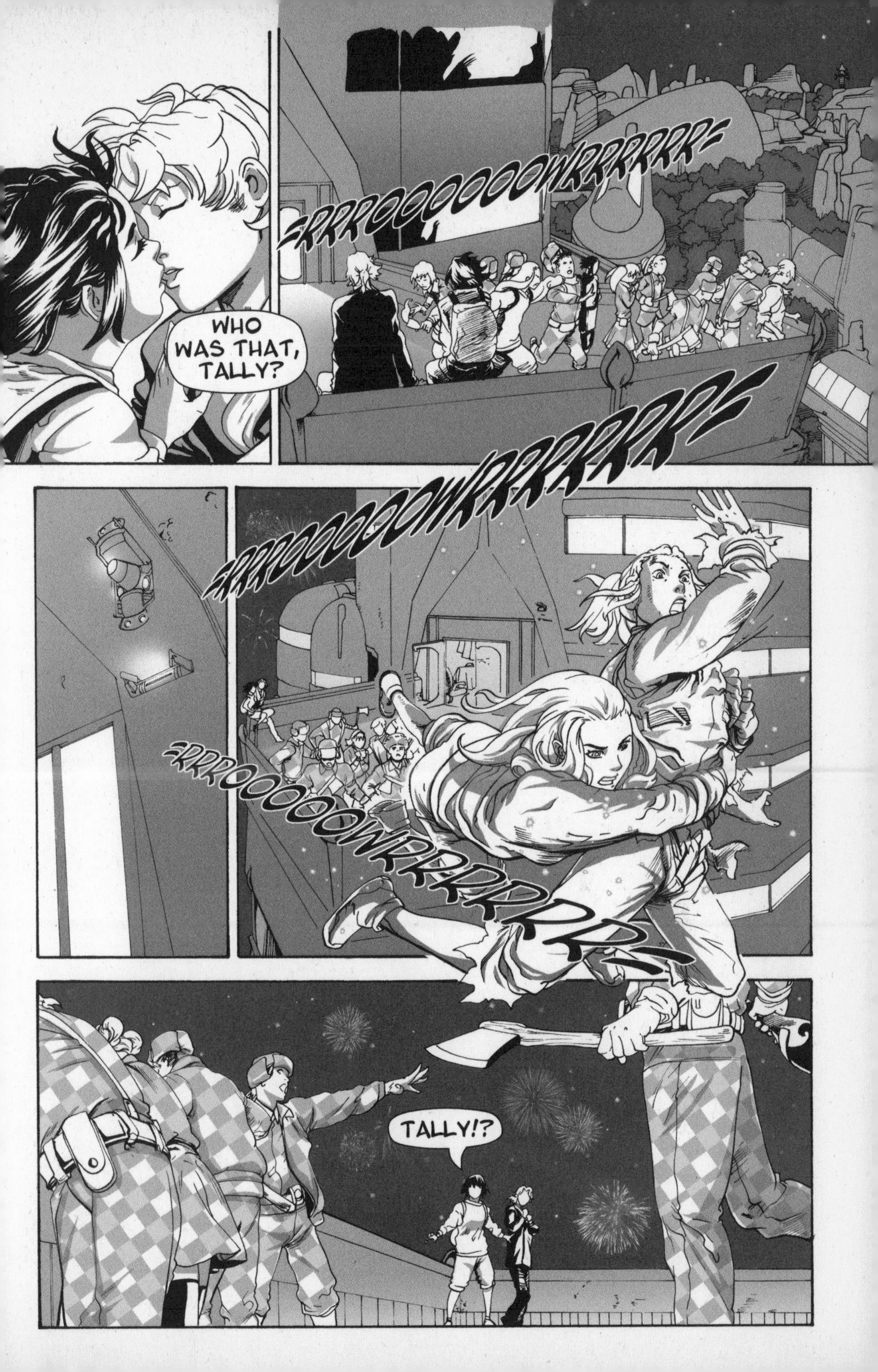
WHO WAS THAT, TALLY?
RRROOOOOOOOWRRRRRRR
RRROOOOOOOWRRRRRRR
RRROOOOOOWRRRRRRR
TALLY!?

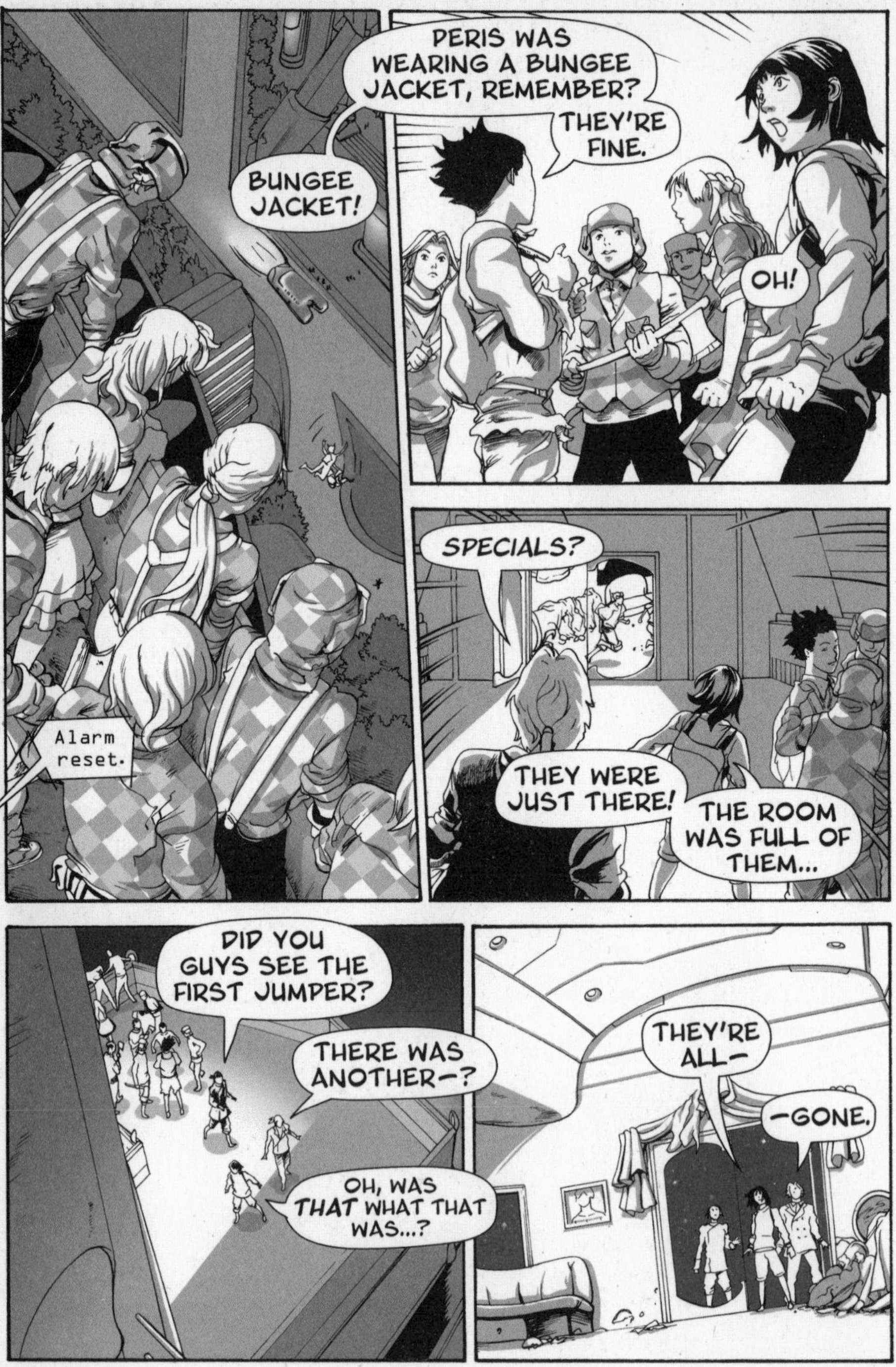
BUNGEE JACKET!
Alarm reset.
PERIS WAS WEARING A BUNGEE JACKET, REMEMBER?
THEY'RE FINE.
OH!
SPECIALS?
THEY WERE JUST THERE!
THE ROOM WAS FULL OF THEM...
DID YOU GUYS SEE THE FIRST JUMPER?
THERE WAS ANOTHER—?
OH, WAS *THAT* WHAT THAT WAS...?
THEY'RE ALL—
—GONE.

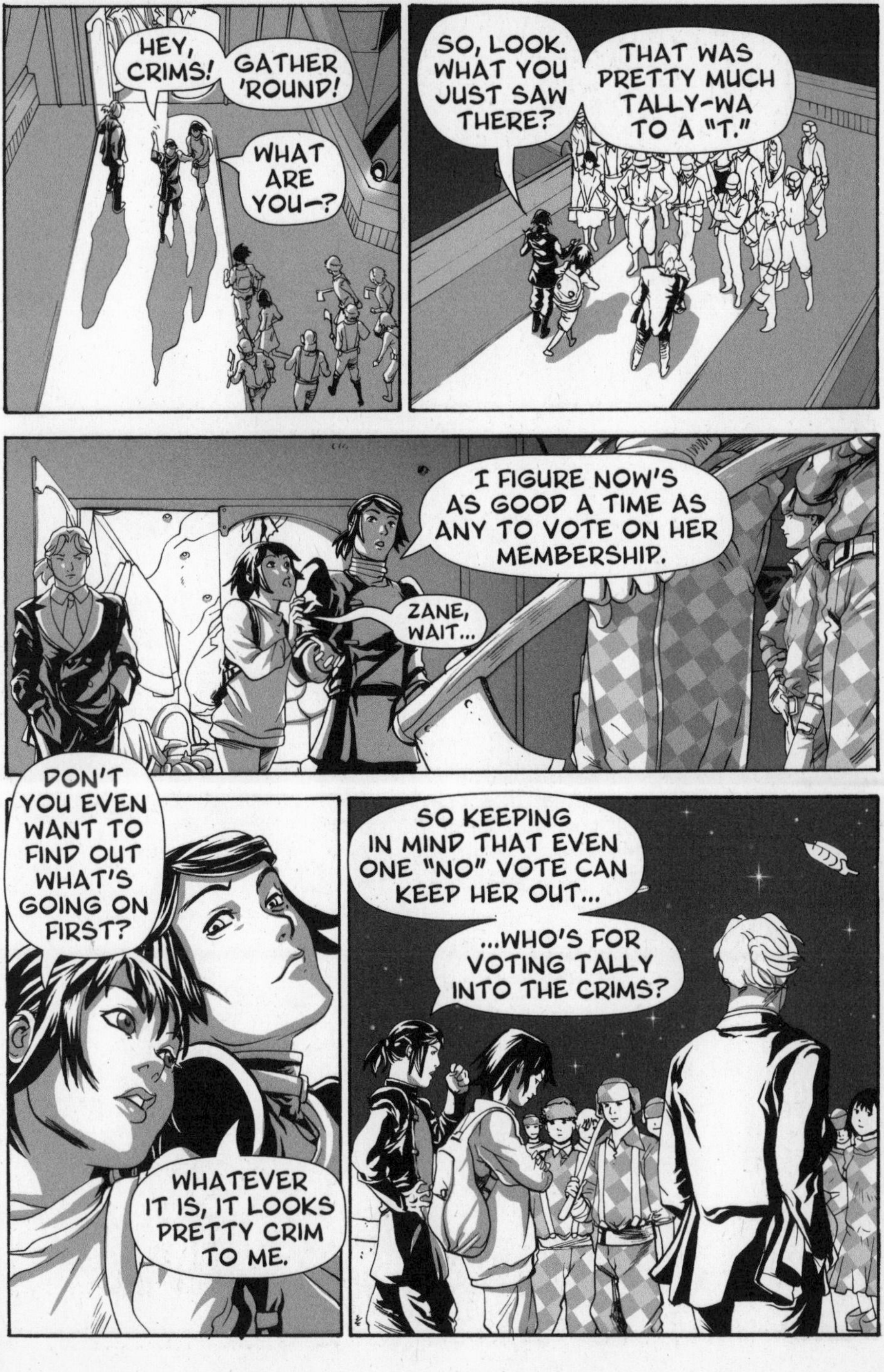
HEY, CRIMS!
GATHER 'ROUND!
WHAT ARE YOU—?
SO, LOOK. WHAT YOU JUST SAW THERE?
THAT WAS PRETTY MUCH TALLY-WA TO A "T."
I FIGURE NOW'S AS GOOD A TIME AS ANY TO VOTE ON HER MEMBERSHIP.
ZANE, WAIT...
DON'T YOU EVEN WANT TO FIND OUT WHAT'S GOING ON FIRST?
WHATEVER IT IS, IT LOOKS PRETTY CRIM TO ME.
SO KEEPING IN MIND THAT EVEN ONE "NO" VOTE CAN KEEP HER OUT...
...WHO'S FOR VOTING TALLY INTO THE CRIMS?

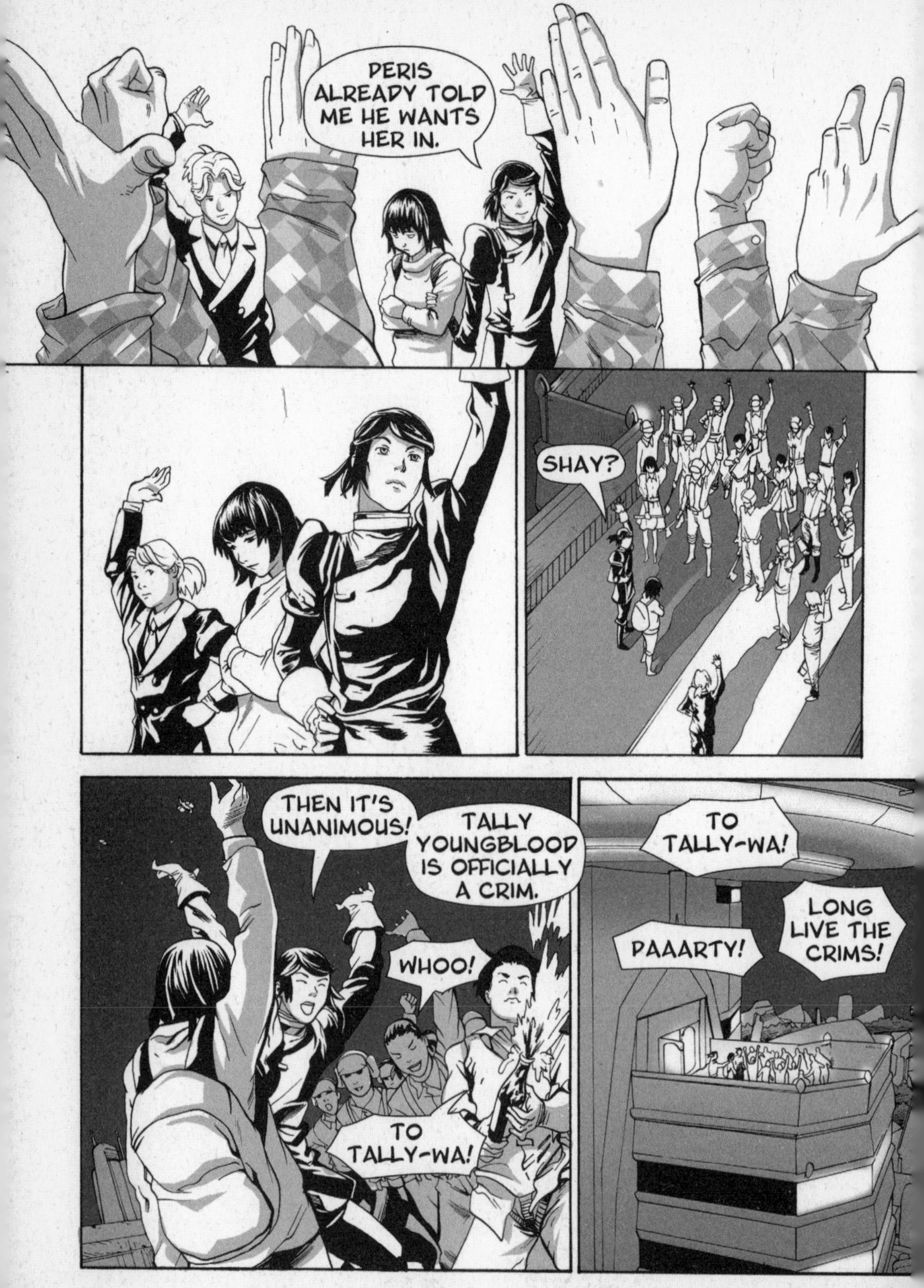
PERIS ALREADY TOLD ME HE WANTS HER IN.
SHAY?
THEN IT'S UNANIMOUS!
TALLY YOUNGBLOOD IS OFFICIALLY A CRIM.
WHOO!
TO TALLY-WA!
TO TALLY-WA!
PAAARTY!
LONG LIVE THE CRIMS!

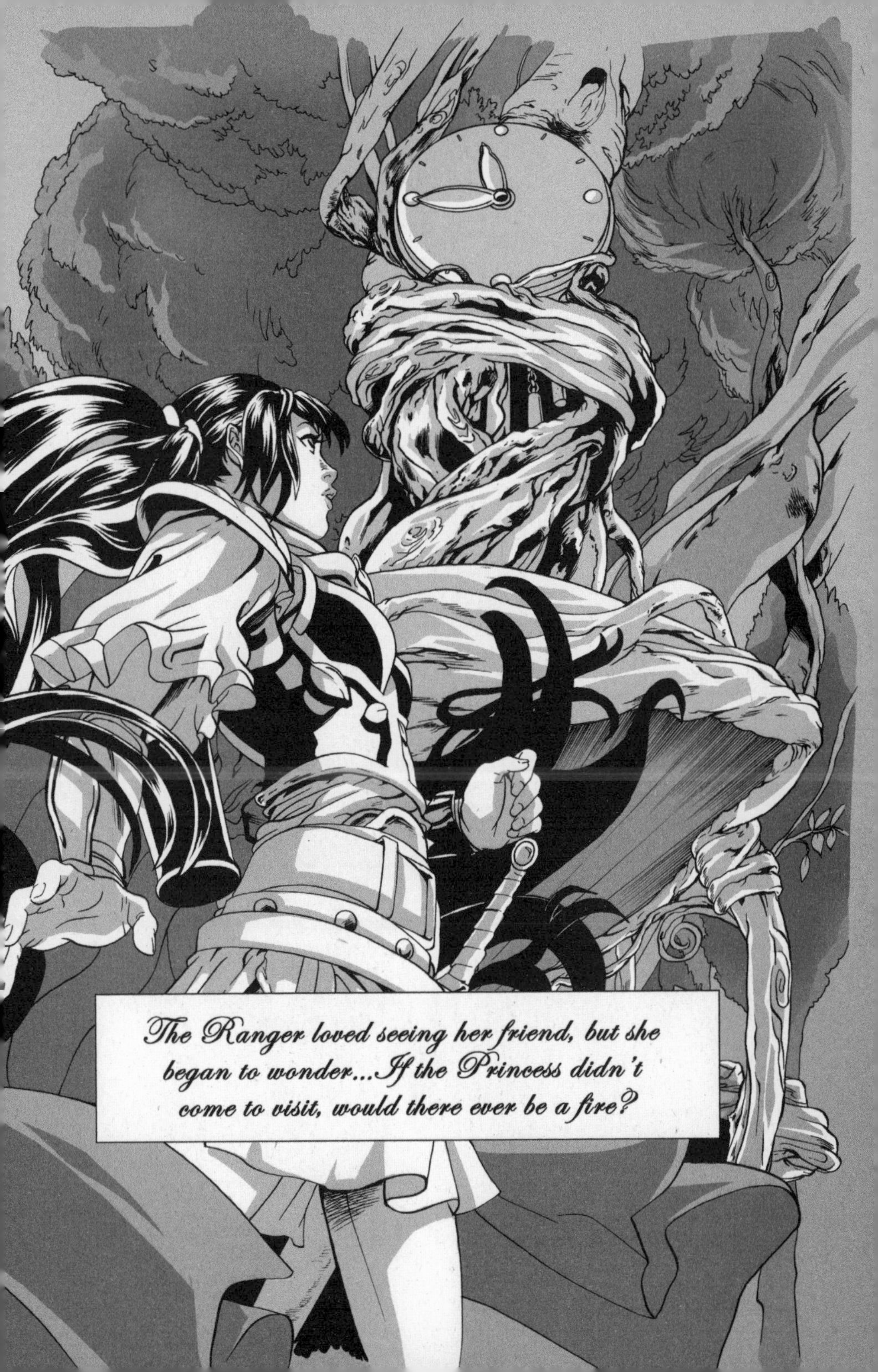
The Ranger loved seeing her friend, but she began to wonder...If the Princess didn't come to visit, would there ever be a fire?

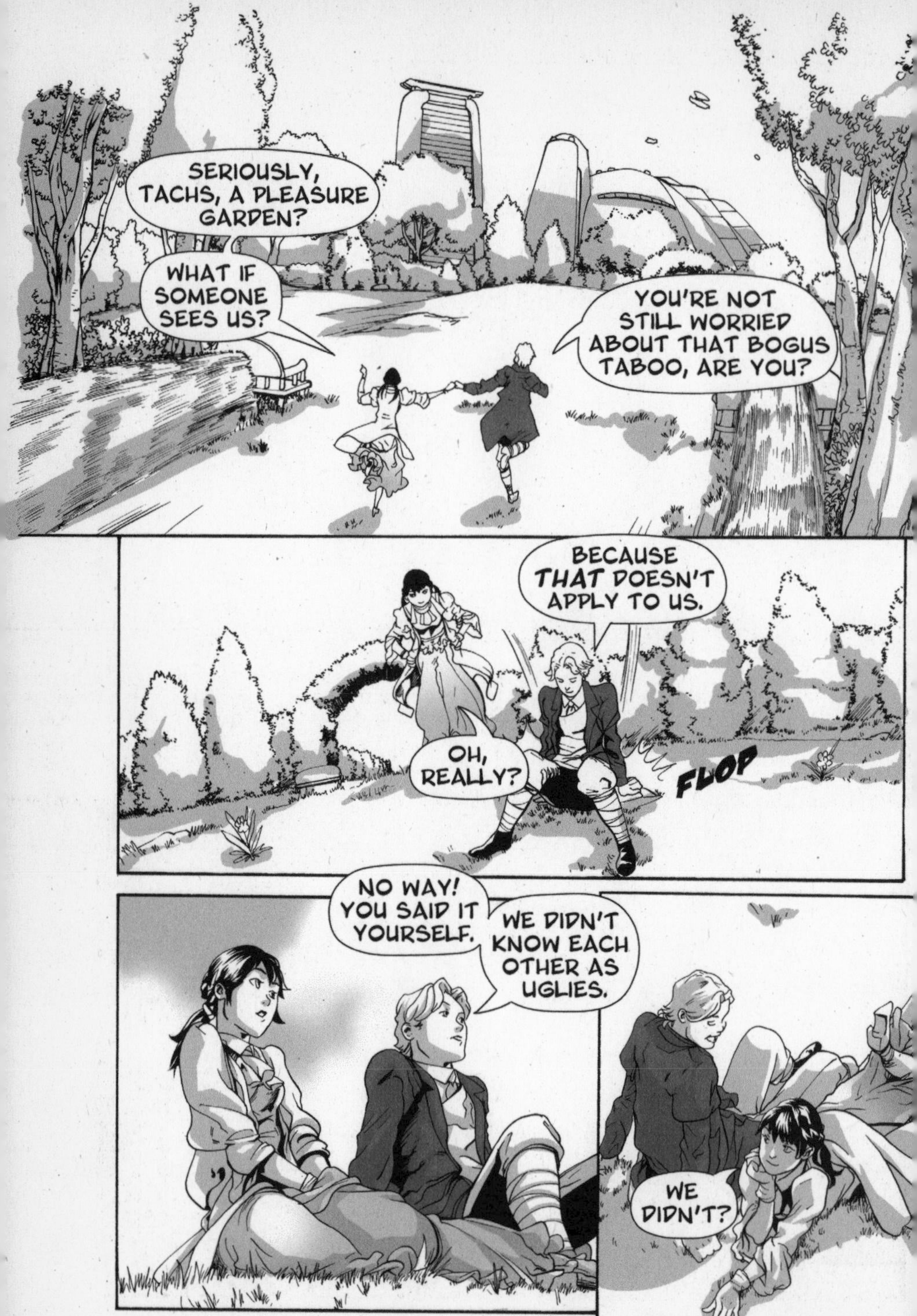
SERIOUSLY, TACHS, A PLEASURE GARDEN?
WHAT IF SOMEONE SEES US?
YOU'RE NOT STILL WORRIED ABOUT THAT BOGUS TABOO, ARE YOU?
BECAUSE THAT DOESN'T APPLY TO US.
OH, REALLY?
FLOP
NO WAY! YOU SAID IT YOURSELF.
WE DIDN'T KNOW EACH OTHER AS UGLIES.
WE DIDN'T?

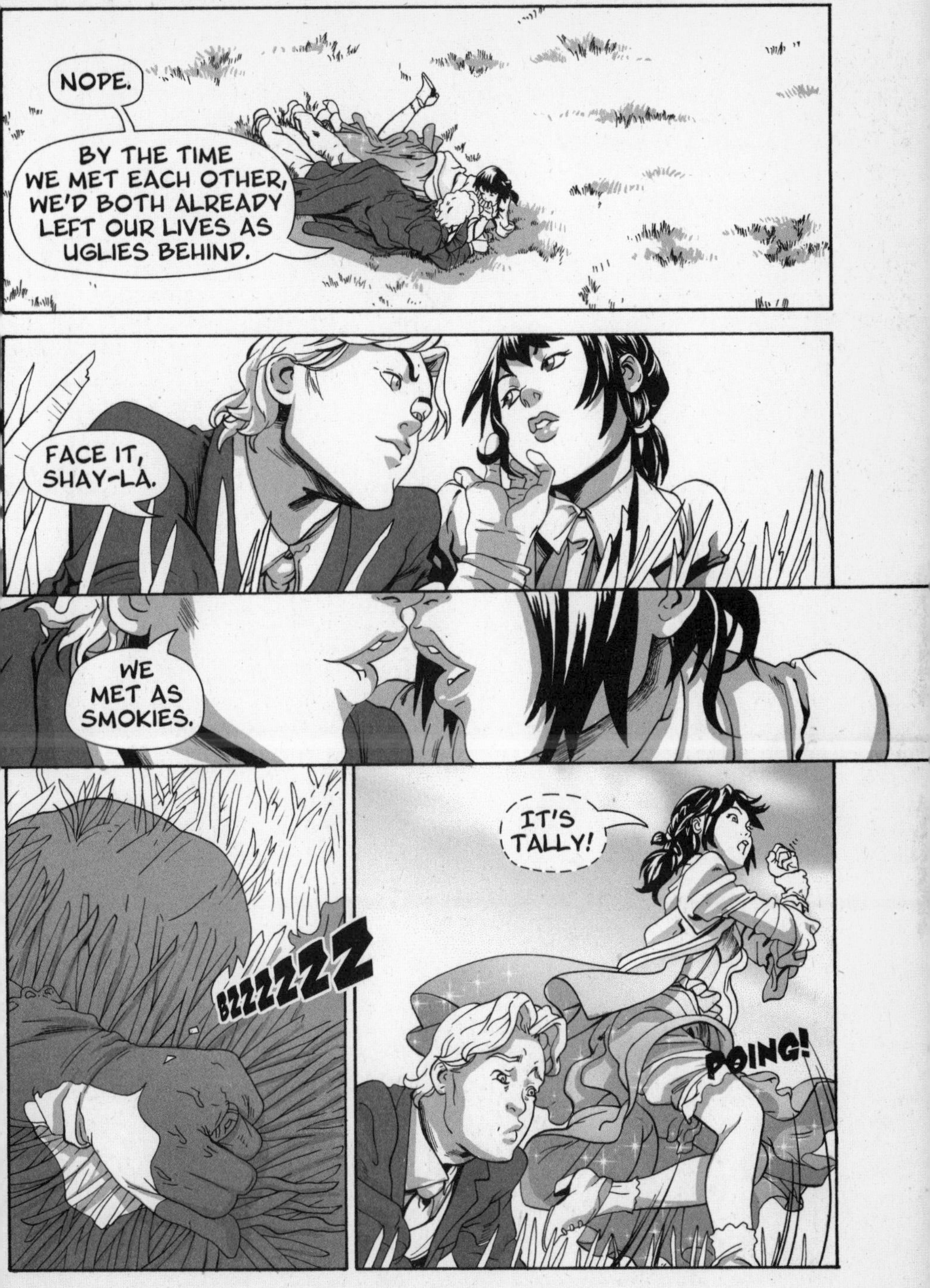
NOPE.
BY THE TIME WE MET EACH OTHER, WE'D BOTH ALREADY LEFT OUR LIVES AS UGLIES BEHIND.
FACE IT, SHAY-LA.
WE MET AS SMOKIES.
BZZZZZZ
IT'S TALLY!
POING!

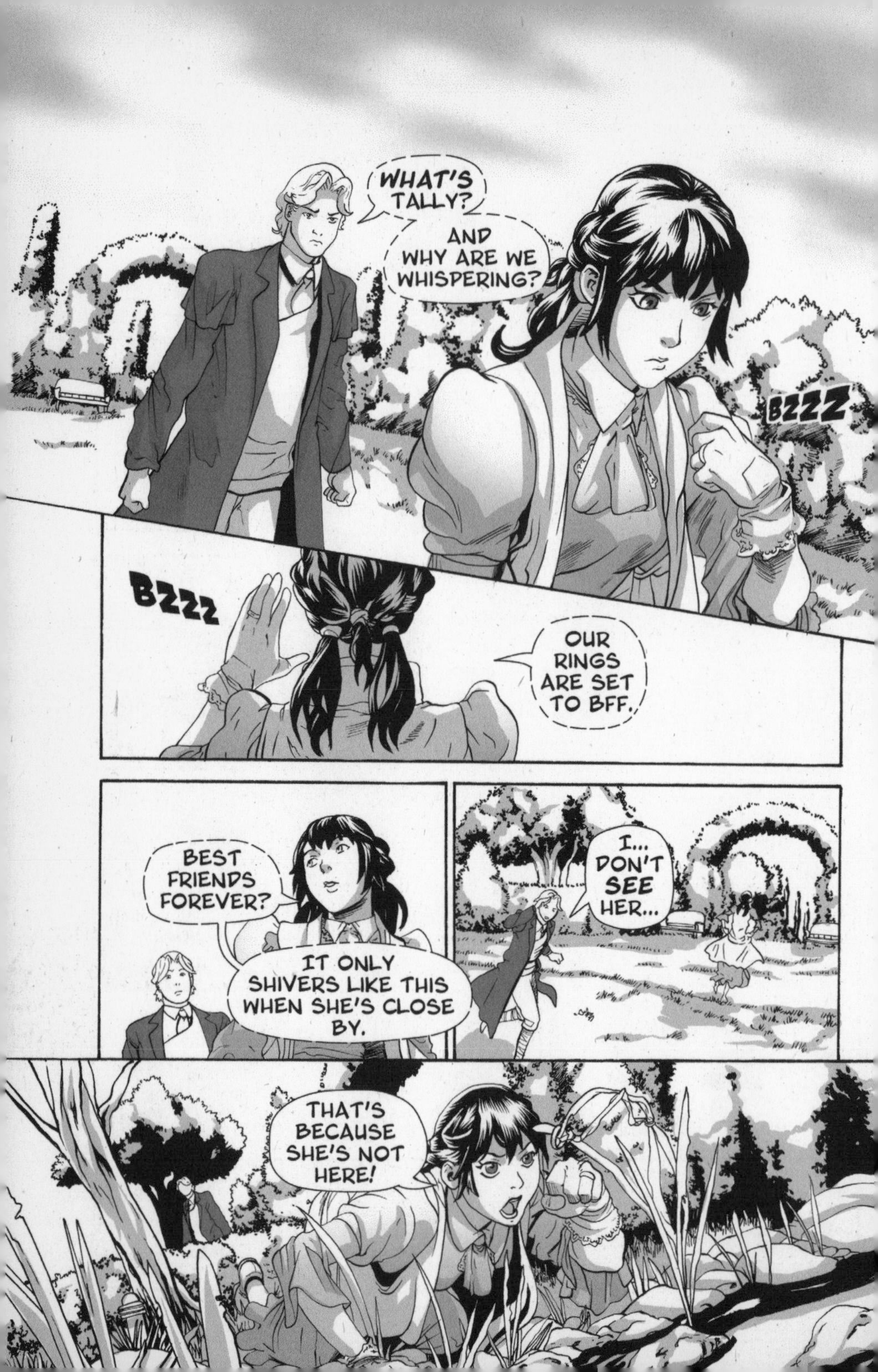
WHAT'S TALLY?
AND WHY ARE WE WHISPERING?
BZZZ
BZZZ
OUR RINGS ARE SET TO BFF.
BEST FRIENDS FOREVER?
IT ONLY SHIVERS LIKE THIS WHEN SHE'S CLOSE BY.
I... DON'T SEE HER...
THAT'S BECAUSE SHE'S NOT HERE!

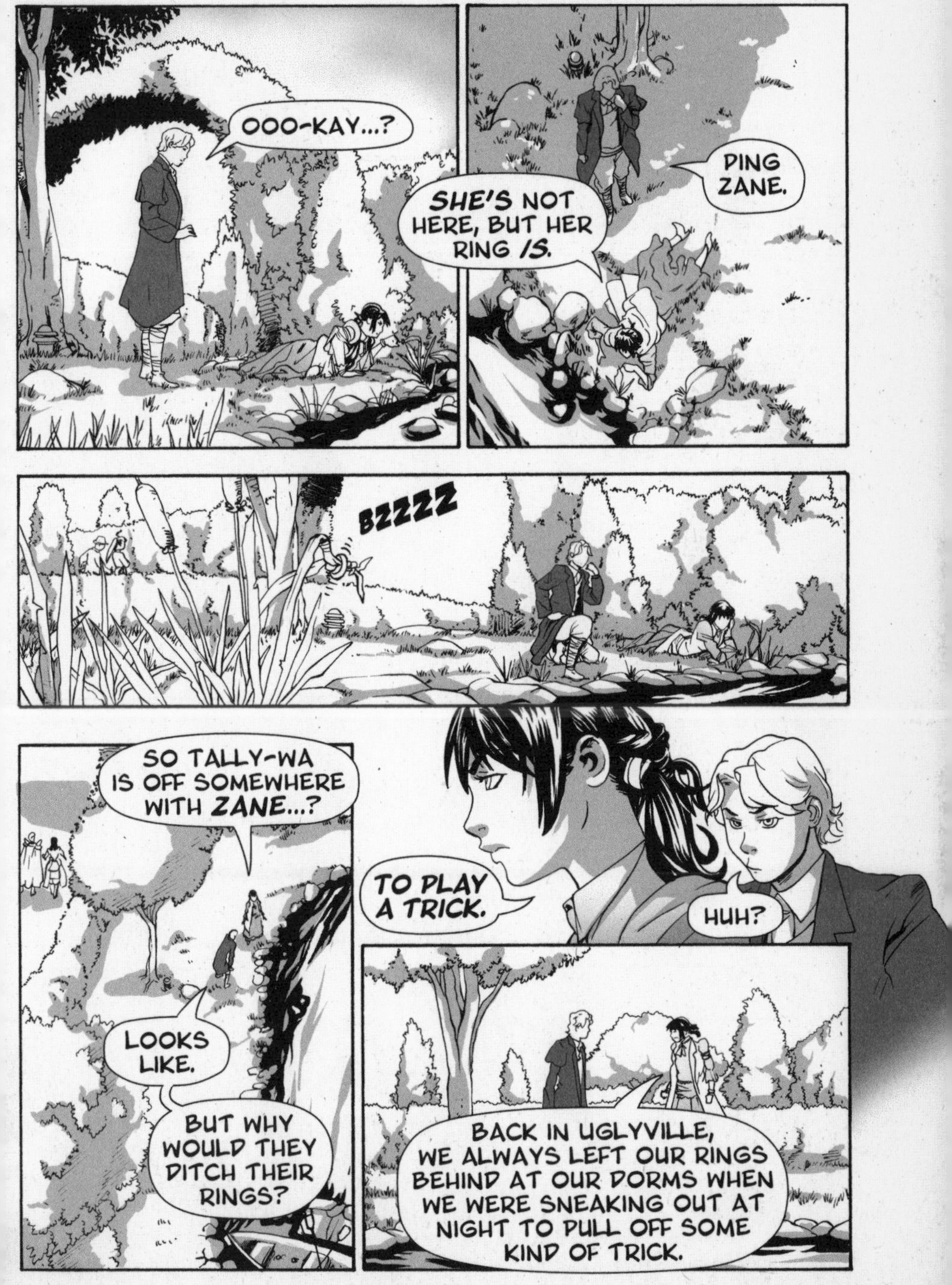
OOO-KAY...?
PING ZANE.
SHE'S NOT HERE, BUT HER RING IS.
BZZZZ
SO TALLY-WA IS OFF SOMEWHERE WITH ZANE...?
LOOKS LIKE.
BUT WHY WOULD THEY DITCH THEIR RINGS?
TO PLAY A TRICK.
HUH?
BACK IN UGLYVILLE, WE ALWAYS LEFT OUR RINGS BEHIND AT OUR DORMS WHEN WE WERE SNEAKING OUT AT NIGHT TO PULL OFF SOME KIND OF TRICK.

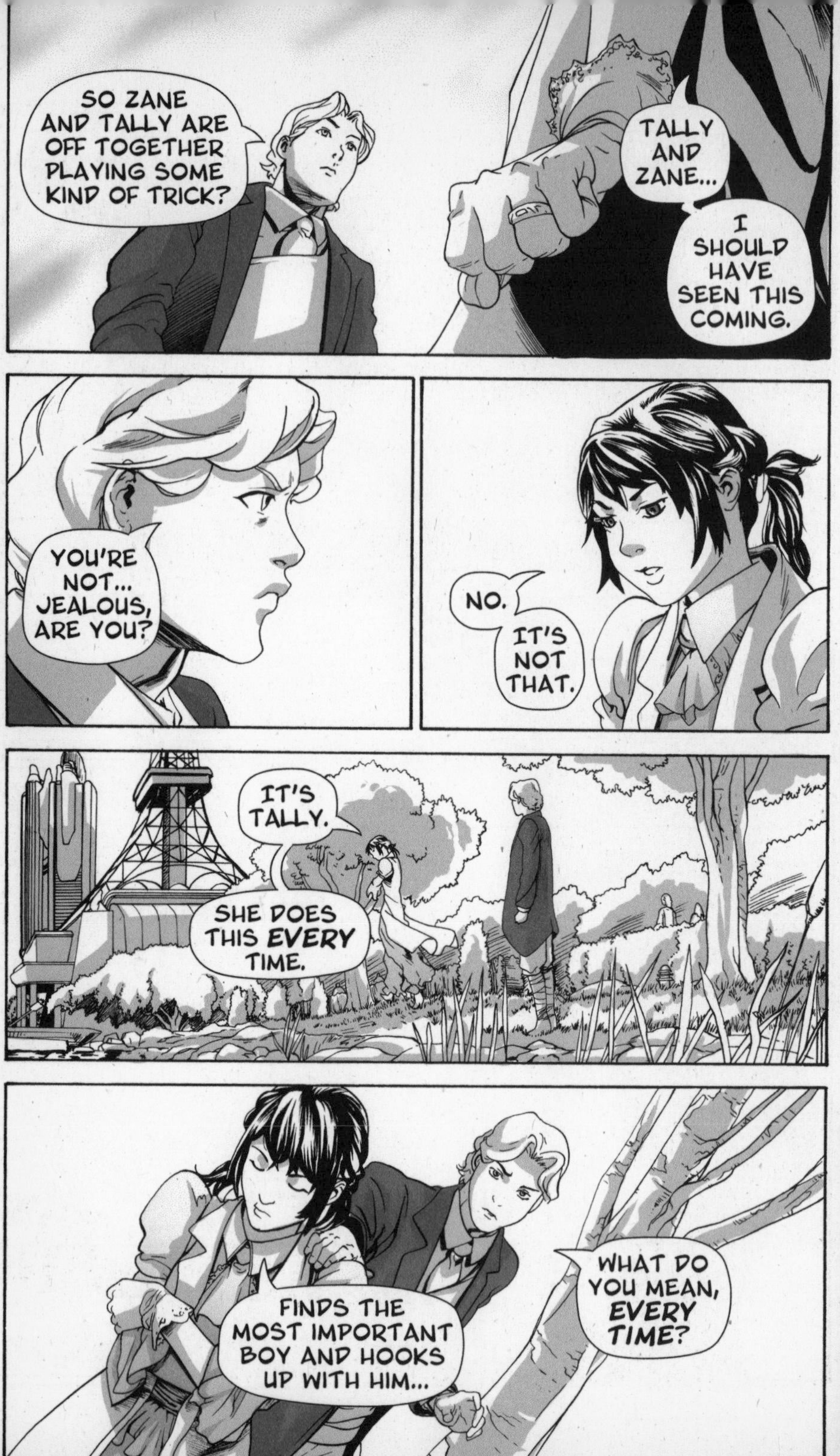
SO ZANE AND TALLY ARE OFF TOGETHER PLAYING SOME KIND OF TRICK?
TALLY AND ZANE...
I SHOULD HAVE SEEN THIS COMING.
YOU'RE NOT... JEALOUS, ARE YOU?
NO.
IT'S NOT THAT.
IT'S TALLY.
SHE DOES THIS EVERY TIME.
FINDS THE MOST IMPORTANT BOY AND HOOKS UP WITH HIM...
WHAT DO YOU MEAN, EVERY TIME?

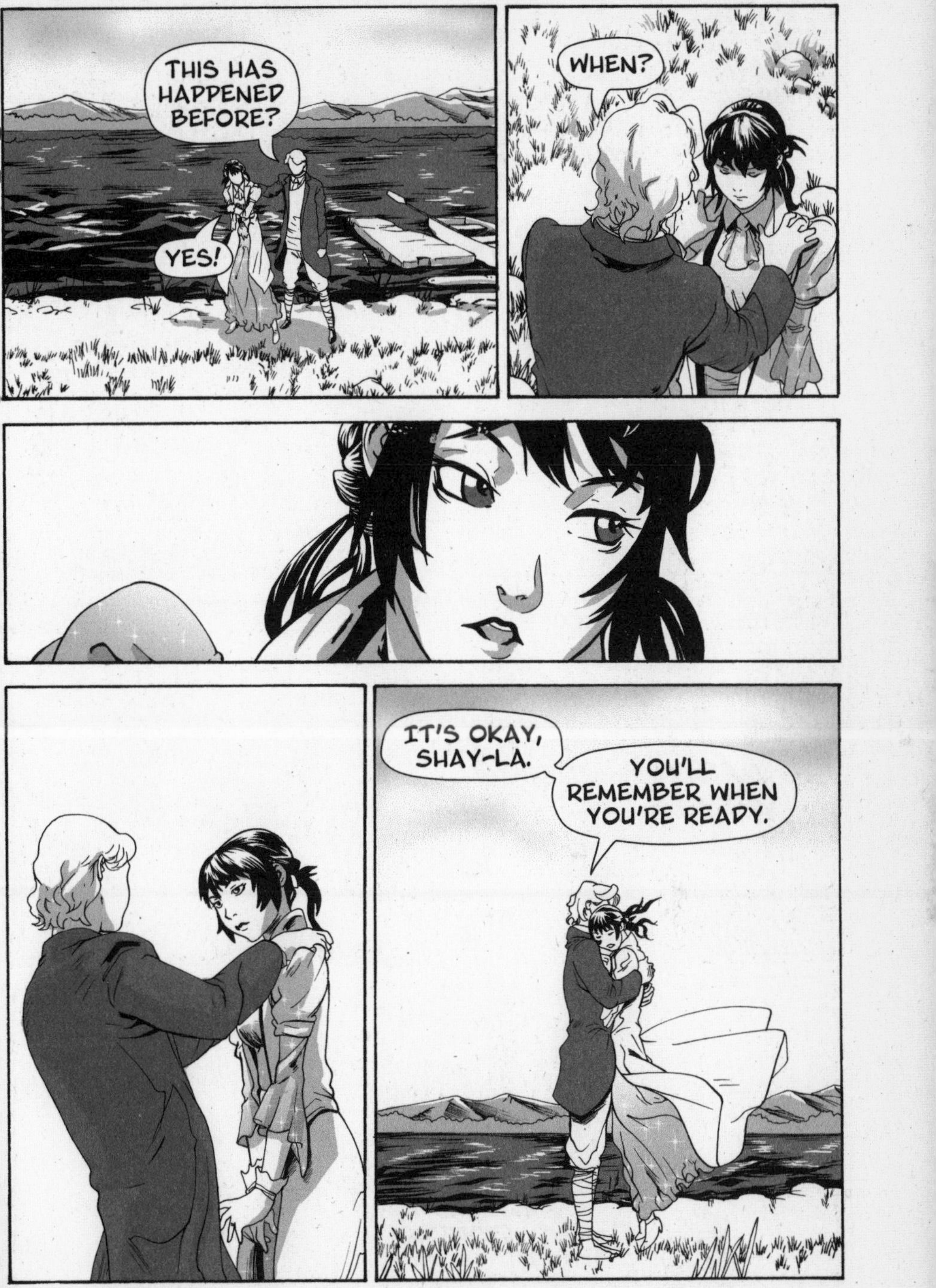
THIS HAS HAPPENED BEFORE?
YES!
WHEN?
IT'S OKAY, SHAY-LA.
YOU'LL REMEMBER WHEN YOU'RE READY.

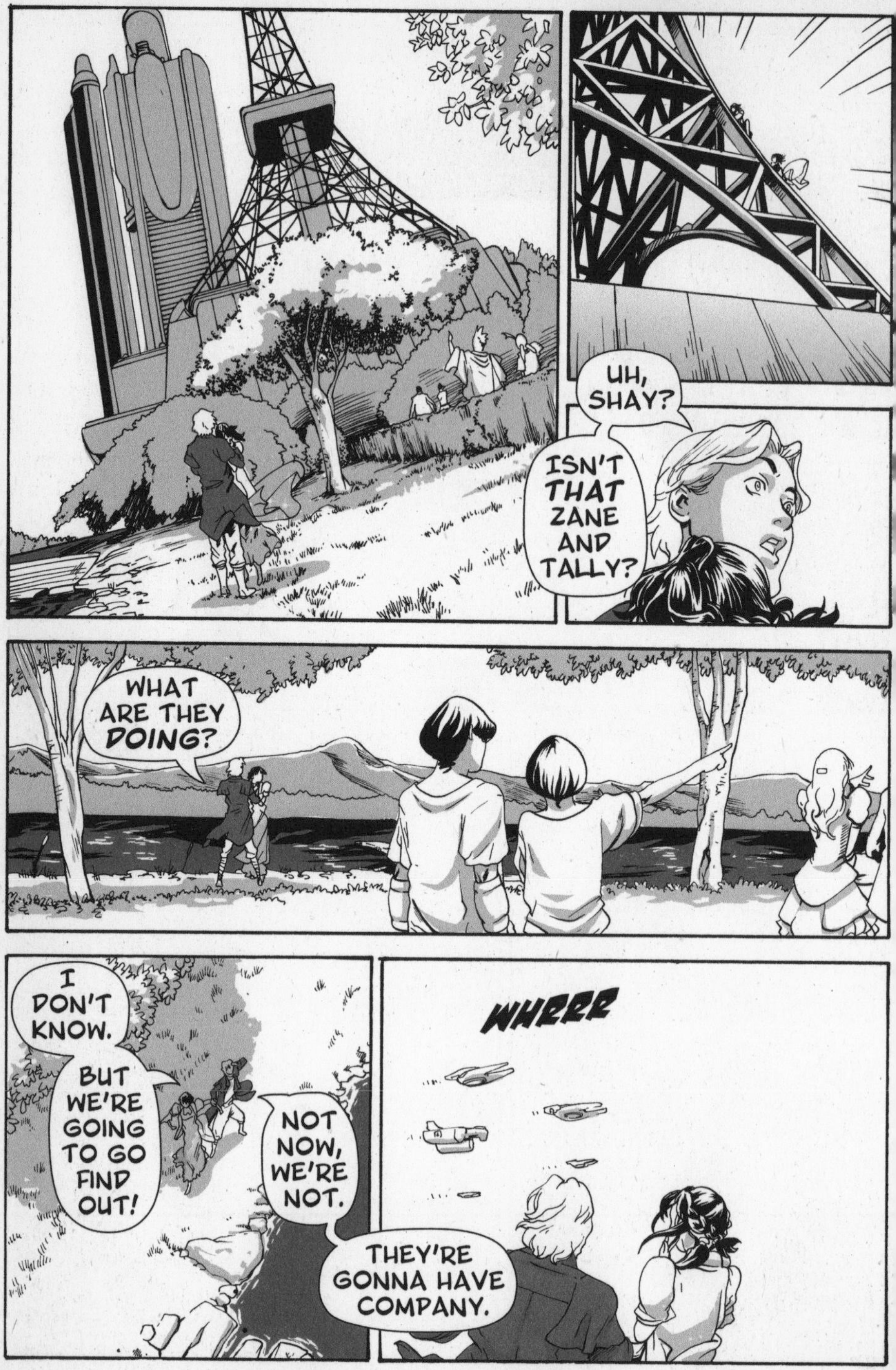
UH, SHAY?
ISN'T THAT ZANE AND TALLY?
WHAT ARE THEY DOING?
I DON'T KNOW.
BUT WE'RE GOING TO GO FIND OUT!
NOT NOW, WE'RE NOT.
THEY'RE GONNA HAVE COMPANY.
WHRRR

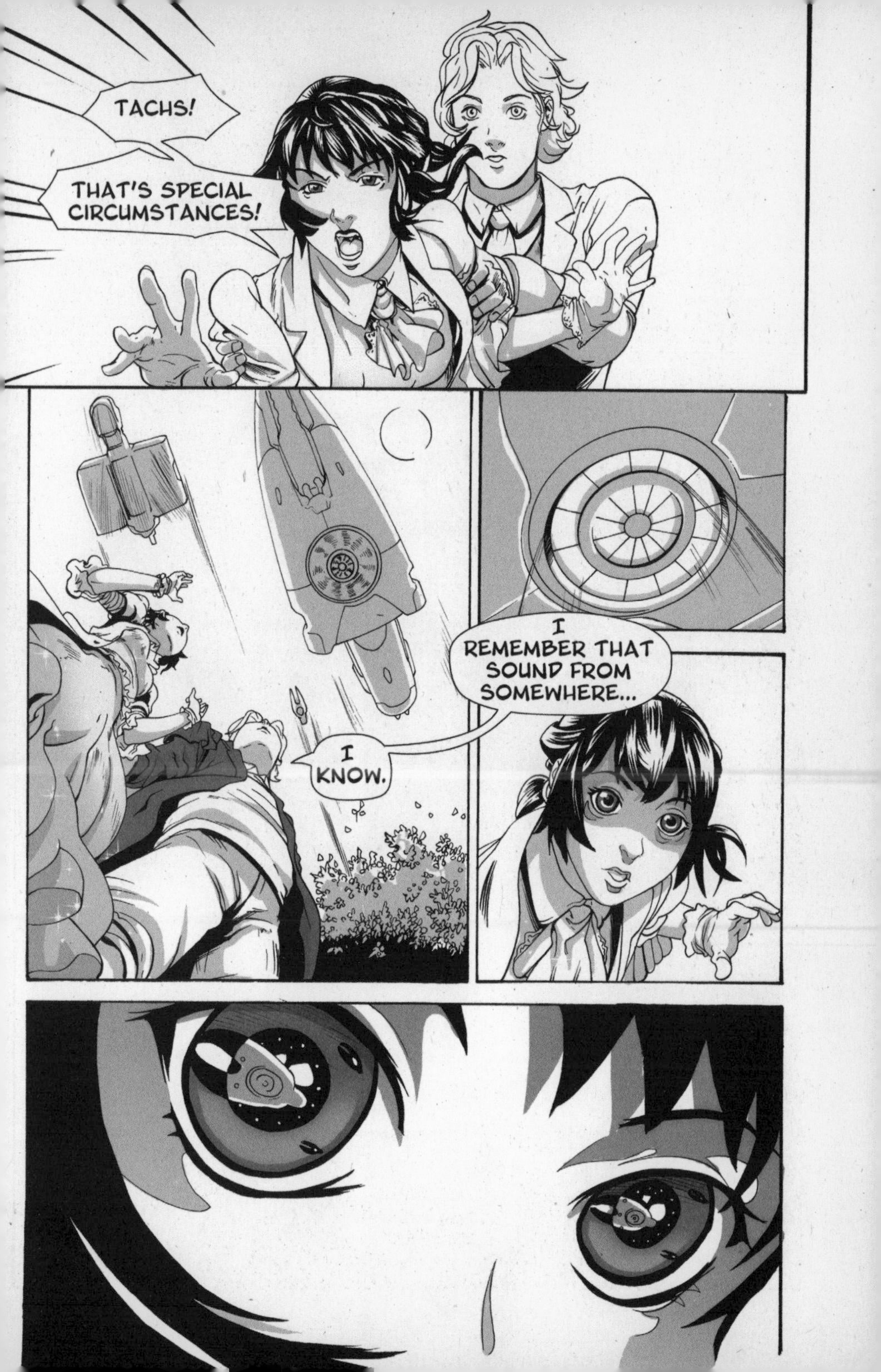

TACHS!
THAT'S SPECIAL CIRCUMSTANCES!
I KNOW.
I REMEMBER THAT SOUND FROM SOMEWHERE...

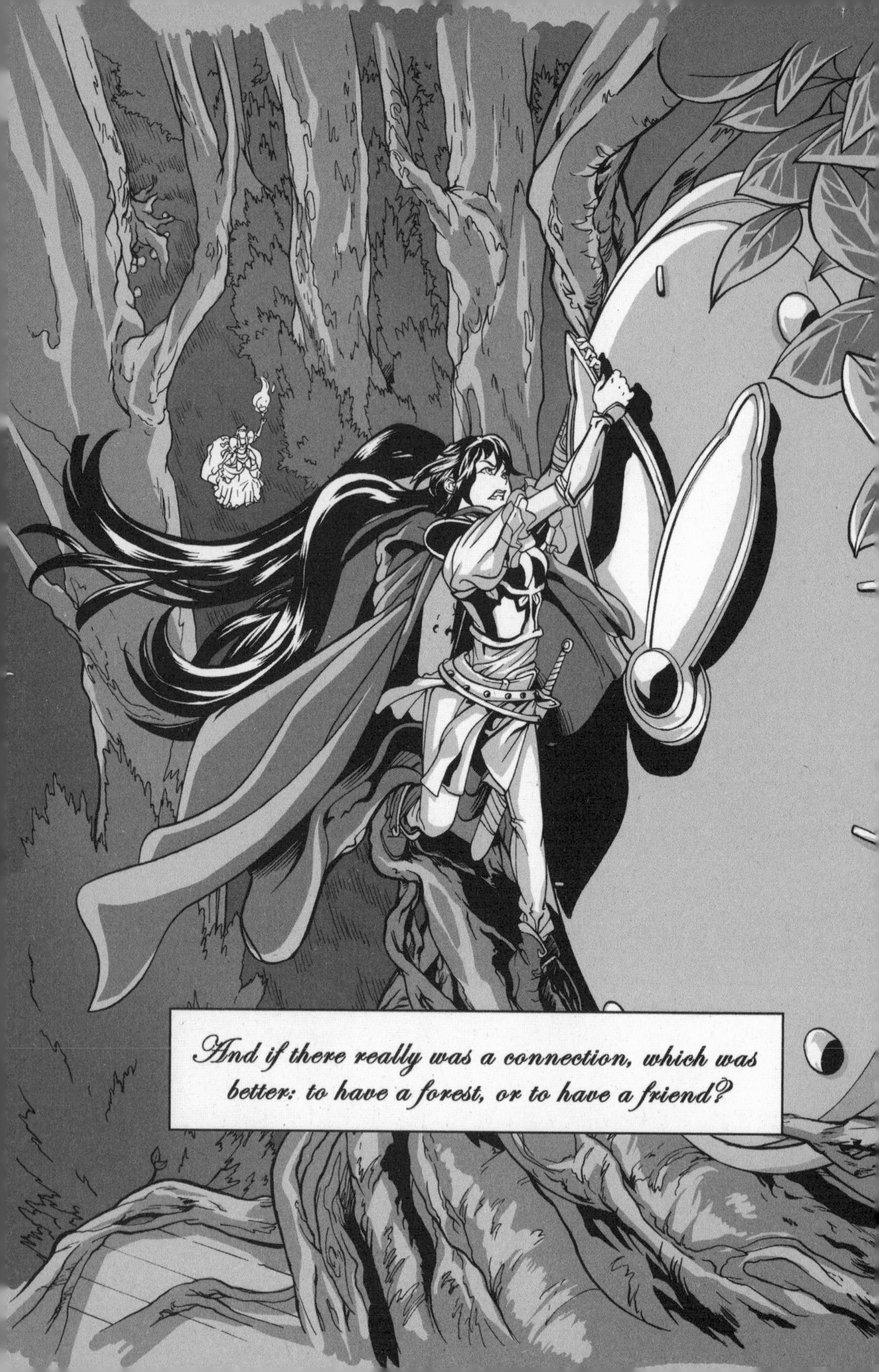
And if there really was a connection, which was better: to have a forest, or to have a friend?

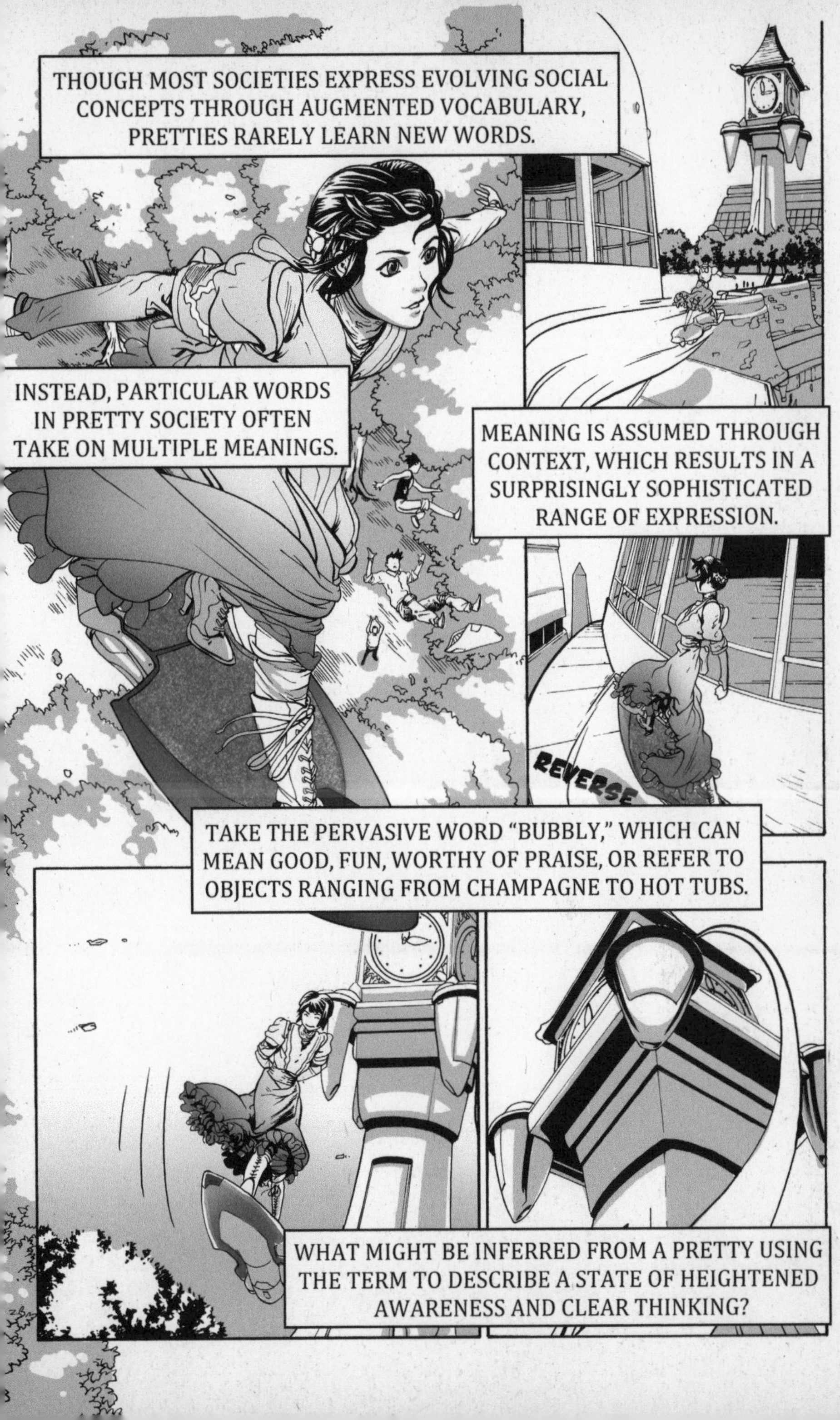
THOUGH MOST SOCIETIES EXPRESS EVOLVING SOCIAL CONCEPTS THROUGH AUGMENTED VOCABULARY, PRETTIES RARELY LEARN NEW WORDS.
INSTEAD, PARTICULAR WORDS IN PRETTY SOCIETY OFTEN TAKE ON MULTIPLE MEANINGS.
MEANING IS ASSUMED THROUGH CONTEXT, WHICH RESULTS IN A SURPRISINGLY SOPHISTICATED RANGE OF EXPRESSION.
REVERSE
TAKE THE PERVASIVE WORD "BUBBLY," WHICH CAN MEAN GOOD, FUN, WORTHY OF PRAISE, OR REFER TO OBJECTS RANGING FROM CHAMPAGNE TO HOT TUBS.
WHAT MIGHT BE INFERRED FROM A PRETTY USING THE TERM TO DESCRIBE A STATE OF HEIGHTENED AWARENESS AND CLEAR THINKING?

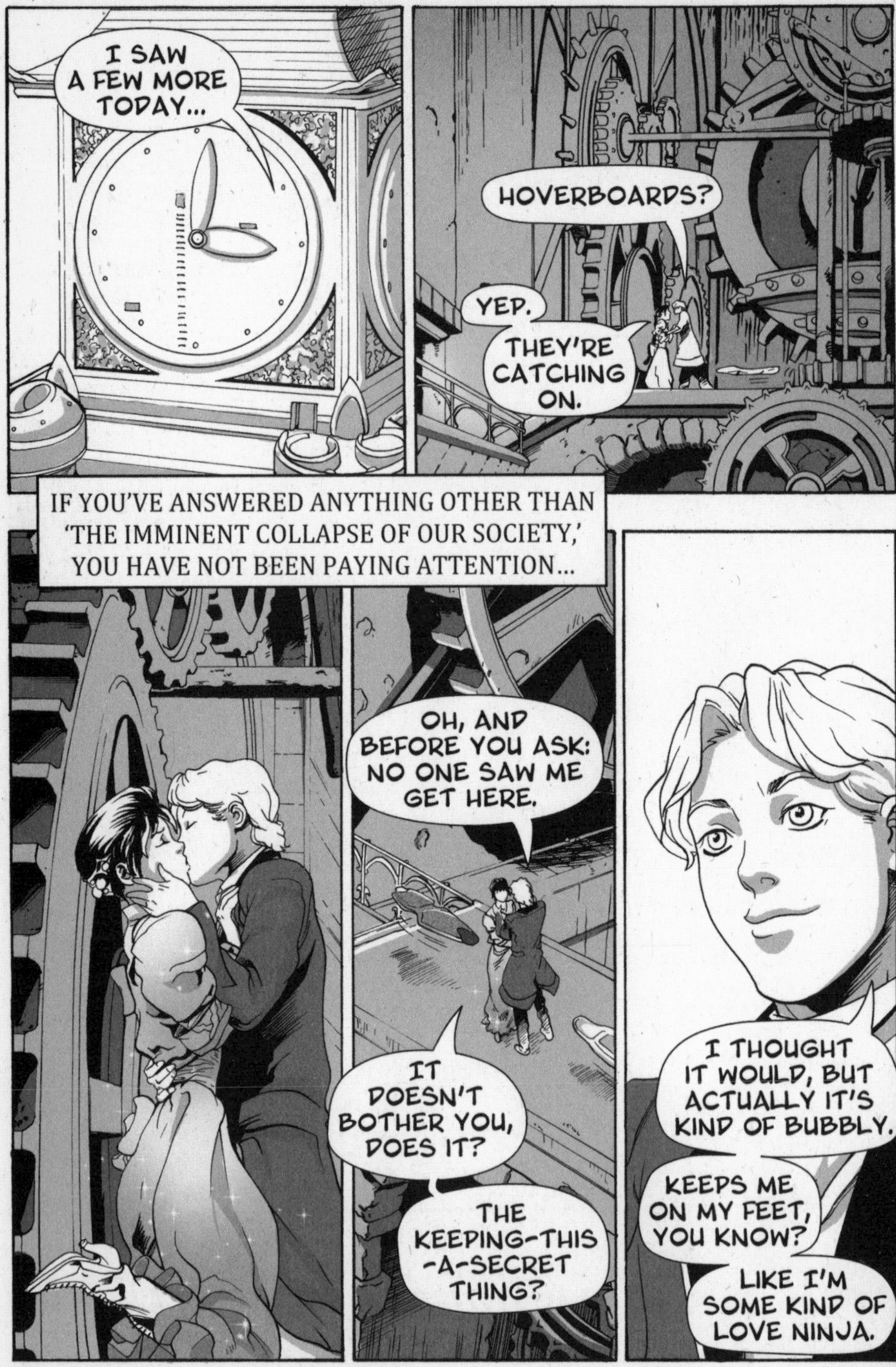
I SAW A FEW MORE TODAY...
HOVERBOARDS?
YEP.
THEY'RE CATCHING ON.
IF YOU'VE ANSWERED ANYTHING OTHER THAN 'THE IMMINENT COLLAPSE OF OUR SOCIETY,' YOU HAVE NOT BEEN PAYING ATTENTION...
OH, AND BEFORE YOU ASK: NO ONE SAW ME GET HERE.
IT DOESN'T BOTHER YOU, DOES IT?
THE KEEPING-THIS-A-SECRET THING?
I THOUGHT IT WOULD, BUT ACTUALLY IT'S KIND OF BUBBLY.
KEEPS ME ON MY FEET, YOU KNOW?
LIKE I'M SOME KIND OF LOVE NINJA.

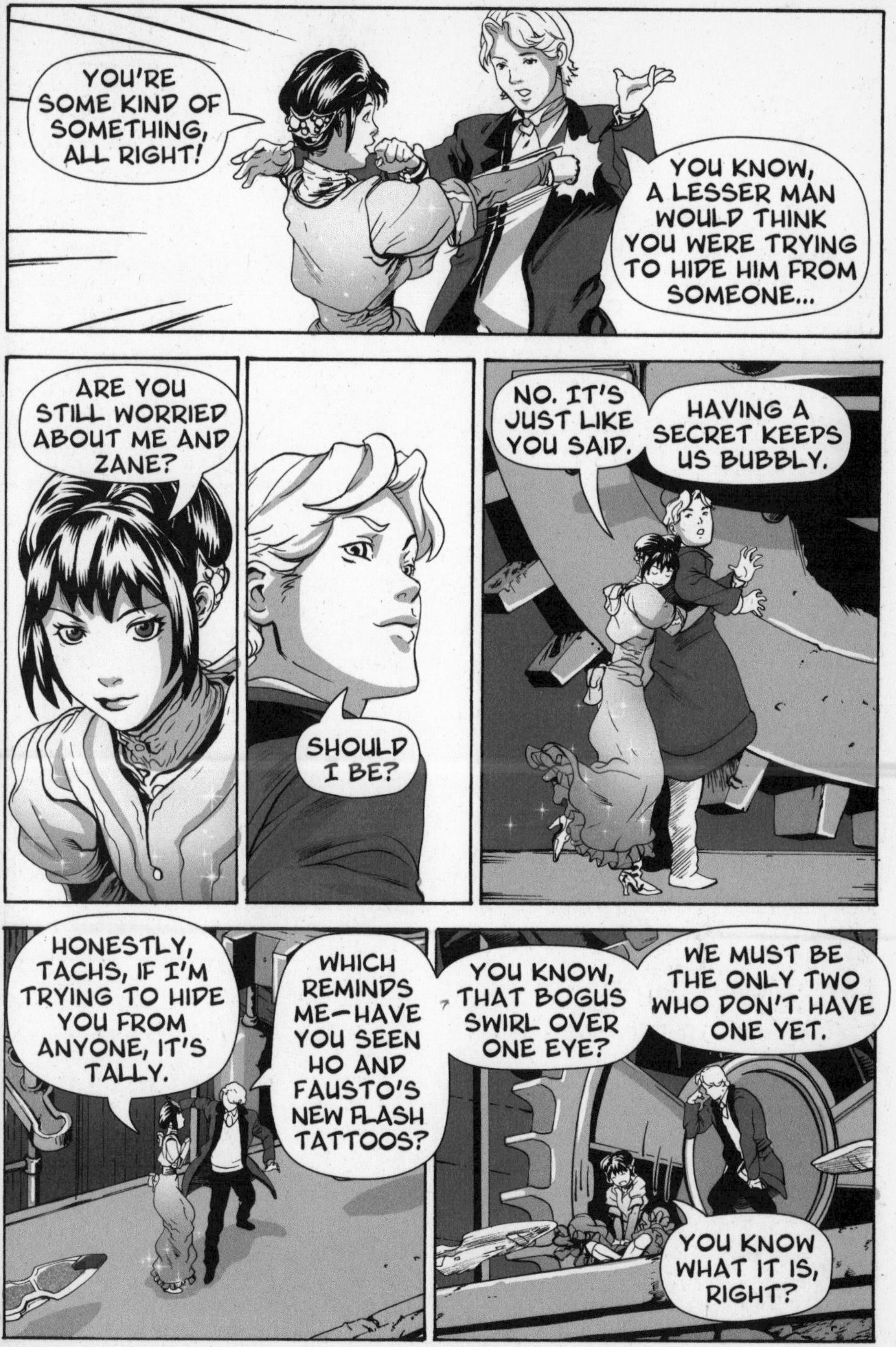
YOU'RE SOME KIND OF SOMETHING, ALL RIGHT!
YOU KNOW, A LESSER MAN WOULD THINK YOU WERE TRYING TO HIDE HIM FROM SOMEONE...
ARE YOU STILL WORRIED ABOUT ME AND ZANE?
SHOULD I BE?
NO. IT'S JUST LIKE YOU SAID.
HAVING A SECRET KEEPS US BUBBLY.
HONESTLY, TACHS, IF I'M TRYING TO HIDE YOU FROM ANYONE, IT'S TALLY.
WHICH REMINDS ME—HAVE YOU SEEN HO AND FAUSTO'S NEW FLASH TATTOOS?
YOU KNOW, THAT BOGUS SWIRL OVER ONE EYE?
WE MUST BE THE ONLY TWO WHO DON'T HAVE ONE YET.
YOU KNOW WHAT IT IS, RIGHT?

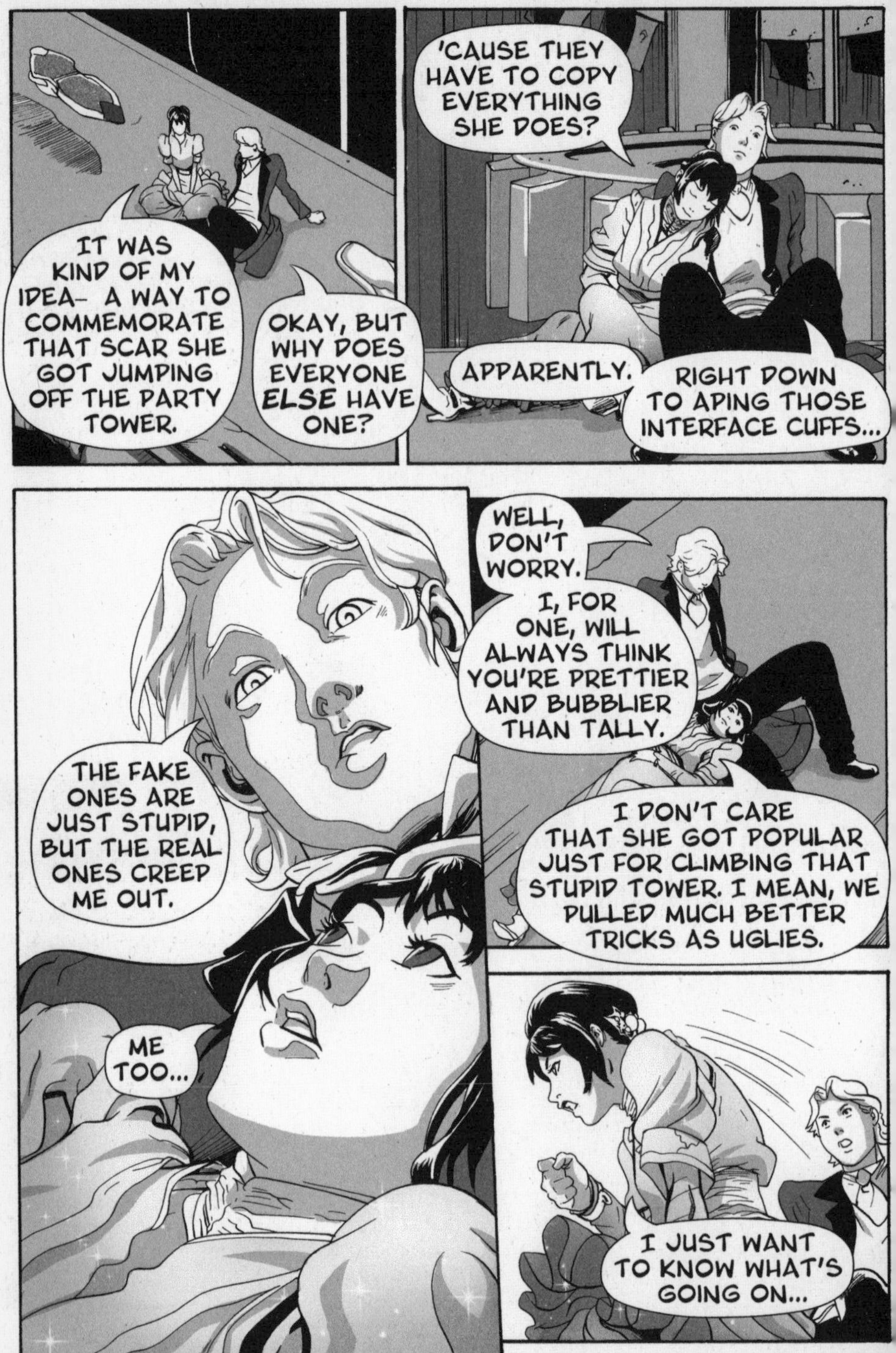
IT WAS KIND OF MY IDEA– A WAY TO COMMEMORATE THAT SCAR SHE GOT JUMPING OFF THE PARTY TOWER.
OKAY, BUT WHY DOES EVERYONE ELSE HAVE ONE?
'CAUSE THEY HAVE TO COPY EVERYTHING SHE DOES?
APPARENTLY.
RIGHT DOWN TO APING THOSE INTERFACE CUFFS...
THE FAKE ONES ARE JUST STUPID, BUT THE REAL ONES CREEP ME OUT.
ME TOO...
WELL, DON'T WORRY.
I, FOR ONE, WILL ALWAYS THINK YOU'RE PRETTIER AND BUBBLIER THAN TALLY.
I DON'T CARE THAT SHE GOT POPULAR JUST FOR CLIMBING THAT STUPID TOWER. I MEAN, WE PULLED MUCH BETTER TRICKS AS UGLIES.
I JUST WANT TO KNOW WHAT'S GOING ON...

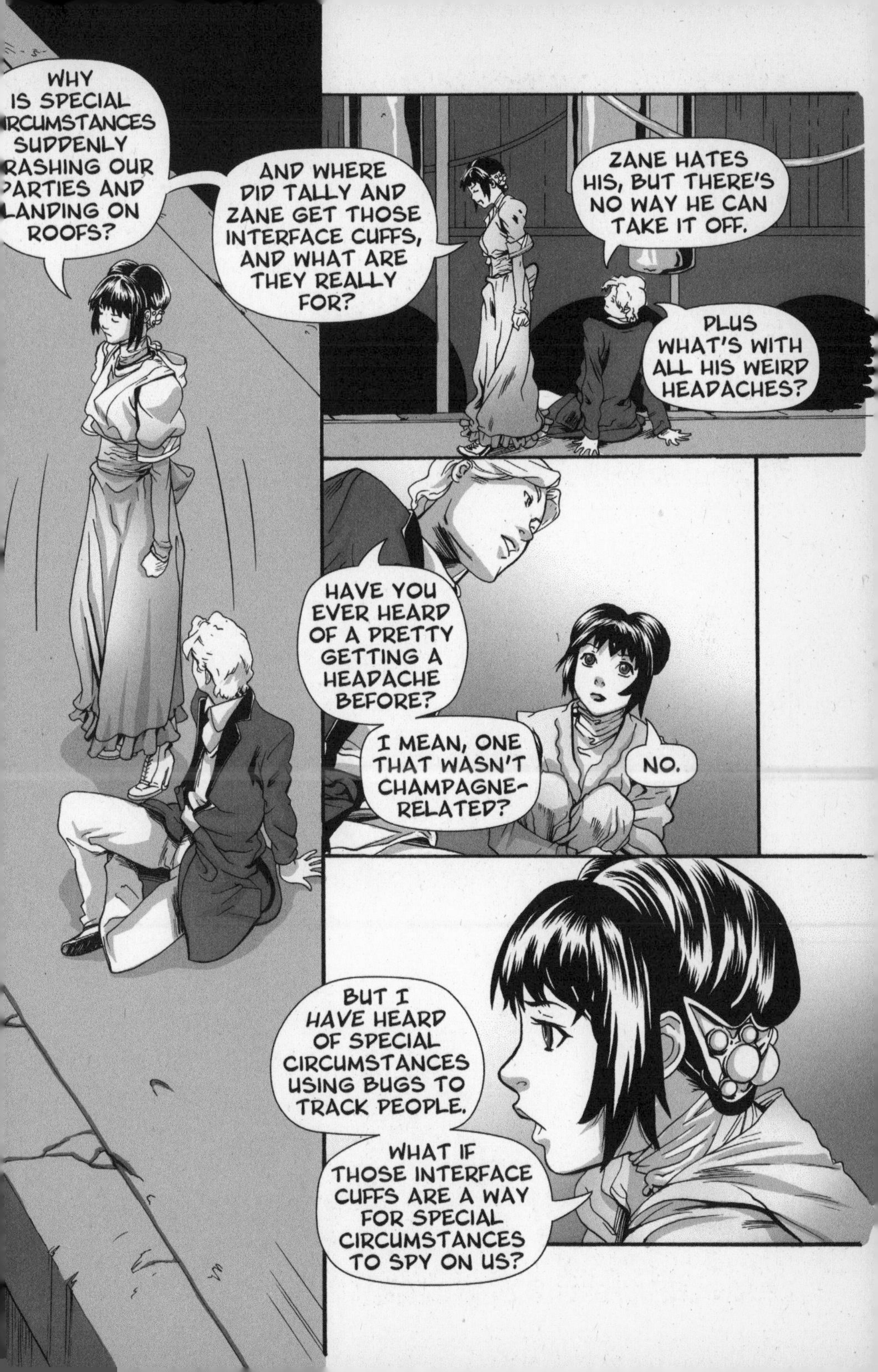

WHY IS SPECIAL IRCUMSTANCES SUDDENLY RASHING OUR PARTIES AND LANDING ON ROOFS?
AND WHERE DID TALLY AND ZANE GET THOSE INTERFACE CUFFS, AND WHAT ARE THEY REALLY FOR?
ZANE HATES HIS, BUT THERE'S NO WAY HE CAN TAKE IT OFF.
PLUS WHAT'S WITH ALL HIS WEIRD HEADACHES?
HAVE YOU EVER HEARD OF A PRETTY GETTING A HEADACHE BEFORE?
I MEAN, ONE THAT WASN'T CHAMPAGNE-RELATED?
NO.
BUT I HAVE HEARD OF SPECIAL CIRCUMSTANCES USING BUGS TO TRACK PEOPLE.
WHAT IF THOSE INTERFACE CUFFS ARE A WAY FOR SPECIAL CIRCUMSTANCES TO SPY ON US?

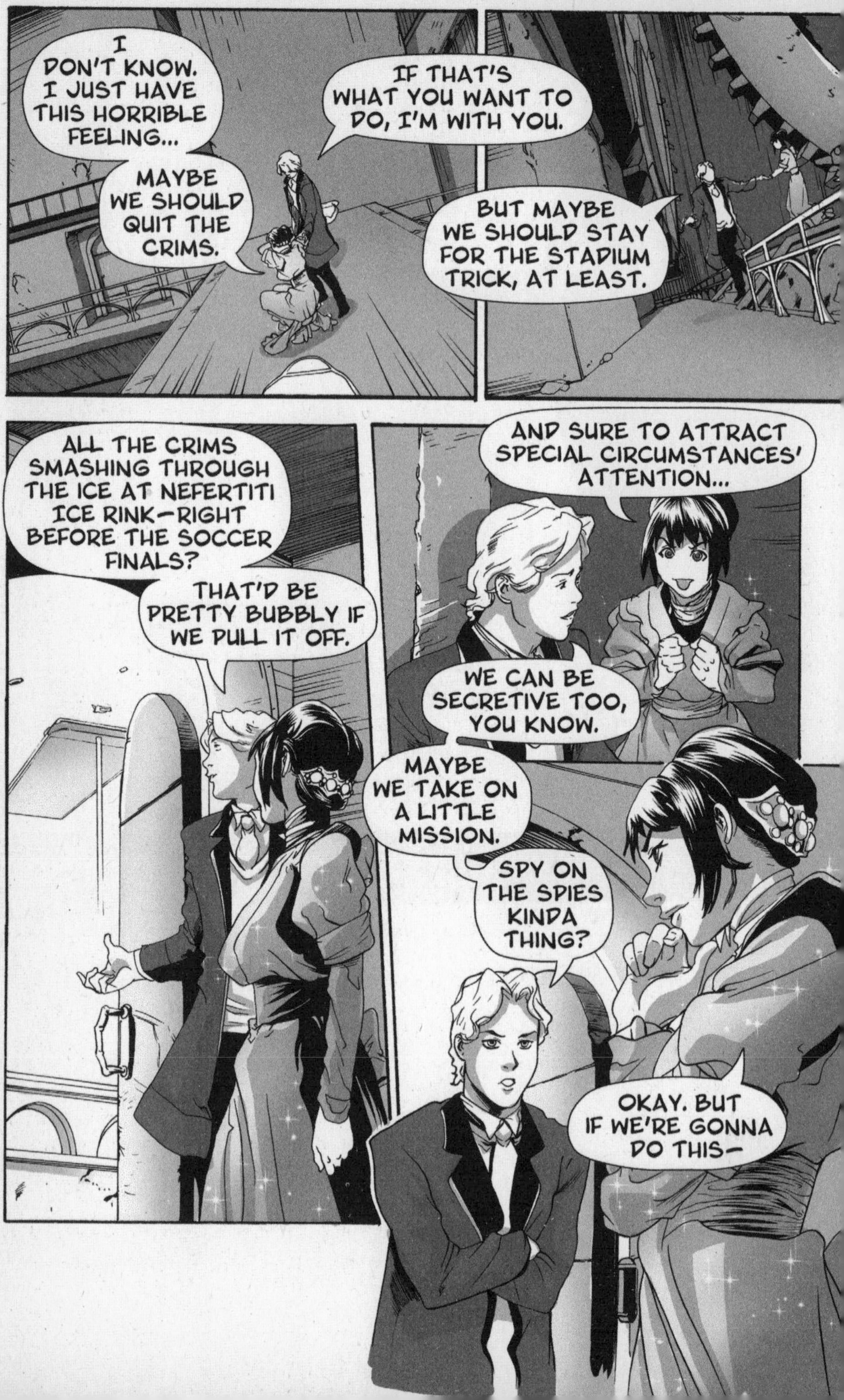
I DON'T KNOW. I JUST HAVE THIS HORRIBLE FEELING...
MAYBE WE SHOULD QUIT THE CRIMS.
IF THAT'S WHAT YOU WANT TO DO, I'M WITH YOU.
BUT MAYBE WE SHOULD STAY FOR THE STADIUM TRICK, AT LEAST.
ALL THE CRIMS SMASHING THROUGH THE ICE AT NEFERTITI ICE RINK—RIGHT BEFORE THE SOCCER FINALS?
THAT'D BE PRETTY BUBBLY IF WE PULL IT OFF.
AND SURE TO ATTRACT SPECIAL CIRCUMSTANCES' ATTENTION...
WE CAN BE SECRETIVE TOO, YOU KNOW.
MAYBE WE TAKE ON A LITTLE MISSION.
SPY ON THE SPIES KINDA THING?
OKAY. BUT IF WE'RE GONNA DO THIS—

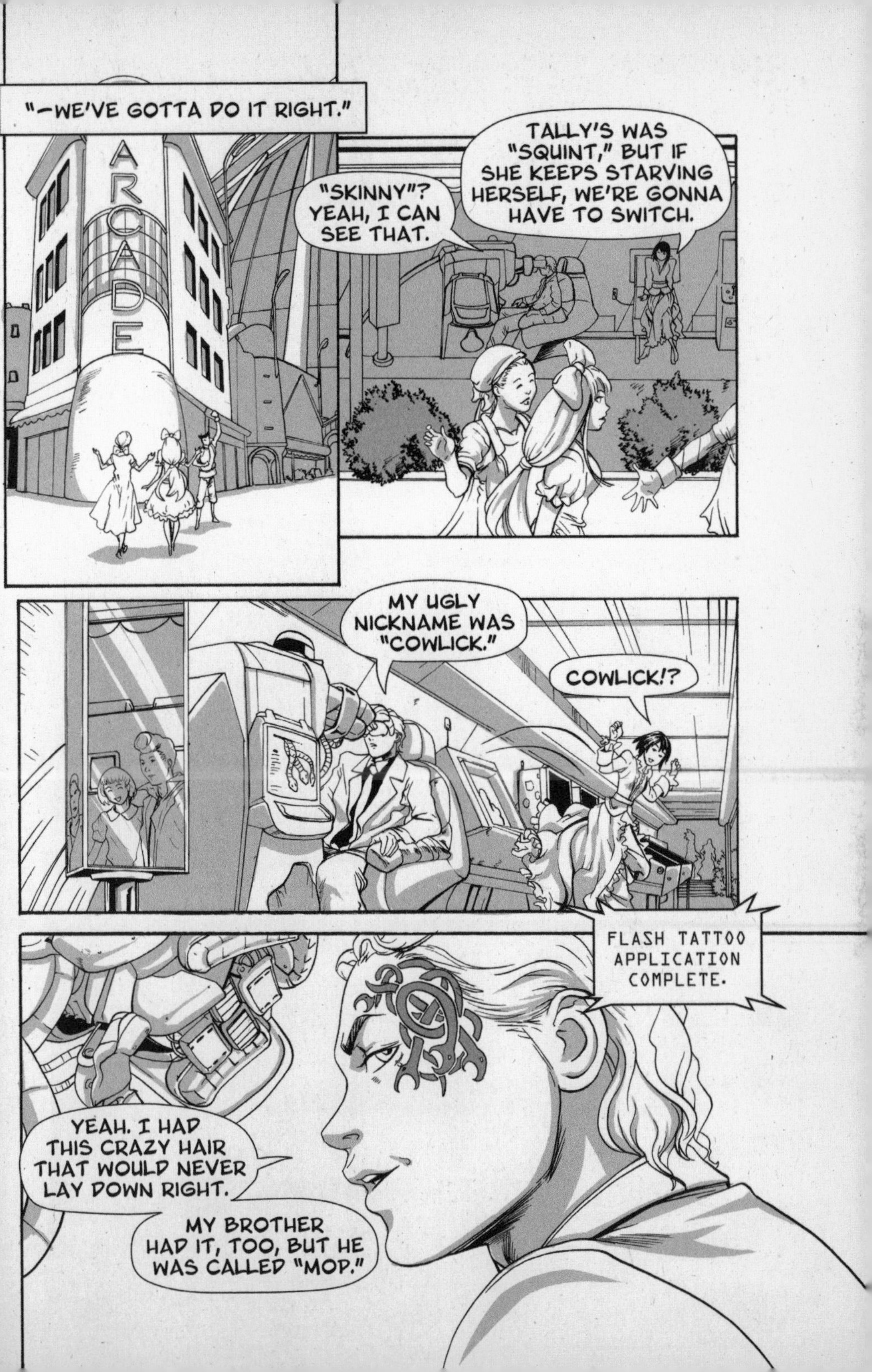
"—WE'VE GOTTA DO IT RIGHT."
ARCADE
"SKINNY"? YEAH, I CAN SEE THAT.
TALLY'S WAS "SQUINT," BUT IF SHE KEEPS STARVING HERSELF, WE'RE GONNA HAVE TO SWITCH.
MY UGLY NICKNAME WAS "COWLICK."
COWLICK!?
FLASH TATTOO APPLICATION COMPLETE.
YEAH. I HAD THIS CRAZY HAIR THAT WOULD NEVER LAY DOWN RIGHT.
MY BROTHER HAD IT, TOO, BUT HE WAS CALLED "MOP."

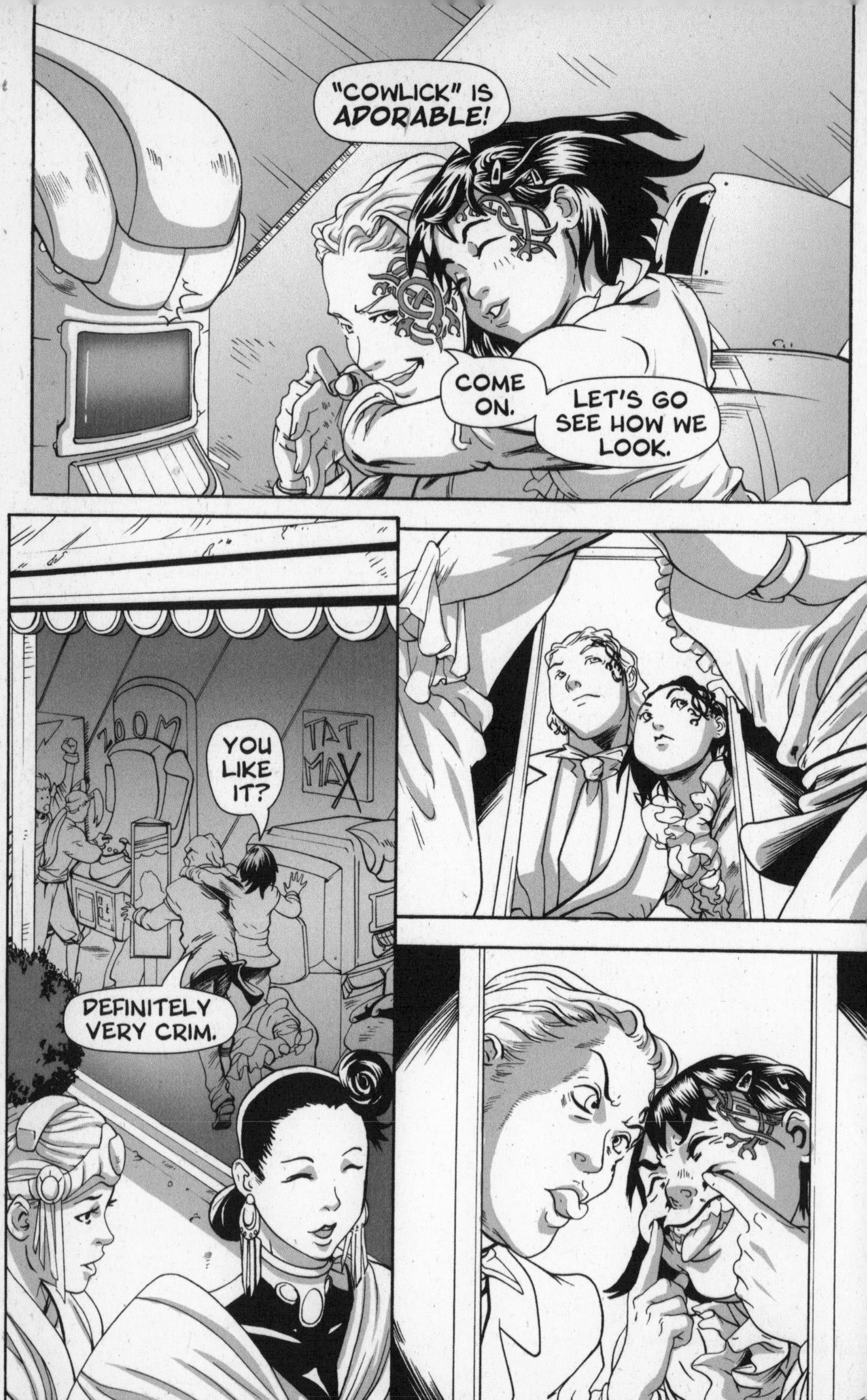
"COWLICK" IS ADORABLE!
COME ON.
LET'S GO SEE HOW WE LOOK.
ZOOM
YOU LIKE IT?
TAT MAX
DEFINITELY VERY CRIM.

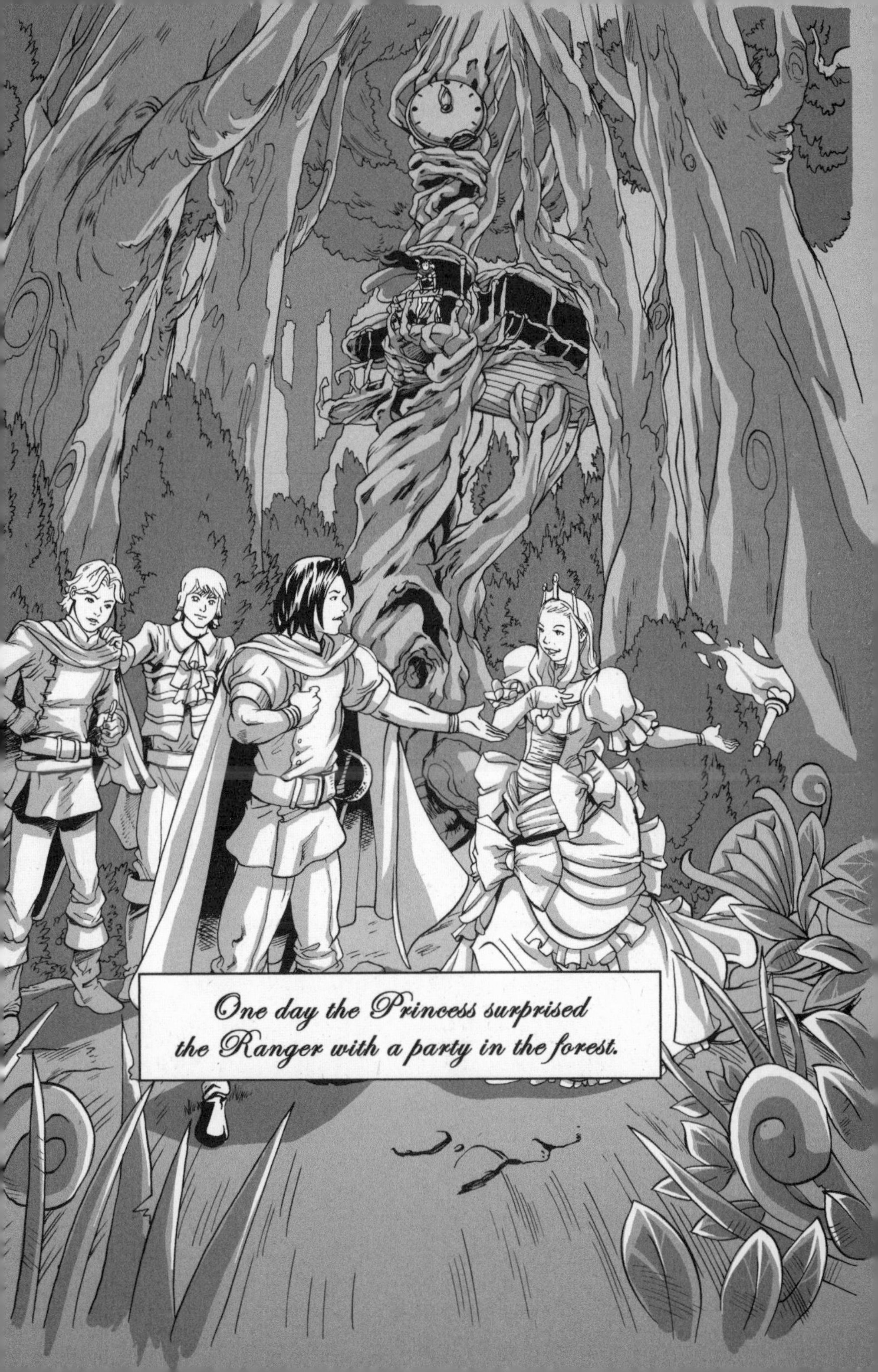
One day the Princess surprised the Ranger with a party in the forest.

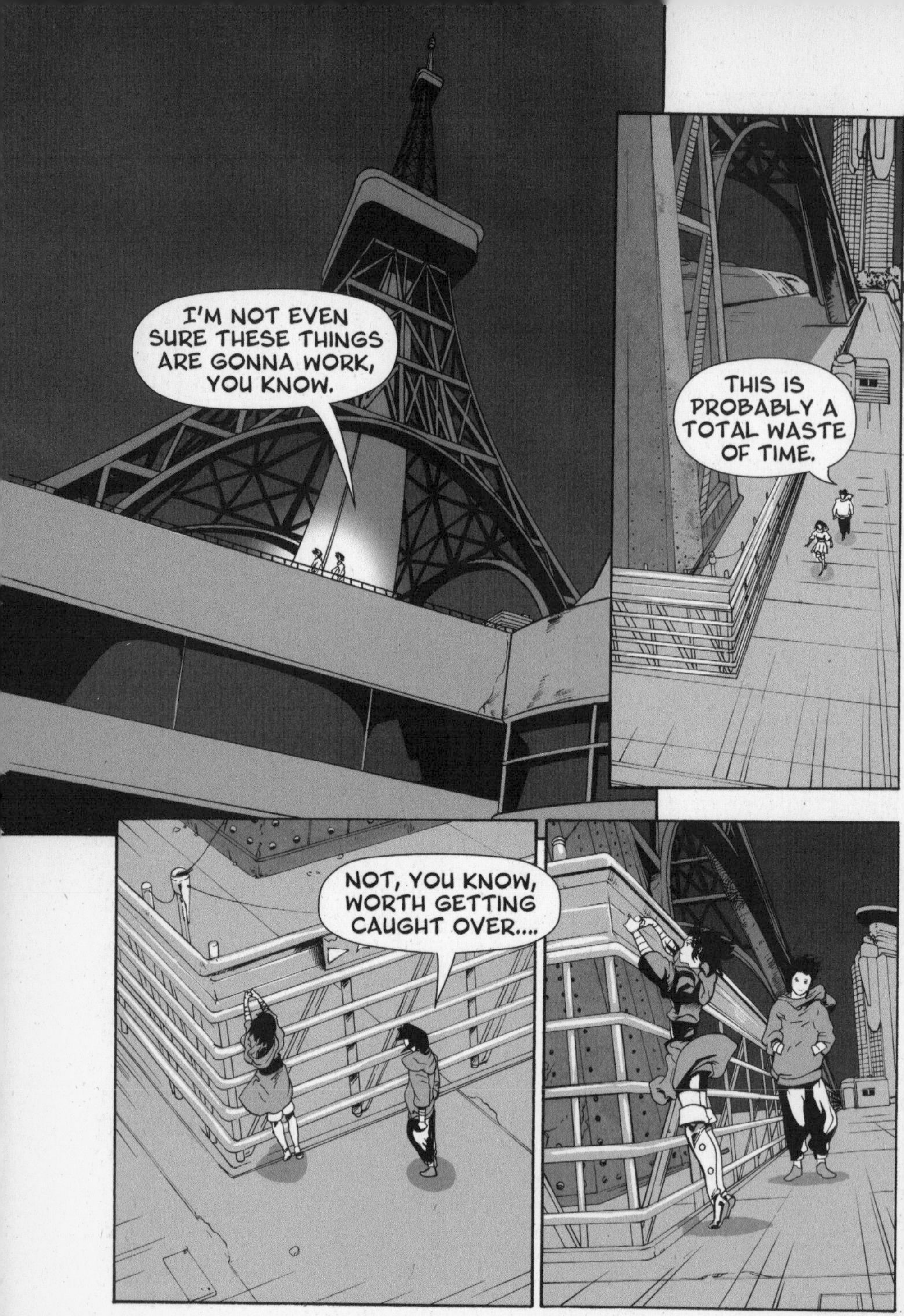
I'M NOT EVEN SURE THESE THINGS ARE GONNA WORK, YOU KNOW.
THIS IS PROBABLY A TOTAL WASTE OF TIME.
NOT, YOU KNOW, WORTH GETTING CAUGHT OVER....

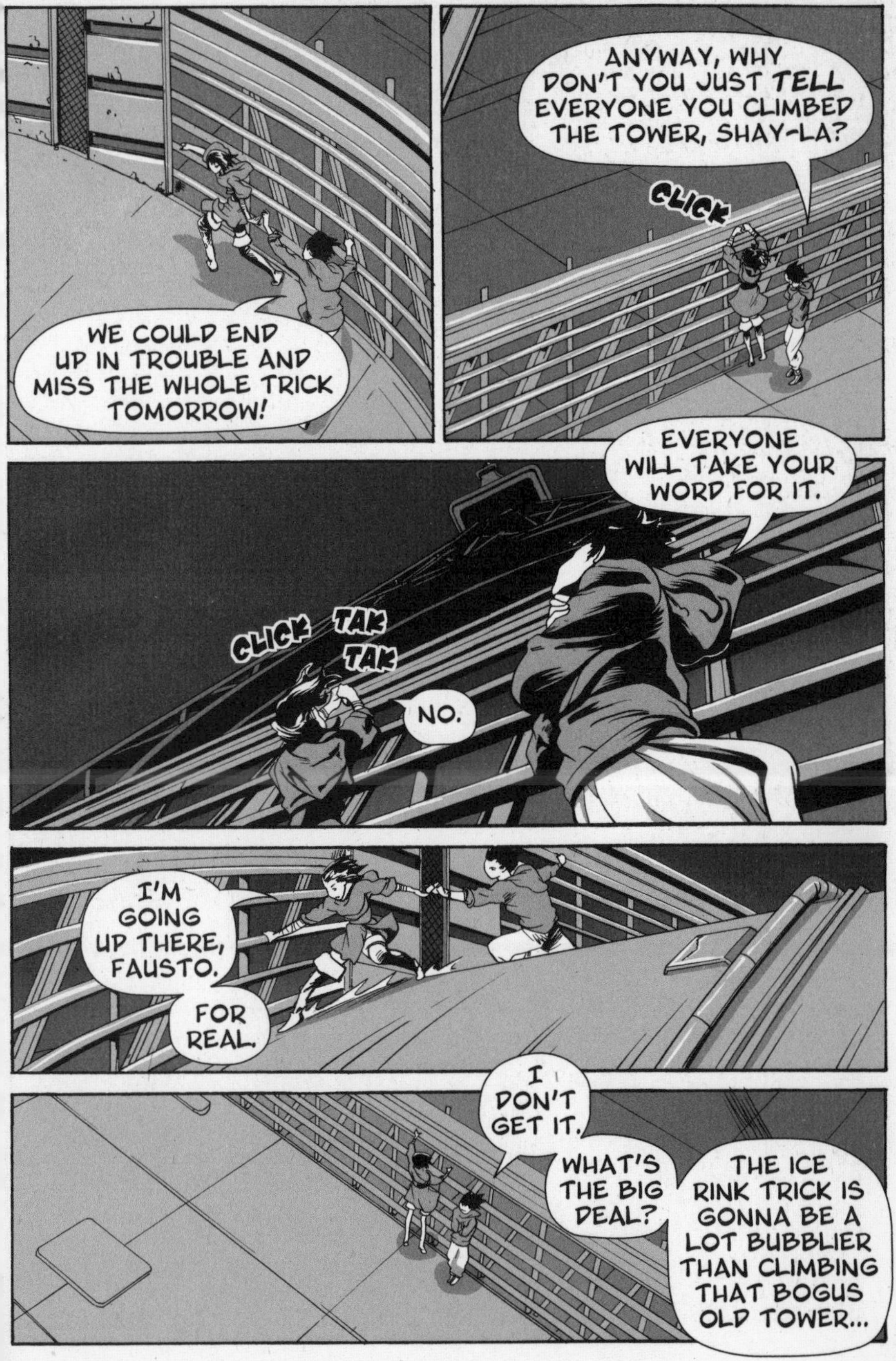
WE COULD END UP IN TROUBLE AND MISS THE WHOLE TRICK TOMORROW!
ANYWAY, WHY DON'T YOU JUST TELL EVERYONE YOU CLIMBED THE TOWER, SHAY-LA?
CLICK
EVERYONE WILL TAKE YOUR WORD FOR IT.
CLICK
TAK
TAK
NO.
I'M GOING UP THERE, FAUSTO.
FOR REAL.
I DON'T GET IT.
WHAT'S THE BIG DEAL?
THE ICE RINK TRICK IS GONNA BE A LOT BUBBLIER THAN CLIMBING THAT BOGUS OLD TOWER...

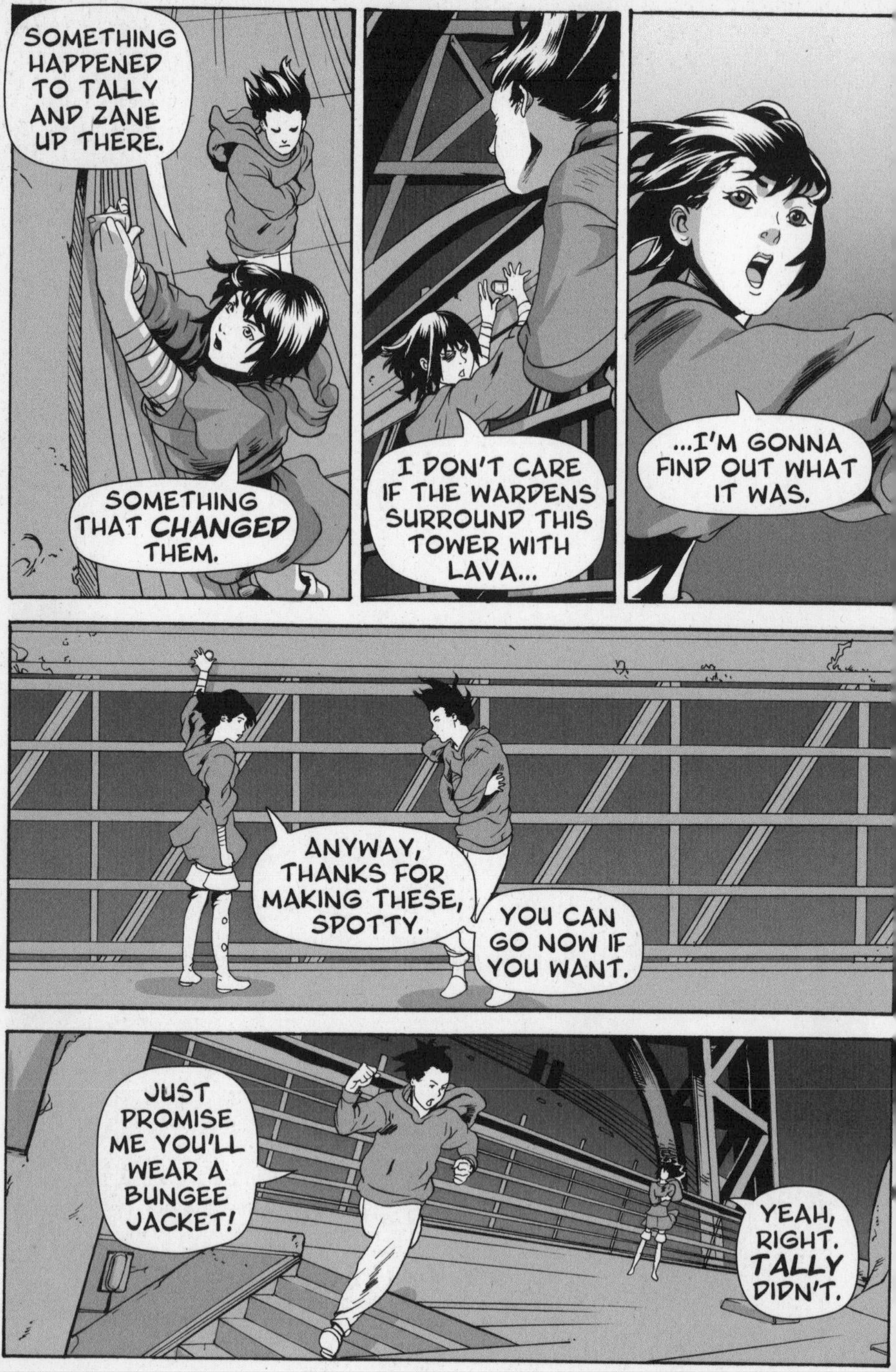
SOMETHING HAPPENED TO TALLY AND ZANE UP THERE.
SOMETHING THAT CHANGED THEM.
I DON'T CARE IF THE WARDENS SURROUND THIS TOWER WITH LAVA...
...I'M GONNA FIND OUT WHAT IT WAS.
ANYWAY, THANKS FOR MAKING THESE, SPOTTY.
YOU CAN GO NOW IF YOU WANT.
JUST PROMISE ME YOU'LL WEAR A BUNGEE JACKET!
YEAH, RIGHT. TALLY DIDN'T.

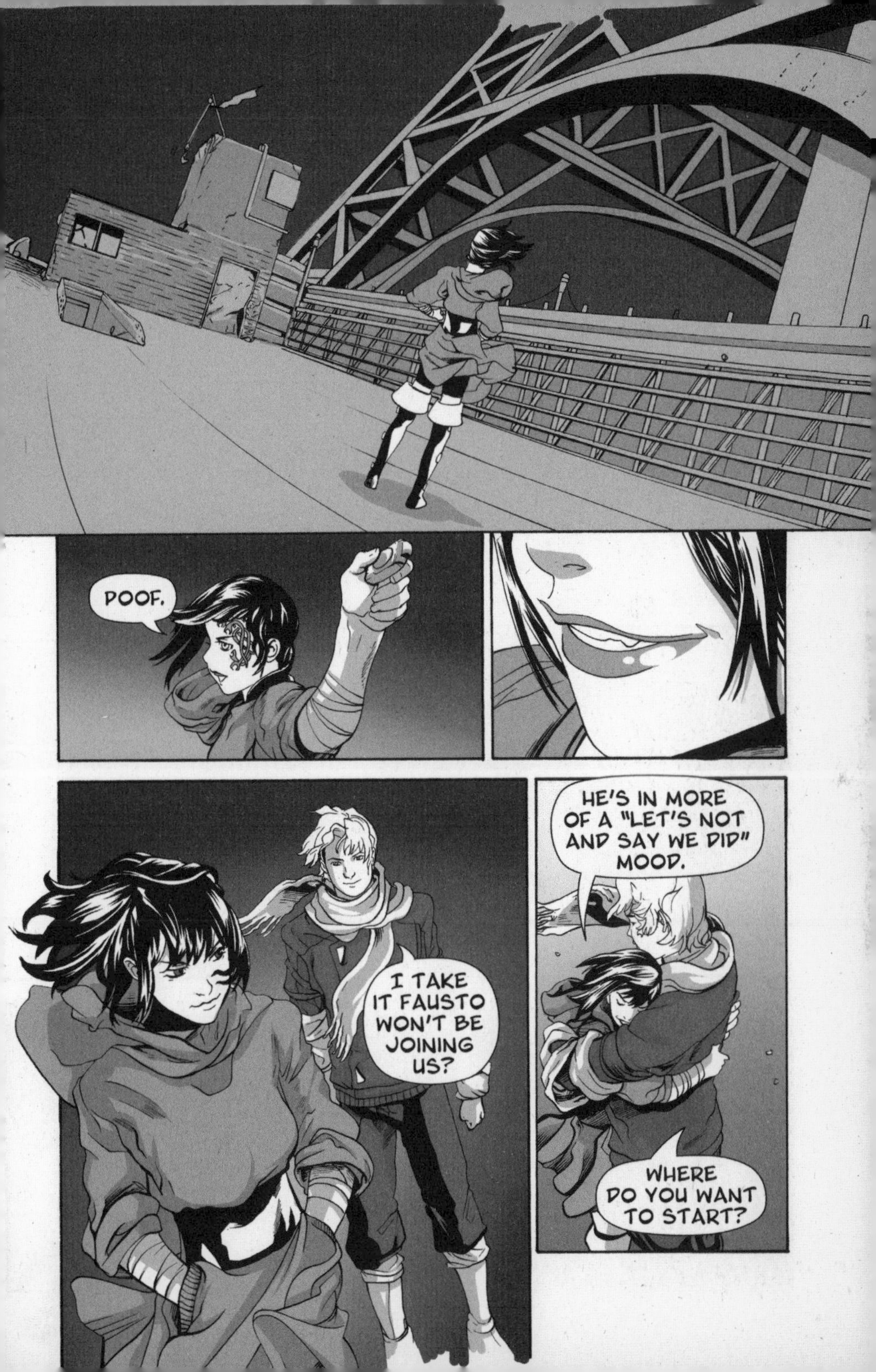
POOF.
I TAKE IT FAUSTO WON'T BE JOINING US?
HE'S IN MORE OF A "LET'S NOT AND SAY WE DID" MOOD.
WHERE DO YOU WANT TO START?

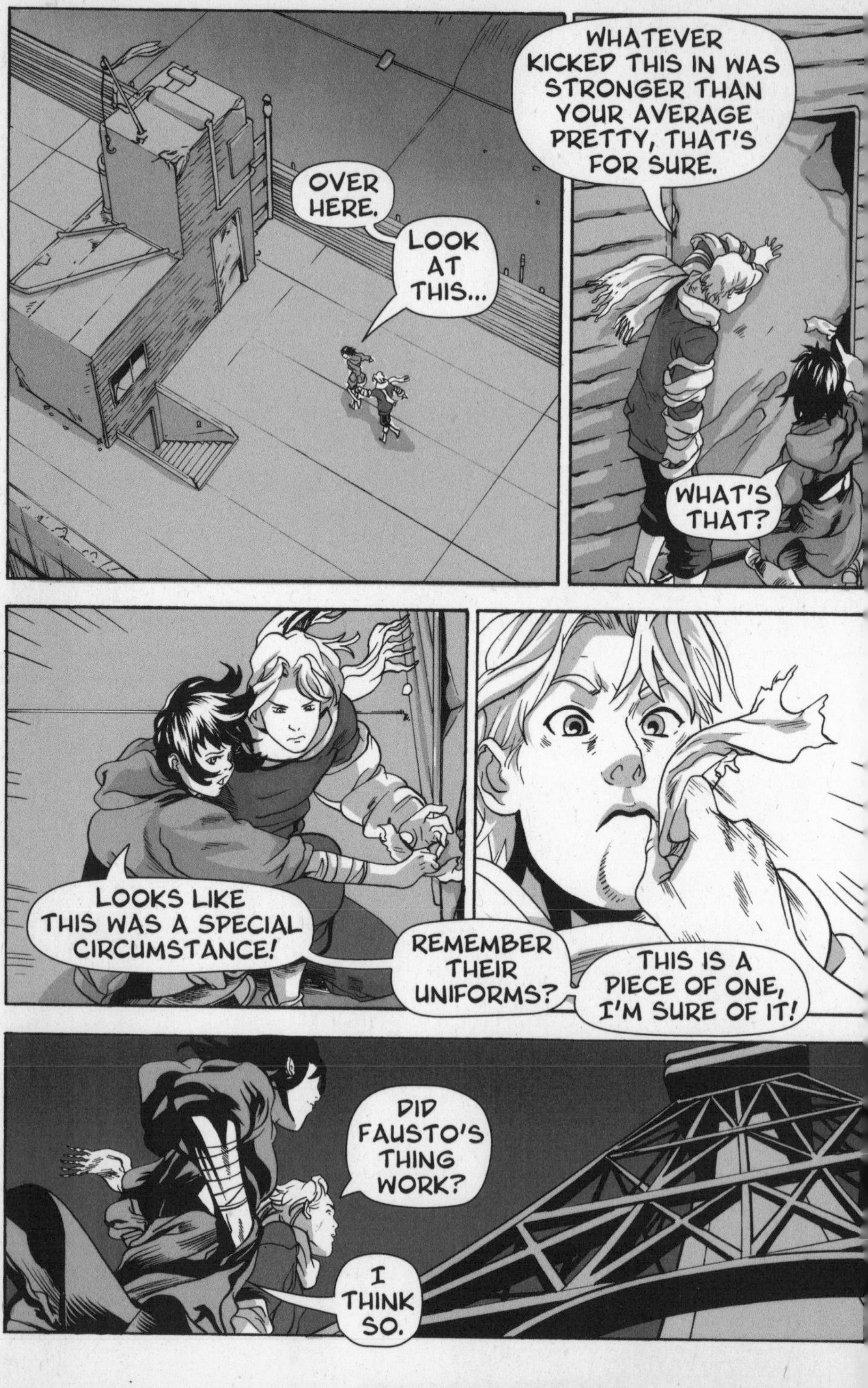
OVER HERE.
LOOK AT THIS...
WHATEVER KICKED THIS IN WAS STRONGER THAN YOUR AVERAGE PRETTY, THAT'S FOR SURE.
WHAT'S THAT?
LOOKS LIKE THIS WAS A SPECIAL CIRCUMSTANCE!
REMEMBER THEIR UNIFORMS?
THIS IS A PIECE OF ONE, I'M SURE OF IT!
DID FAUSTO'S THING WORK?
I THINK SO.

YOU THINK SO?

WHAT'LL HAPPEN IF THE MINDERS ARE STILL ON?

I DON'T KNOW.

LET'S BE CLEAR.

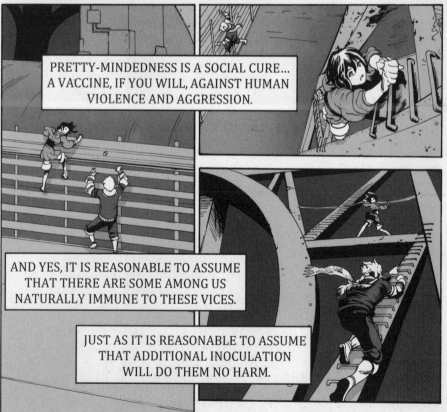

PRETTY-MINDEDNESS IS A SOCIAL CURE... A VACCINE, IF YOU WILL, AGAINST HUMAN VIOLENCE AND AGGRESSION.

AND YES, IT IS REASONABLE TO ASSUME THAT THERE ARE SOME AMONG US NATURALLY IMMUNE TO THESE VICES.

JUST AS IT IS REASONABLE TO ASSUME THAT ADDITIONAL INOCULATION WILL DO THEM NO HARM.

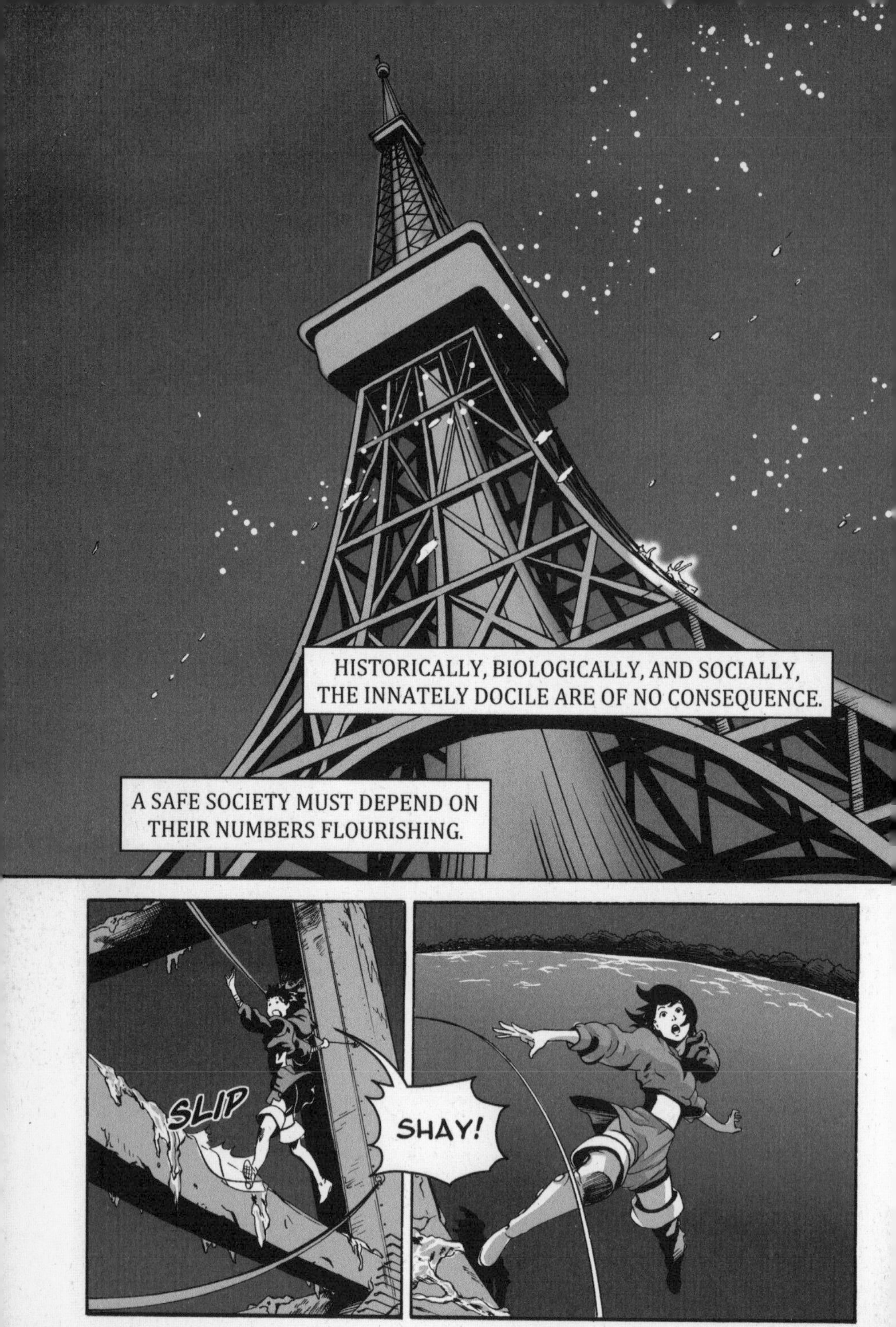
HISTORICALLY, BIOLOGICALLY, AND SOCIALLY, THE INNATELY DOCILE ARE OF NO CONSEQUENCE.
A SAFE SOCIETY MUST DEPEND ON THEIR NUMBERS FLOURISHING.
SLIP
SHAY!

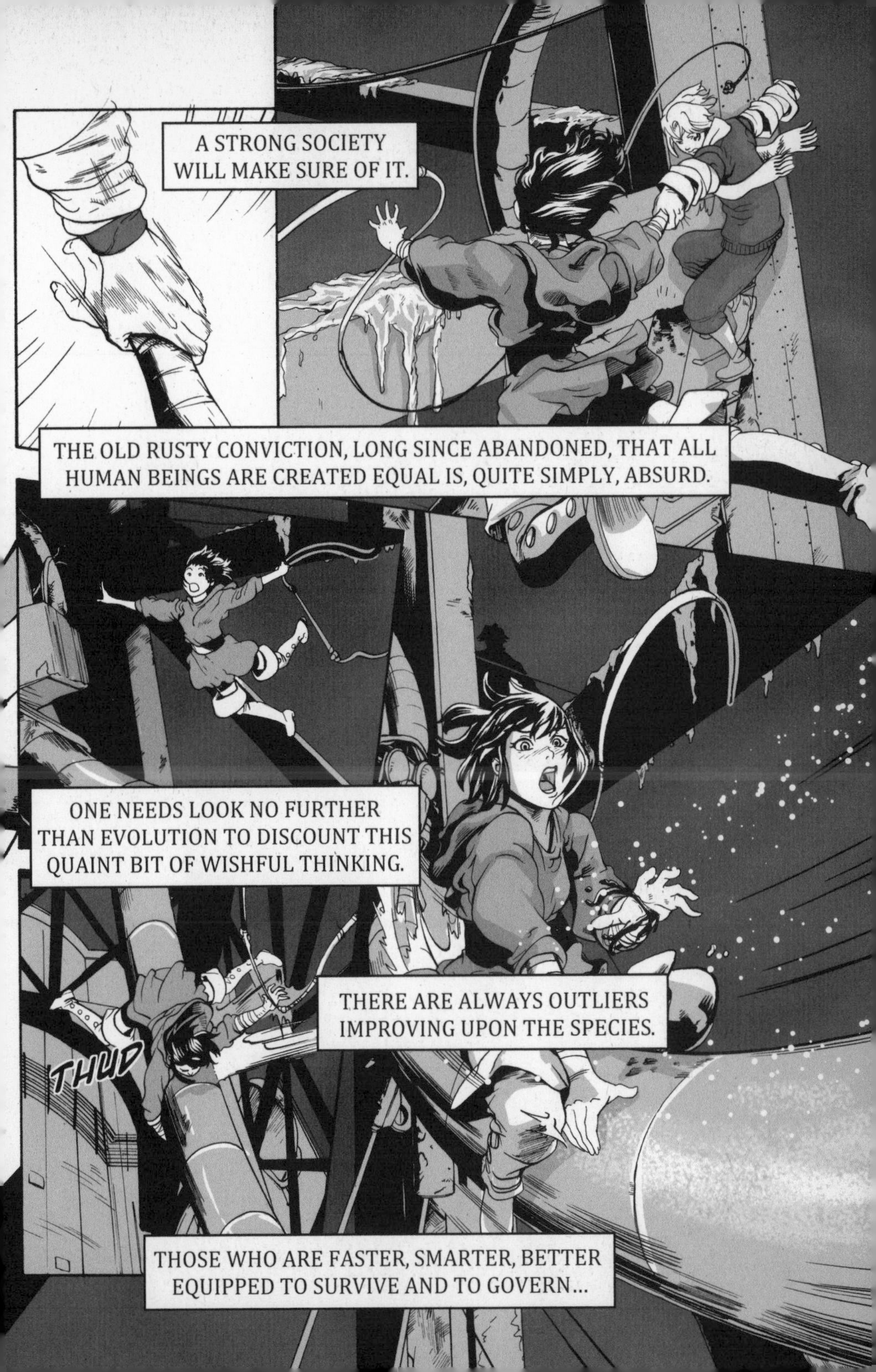
A STRONG SOCIETY WILL MAKE SURE OF IT.
THE OLD RUSTY CONVICTION, LONG SINCE ABANDONED, THAT ALL HUMAN BEINGS ARE CREATED EQUAL IS, QUITE SIMPLY, ABSURD.
ONE NEEDS LOOK NO FURTHER THAN EVOLUTION TO DISCOUNT THIS QUAINT BIT OF WISHFUL THINKING.
THERE ARE ALWAYS OUTLIERS IMPROVING UPON THE SPECIES.
THUD
THOSE WHO ARE FASTER, SMARTER, BETTER EQUIPPED TO SURVIVE AND TO GOVERN...

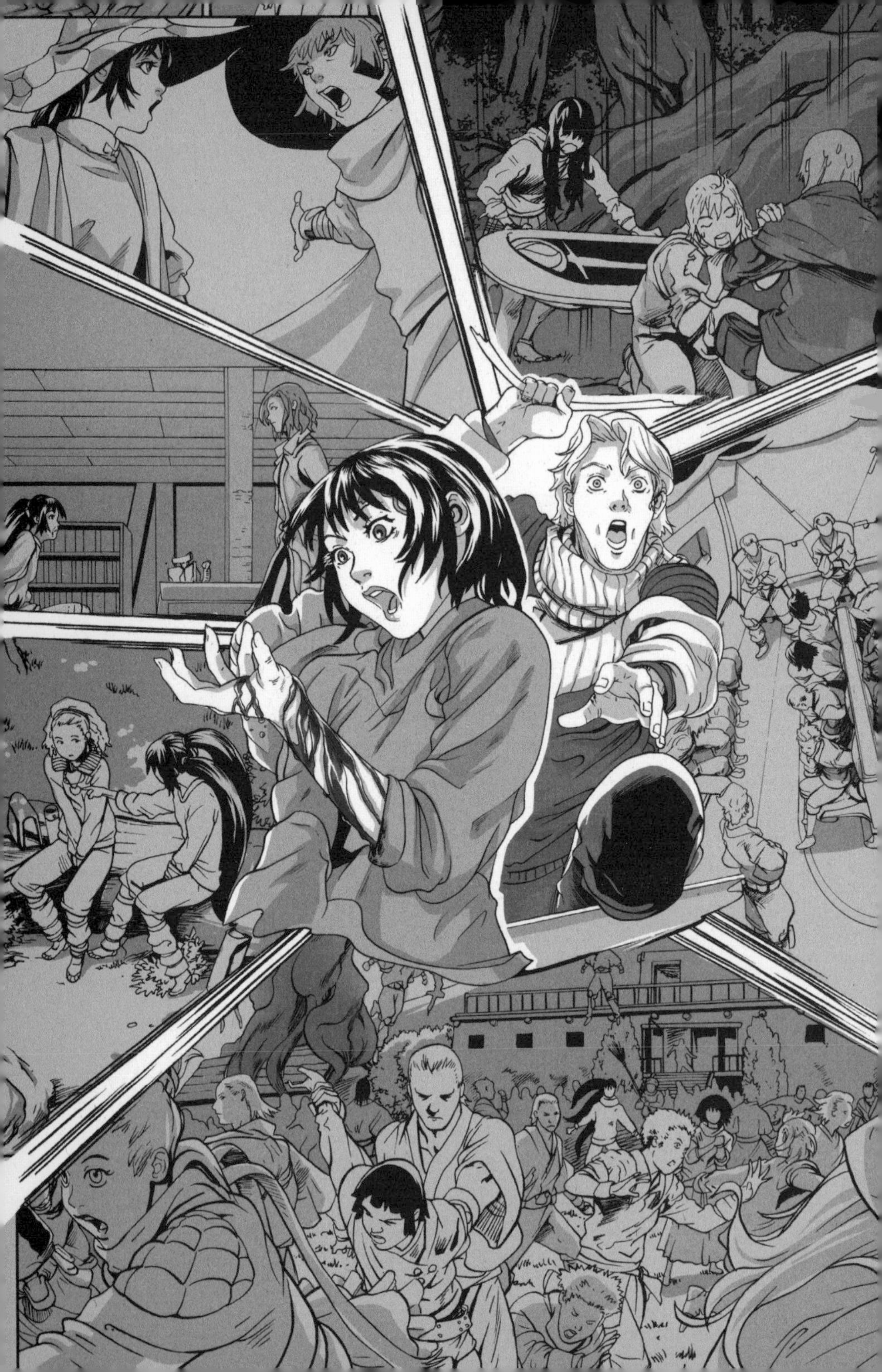

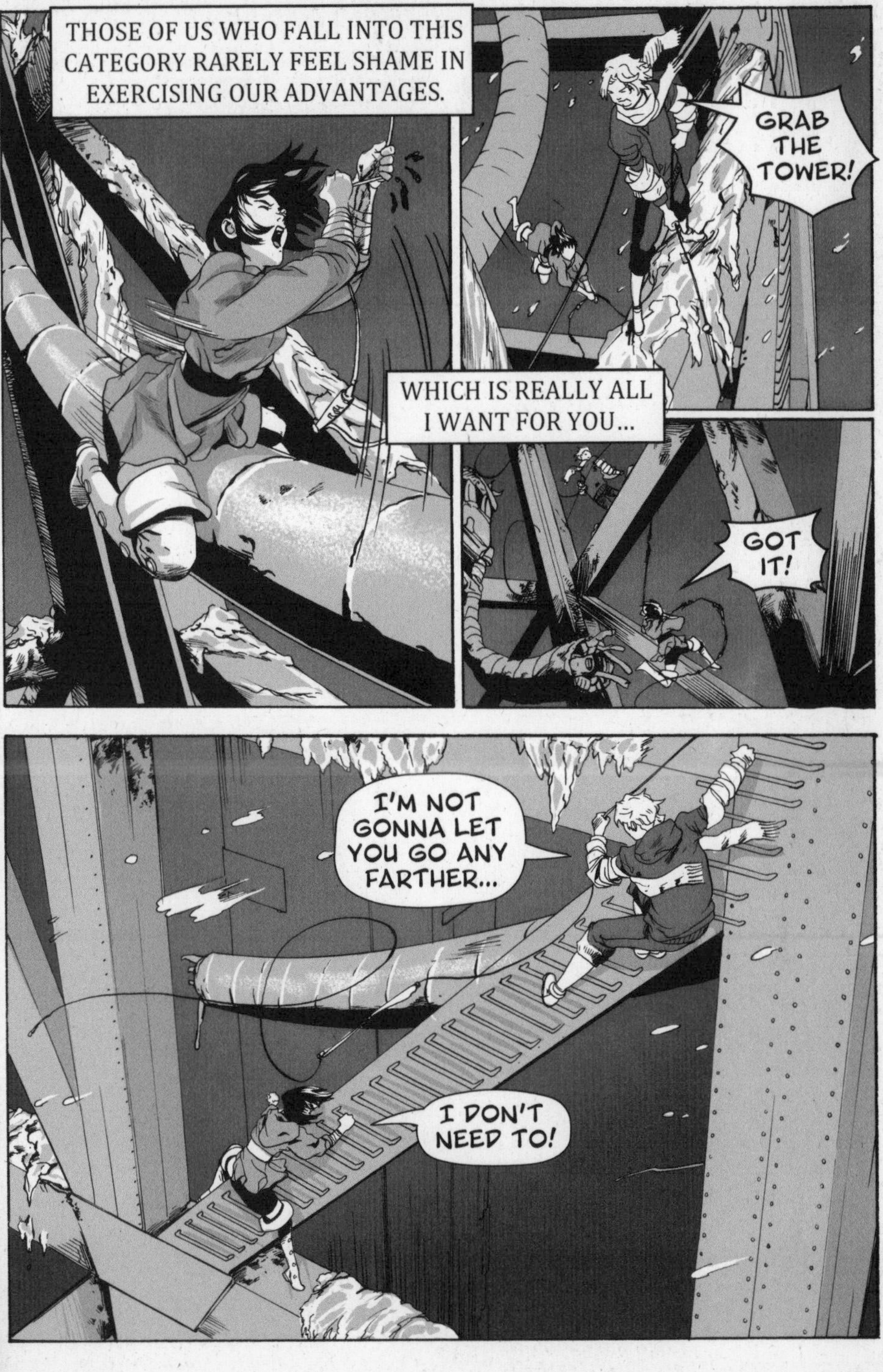
THOSE OF US WHO FALL INTO THIS CATEGORY RARELY FEEL SHAME IN EXERCISING OUR ADVANTAGES.
GRAB THE TOWER!
WHICH IS REALLY ALL I WANT FOR YOU...
GOT IT!
I'M NOT GONNA LET YOU GO ANY FARTHER...
I DON'T NEED TO!

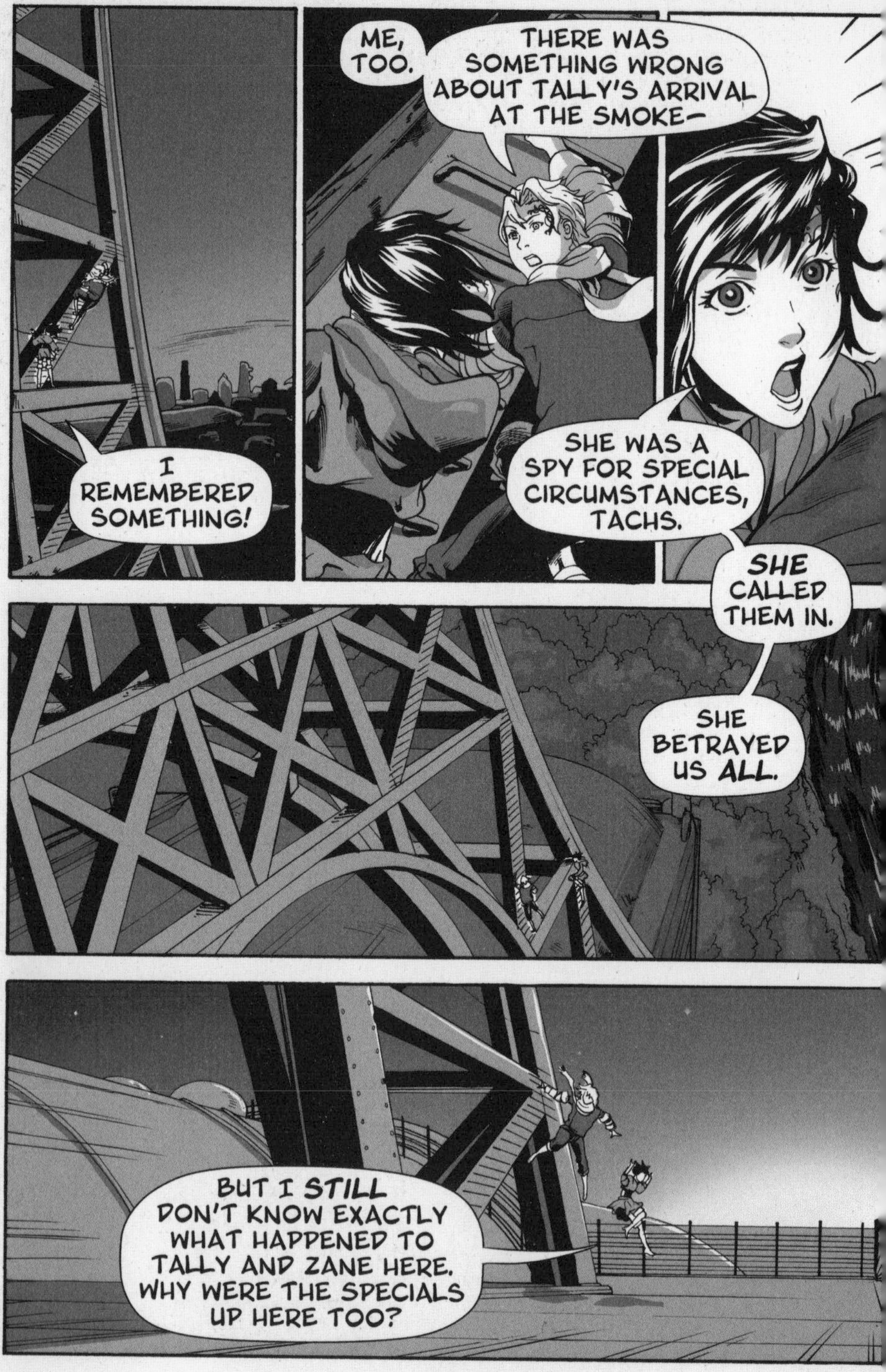
I REMEMBERED SOMETHING!
ME, TOO.
THERE WAS SOMETHING WRONG ABOUT TALLY'S ARRIVAL AT THE SMOKE—
SHE WAS A SPY FOR SPECIAL CIRCUMSTANCES, TACHS.
SHE CALLED THEM IN.
SHE BETRAYED US **ALL**.
BUT I **STILL** DON'T KNOW EXACTLY WHAT HAPPENED TO TALLY AND ZANE HERE. WHY WERE THE SPECIALS UP HERE TOO?

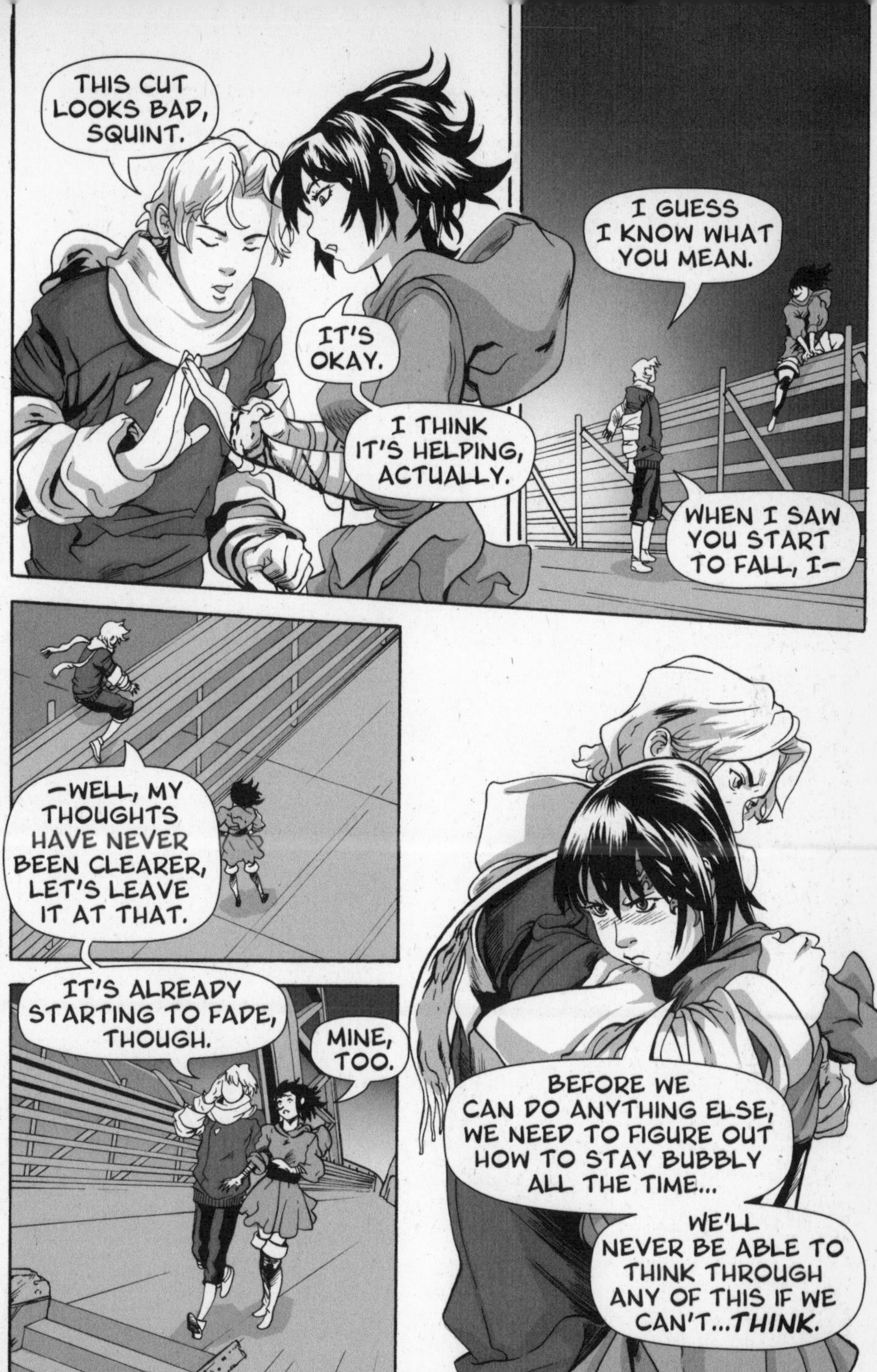
THIS CUT LOOKS BAD, SQUINT.
IT'S OKAY.
I THINK IT'S HELPING, ACTUALLY.
I GUESS I KNOW WHAT YOU MEAN.
WHEN I SAW YOU START TO FALL, I—
—WELL, MY THOUGHTS HAVE NEVER BEEN CLEARER, LET'S LEAVE IT AT THAT.
IT'S ALREADY STARTING TO FADE, THOUGH.
MINE, TOO.
BEFORE WE CAN DO ANYTHING ELSE, WE NEED TO FIGURE OUT HOW TO STAY BUBBLY ALL THE TIME...
WE'LL NEVER BE ABLE TO THINK THROUGH ANY OF THIS IF WE CAN'T...*THINK*.

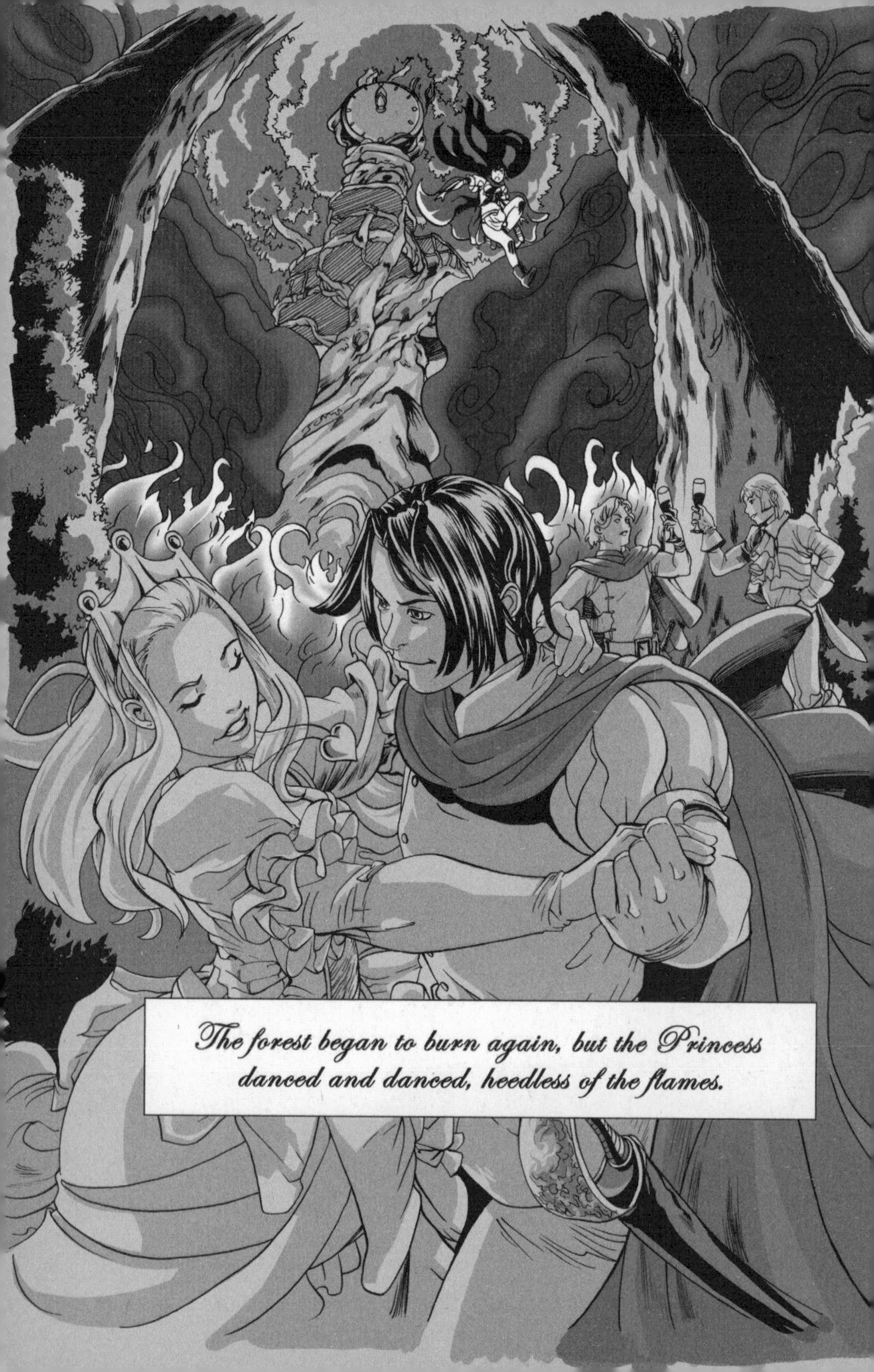
The forest began to burn again, but the Princess danced and danced, heedless of the flames.

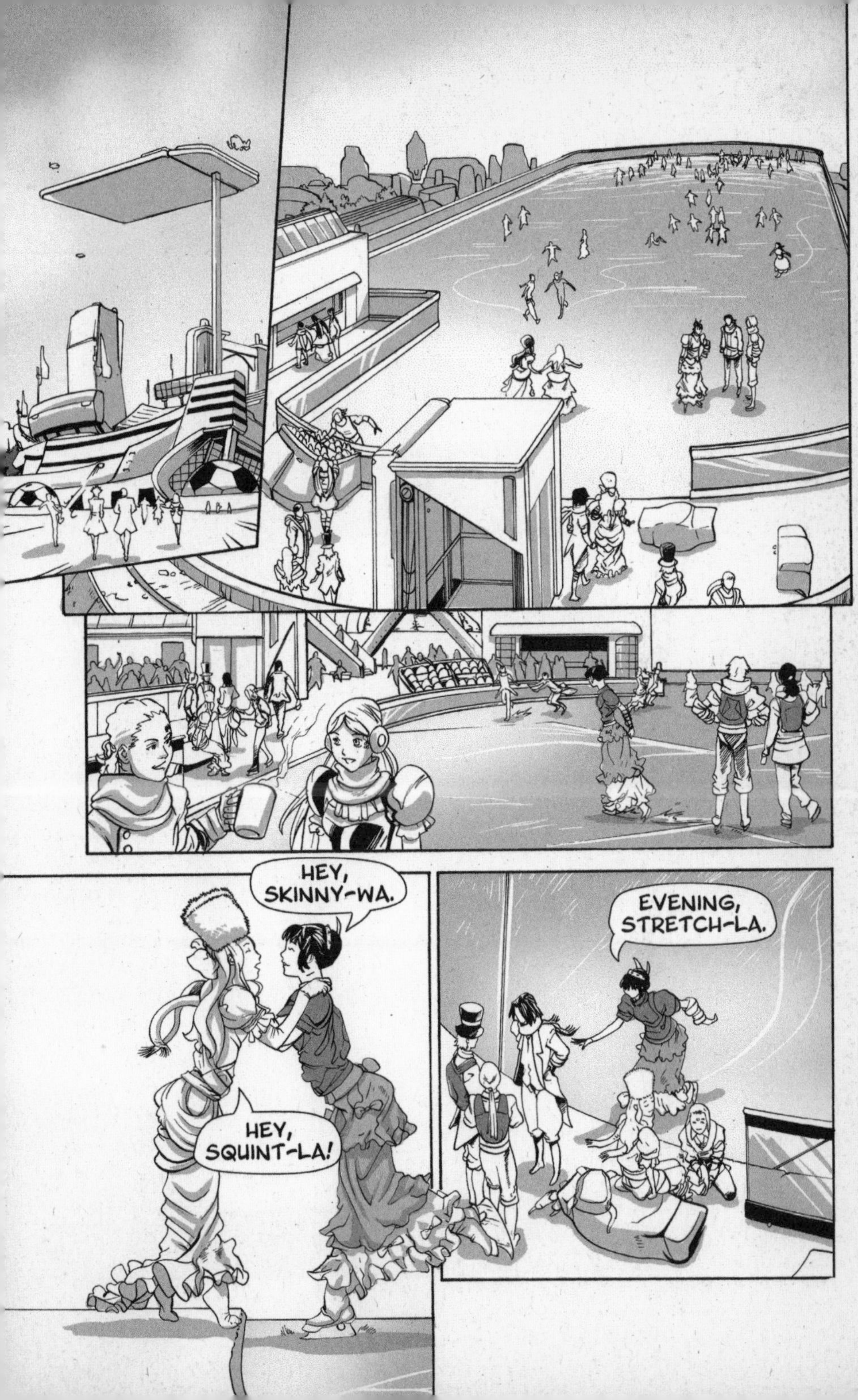
HEY, SKINNY-WA.
HEY, SQUINT-LA!
EVENING, STRETCH-LA.

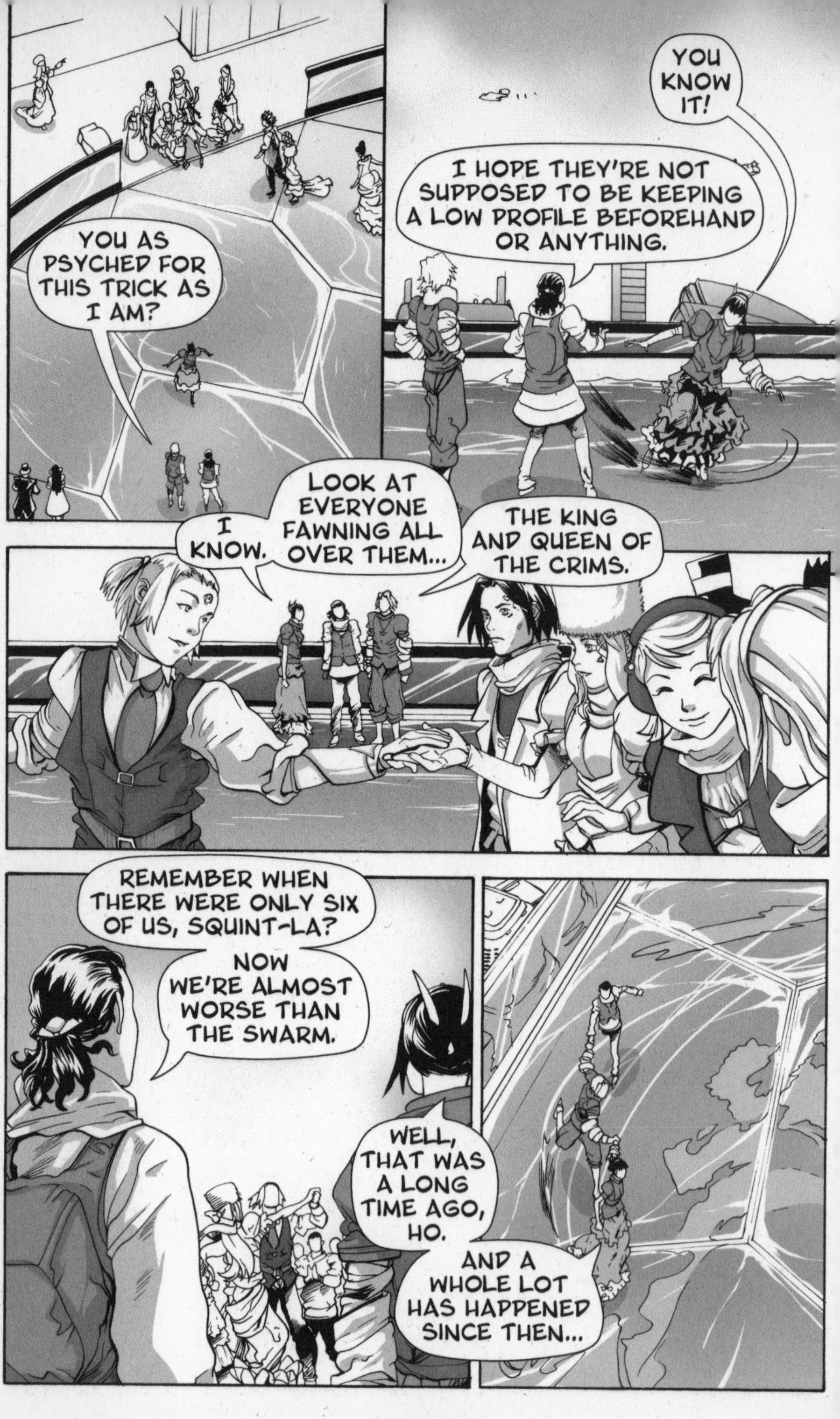
YOU AS PSYCHED FOR THIS TRICK AS I AM?
YOU KNOW IT!
I HOPE THEY'RE NOT SUPPOSED TO BE KEEPING A LOW PROFILE BEFOREHAND OR ANYTHING.
LOOK AT EVERYONE FAWNING ALL OVER THEM...
I KNOW.
THE KING AND QUEEN OF THE CRIMS.
REMEMBER WHEN THERE WERE ONLY SIX OF US, SQUINT-LA?
NOW WE'RE ALMOST WORSE THAN THE SWARM.
WELL, THAT WAS A LONG TIME AGO, HO.
AND A WHOLE LOT HAS HAPPENED SINCE THEN...

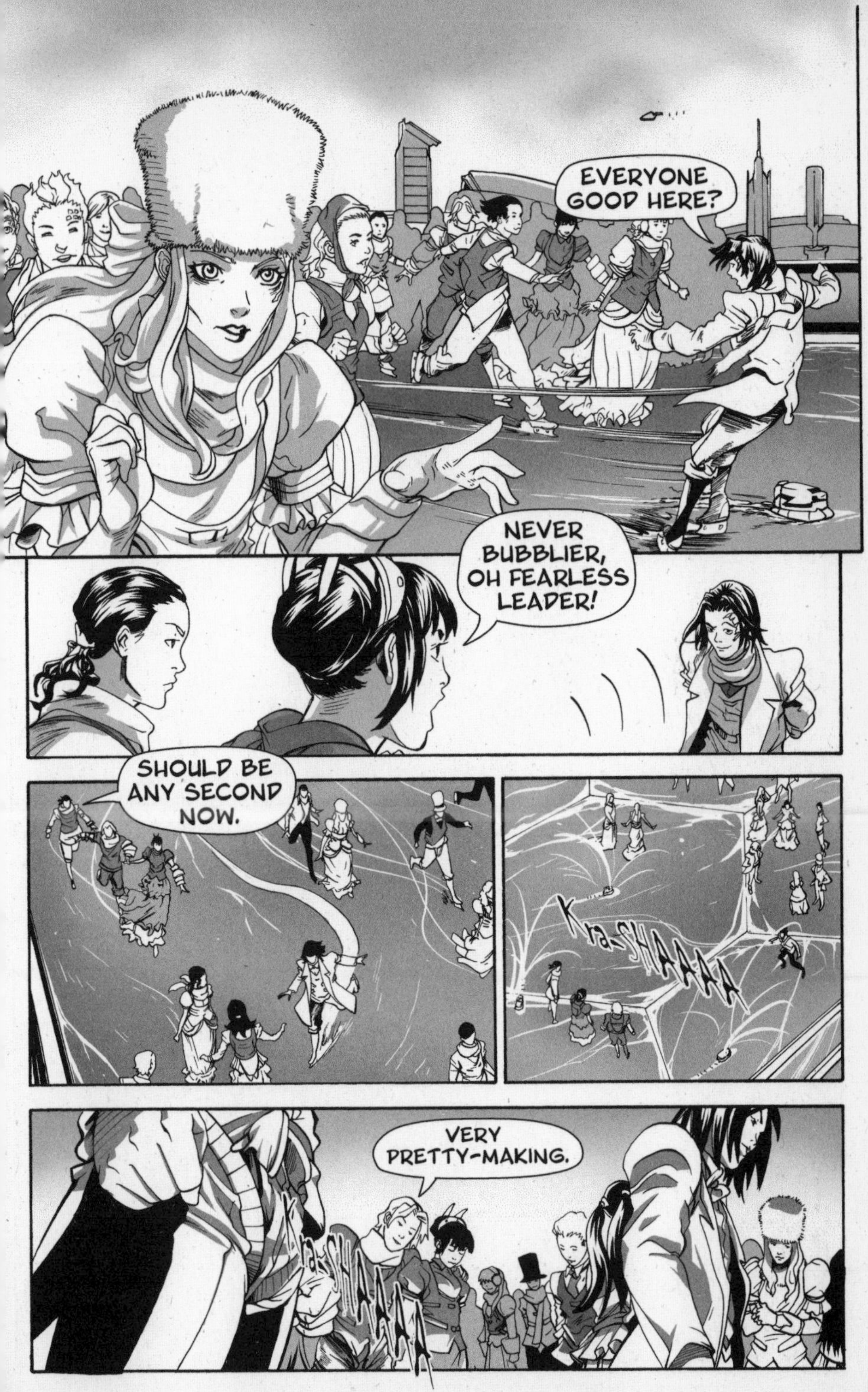
EVERYONE GOOD HERE?
NEVER BUBBLIER, OH FEARLESS LEADER!
SHOULD BE ANY SECOND NOW.
Kra-SHAAAAA
VERY PRETTY-MAKING.
Kra-SHAAAAA

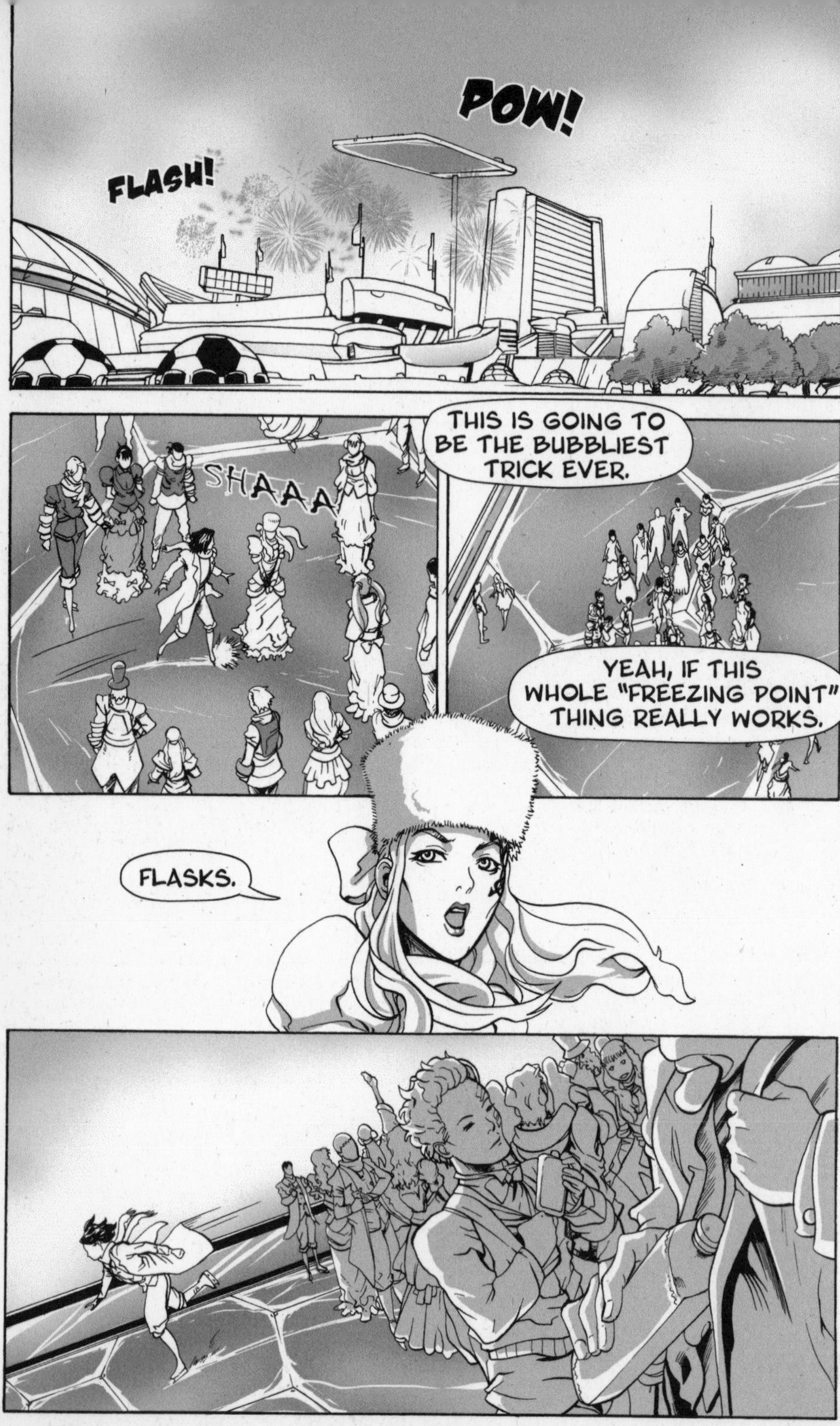
FLASH!
POW!
SHAAAA
THIS IS GOING TO BE THE BUBBLIEST TRICK EVER.
YEAH, IF THIS WHOLE "FREEZING POINT" THING REALLY WORKS.
FLASKS.

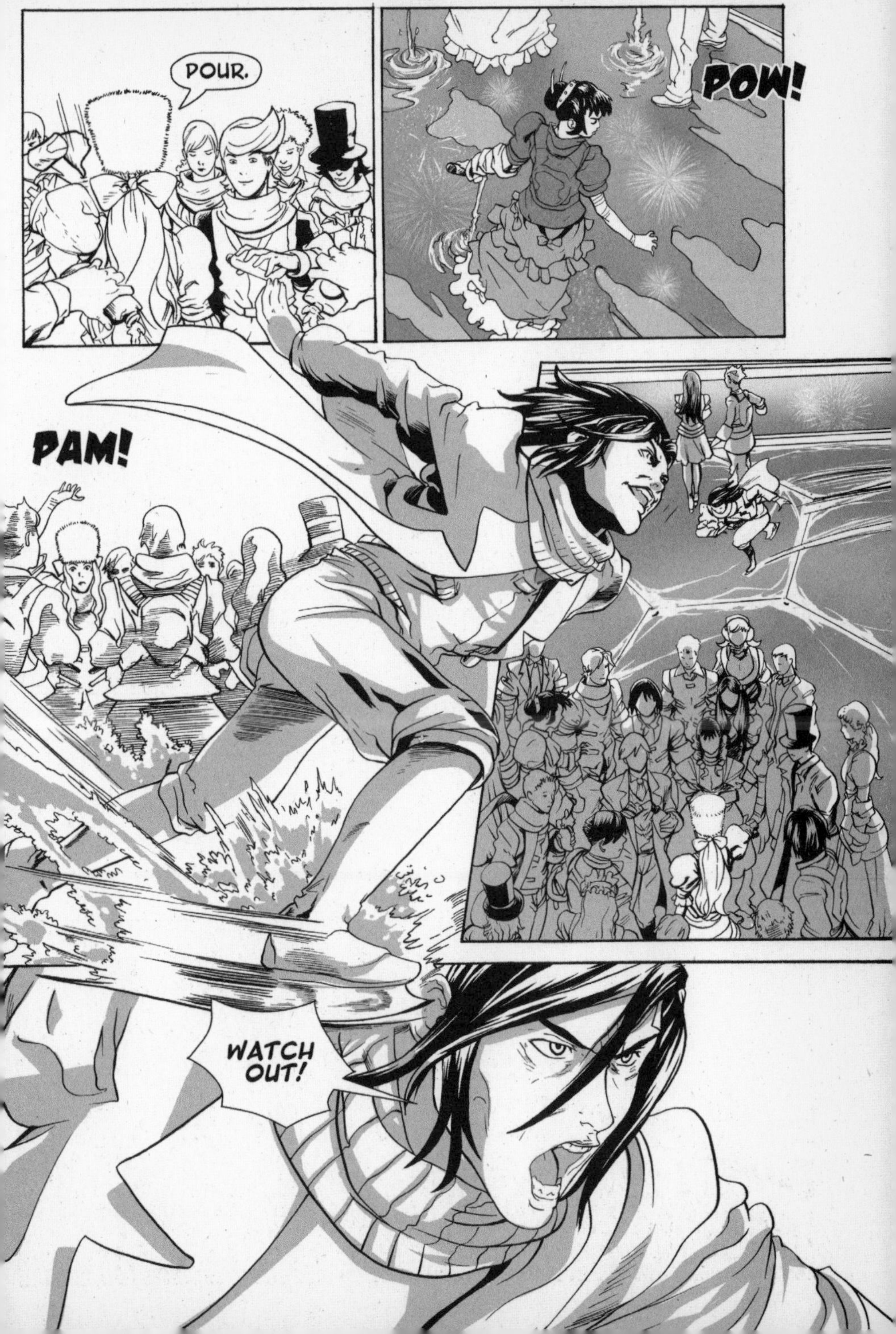
POUR.
POW!
PAM!
WATCH OUT!

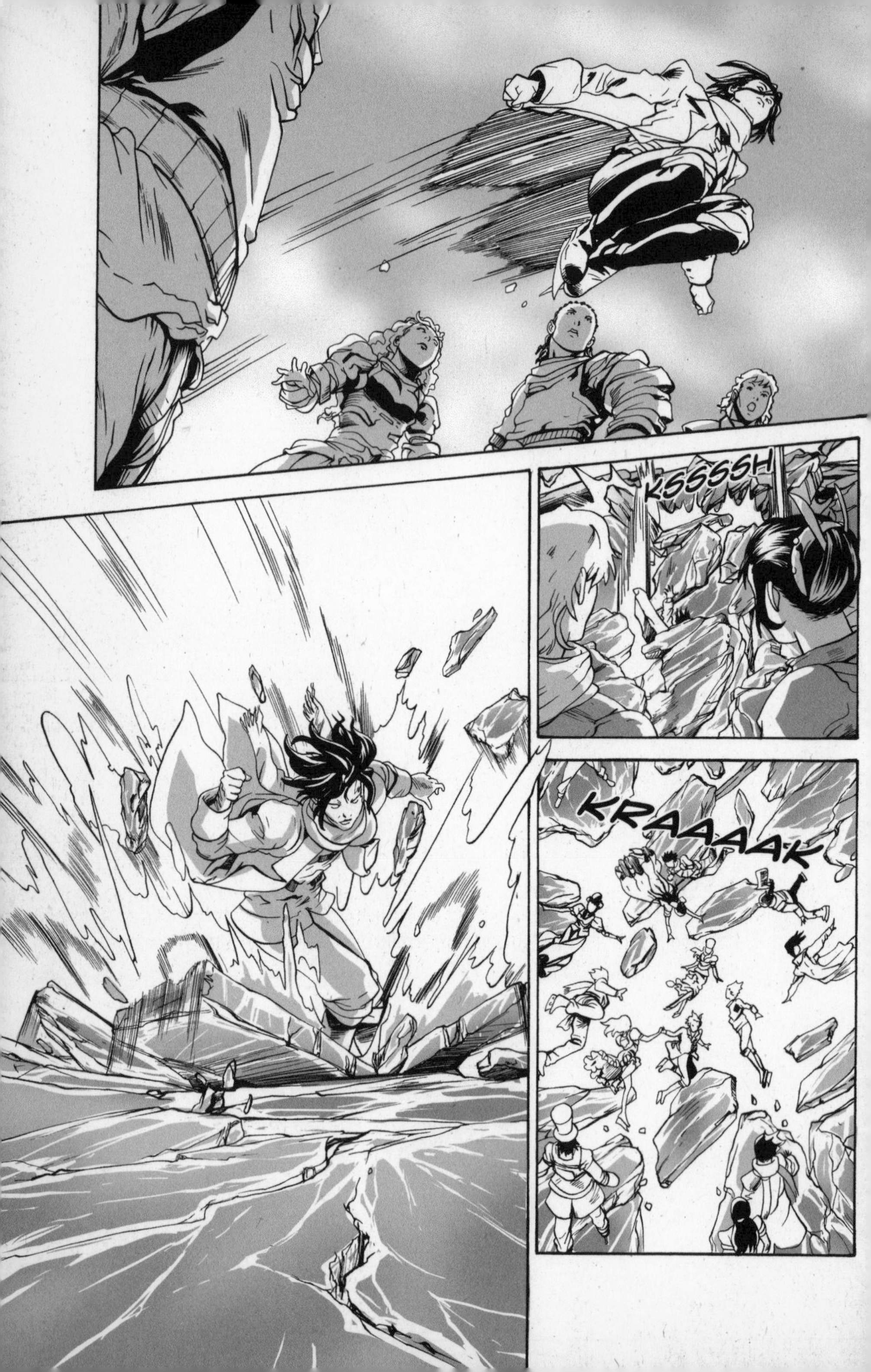
KSSSSH
KRAAAAAK

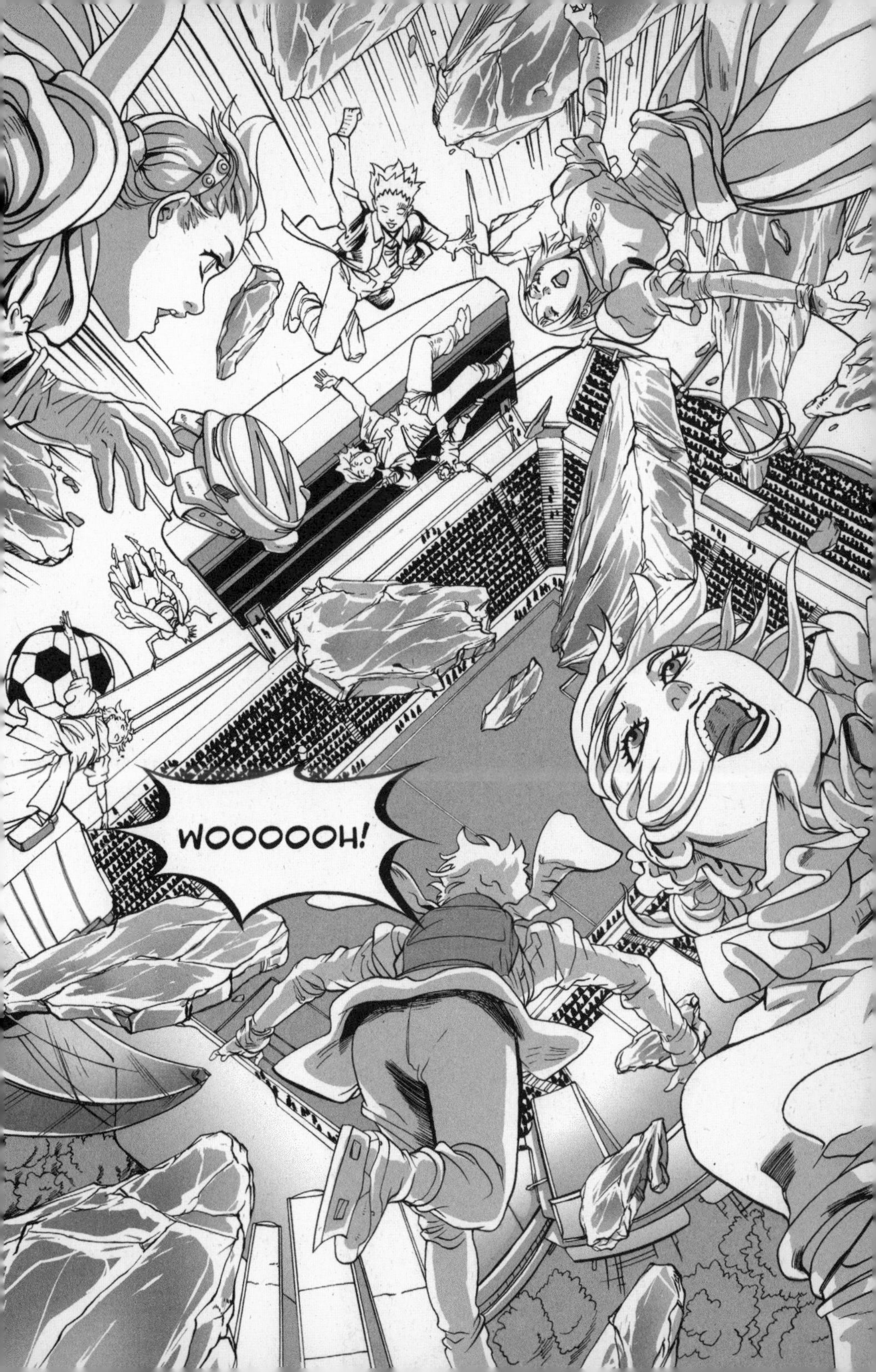
WOOOOOH!

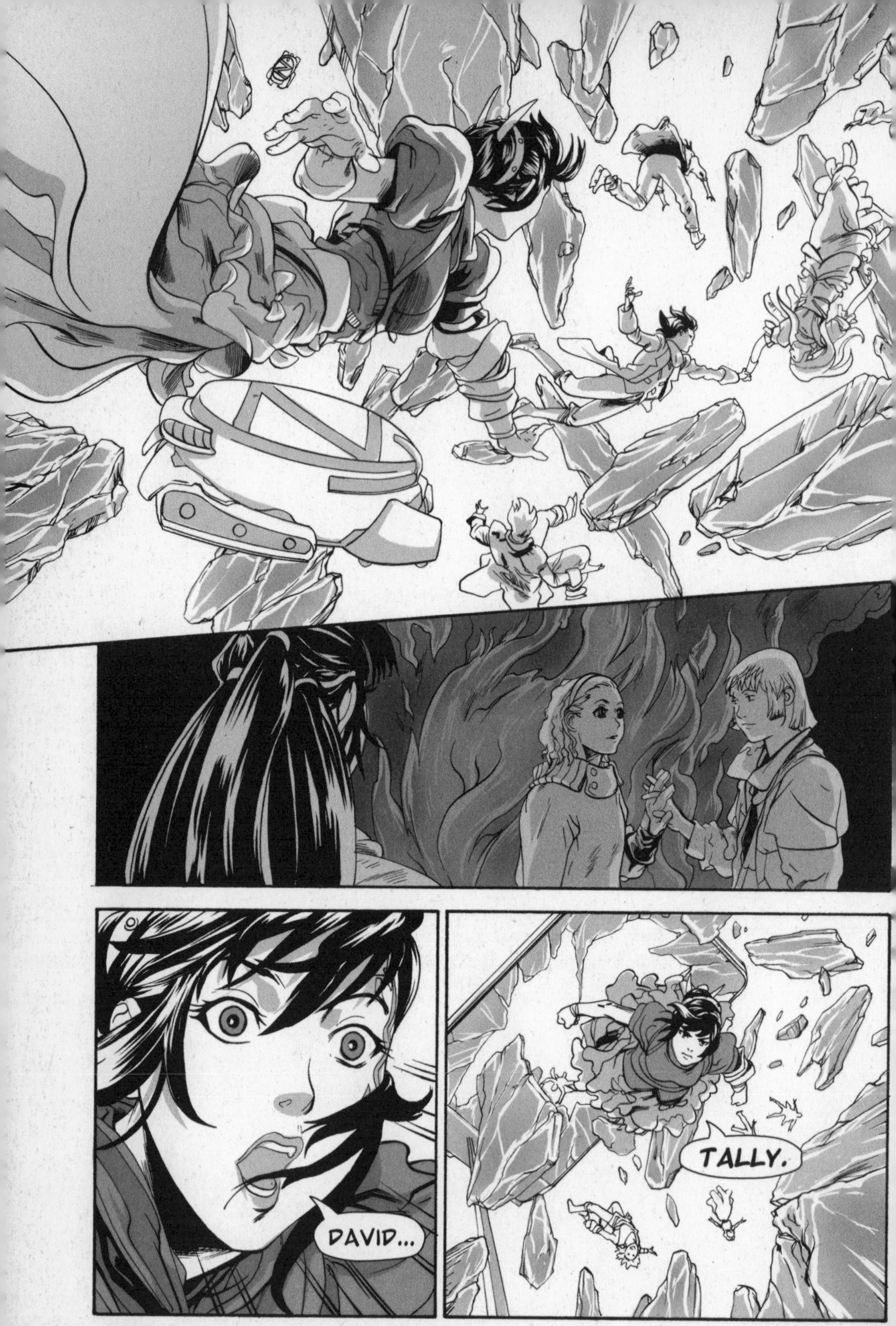
DAVID...
TALLY.

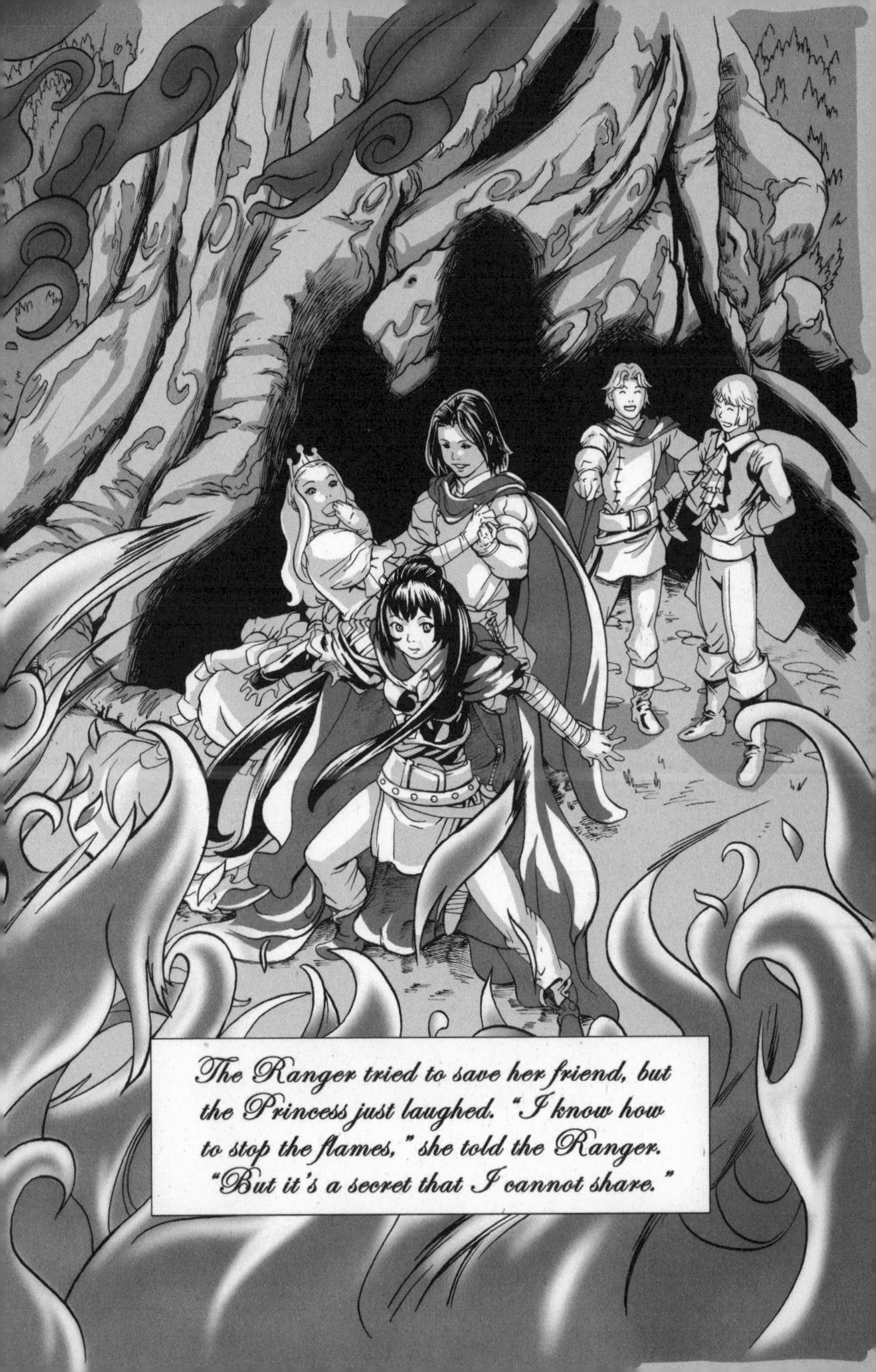
The Ranger tried to save her friend, but the Princess just laughed. "I know how to stop the flames," she told the Ranger. "But it's a secret that I cannot share."

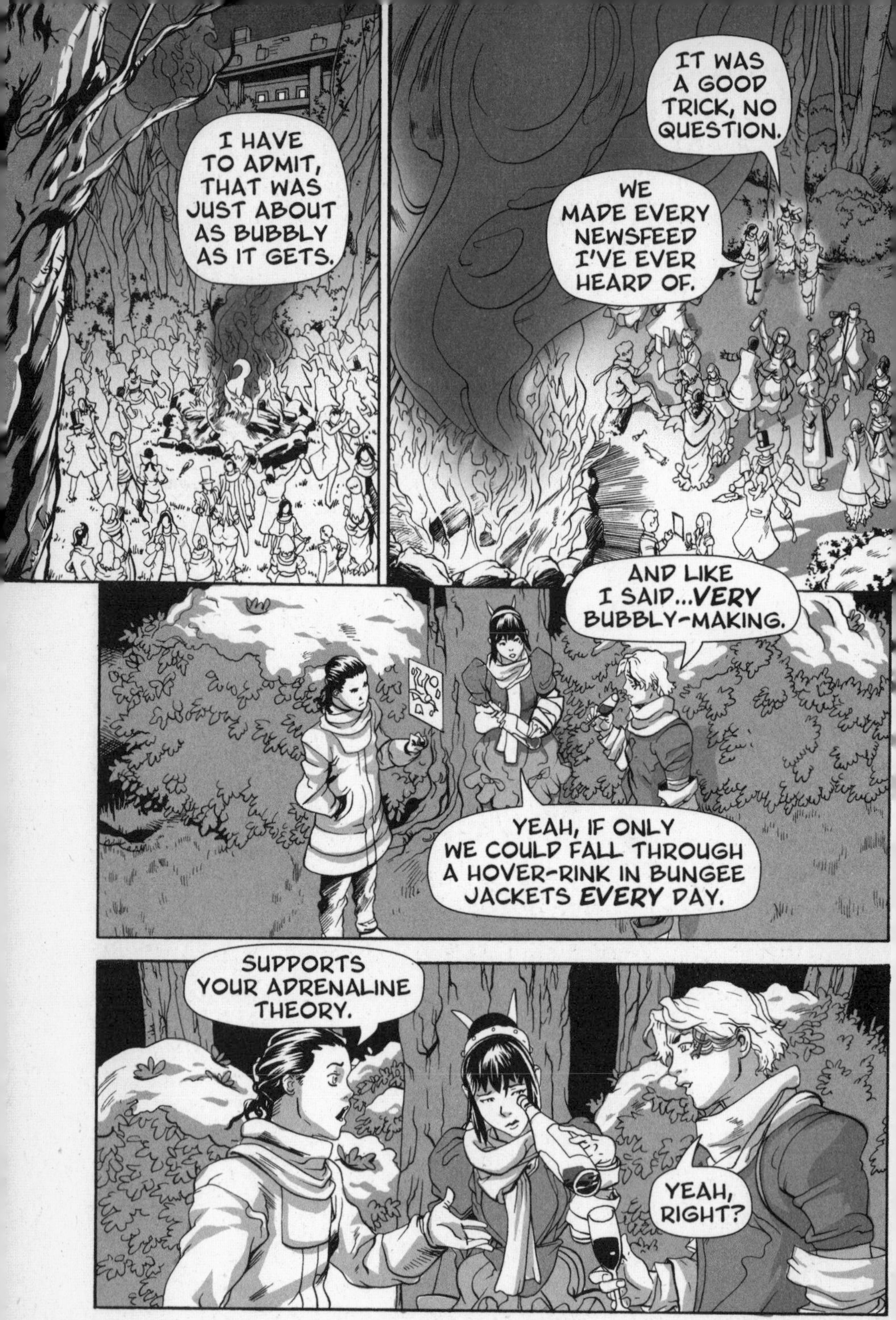
I HAVE TO ADMIT, THAT WAS JUST ABOUT AS BUBBLY AS IT GETS.
IT WAS A GOOD TRICK, NO QUESTION.
WE MADE EVERY NEWSFEED I'VE EVER HEARD OF.
AND LIKE I SAID...VERY BUBBLY-MAKING.
YEAH, IF ONLY WE COULD FALL THROUGH A HOVER-RINK IN BUNGEE JACKETS EVERY DAY.
SUPPORTS YOUR ADRENALINE THEORY.
YEAH, RIGHT?

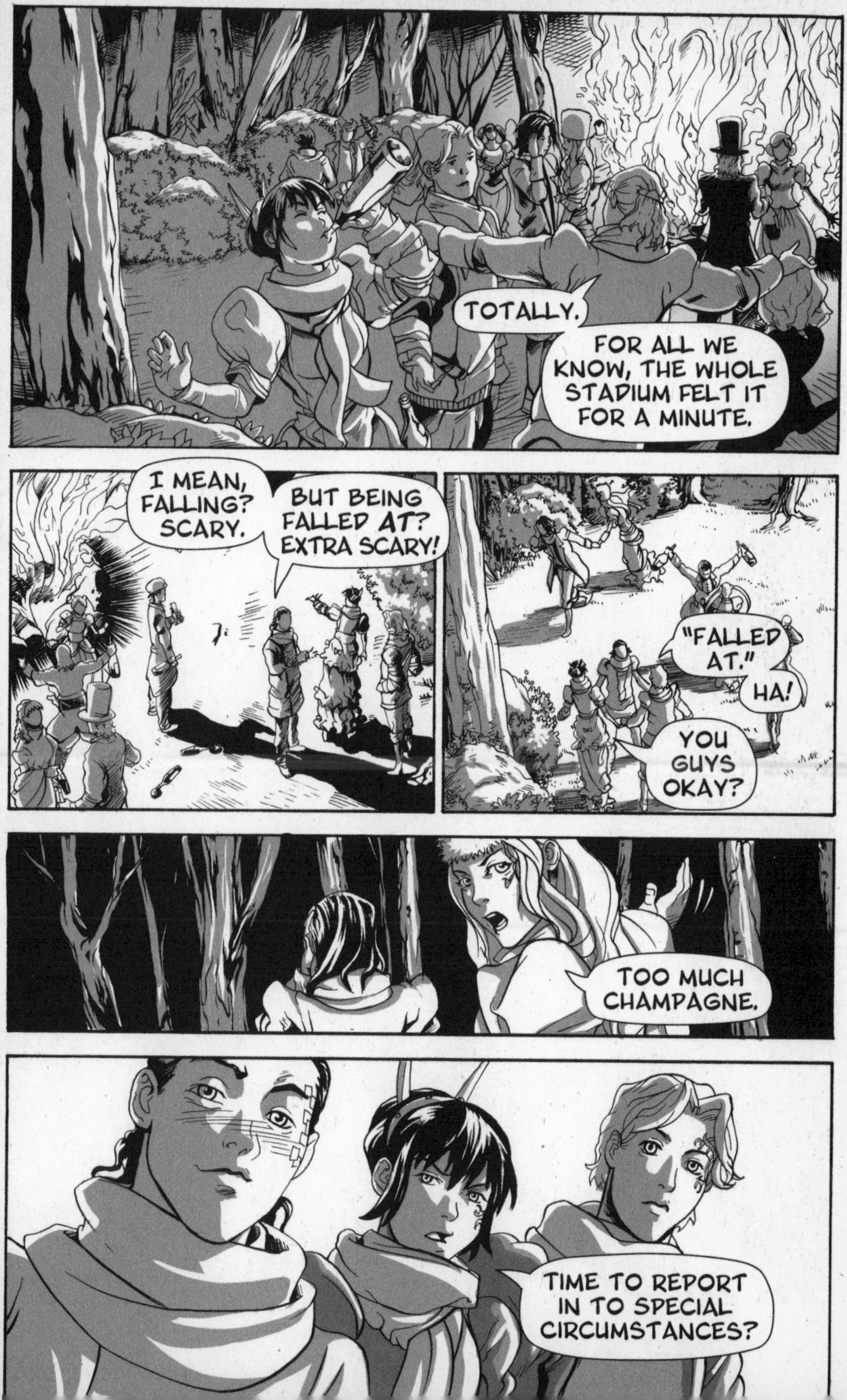

TOTALLY.
FOR ALL WE KNOW, THE WHOLE STADIUM FELT IT FOR A MINUTE.
I MEAN, FALLING? SCARY.
BUT BEING FALLED AT? EXTRA SCARY!
"FALLED AT."
HA!
YOU GUYS OKAY?
TOO MUCH CHAMPAGNE.
TIME TO REPORT IN TO SPECIAL CIRCUMSTANCES?

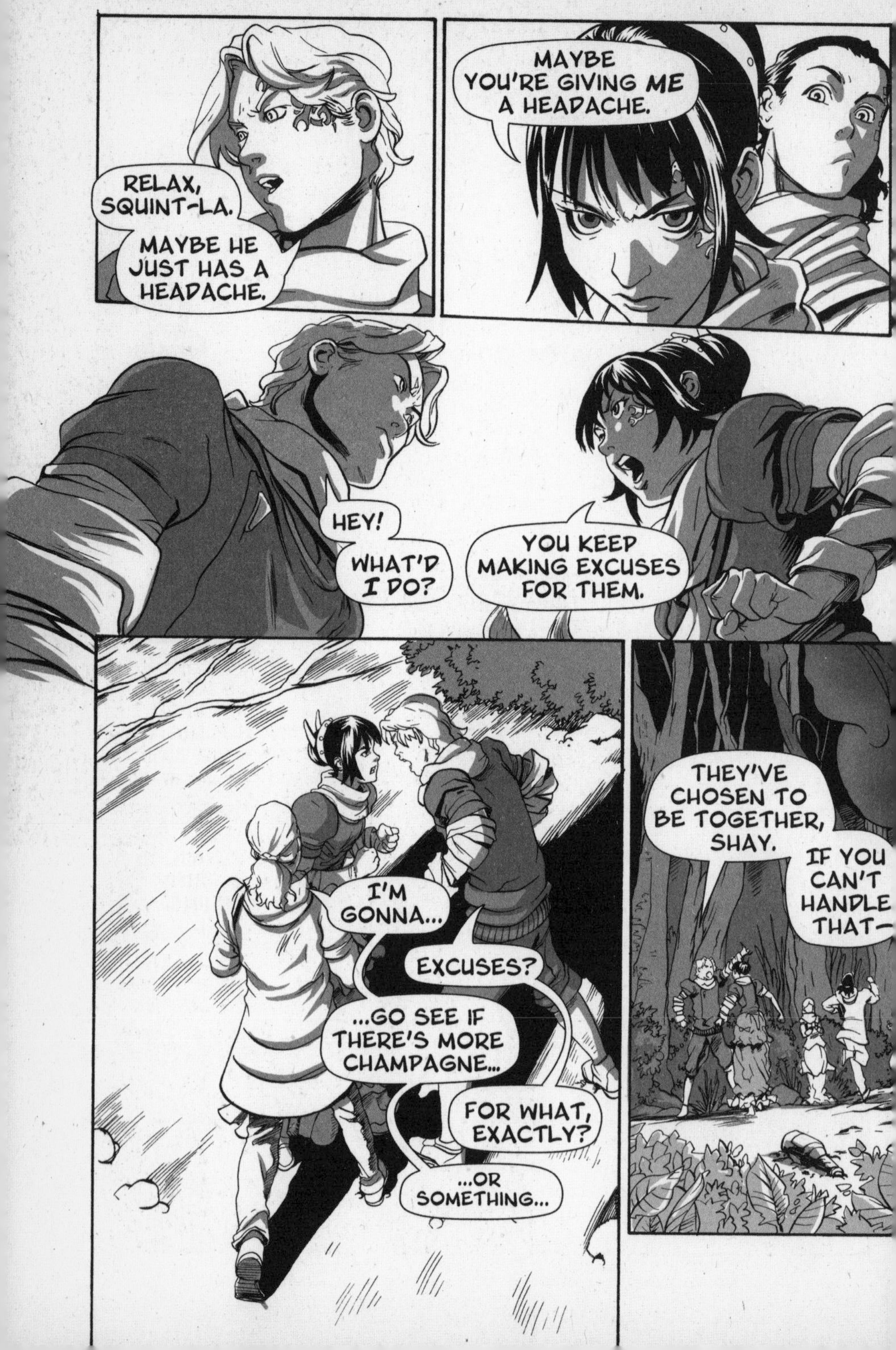
RELAX, SQUINT-LA.
MAYBE HE JUST HAS A HEADACHE.
MAYBE YOU'RE GIVING ME A HEADACHE.
HEY!
WHAT'D I DO?
YOU KEEP MAKING EXCUSES FOR THEM.
I'M GONNA...
EXCUSES?
...GO SEE IF THERE'S MORE CHAMPAGNE...
FOR WHAT, EXACTLY?
...OR SOMETHING...
THEY'VE CHOSEN TO BE TOGETHER, SHAY.
IF YOU CAN'T HANDLE THAT—

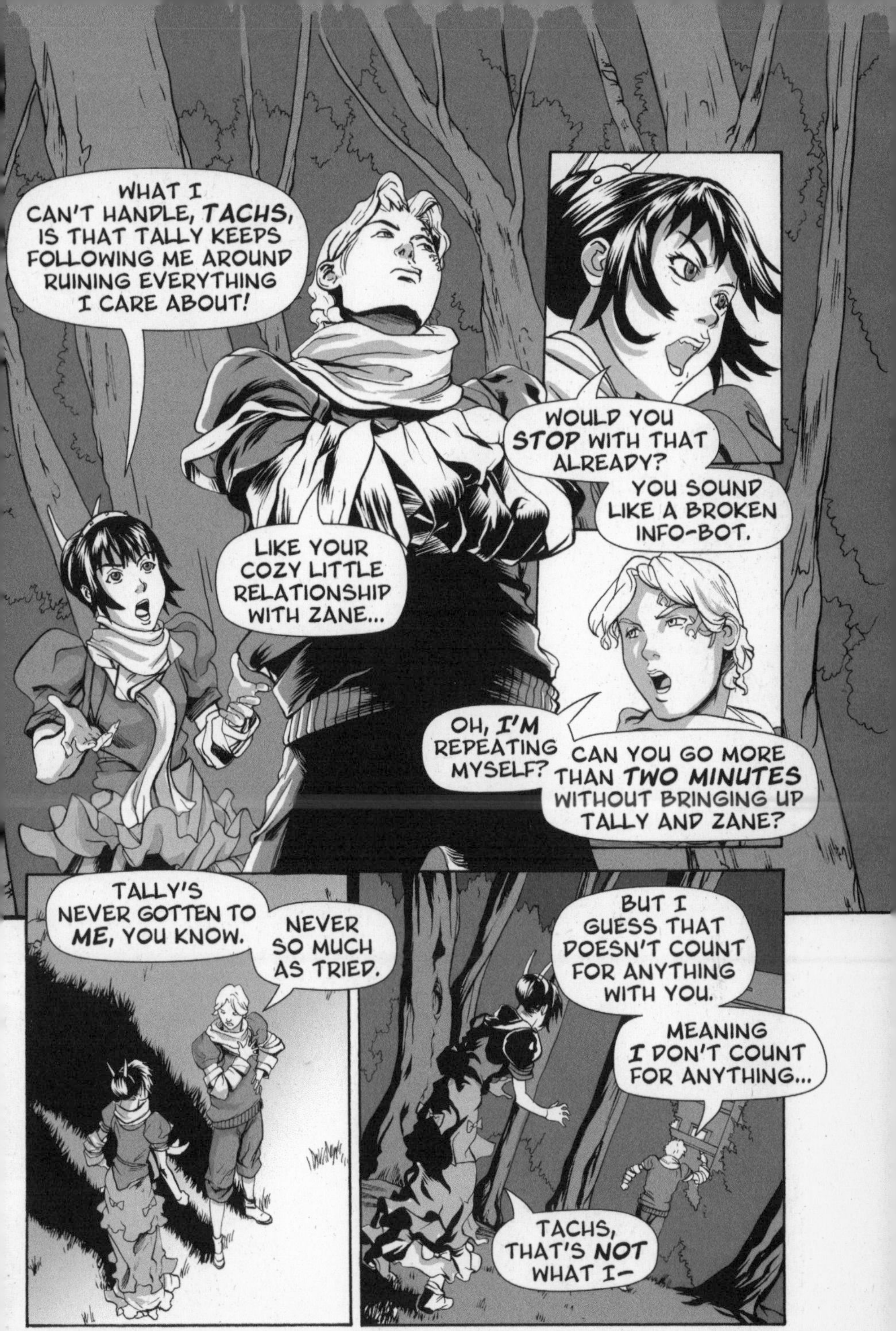
WHAT I CAN'T HANDLE, TACHS, IS THAT TALLY KEEPS FOLLOWING ME AROUND RUINING EVERYTHING I CARE ABOUT!
LIKE YOUR COZY LITTLE RELATIONSHIP WITH ZANE...
WOULD YOU STOP WITH THAT ALREADY?
YOU SOUND LIKE A BROKEN INFO-BOT.
OH, I'M REPEATING MYSELF?
CAN YOU GO MORE THAN TWO MINUTES WITHOUT BRINGING UP TALLY AND ZANE?
TALLY'S NEVER GOTTEN TO ME, YOU KNOW.
NEVER SO MUCH AS TRIED.
BUT I GUESS THAT DOESN'T COUNT FOR ANYTHING WITH YOU.
MEANING I DON'T COUNT FOR ANYTHING...
TACHS, THAT'S NOT WHAT I-

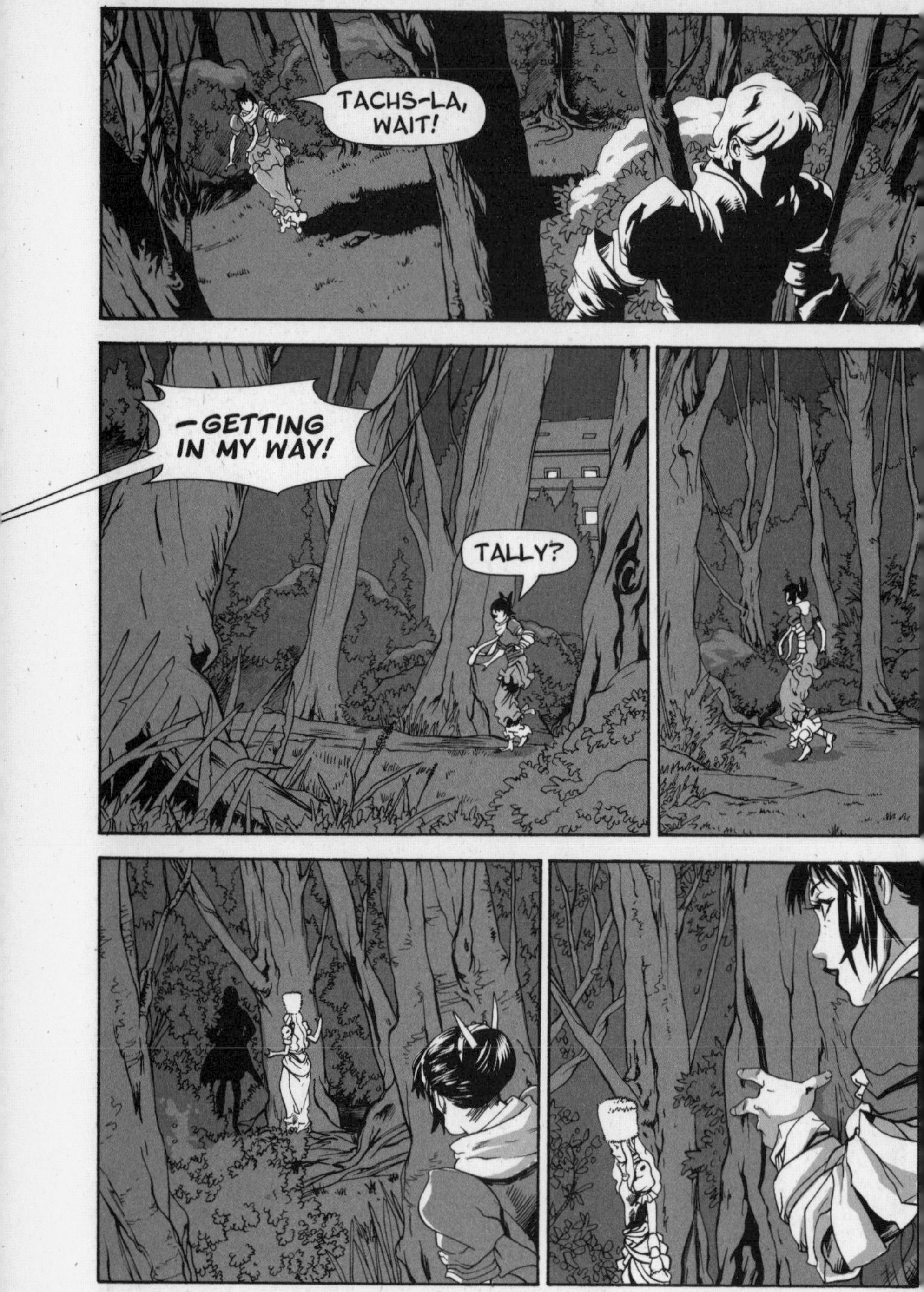
TACHS-LA, WAIT!
—GETTING IN MY WAY!
TALLY?

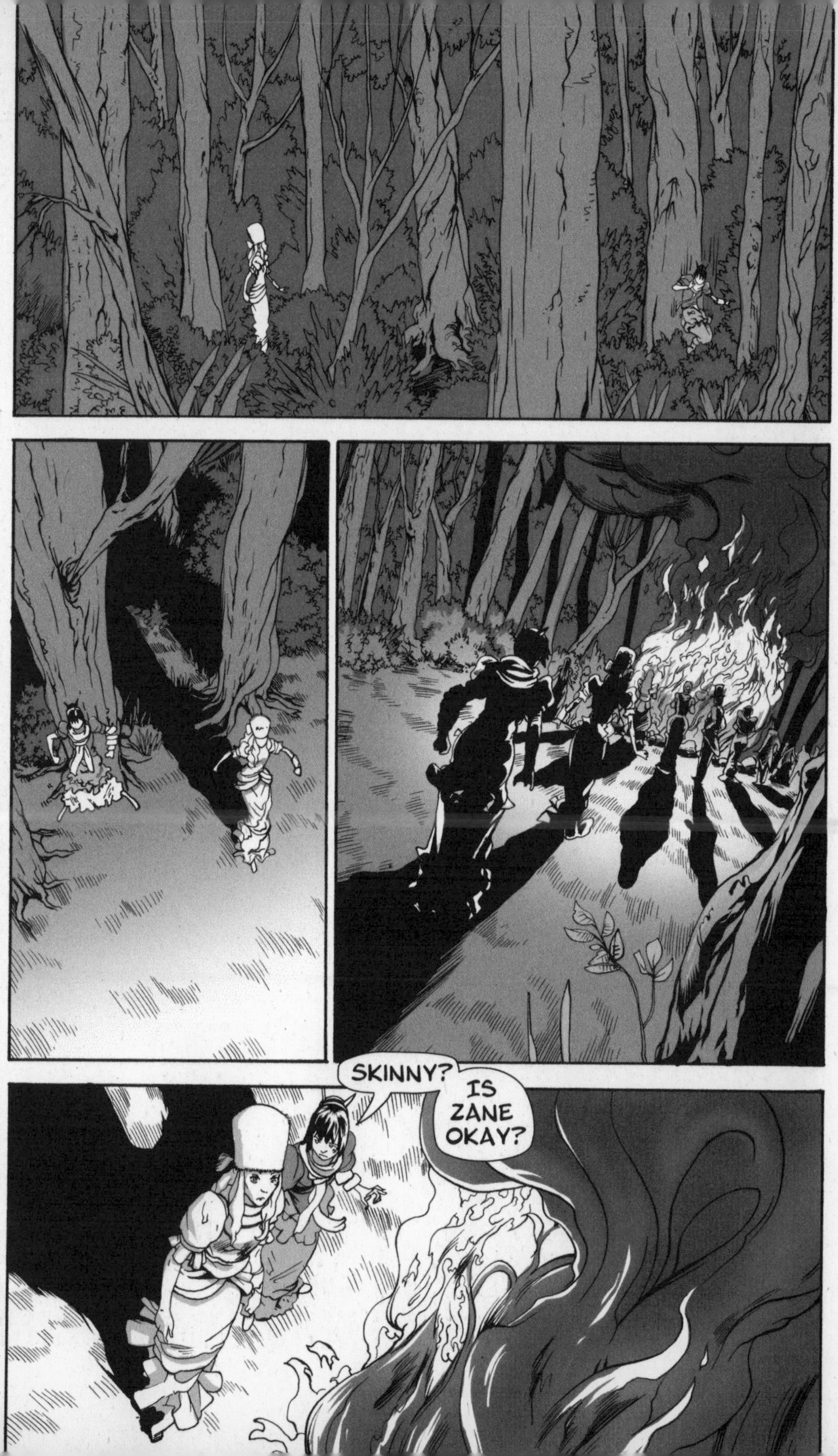
SKINNY?
IS ZANE OKAY?

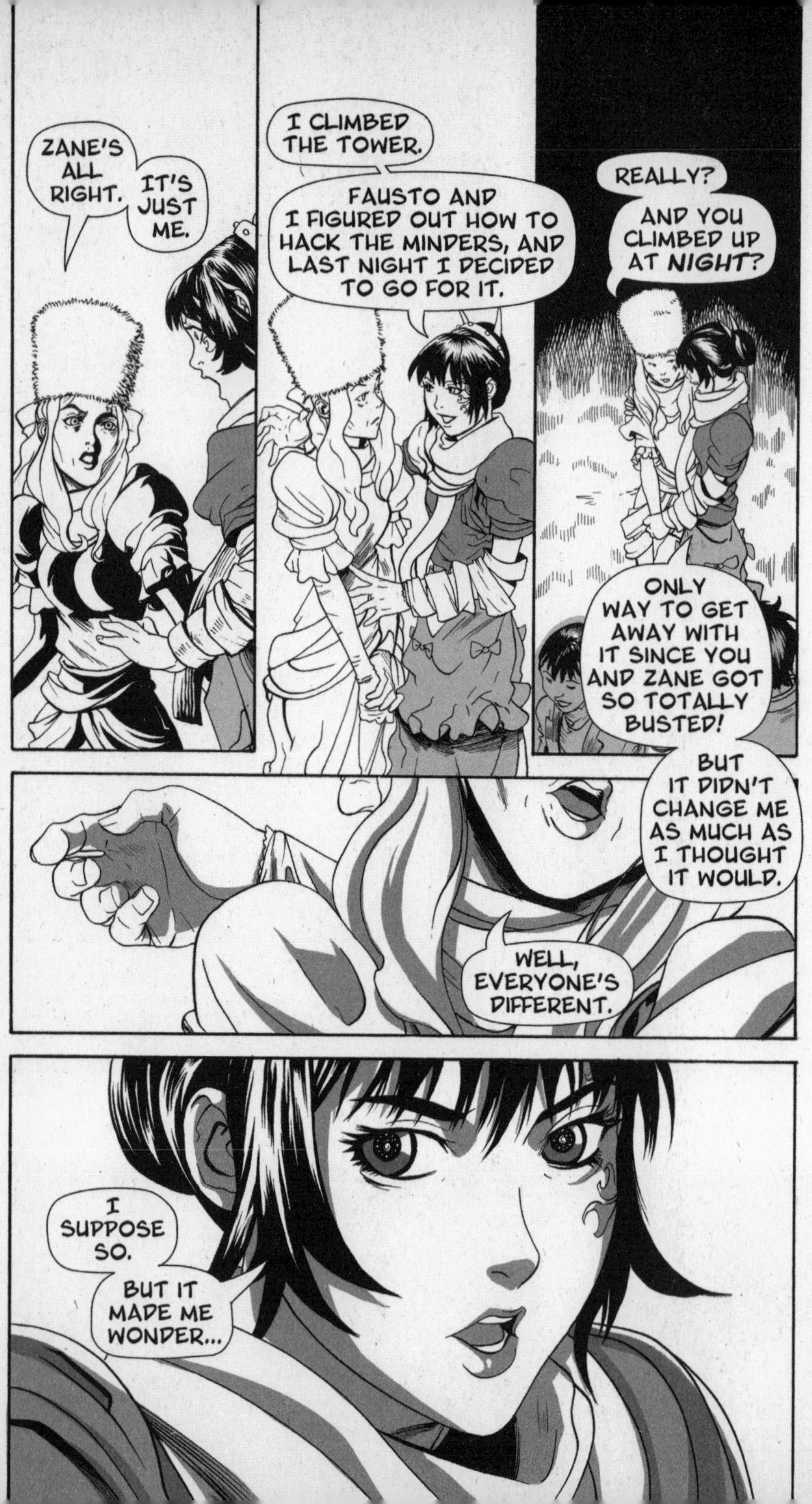
ZANE'S ALL RIGHT.
IT'S JUST ME.
I CLIMBED THE TOWER.
FAUSTO AND I FIGURED OUT HOW TO HACK THE MINDERS, AND LAST NIGHT I DECIDED TO GO FOR IT.
REALLY?
AND YOU CLIMBED UP AT NIGHT?
ONLY WAY TO GET AWAY WITH IT SINCE YOU AND ZANE GOT SO TOTALLY BUSTED!
BUT IT DIDN'T CHANGE ME AS MUCH AS I THOUGHT IT WOULD.
WELL, EVERYONE'S DIFFERENT.
I SUPPOSE SO.
BUT IT MADE ME WONDER...

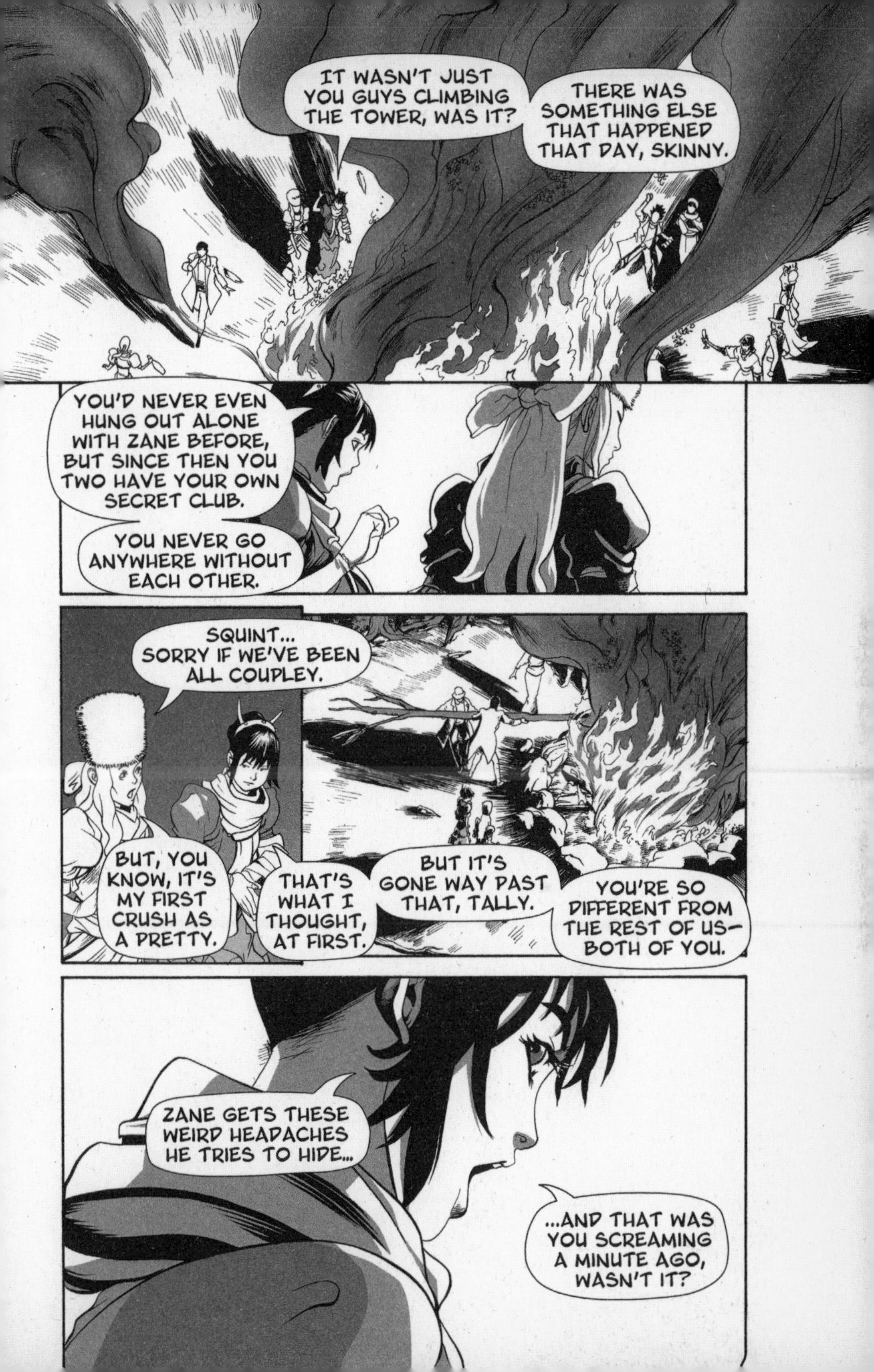
IT WASN'T JUST YOU GUYS CLIMBING THE TOWER, WAS IT?
THERE WAS SOMETHING ELSE THAT HAPPENED THAT DAY, SKINNY.
YOU'D NEVER EVEN HUNG OUT ALONE WITH ZANE BEFORE, BUT SINCE THEN YOU TWO HAVE YOUR OWN SECRET CLUB.
YOU NEVER GO ANYWHERE WITHOUT EACH OTHER.
SQUINT... SORRY IF WE'VE BEEN ALL COUPLEY.
BUT, YOU KNOW, IT'S MY FIRST CRUSH AS A PRETTY.
THAT'S WHAT I THOUGHT, AT FIRST.
BUT IT'S GONE WAY PAST THAT, TALLY.
YOU'RE SO DIFFERENT FROM THE REST OF US—BOTH OF YOU.
ZANE GETS THESE WEIRD HEADACHES HE TRIES TO HIDE...
...AND THAT WAS YOU SCREAMING A MINUTE AGO, WASN'T IT?

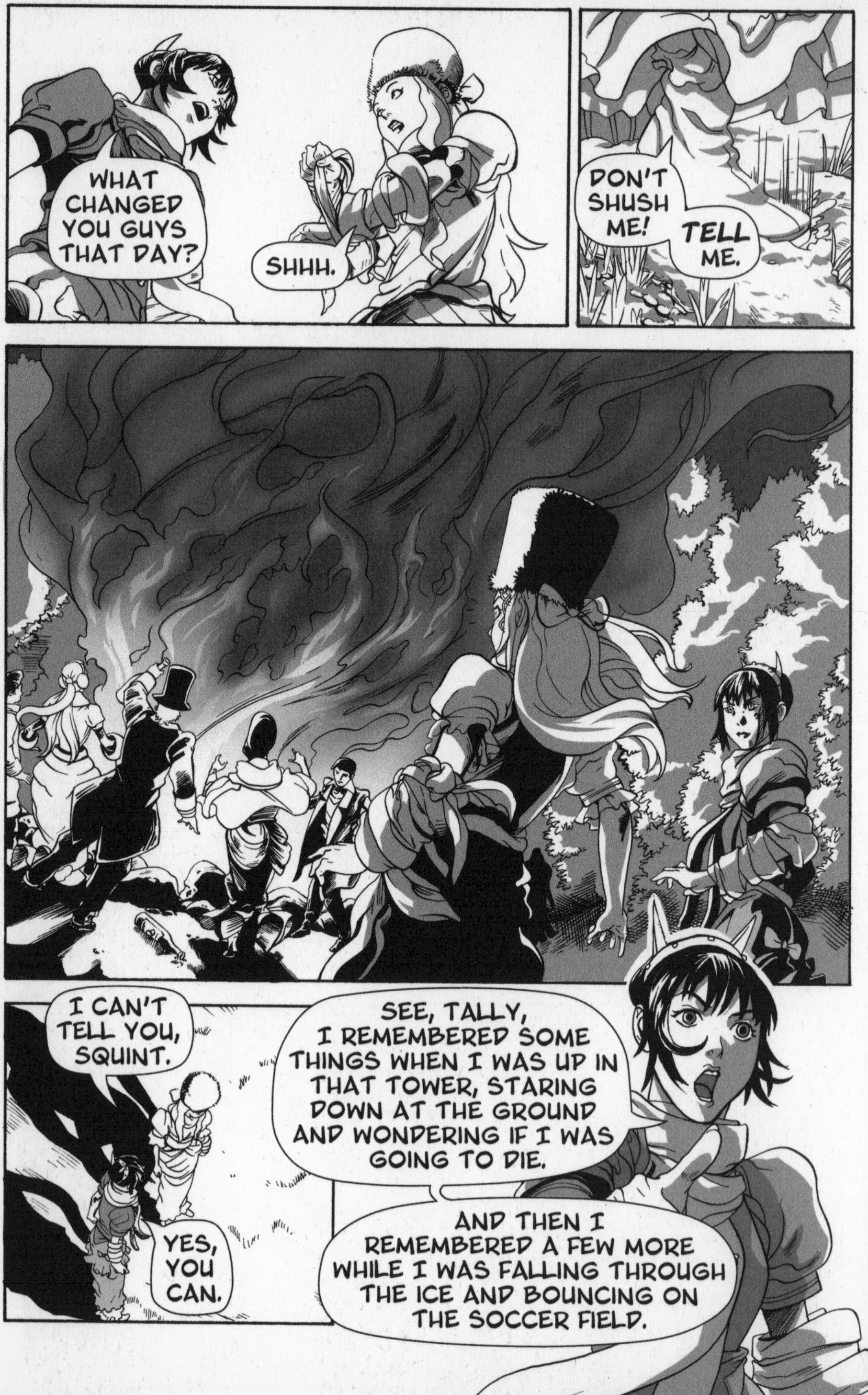
WHAT CHANGED YOU GUYS THAT DAY?
SHHH.
DON'T SHUSH ME!
TELL ME.
I CAN'T TELL YOU, SQUINT.
YES, YOU CAN.
SEE, TALLY, I REMEMBERED SOME THINGS WHEN I WAS UP IN THAT TOWER, STARING DOWN AT THE GROUND AND WONDERING IF I WAS GOING TO DIE.
AND THEN I REMEMBERED A FEW MORE WHILE I WAS FALLING THROUGH THE ICE AND BOUNCING ON THE SOCCER FIELD.

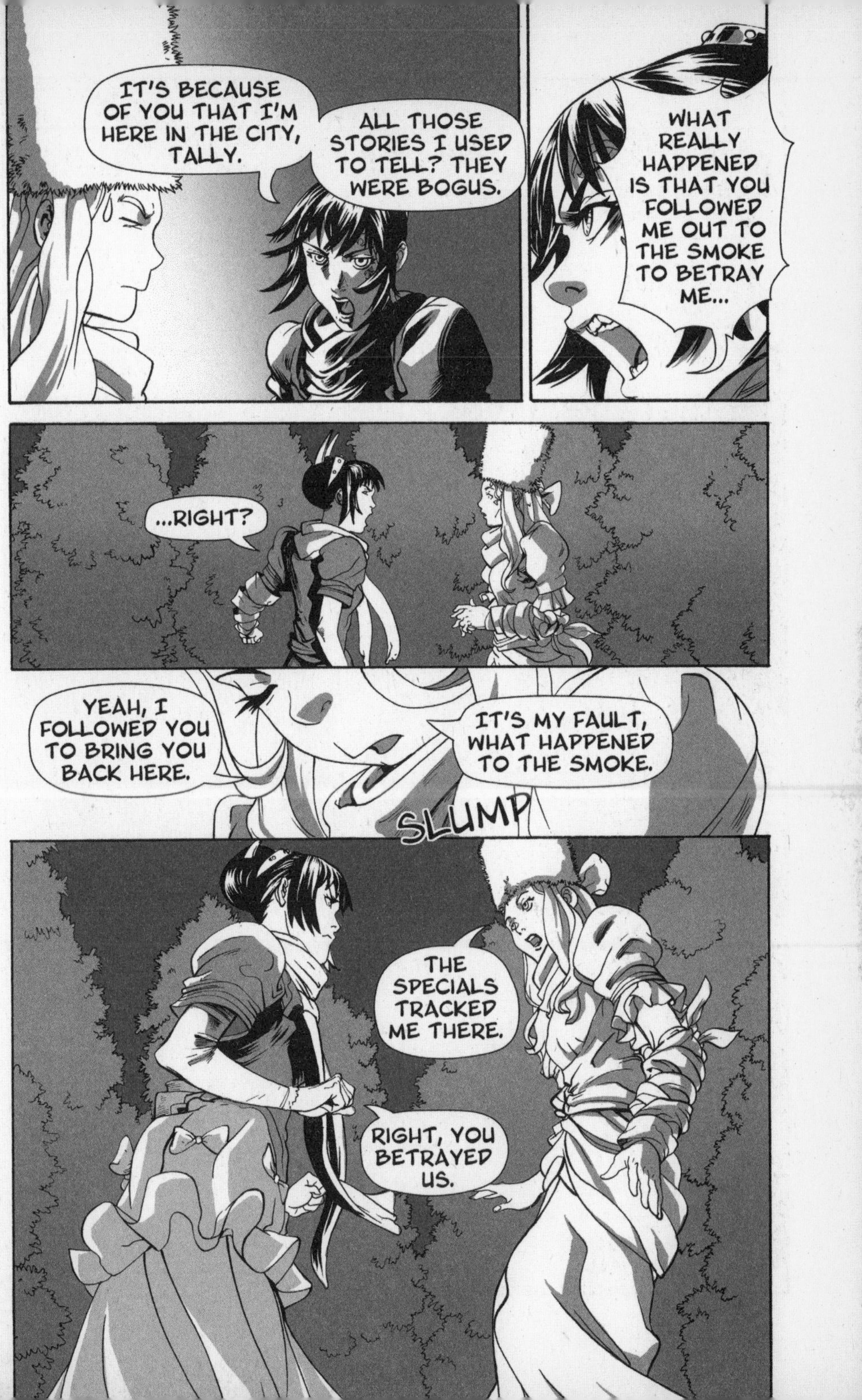
IT'S BECAUSE OF YOU THAT I'M HERE IN THE CITY, TALLY.
ALL THOSE STORIES I USED TO TELL? THEY WERE BOGUS.
WHAT REALLY HAPPENED IS THAT YOU FOLLOWED ME OUT TO THE SMOKE TO BETRAY ME...
...RIGHT?
YEAH, I FOLLOWED YOU TO BRING YOU BACK HERE.
IT'S MY FAULT, WHAT HAPPENED TO THE SMOKE.
SLUMP
THE SPECIALS TRACKED ME THERE.
RIGHT, YOU BETRAYED US.

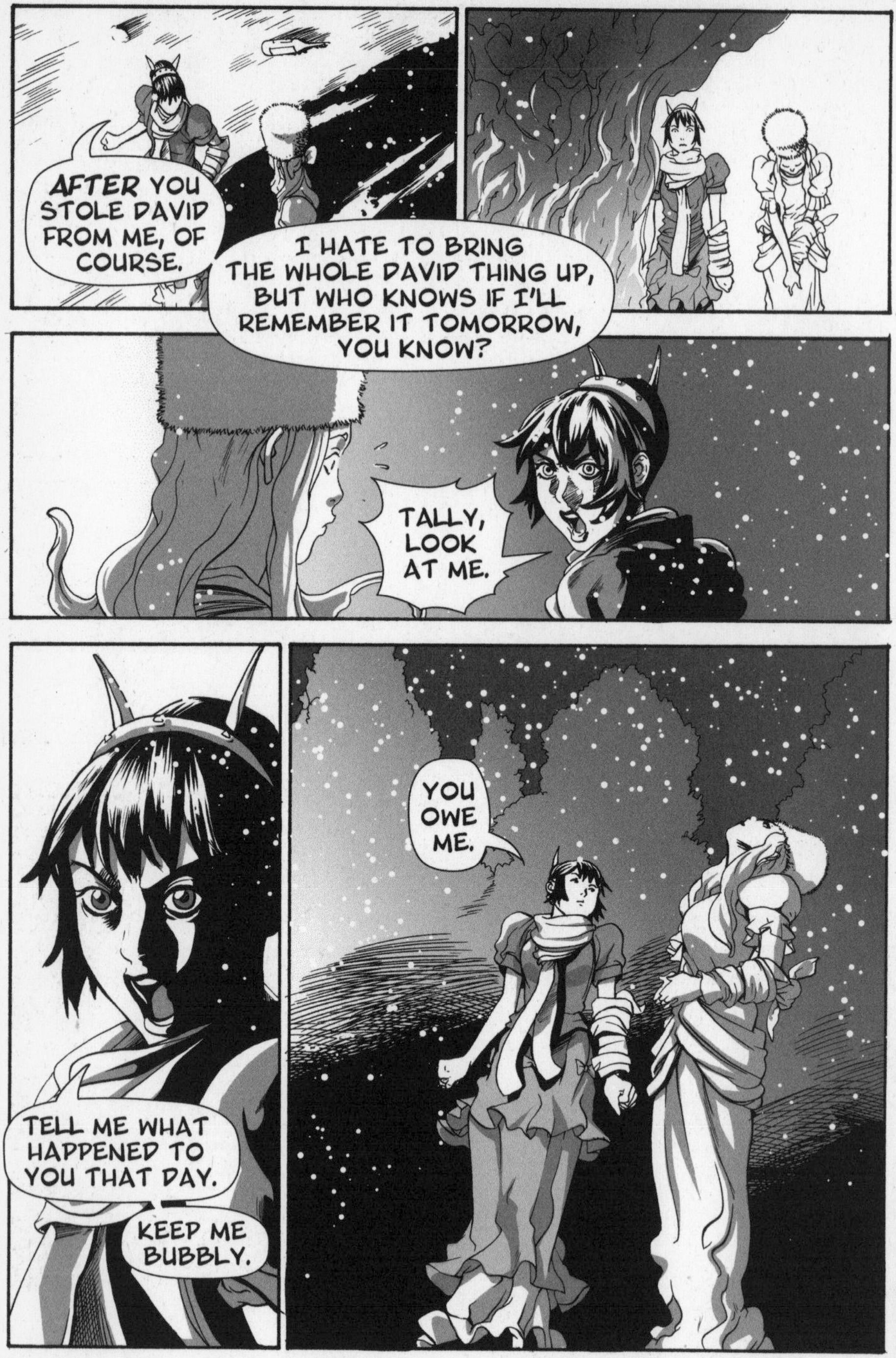
AFTER YOU STOLE DAVID FROM ME, OF COURSE.
I HATE TO BRING THE WHOLE DAVID THING UP, BUT WHO KNOWS IF I'LL REMEMBER IT TOMORROW, YOU KNOW?
TALLY, LOOK AT ME.
TELL ME WHAT HAPPENED TO YOU THAT DAY.
KEEP ME BUBBLY.
YOU OWE ME.

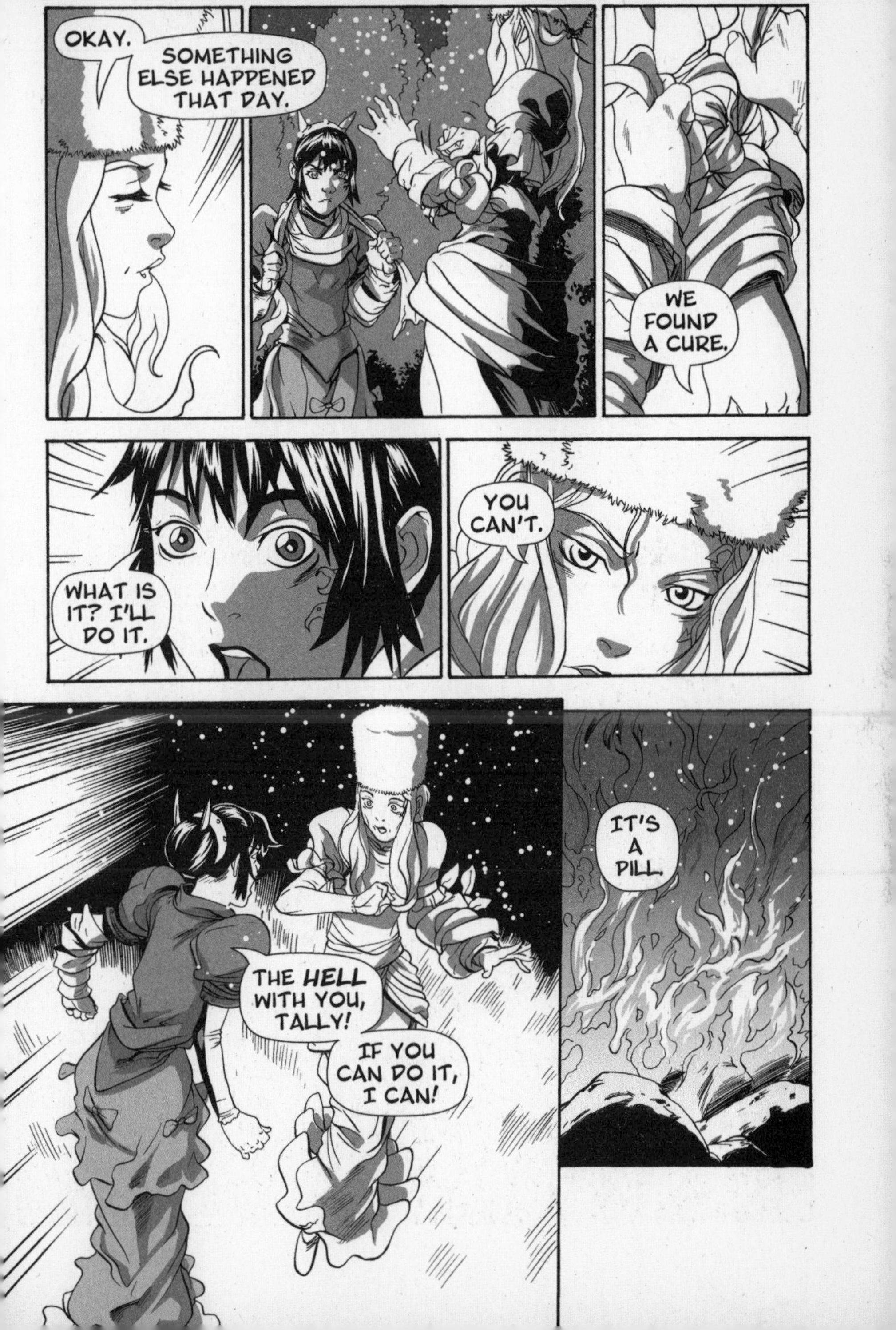
OKAY.
SOMETHING ELSE HAPPENED THAT DAY.
WE FOUND A CURE.
WHAT IS IT? I'LL DO IT.
YOU CAN'T.
THE HELL WITH YOU, TALLY!
IF YOU CAN DO IT, I CAN!
IT'S A PILL.

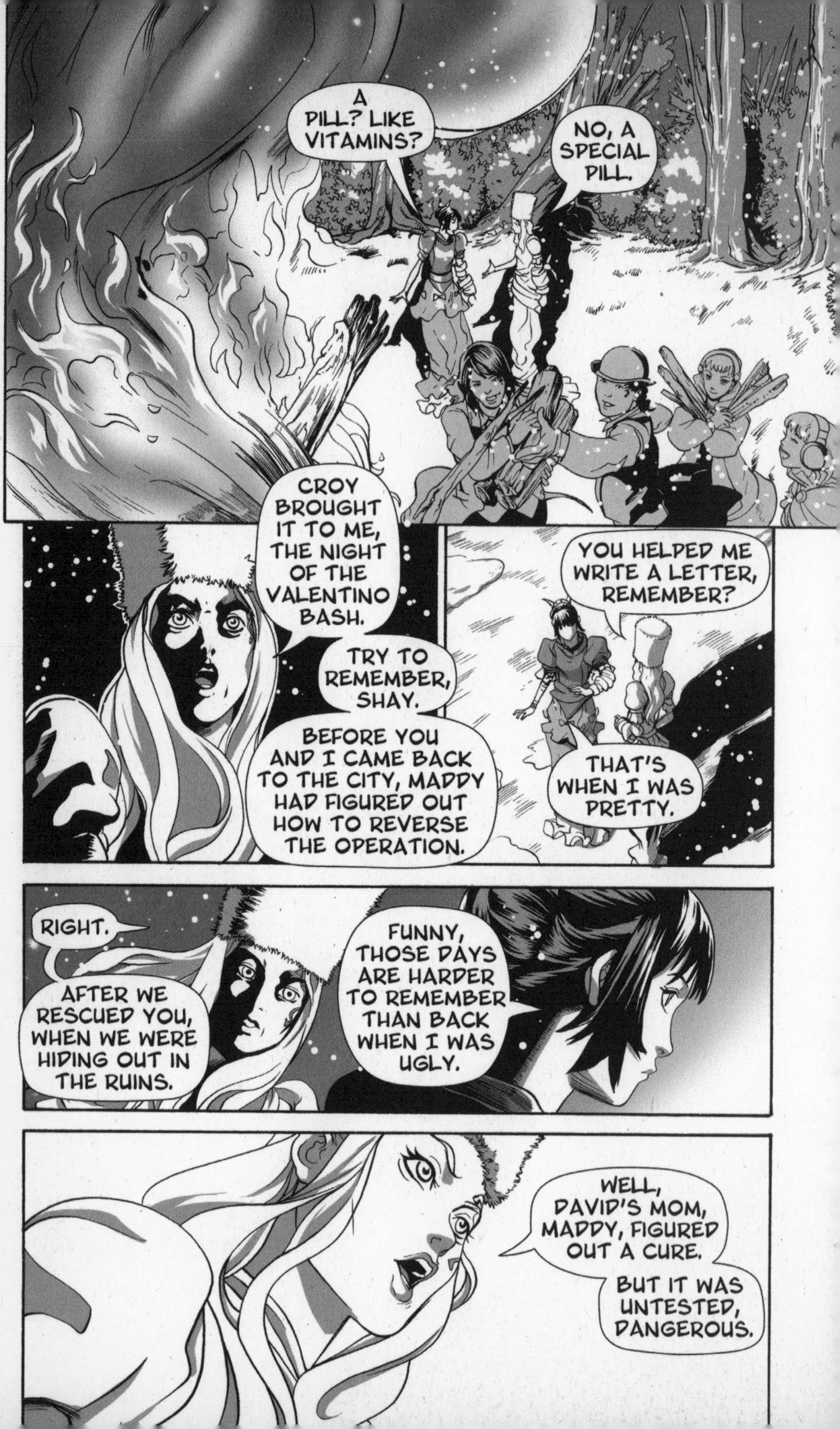
A PILL? LIKE VITAMINS?
NO, A SPECIAL PILL.
CROY BROUGHT IT TO ME, THE NIGHT OF THE VALENTINO BASH.
TRY TO REMEMBER, SHAY.
BEFORE YOU AND I CAME BACK TO THE CITY, MADDY HAD FIGURED OUT HOW TO REVERSE THE OPERATION.
YOU HELPED ME WRITE A LETTER, REMEMBER?
THAT'S WHEN I WAS PRETTY.
RIGHT.
AFTER WE RESCUED YOU, WHEN WE WERE HIDING OUT IN THE RUINS.
FUNNY, THOSE DAYS ARE HARDER TO REMEMBER THAN BACK WHEN I WAS UGLY.
WELL, DAVID'S MOM, MADDY, FIGURED OUT A CURE.
BUT IT WAS UNTESTED, DANGEROUS.

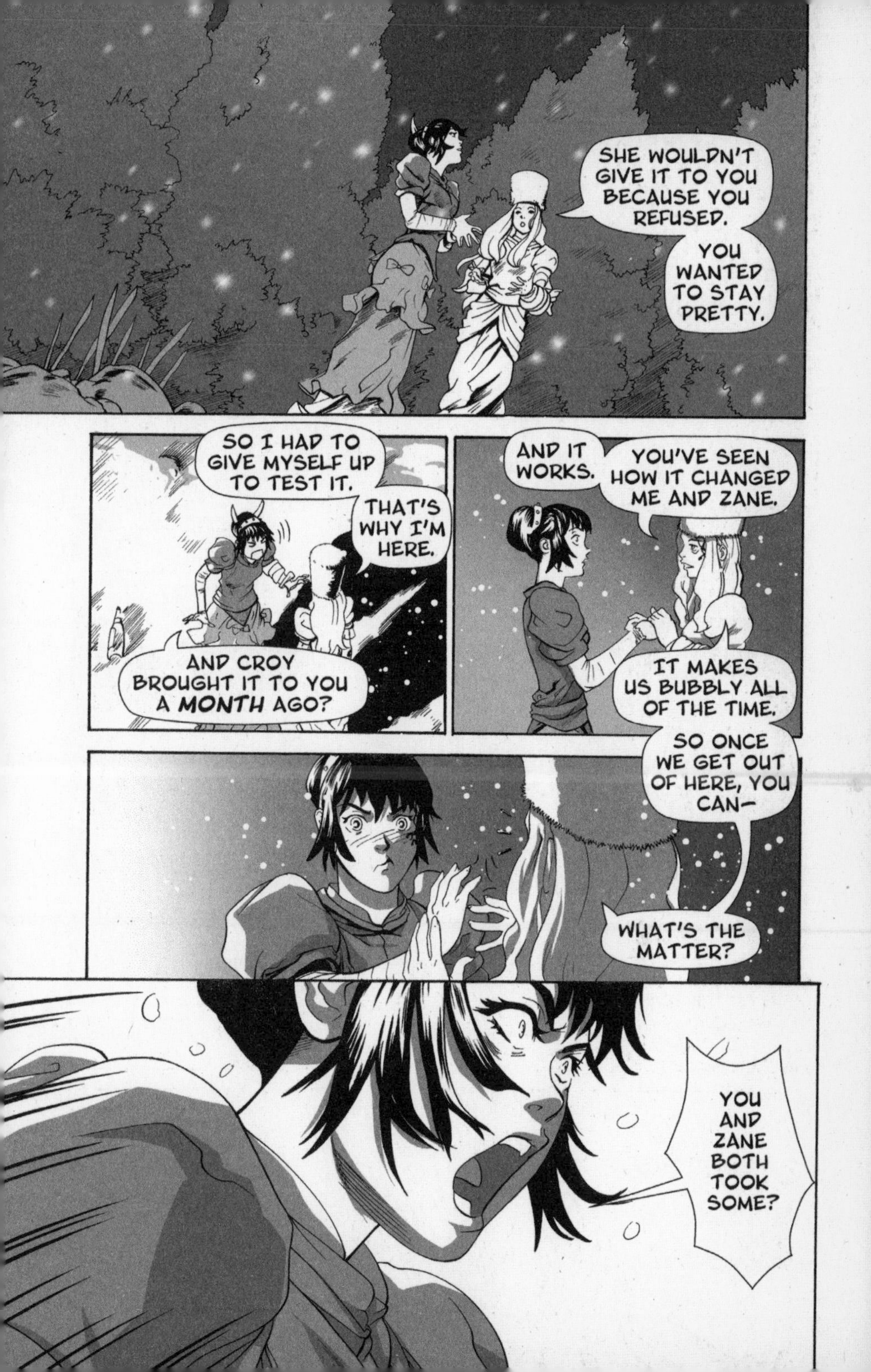
SHE WOULDN'T GIVE IT TO YOU BECAUSE YOU REFUSED.
YOU WANTED TO STAY PRETTY.
SO I HAD TO GIVE MYSELF UP TO TEST IT.
THAT'S WHY I'M HERE.
AND CROY BROUGHT IT TO YOU A MONTH AGO?
AND IT WORKS.
YOU'VE SEEN HOW IT CHANGED ME AND ZANE.
IT MAKES US BUBBLY ALL OF THE TIME.
SO ONCE WE GET OUT OF HERE, YOU CAN—
WHAT'S THE MATTER?
YOU AND ZANE BOTH TOOK SOME?

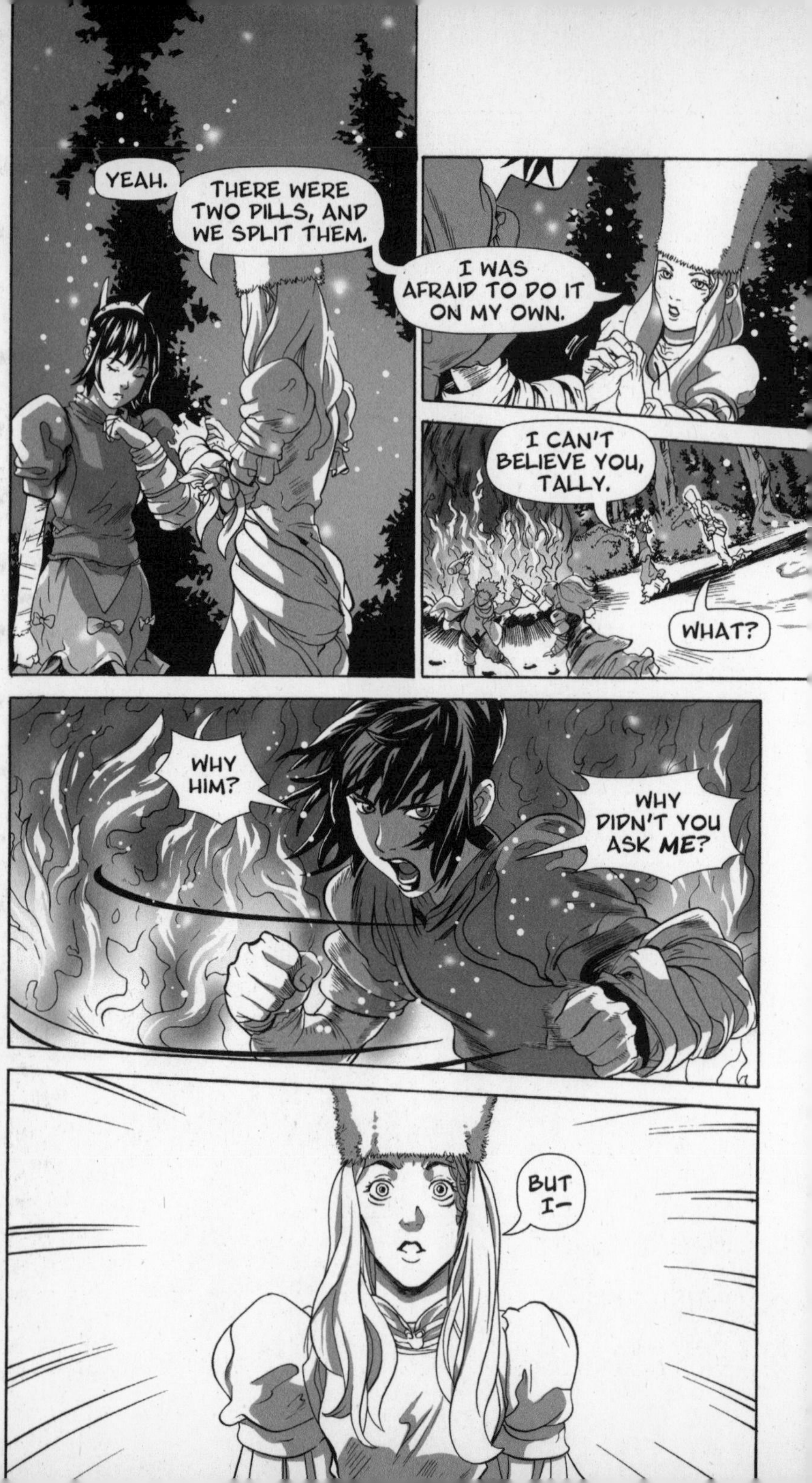
YEAH.
THERE WERE TWO PILLS, AND WE SPLIT THEM.
I WAS AFRAID TO DO IT ON MY OWN.
I CAN'T BELIEVE YOU, TALLY.
WHAT?
WHY HIM?
WHY DIDN'T YOU ASK ME?
BUT I—

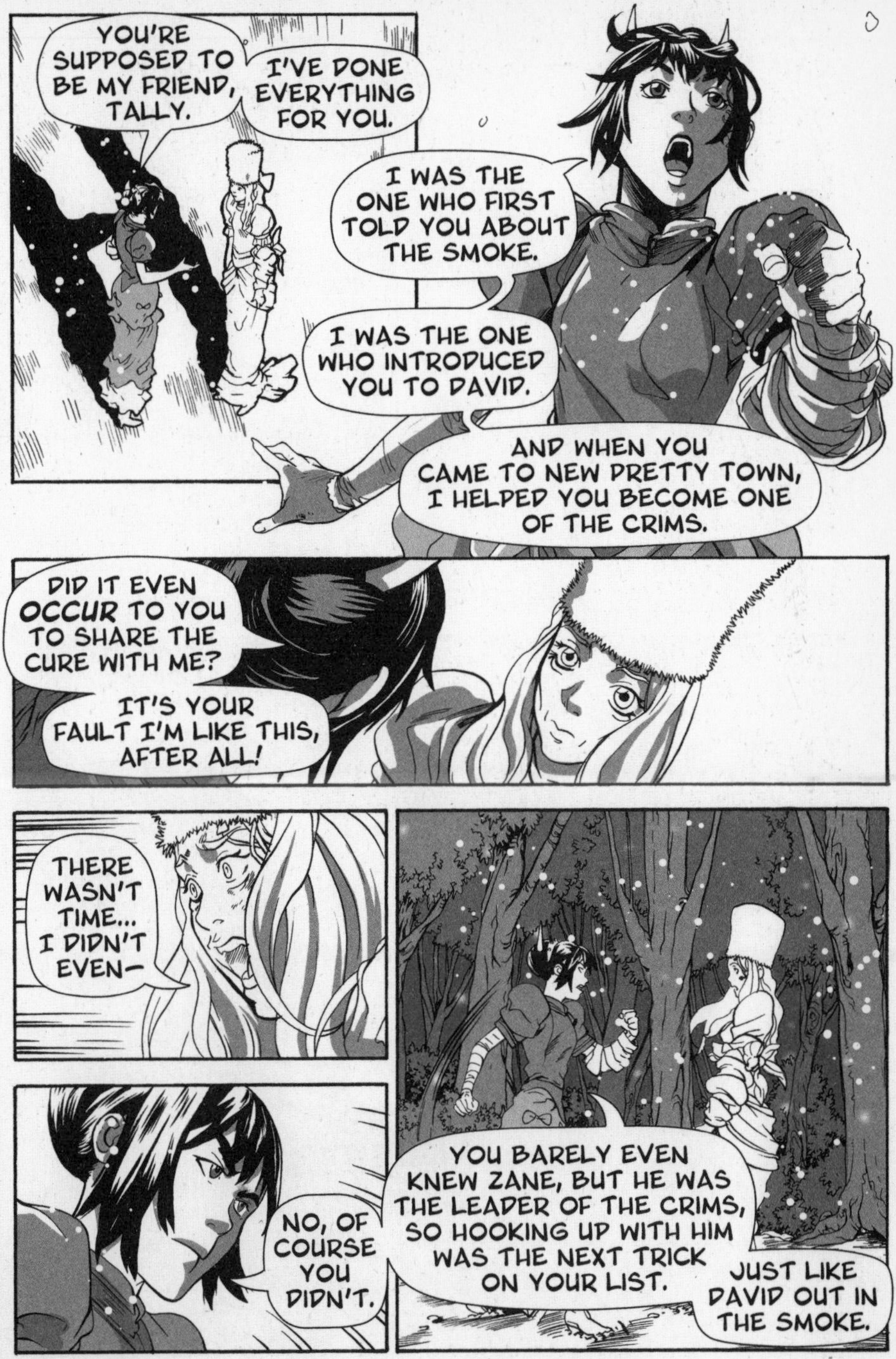
YOU'RE SUPPOSED TO BE MY FRIEND, TALLY.
I'VE DONE EVERYTHING FOR YOU.
I WAS THE ONE WHO FIRST TOLD YOU ABOUT THE SMOKE.
I WAS THE ONE WHO INTRODUCED YOU TO DAVID.
AND WHEN YOU CAME TO NEW PRETTY TOWN, I HELPED YOU BECOME ONE OF THE CRIMS.
DID IT EVEN OCCUR TO YOU TO SHARE THE CURE WITH ME?
IT'S YOUR FAULT I'M LIKE THIS, AFTER ALL!
THERE WASN'T TIME... I DIDN'T EVEN—
NO, OF COURSE YOU DIDN'T.
YOU BARELY EVEN KNEW ZANE, BUT HE WAS THE LEADER OF THE CRIMS, SO HOOKING UP WITH HIM WAS THE NEXT TRICK ON YOUR LIST.
JUST LIKE DAVID OUT IN THE SMOKE.

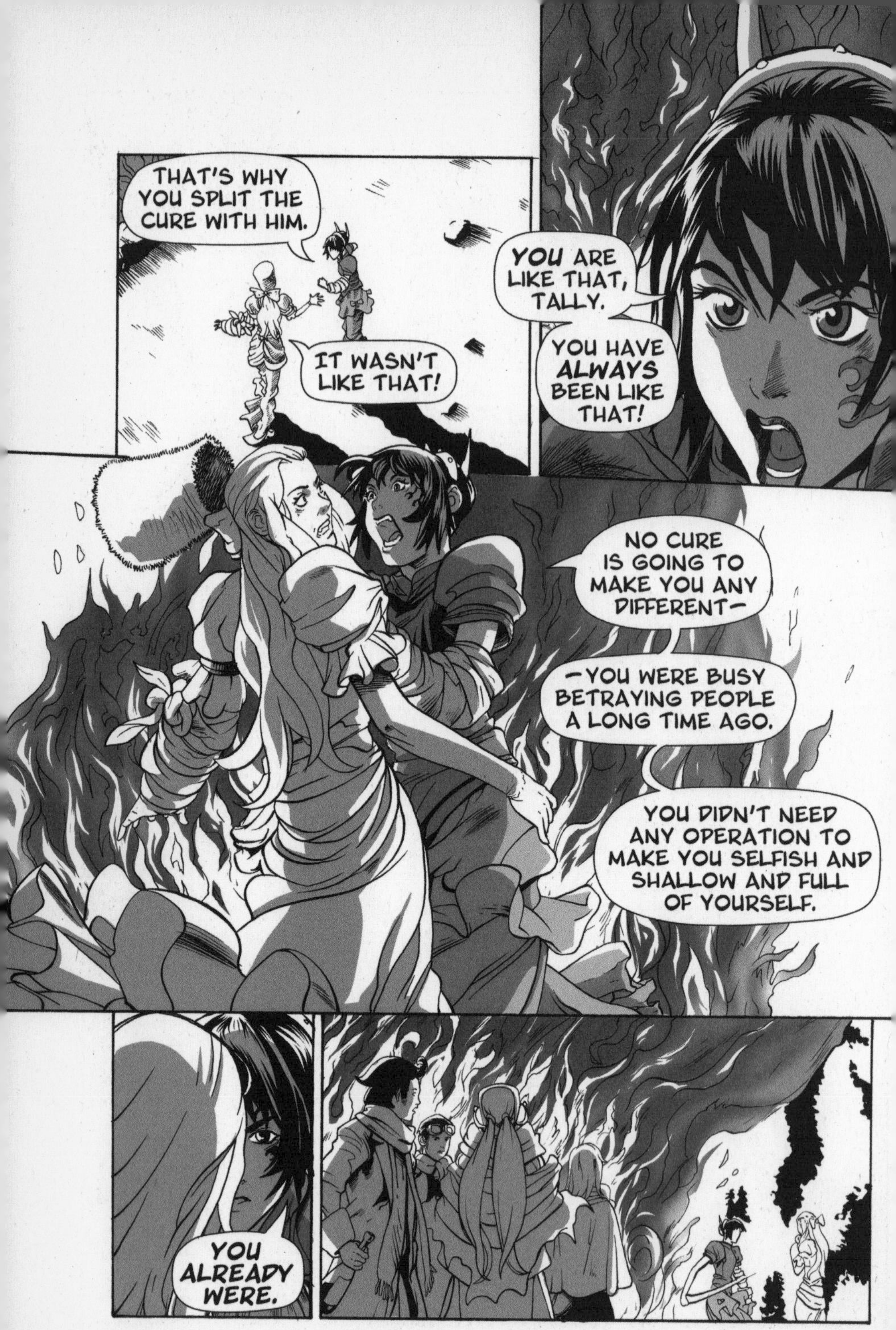
THAT'S WHY YOU SPLIT THE CURE WITH HIM.
IT WASN'T LIKE THAT!
YOU ARE LIKE THAT, TALLY.
YOU HAVE ALWAYS BEEN LIKE THAT!
NO CURE IS GOING TO MAKE YOU ANY DIFFERENT—
—YOU WERE BUSY BETRAYING PEOPLE A LONG TIME AGO.
YOU DIDN'T NEED ANY OPERATION TO MAKE YOU SELFISH AND SHALLOW AND FULL OF YOURSELF.
YOU ALREADY WERE.

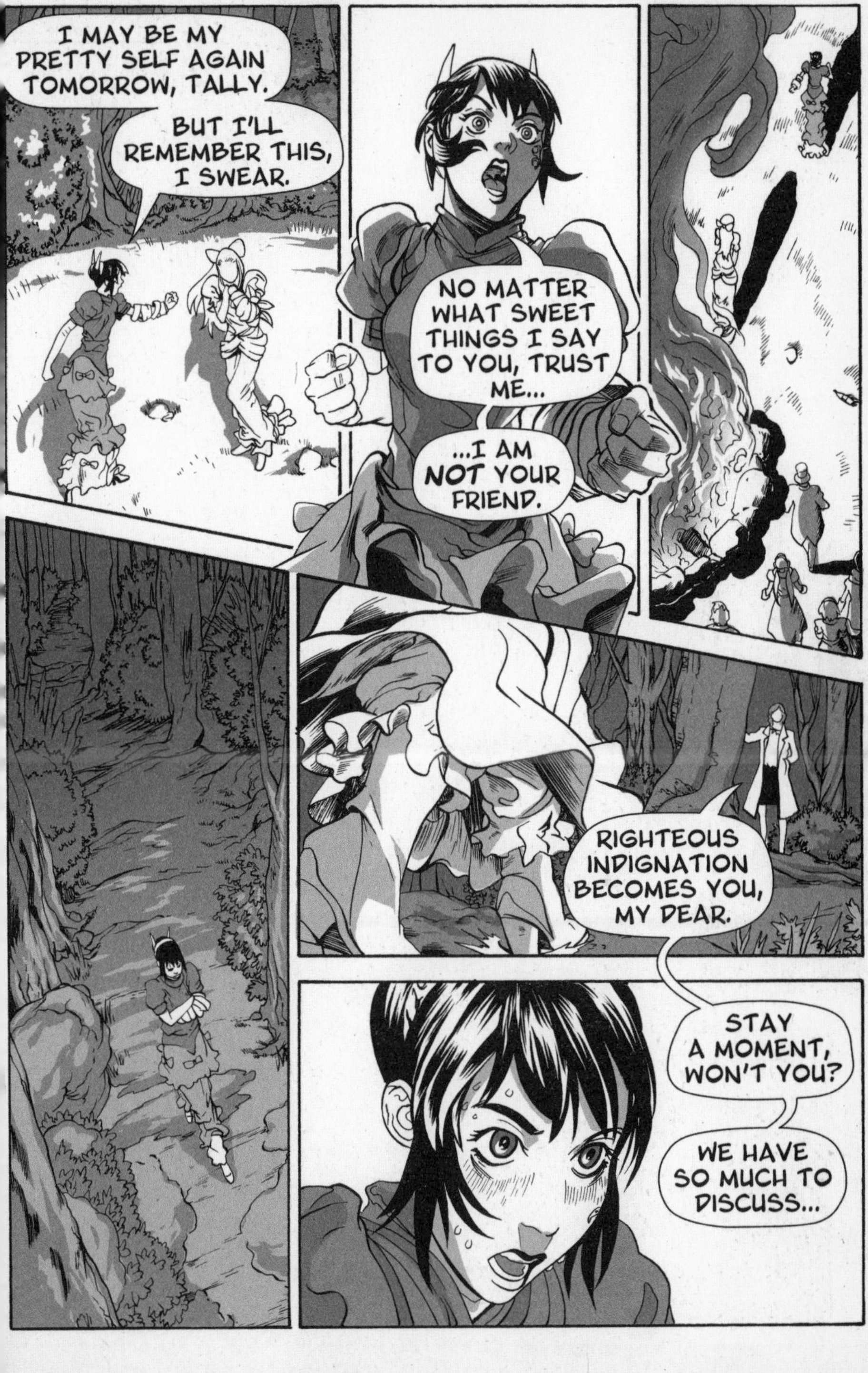
I MAY BE MY PRETTY SELF AGAIN TOMORROW, TALLY.
BUT I'LL REMEMBER THIS, I SWEAR.
NO MATTER WHAT SWEET THINGS I SAY TO YOU, TRUST ME...
...I AM NOT YOUR FRIEND.
RIGHTEOUS INDIGNATION BECOMES YOU, MY DEAR.
STAY A MOMENT, WON'T YOU?
WE HAVE SO MUCH TO DISCUSS...

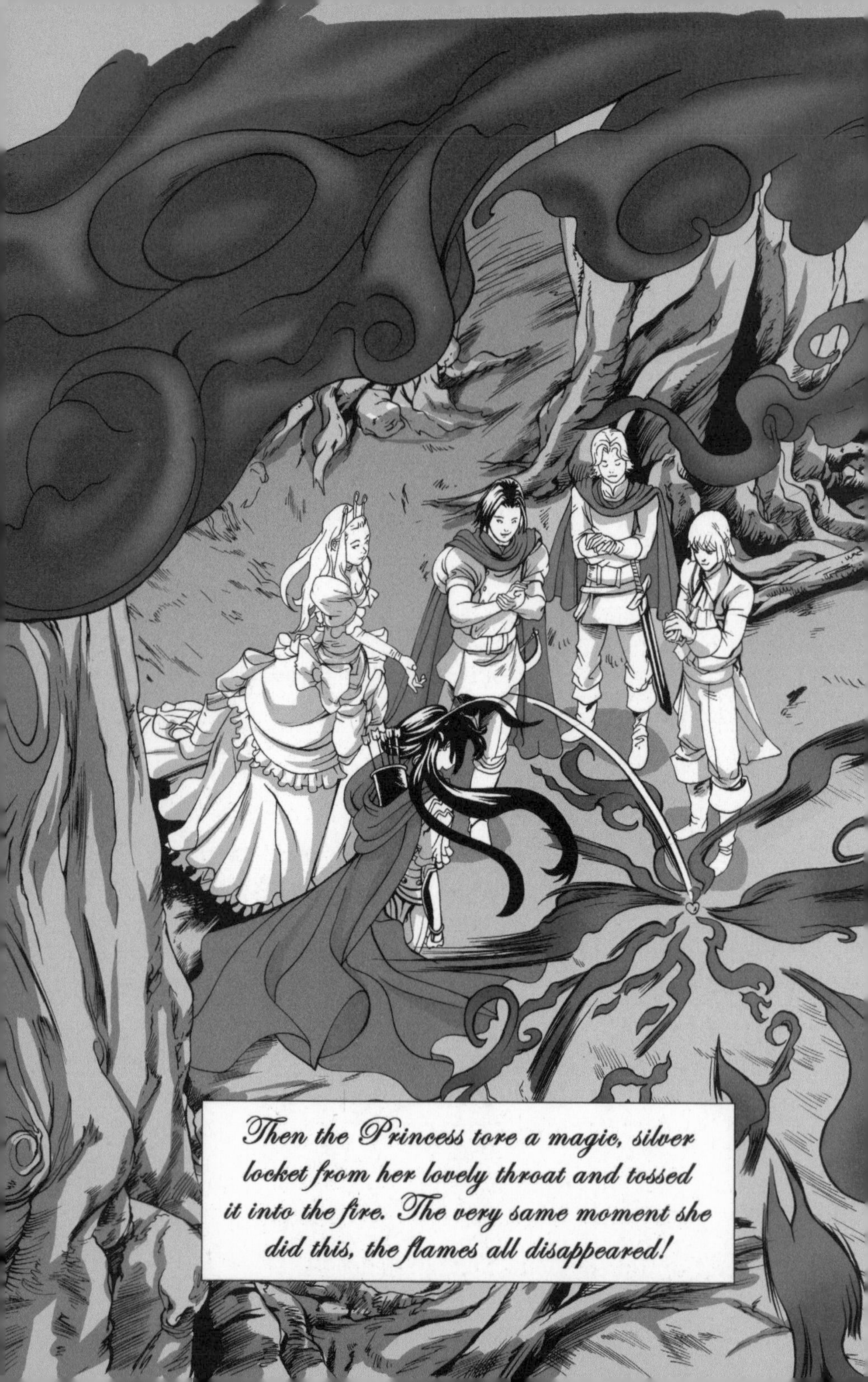
Then the Princess tore a magic, silver locket from her lovely throat and tossed it into the fire. The very same moment she did this, the flames all disappeared!

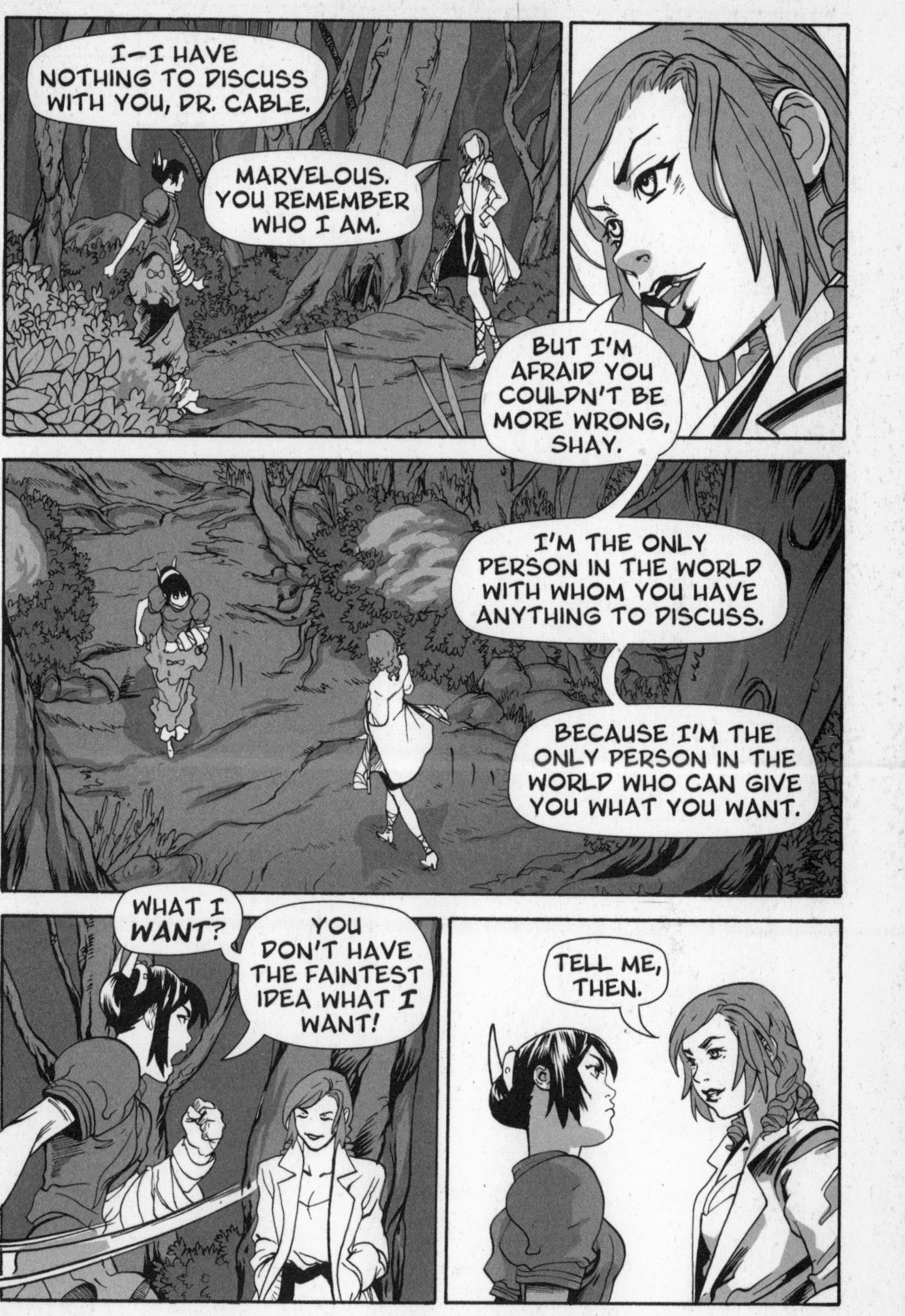
I—I HAVE NOTHING TO DISCUSS WITH YOU, DR. CABLE.
MARVELOUS. YOU REMEMBER WHO I AM.
BUT I'M AFRAID YOU COULDN'T BE MORE WRONG, SHAY.
I'M THE ONLY PERSON IN THE WORLD WITH WHOM YOU HAVE ANYTHING TO DISCUSS.
BECAUSE I'M THE ONLY PERSON IN THE WORLD WHO CAN GIVE YOU WHAT YOU WANT.
WHAT I *WANT*?
YOU DON'T HAVE THE FAINTEST IDEA WHAT *I* WANT!
TELL ME, THEN.

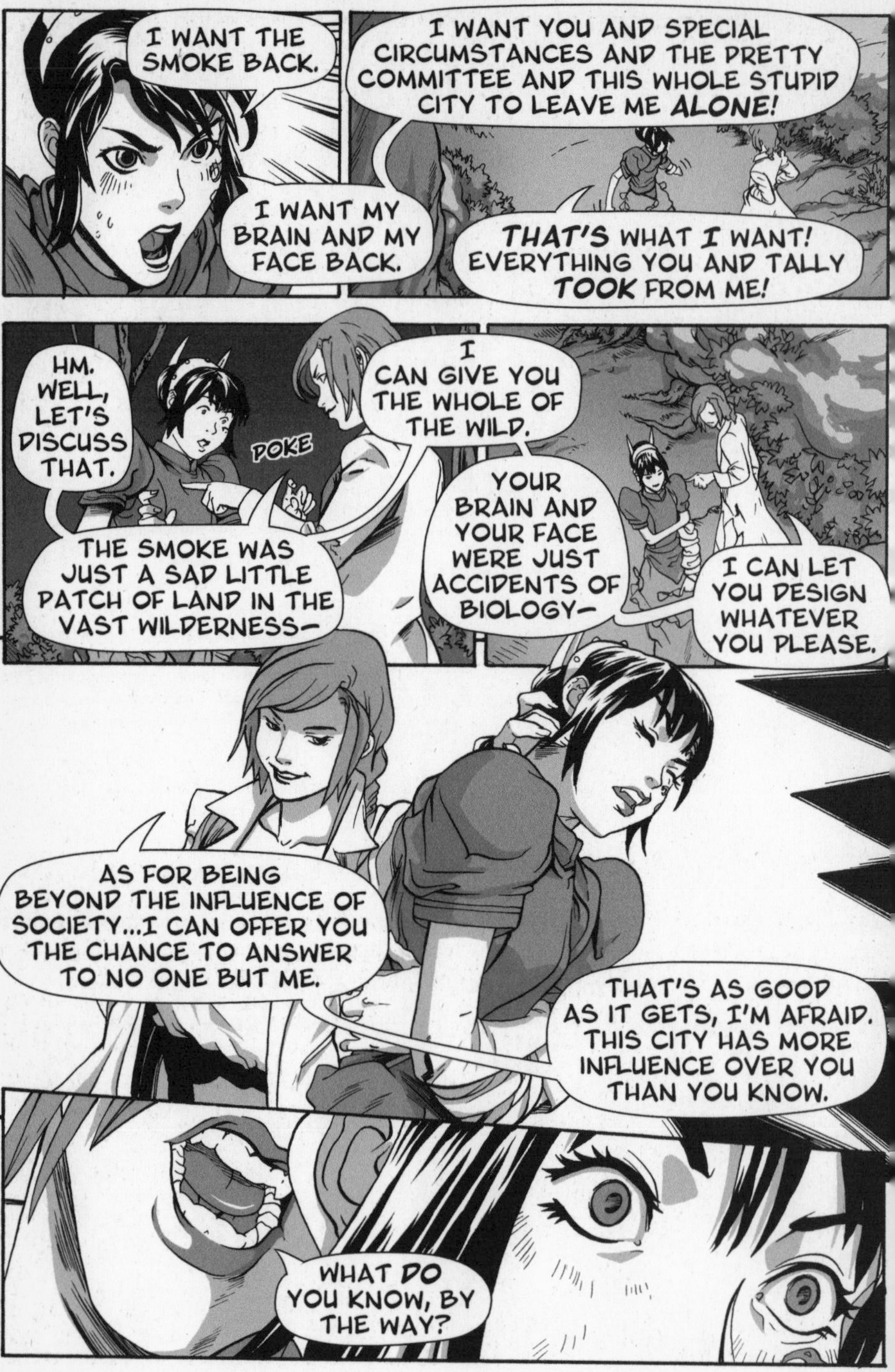
I WANT THE SMOKE BACK.
I WANT MY BRAIN AND MY FACE BACK.
I WANT YOU AND SPECIAL CIRCUMSTANCES AND THE PRETTY COMMITTEE AND THIS WHOLE STUPID CITY TO LEAVE ME ALONE!
THAT'S WHAT I WANT! EVERYTHING YOU AND TALLY TOOK FROM ME!
HM. WELL, LET'S DISCUSS THAT.
POKE
THE SMOKE WAS JUST A SAD LITTLE PATCH OF LAND IN THE VAST WILDERNESS—
I CAN GIVE YOU THE WHOLE OF THE WILD.
YOUR BRAIN AND YOUR FACE WERE JUST ACCIDENTS OF BIOLOGY—
I CAN LET YOU DESIGN WHATEVER YOU PLEASE.
AS FOR BEING BEYOND THE INFLUENCE OF SOCIETY...I CAN OFFER YOU THE CHANCE TO ANSWER TO NO ONE BUT ME.
THAT'S AS GOOD AS IT GETS, I'M AFRAID. THIS CITY HAS MORE INFLUENCE OVER YOU THAN YOU KNOW.
WHAT DO YOU KNOW, BY THE WAY?

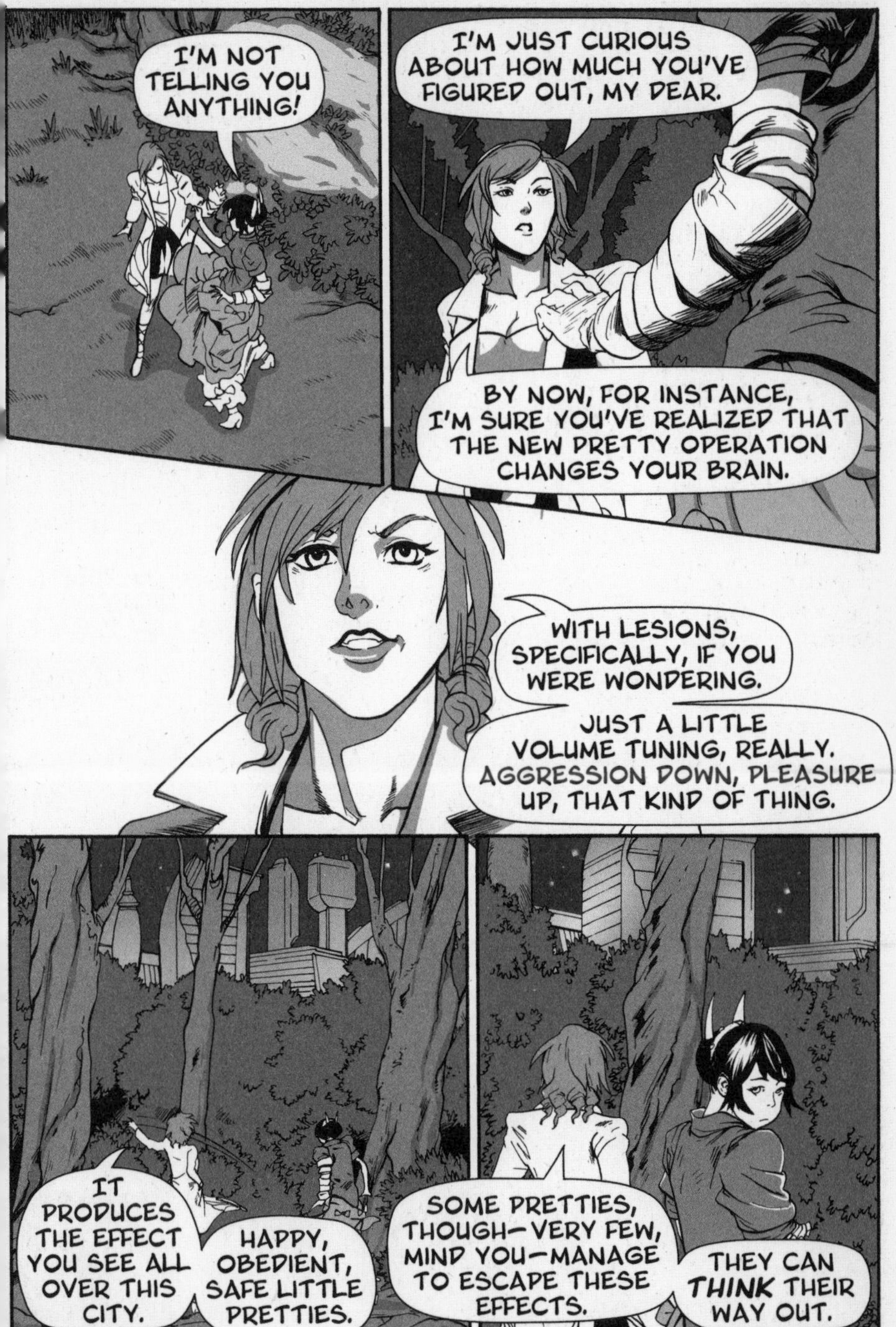
I'M NOT TELLING YOU ANYTHING!
I'M JUST CURIOUS ABOUT HOW MUCH YOU'VE FIGURED OUT, MY DEAR.
BY NOW, FOR INSTANCE, I'M SURE YOU'VE REALIZED THAT THE NEW PRETTY OPERATION CHANGES YOUR BRAIN.
WITH LESIONS, SPECIFICALLY, IF YOU WERE WONDERING.
JUST A LITTLE VOLUME TUNING, REALLY. AGGRESSION DOWN, PLEASURE UP, THAT KIND OF THING.
IT PRODUCES THE EFFECT YOU SEE ALL OVER THIS CITY.
HAPPY, OBEDIENT, SAFE LITTLE PRETTIES.
SOME PRETTIES, THOUGH—VERY FEW, MIND YOU—MANAGE TO ESCAPE THESE EFFECTS.
THEY CAN THINK THEIR WAY OUT.

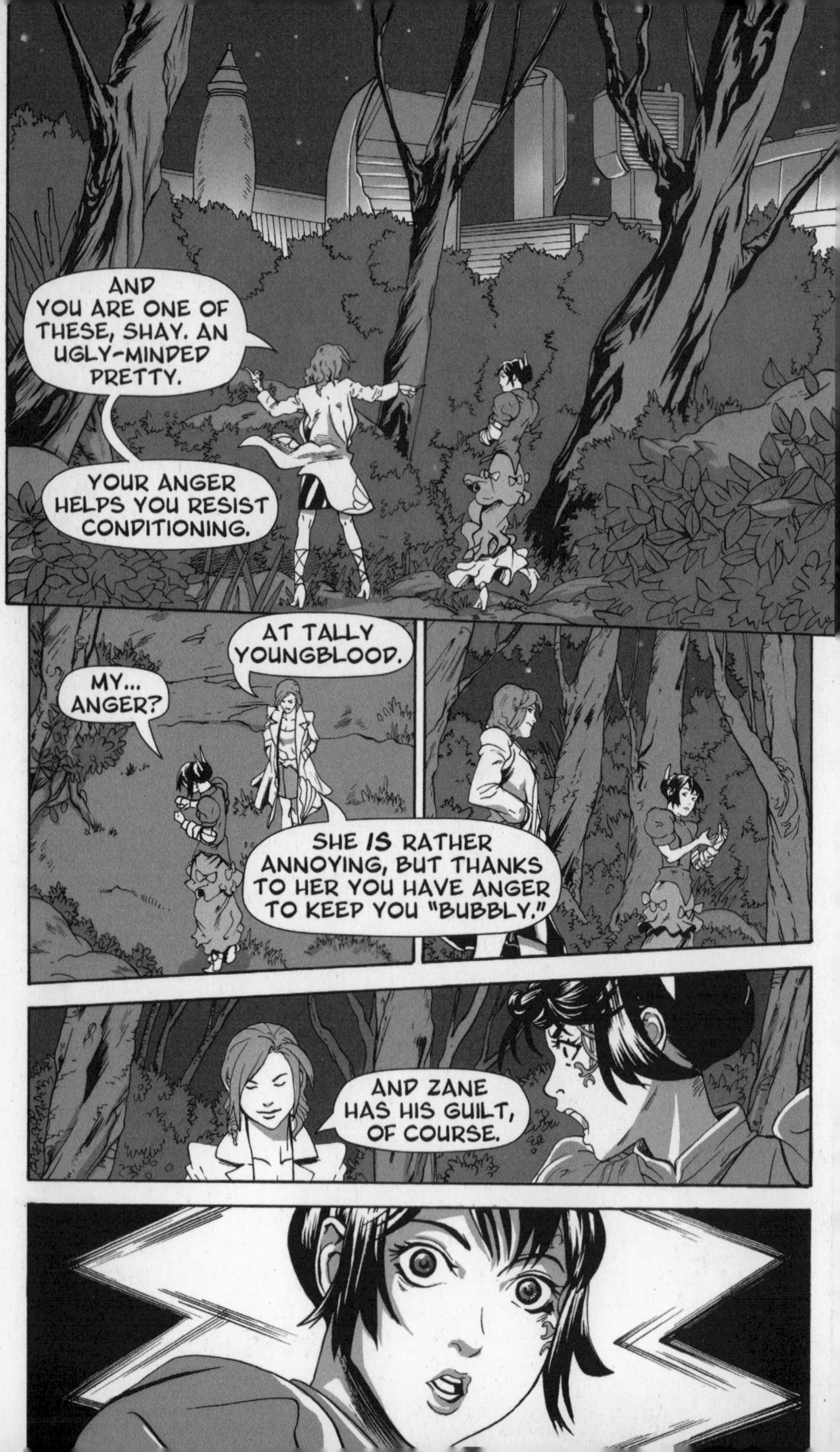
AND YOU ARE ONE OF THESE, SHAY. AN UGLY-MINDED PRETTY.
YOUR ANGER HELPS YOU RESIST CONDITIONING.
MY... ANGER?
AT TALLY YOUNGBLOOD.
SHE IS RATHER ANNOYING, BUT THANKS TO HER YOU HAVE ANGER TO KEEP YOU "BUBBLY."
AND ZANE HAS HIS GUILT, OF COURSE.

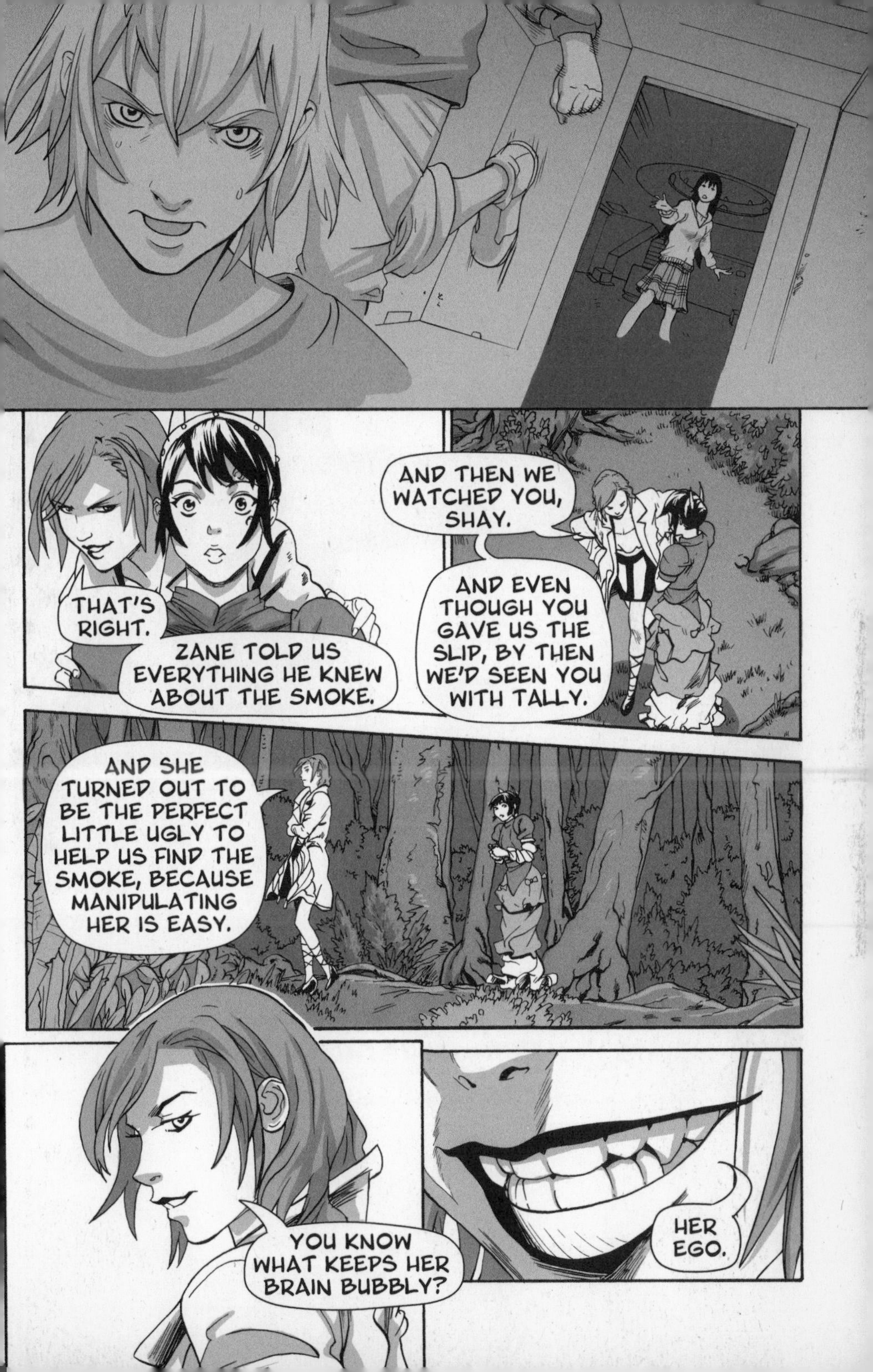
THAT'S RIGHT.
ZANE TOLD US EVERYTHING HE KNEW ABOUT THE SMOKE.
AND THEN WE WATCHED YOU, SHAY.
AND EVEN THOUGH YOU GAVE US THE SLIP, BY THEN WE'D SEEN YOU WITH TALLY.
AND SHE TURNED OUT TO BE THE PERFECT LITTLE UGLY TO HELP US FIND THE SMOKE, BECAUSE MANIPULATING HER IS EASY.
YOU KNOW WHAT KEEPS HER BRAIN BUBBLY?
HER EGO.

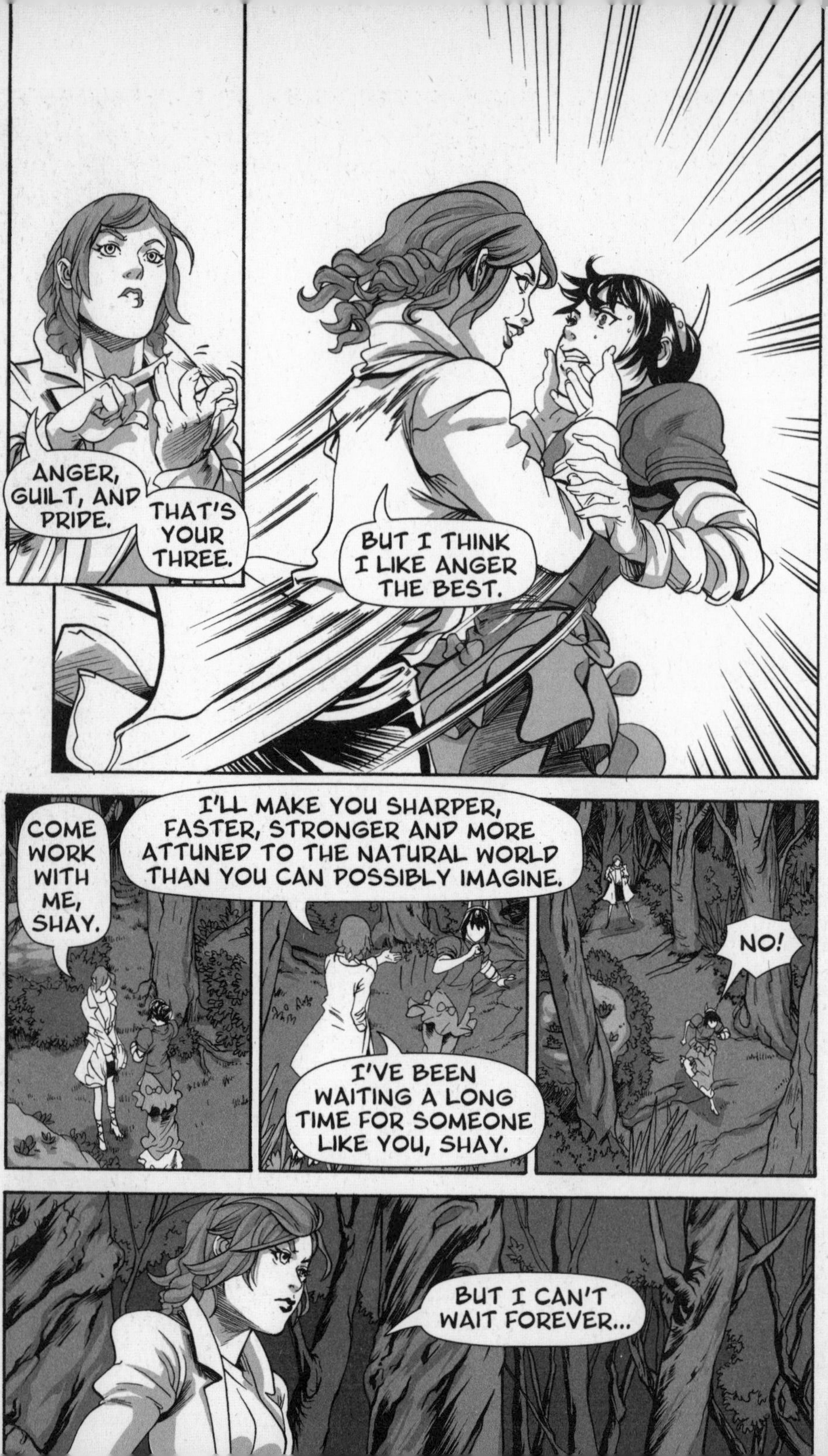
ANGER, GUILT, AND PRIDE.
THAT'S YOUR THREE.
BUT I THINK I LIKE ANGER THE BEST.
COME WORK WITH ME, SHAY.
I'LL MAKE YOU SHARPER, FASTER, STRONGER AND MORE ATTUNED TO THE NATURAL WORLD THAN YOU CAN POSSIBLY IMAGINE.
I'VE BEEN WAITING A LONG TIME FOR SOMEONE LIKE YOU, SHAY.
NO!
BUT I CAN'T WAIT FOREVER...

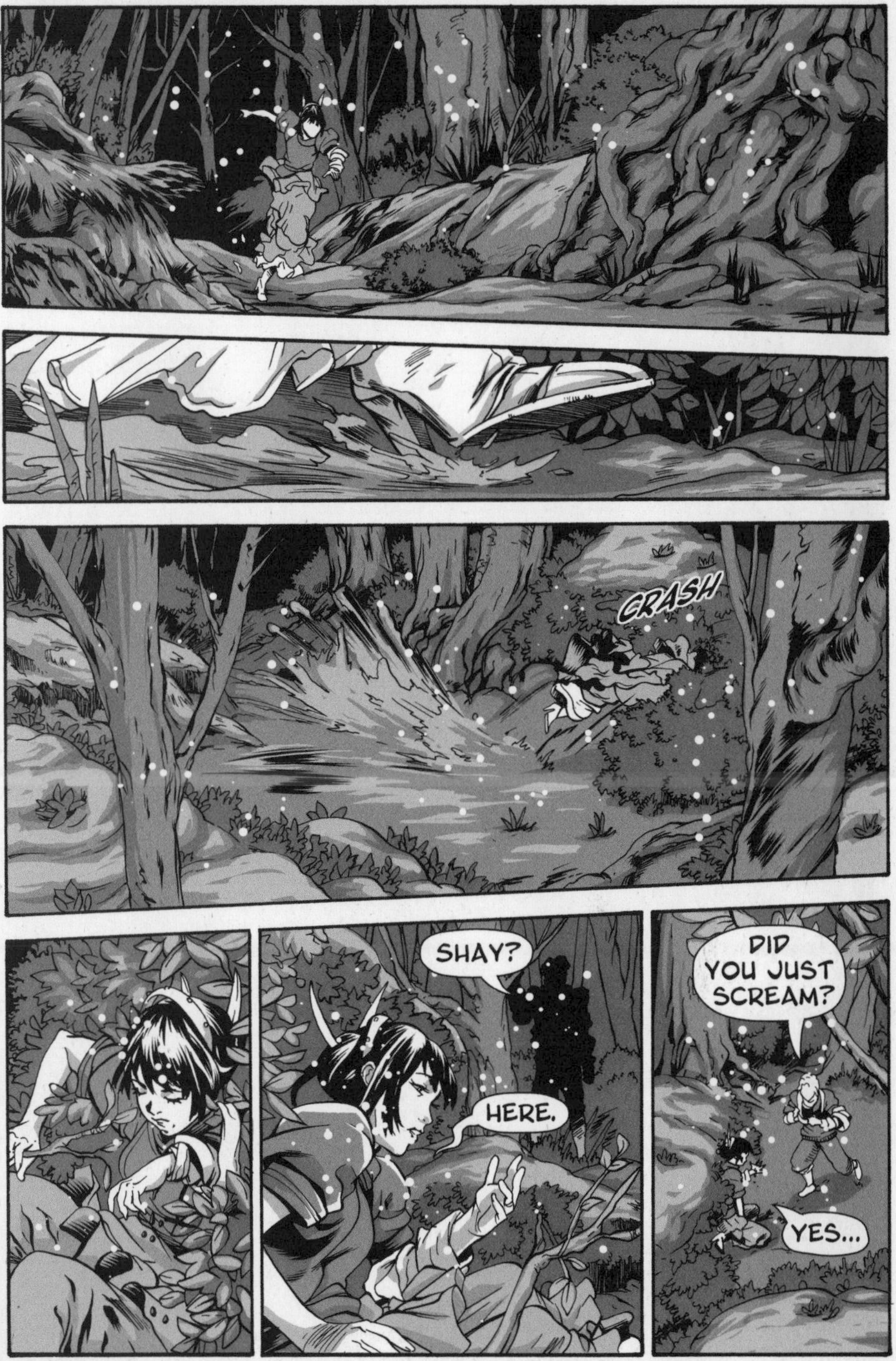
CRASH
SHAY?
HERE.
DID YOU JUST SCREAM?
YES...

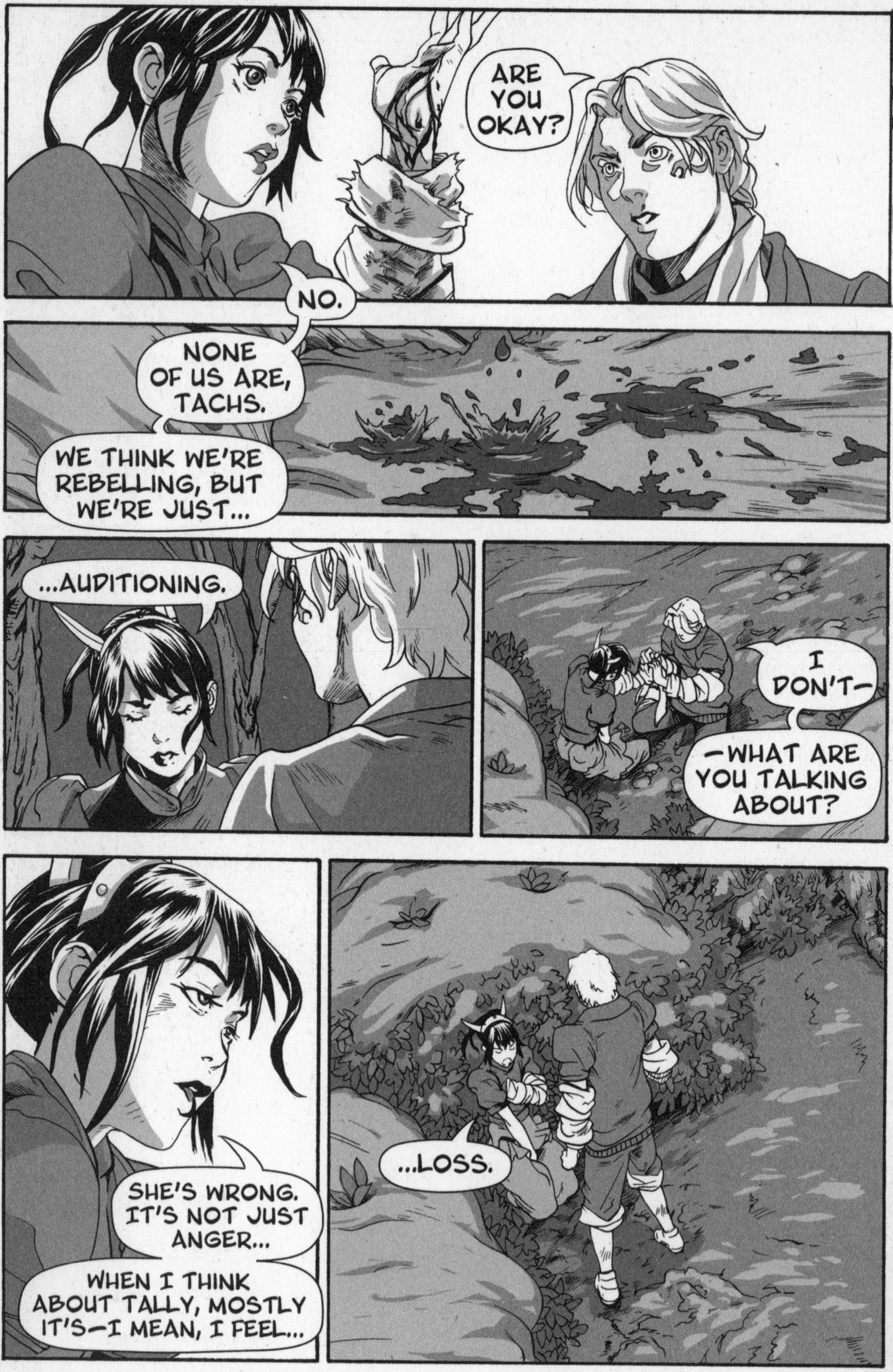
ARE YOU OKAY?
NO.
NONE OF US ARE, TACHS.
WE THINK WE'RE REBELLING, BUT WE'RE JUST...
...AUDITIONING.
I DON'T—
—WHAT ARE YOU TALKING ABOUT?
SHE'S WRONG. IT'S NOT JUST ANGER...
WHEN I THINK ABOUT TALLY, MOSTLY IT'S—I MEAN, I FEEL...
...LOSS.

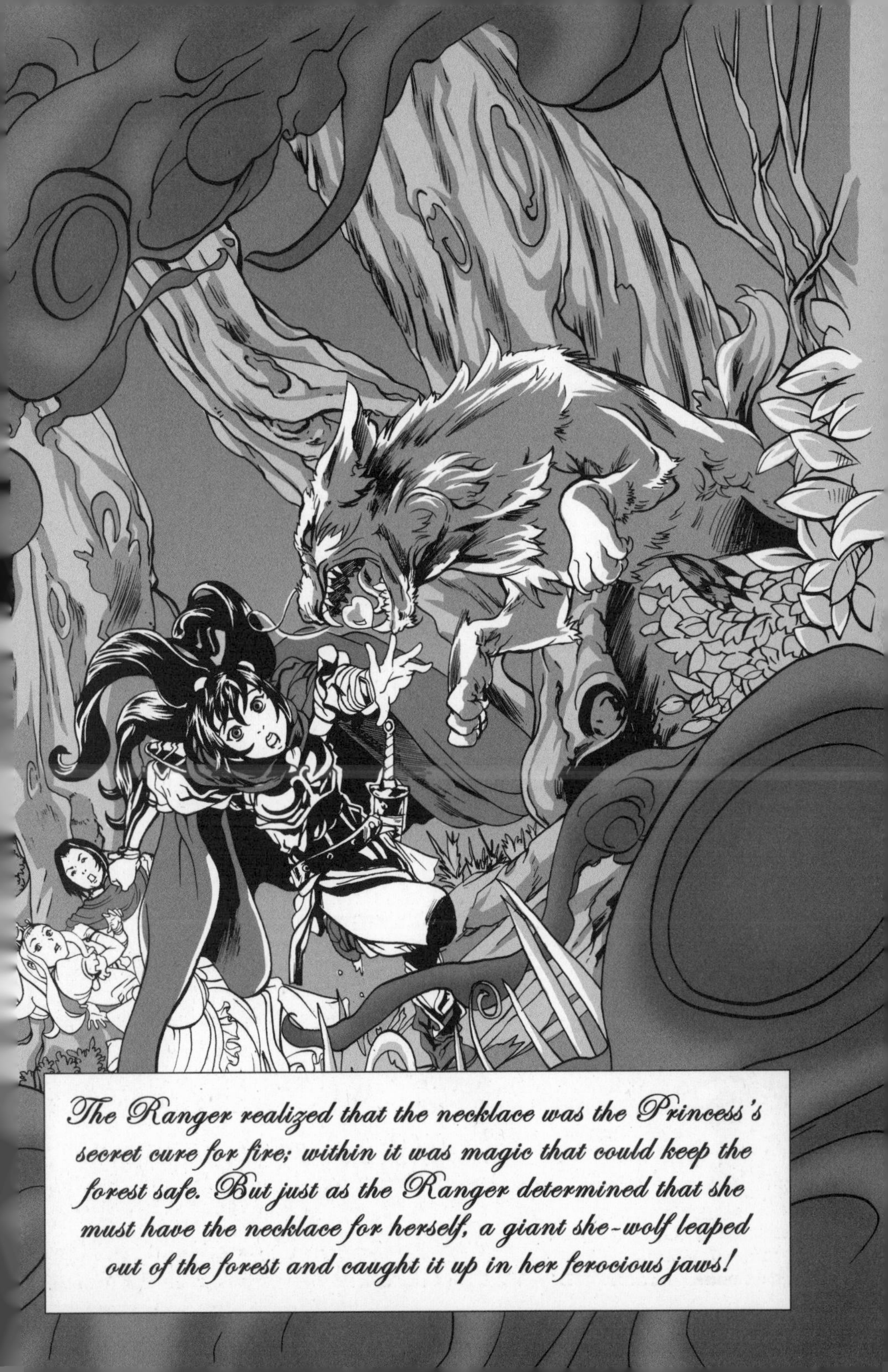
The Ranger realized that the necklace was the Princess's secret cure for fire; within it was magic that could keep the forest safe. But just as the Ranger determined that she must have the necklace for herself, a giant she-wolf leaped out of the forest and caught it up in her ferocious jaws!

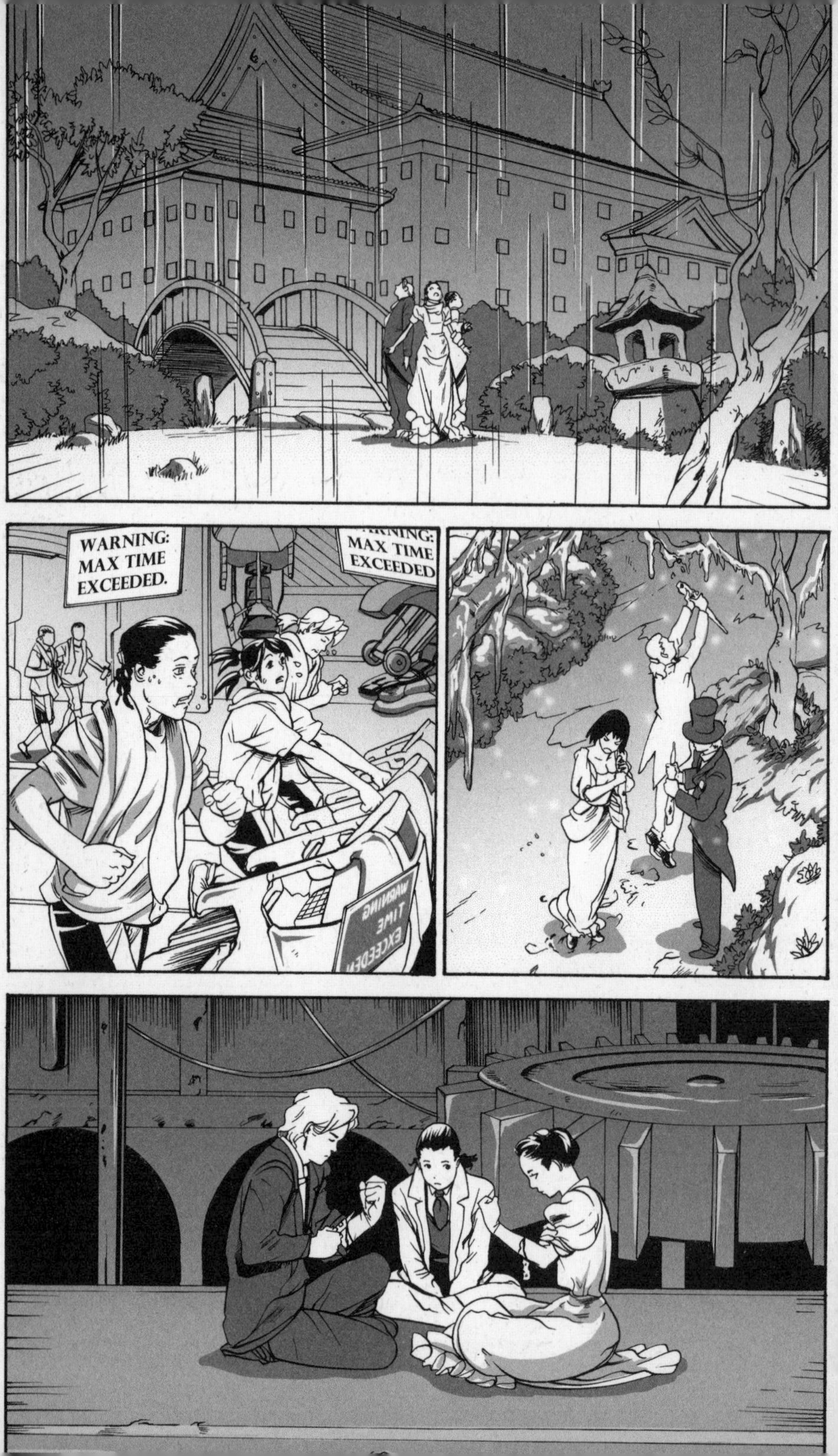
WARNING: MAX TIME EXCEEDED.
MAX TIME EXCEEDED

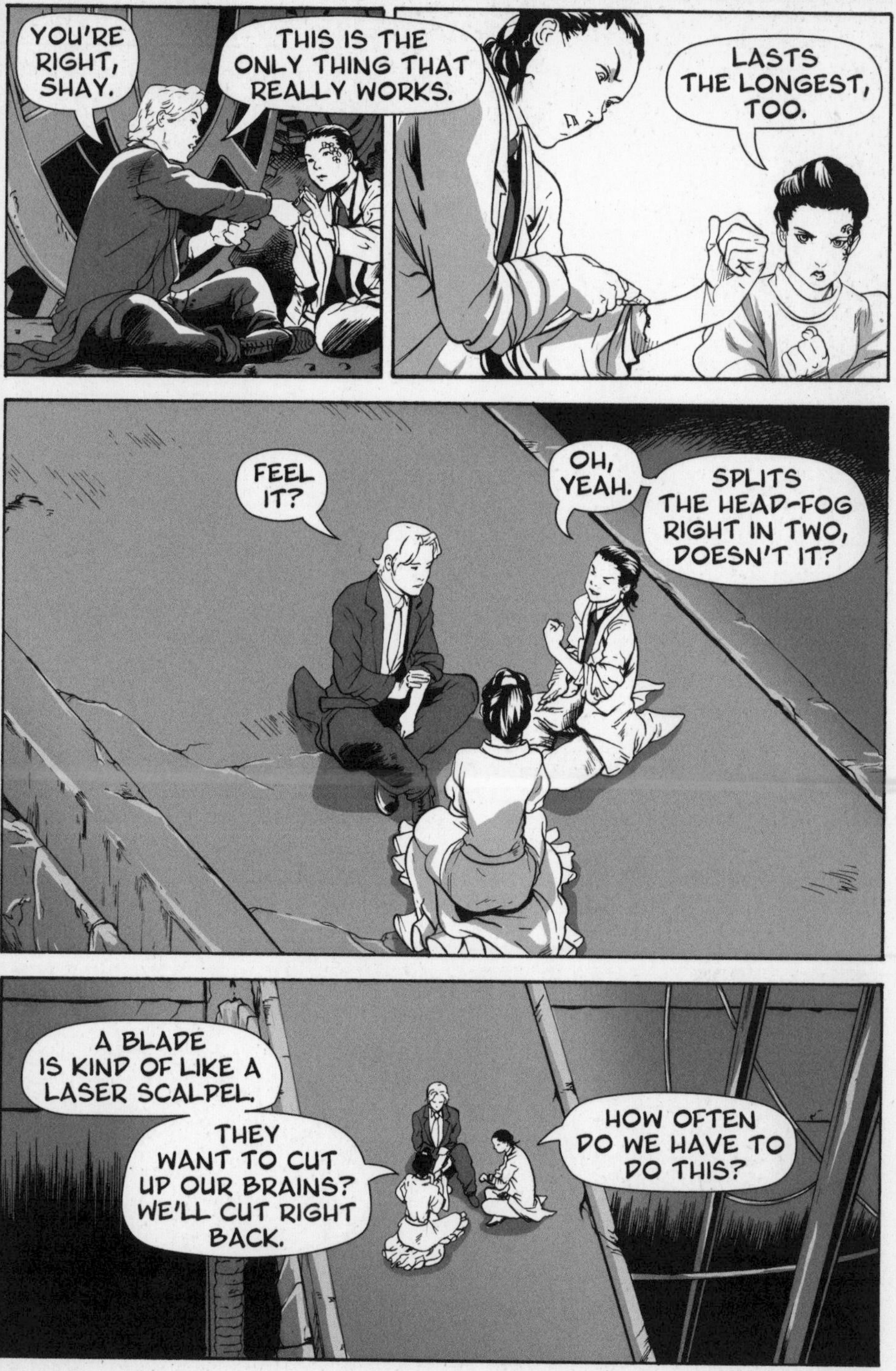
YOU'RE RIGHT, SHAY.
THIS IS THE ONLY THING THAT REALLY WORKS.
LASTS THE LONGEST, TOO.
FEEL IT?
OH, YEAH.
SPLITS THE HEAD-FOG RIGHT IN TWO, DOESN'T IT?
A BLADE IS KIND OF LIKE A LASER SCALPEL.
THEY WANT TO CUT UP OUR BRAINS? WE'LL CUT RIGHT BACK.
HOW OFTEN DO WE HAVE TO DO THIS?

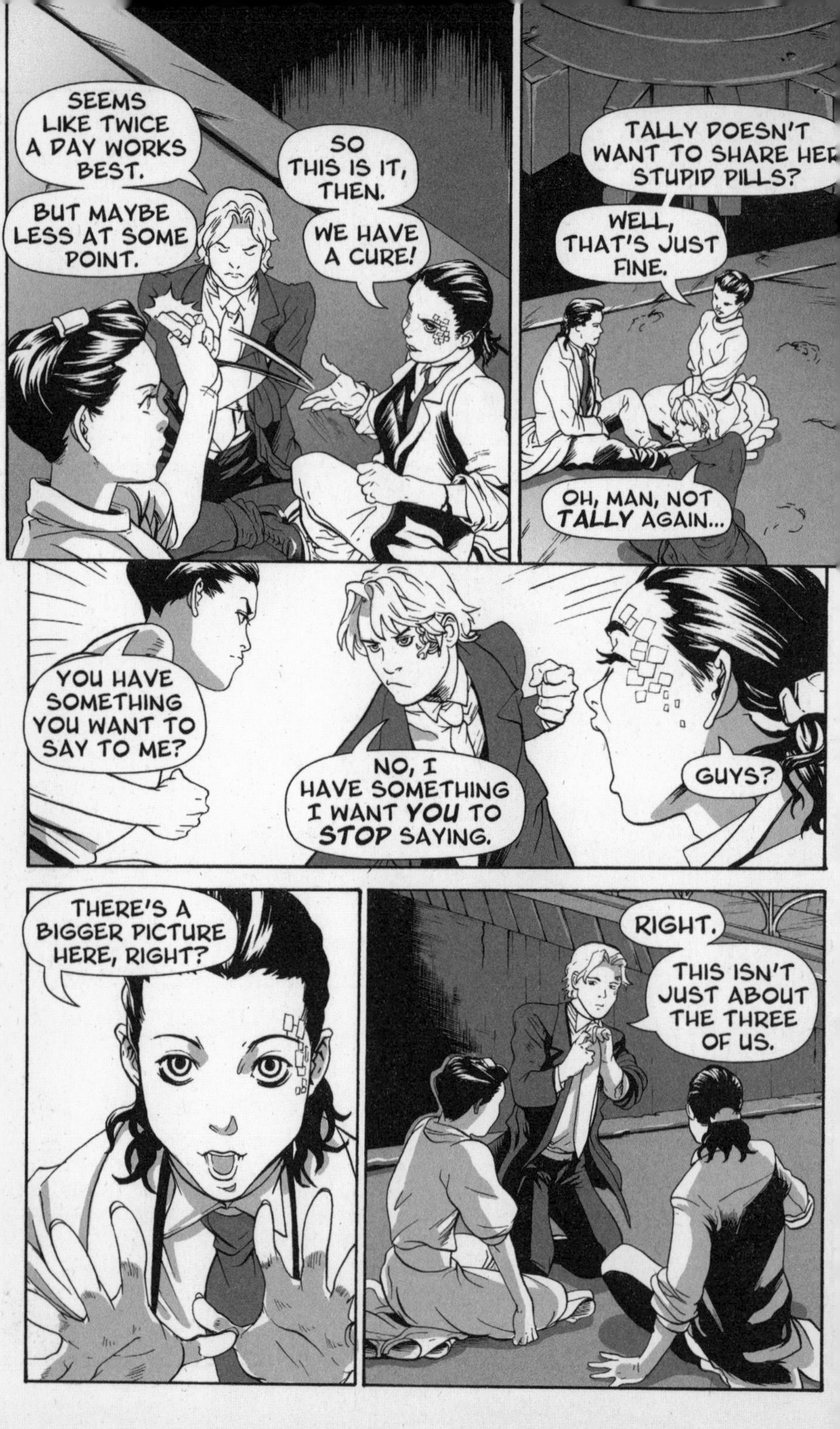
SEEMS LIKE TWICE A DAY WORKS BEST.
BUT MAYBE LESS AT SOME POINT.
SO THIS IS IT, THEN.
WE HAVE A CURE!
TALLY DOESN'T WANT TO SHARE HER STUPID PILLS?
WELL, THAT'S JUST FINE.
OH, MAN, NOT TALLY AGAIN...
YOU HAVE SOMETHING YOU WANT TO SAY TO ME?
NO, I HAVE SOMETHING I WANT YOU TO STOP SAYING.
GUYS?
THERE'S A BIGGER PICTURE HERE, RIGHT?
RIGHT.
THIS ISN'T JUST ABOUT THE THREE OF US.

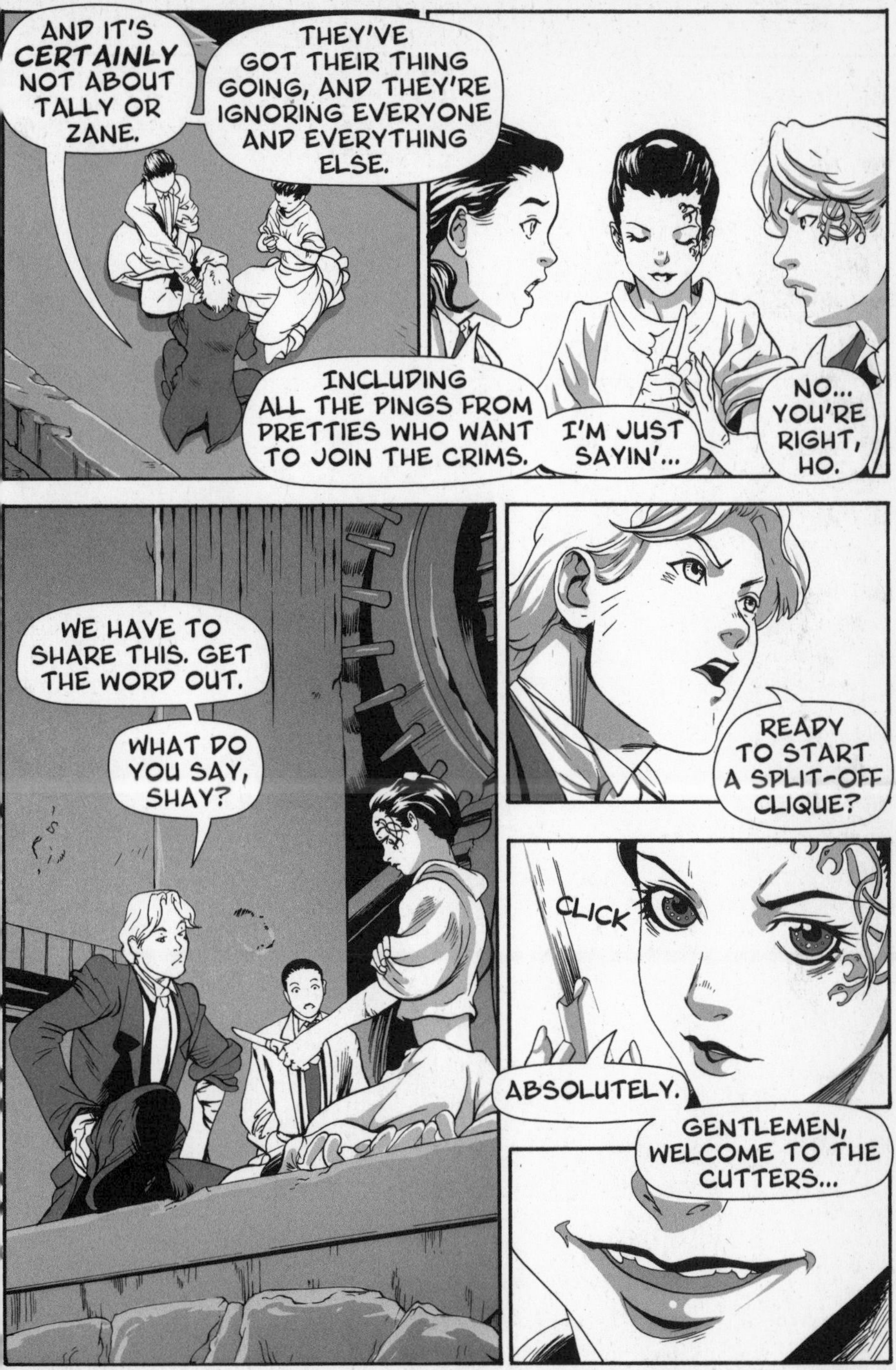
AND IT'S **CERTAINLY** NOT ABOUT TALLY OR ZANE.
THEY'VE GOT THEIR THING GOING, AND THEY'RE IGNORING EVERYONE AND EVERYTHING ELSE.
INCLUDING ALL THE PINGS FROM PRETTIES WHO WANT TO JOIN THE CRIMS.
I'M JUST SAYIN'...
NO... YOU'RE RIGHT, HO.
WE HAVE TO SHARE THIS. GET THE WORD OUT.
WHAT DO YOU SAY, SHAY?
READY TO START A SPLIT-OFF CLIQUE?
CLICK
ABSOLUTELY.
GENTLEMEN, WELCOME TO THE CUTTERS...

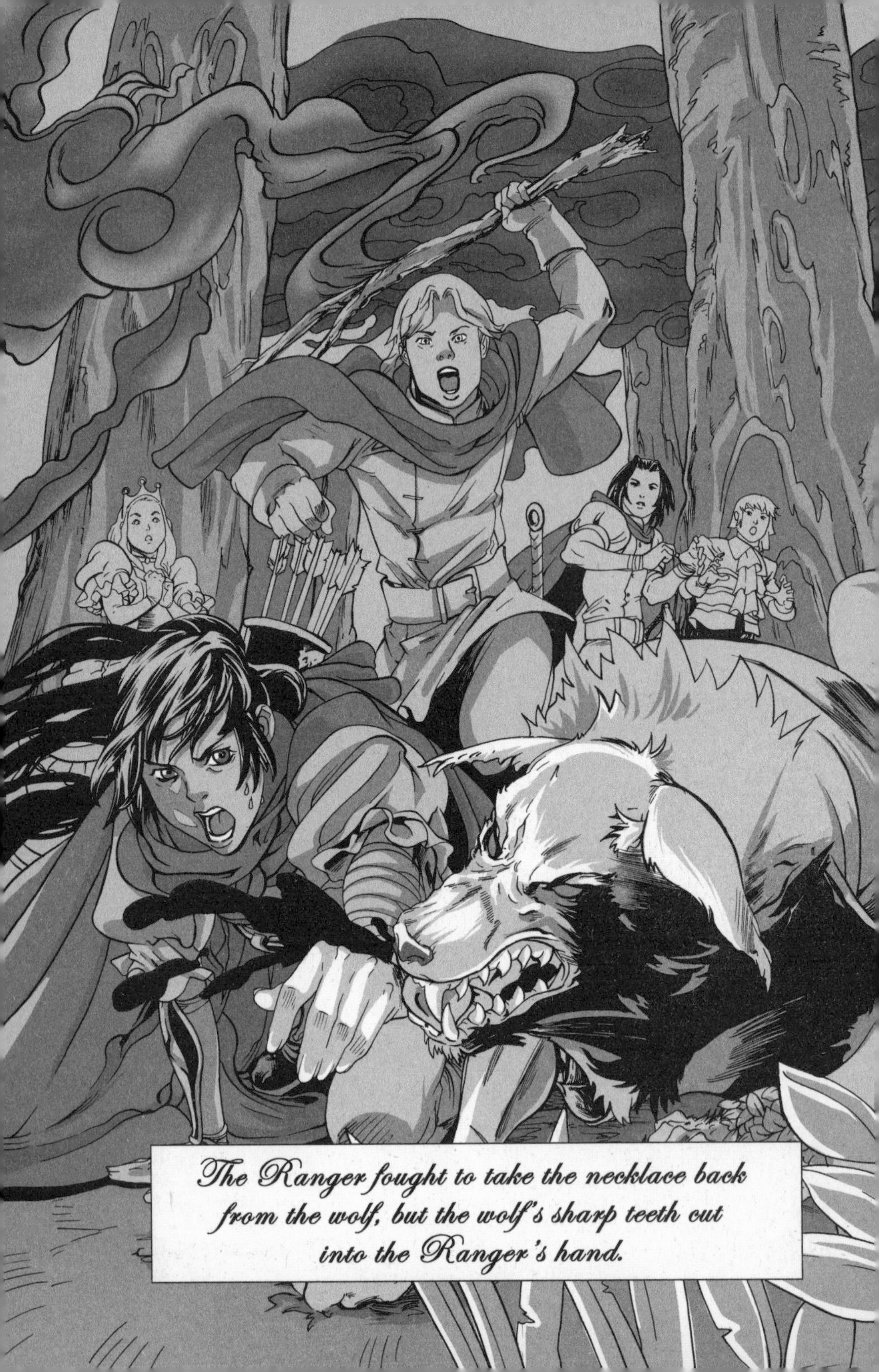
The Ranger fought to take the necklace back from the wolf, but the wolf's sharp teeth cut into the Ranger's hand.

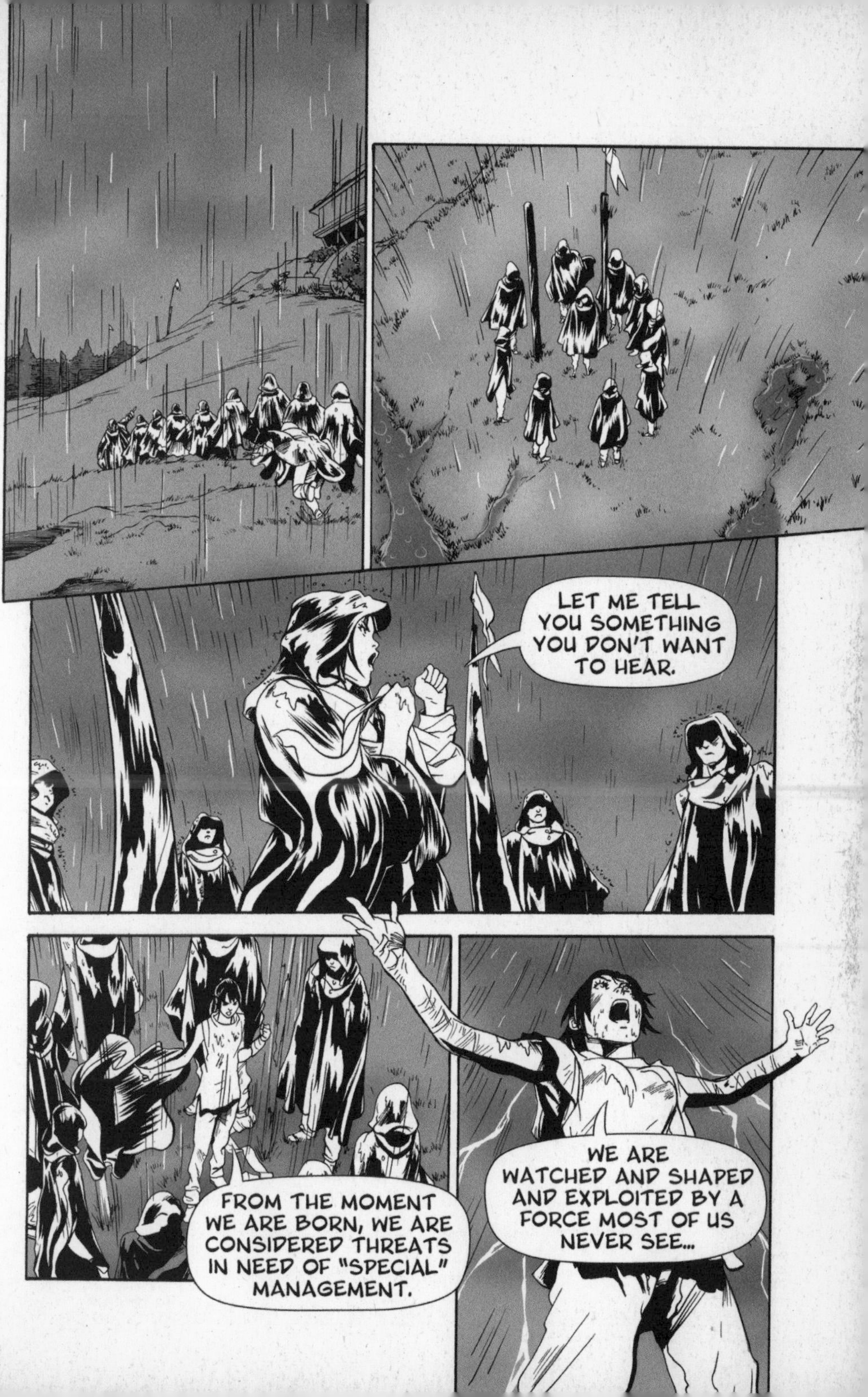
LET ME TELL YOU SOMETHING YOU DON'T WANT TO HEAR.
FROM THE MOMENT WE ARE BORN, WE ARE CONSIDERED THREATS IN NEED OF "SPECIAL" MANAGEMENT.
WE ARE WATCHED AND SHAPED AND EXPLOITED BY A FORCE MOST OF US NEVER SEE...

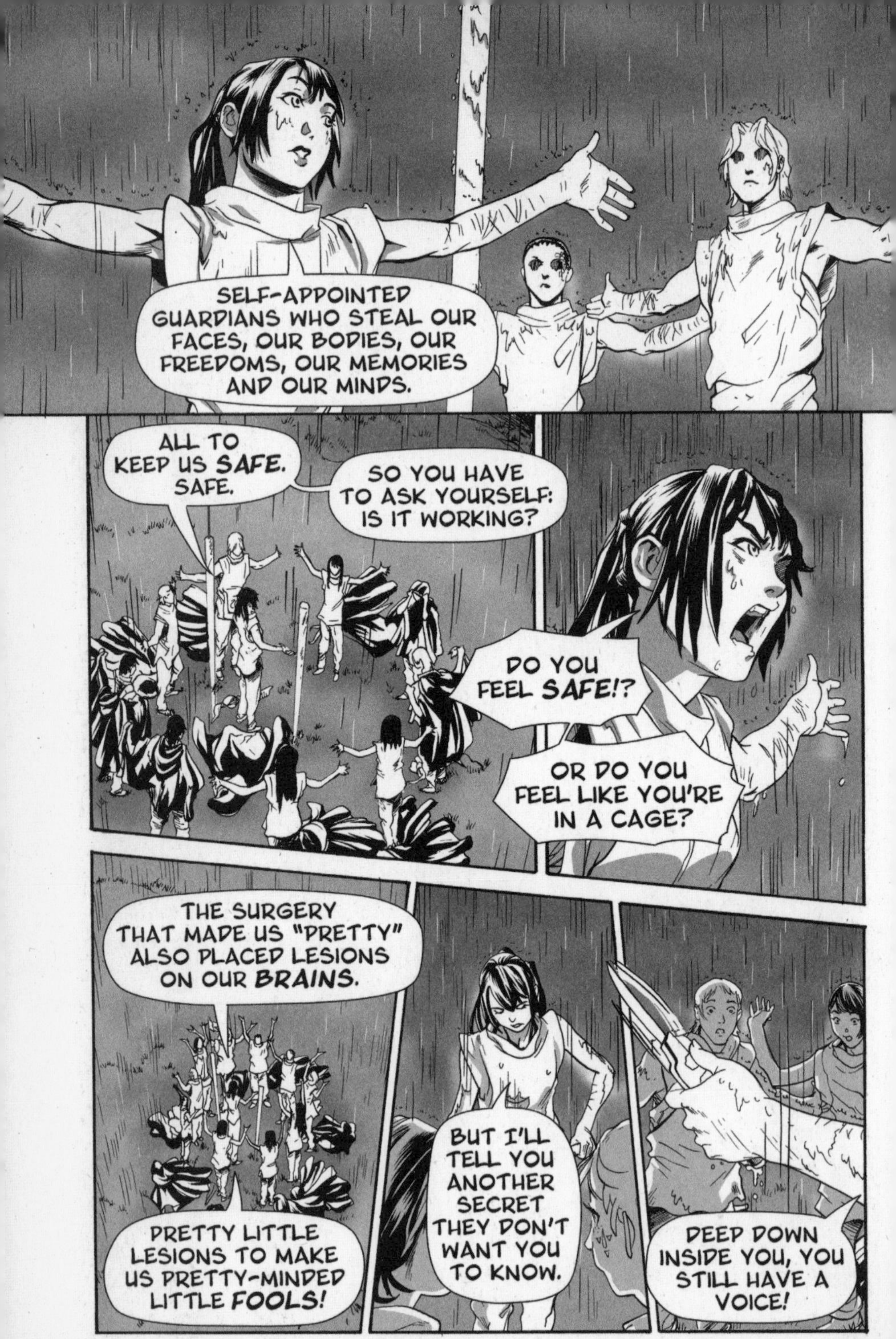
SELF-APPOINTED GUARDIANS WHO STEAL OUR FACES, OUR BODIES, OUR FREEDOMS, OUR MEMORIES AND OUR MINDS.
ALL TO KEEP US SAFE. SAFE.
SO YOU HAVE TO ASK YOURSELF: IS IT WORKING?
DO YOU FEEL SAFE!?
OR DO YOU FEEL LIKE YOU'RE IN A CAGE?
THE SURGERY THAT MADE US "PRETTY" ALSO PLACED LESIONS ON OUR BRAINS.
PRETTY LITTLE LESIONS TO MAKE US PRETTY-MINDED LITTLE FOOLS!
BUT I'LL TELL YOU ANOTHER SECRET THEY DON'T WANT YOU TO KNOW.
DEEP DOWN INSIDE YOU, YOU STILL HAVE A VOICE!

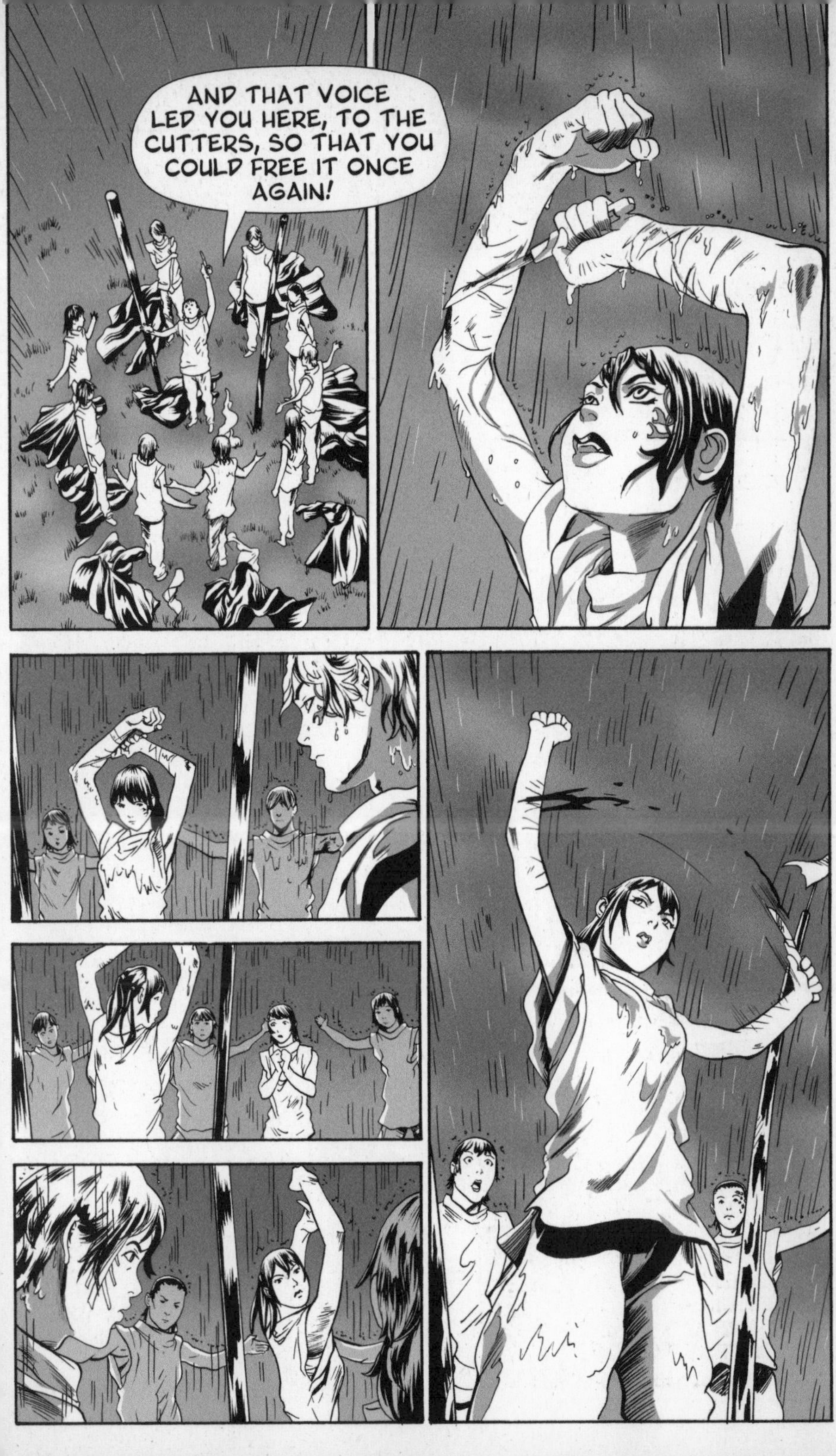
AND THAT VOICE LED YOU HERE, TO THE CUTTERS, SO THAT YOU COULD FREE IT ONCE AGAIN!

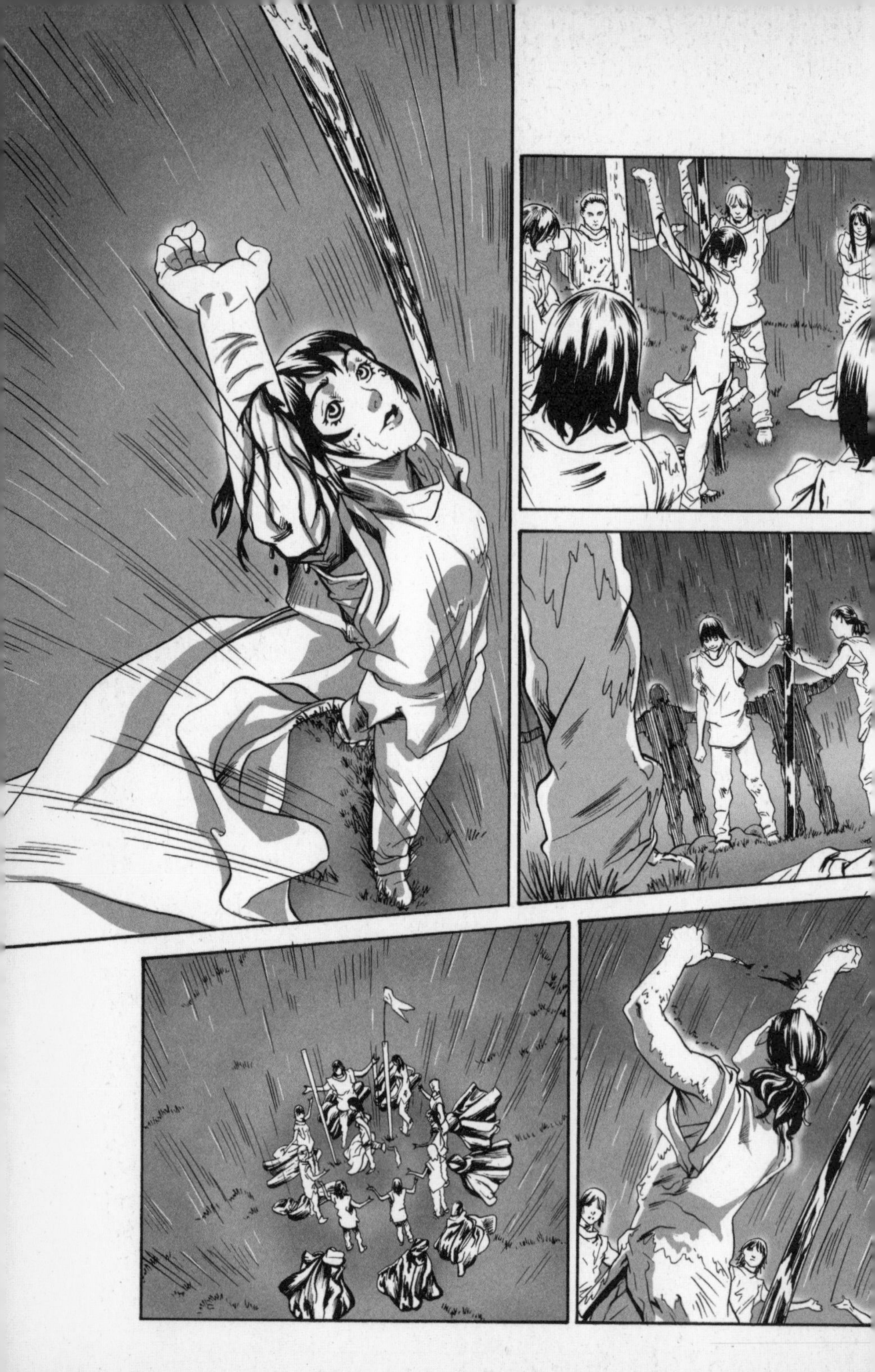

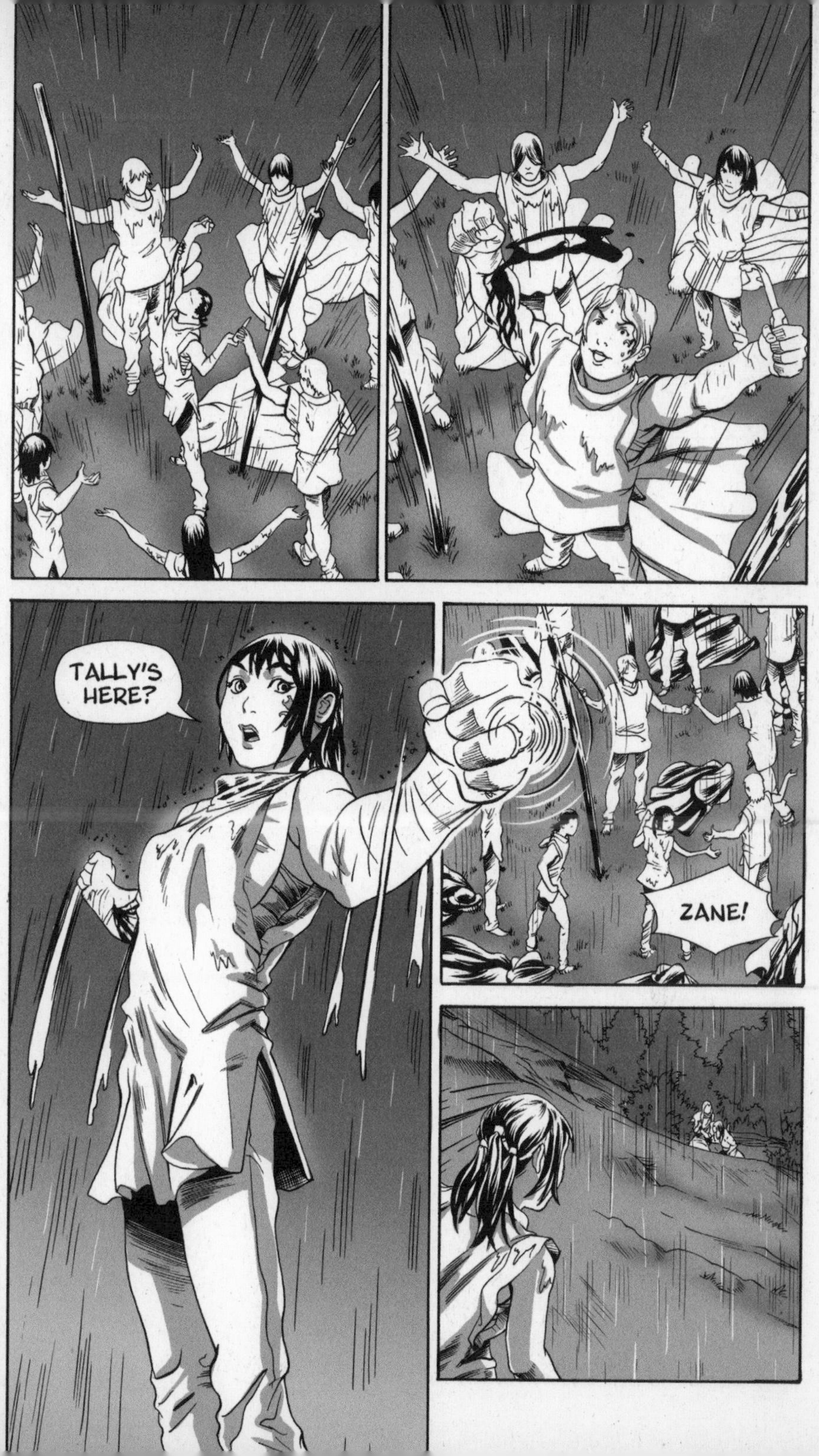
TALLY'S HERE?
ZANE!

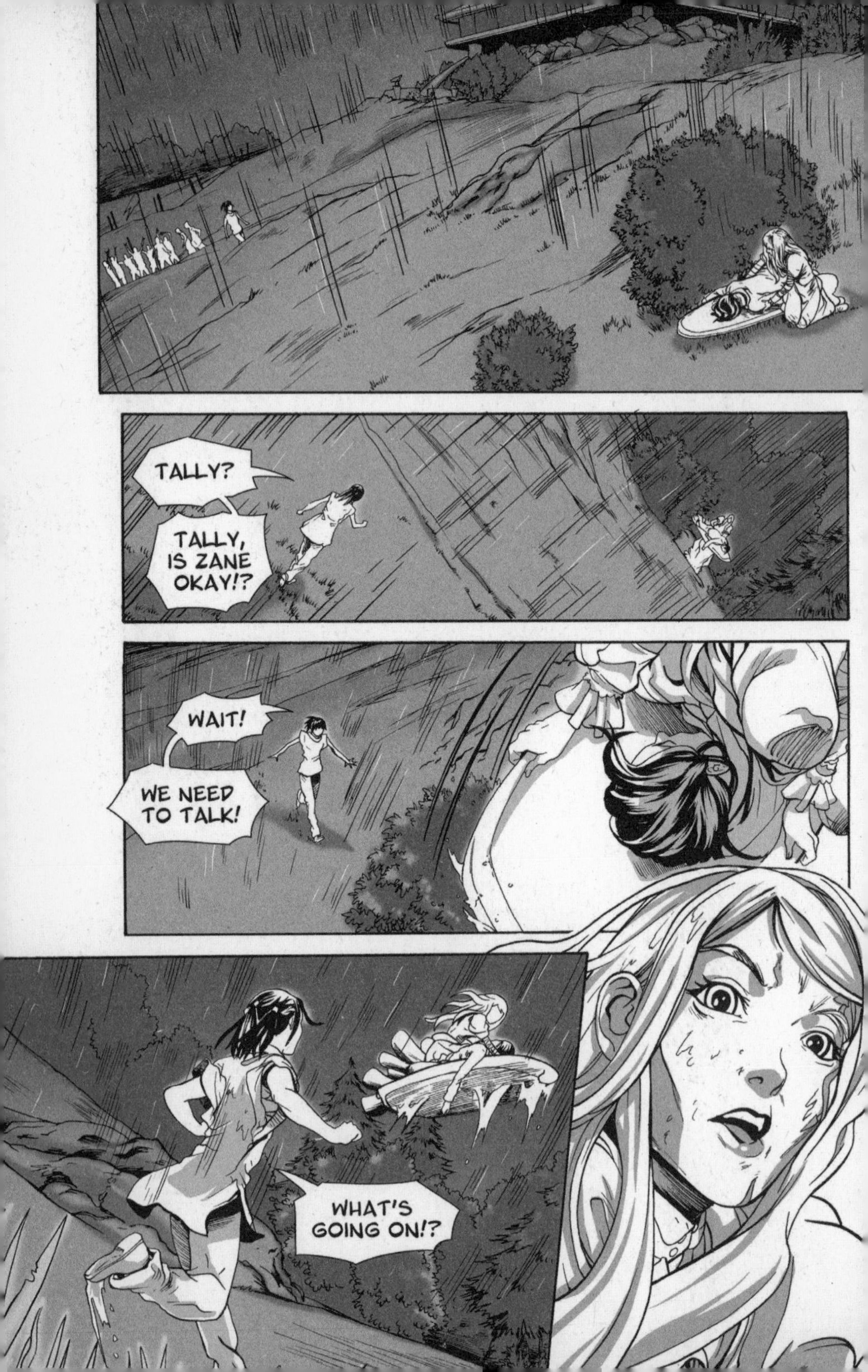
TALLY?
TALLY, IS ZANE OKAY!?
WAIT!
WE NEED TO TALK!
WHAT'S GOING ON!?

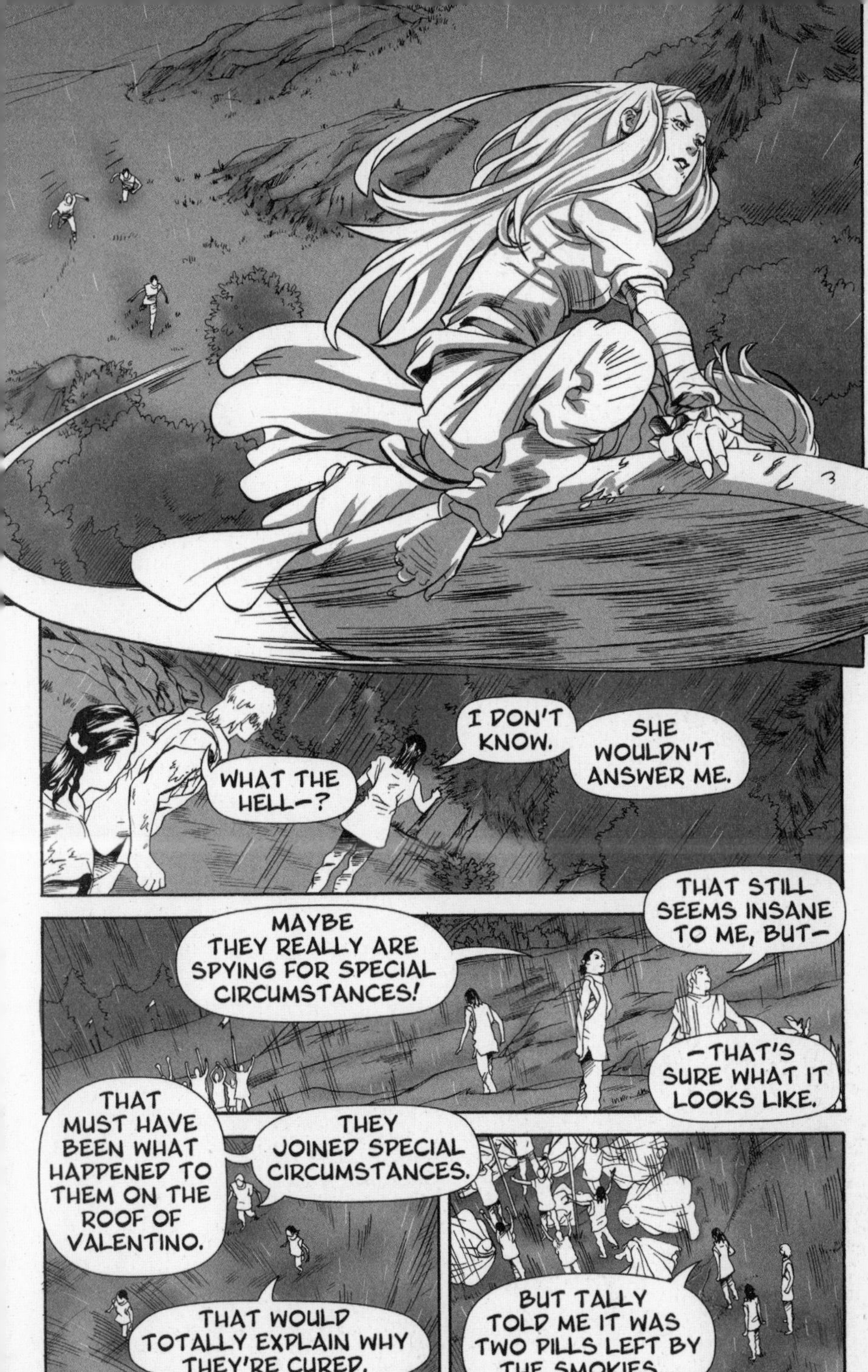
WHAT THE HELL-?
I DON'T KNOW.
SHE WOULDN'T ANSWER ME.
MAYBE THEY REALLY ARE SPYING FOR SPECIAL CIRCUMSTANCES!
THAT STILL SEEMS INSANE TO ME, BUT-
-THAT'S SURE WHAT IT LOOKS LIKE.
THAT MUST HAVE BEEN WHAT HAPPENED TO THEM ON THE ROOF OF VALENTINO.
THEY JOINED SPECIAL CIRCUMSTANCES.
THAT WOULD TOTALLY EXPLAIN WHY THEY'RE CURED.
BUT TALLY TOLD ME IT WAS TWO PILLS LEFT BY THE SMOKIES...

THAT DOESN'T MAKE ANY SENSE.

WHY WOULD THERE BE ONLY *TWO* PILLS?

AND WHY WOULD YOU BELIEVE *ANYTHING* THAT LITTLE TRAITOR SAYS?

YOU'RE RIGHT.

DR. CABLE OFFERED ME A DEAL. WHAT IF SHE OFFERED ONE TO TALLY, TOO?

ZANE AND TALLY COULD BE HEADED STRAIGHT TO DR. CABLE TO TELL HER EVERYTHING THEY JUST SAW.

WE HAVE TO DO SOMETHING...

CUTTERS... OUR ENEMIES KNOW WE HAVE A CURE.

WE HAVE TO LEAVE THE CITY.

NOW.

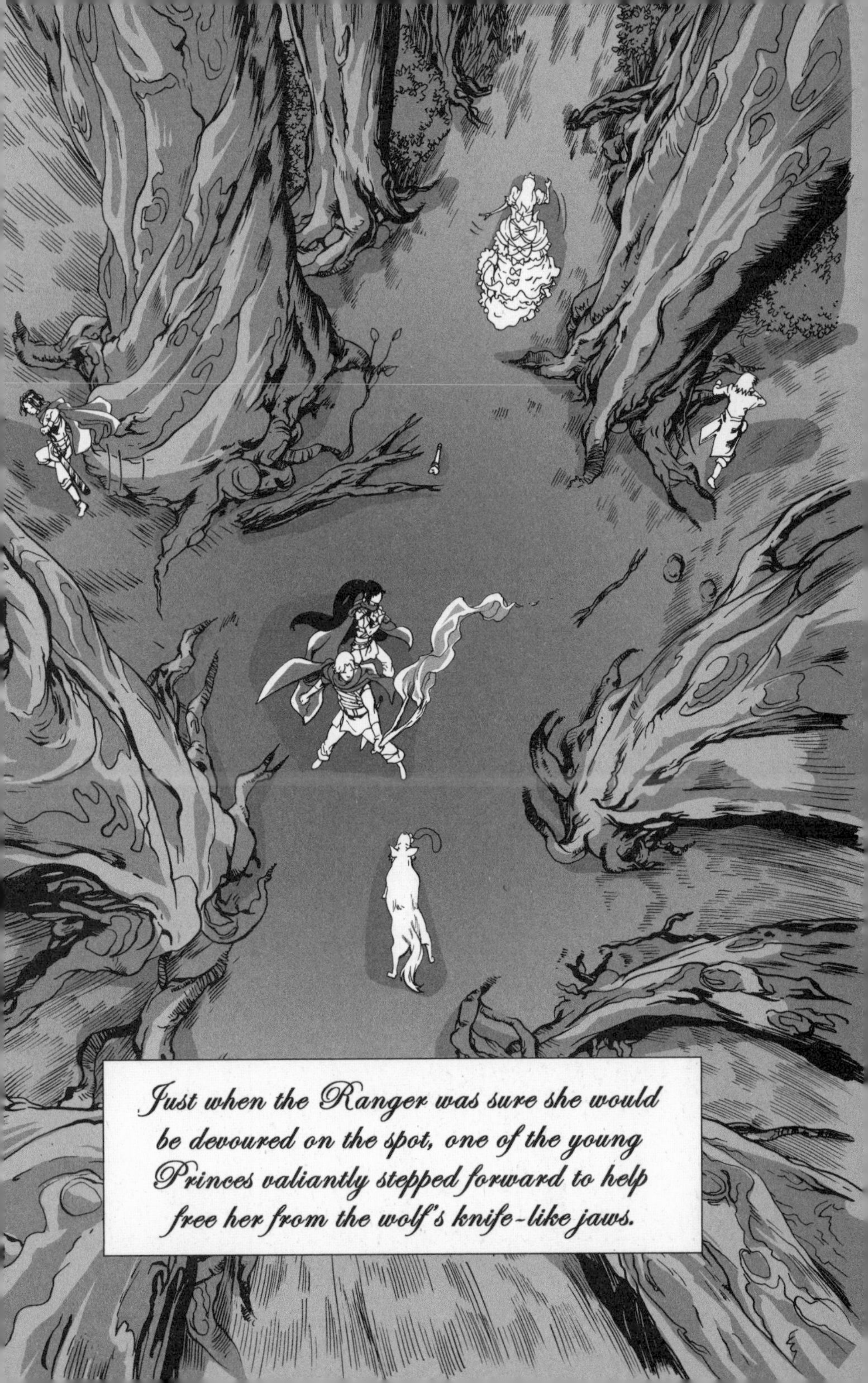
Just when the Ranger was sure she would be devoured on the spot, one of the young Princes valiantly stepped forward to help free her from the wolf's knife-like jaws.

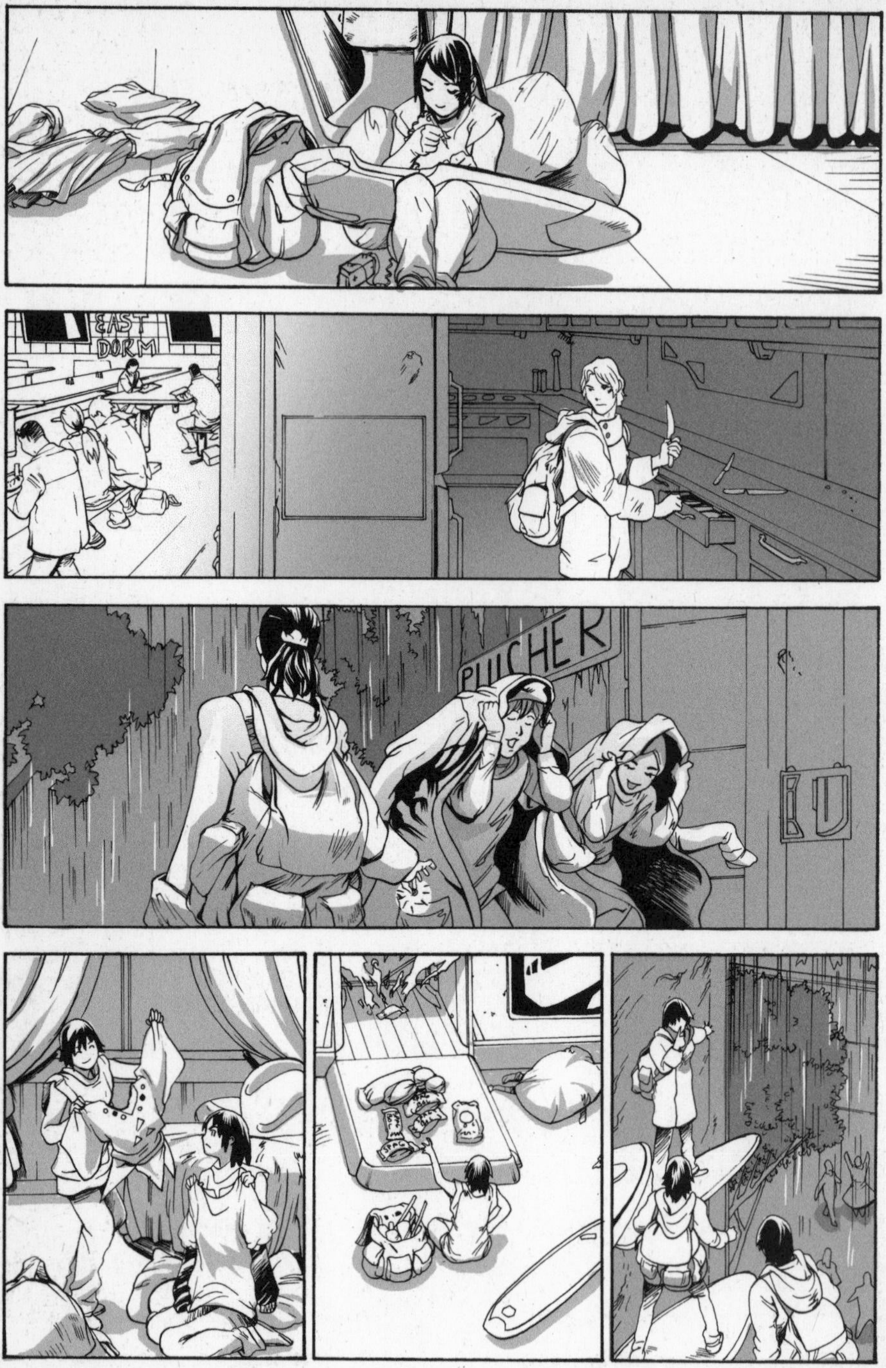
EAST DORM
PULCHER

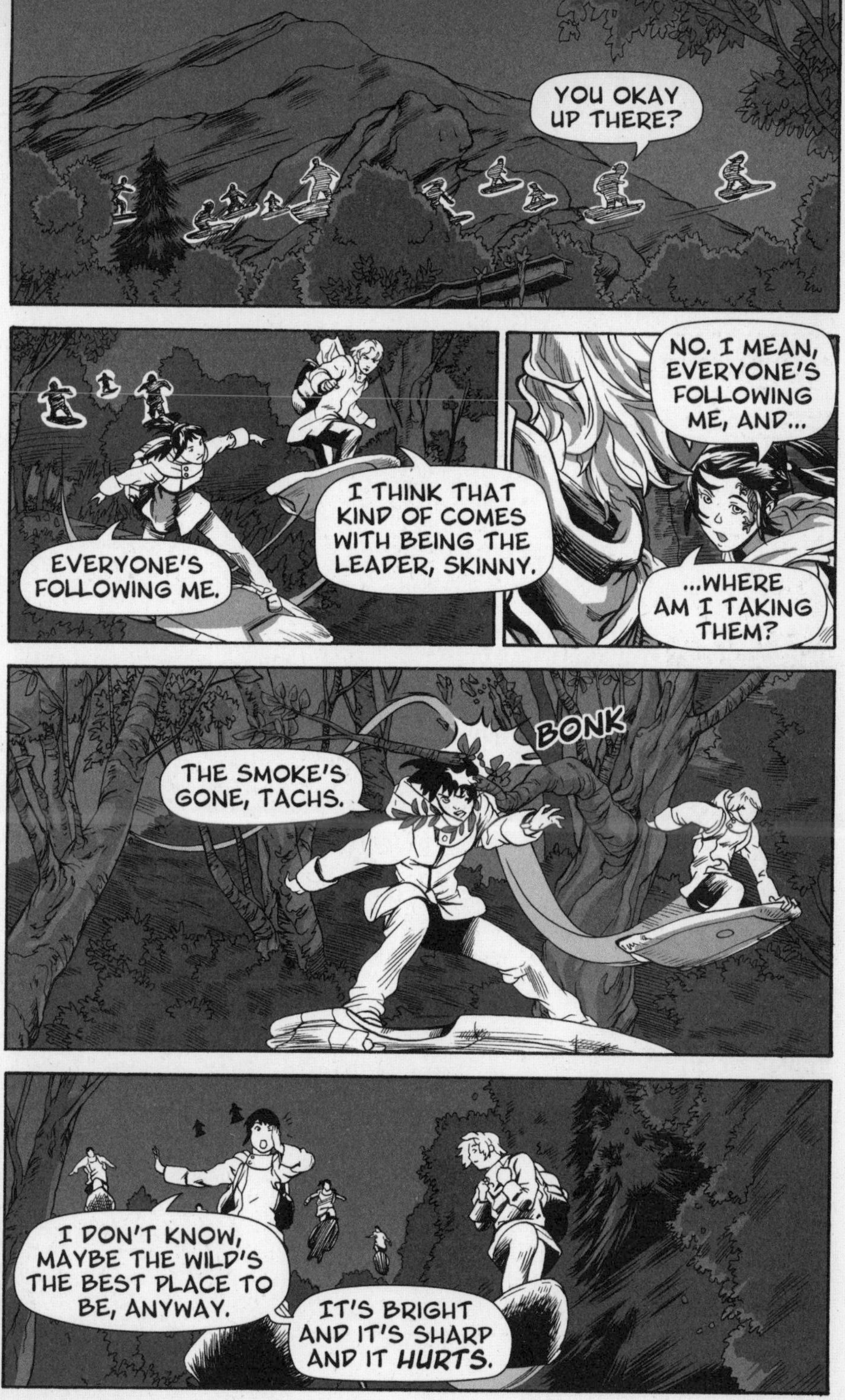
YOU OKAY UP THERE?
EVERYONE'S FOLLOWING ME.
I THINK THAT KIND OF COMES WITH BEING THE LEADER, SKINNY.
NO. I MEAN, EVERYONE'S FOLLOWING ME, AND...
...WHERE AM I TAKING THEM?
BONK
THE SMOKE'S GONE, TACHS.
I DON'T KNOW, MAYBE THE WILD'S THE BEST PLACE TO BE, ANYWAY.
IT'S BRIGHT AND IT'S SHARP AND IT HURTS.

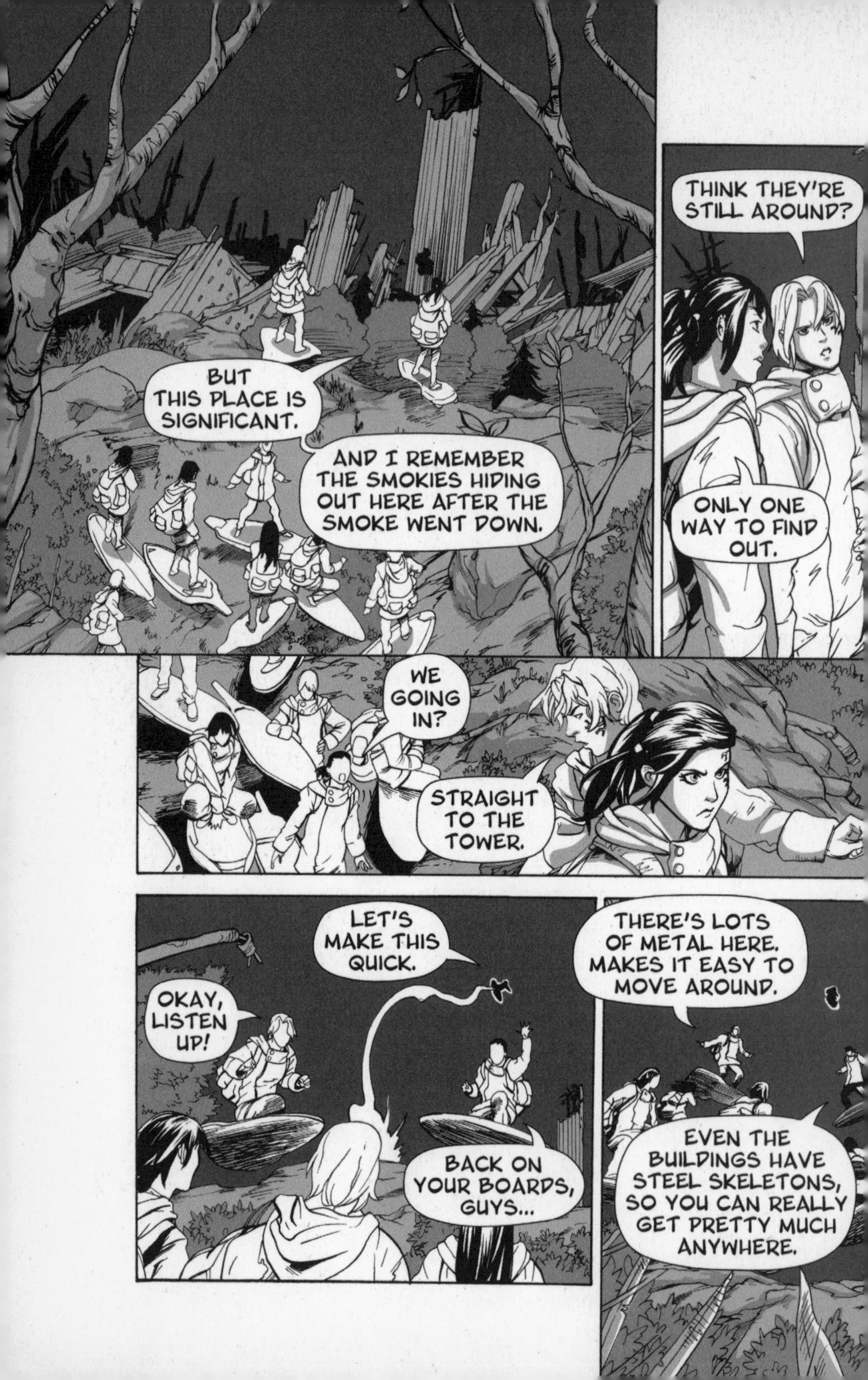
BUT THIS PLACE IS SIGNIFICANT.
AND I REMEMBER THE SMOKIES HIDING OUT HERE AFTER THE SMOKE WENT DOWN.
THINK THEY'RE STILL AROUND?
ONLY ONE WAY TO FIND OUT.
WE GOING IN?
STRAIGHT TO THE TOWER.
LET'S MAKE THIS QUICK.
OKAY, LISTEN UP!
BACK ON YOUR BOARDS, GUYS...
THERE'S LOTS OF METAL HERE. MAKES IT EASY TO MOVE AROUND.
EVEN THE BUILDINGS HAVE STEEL SKELETONS, SO YOU CAN REALLY GET PRETTY MUCH ANYWHERE.

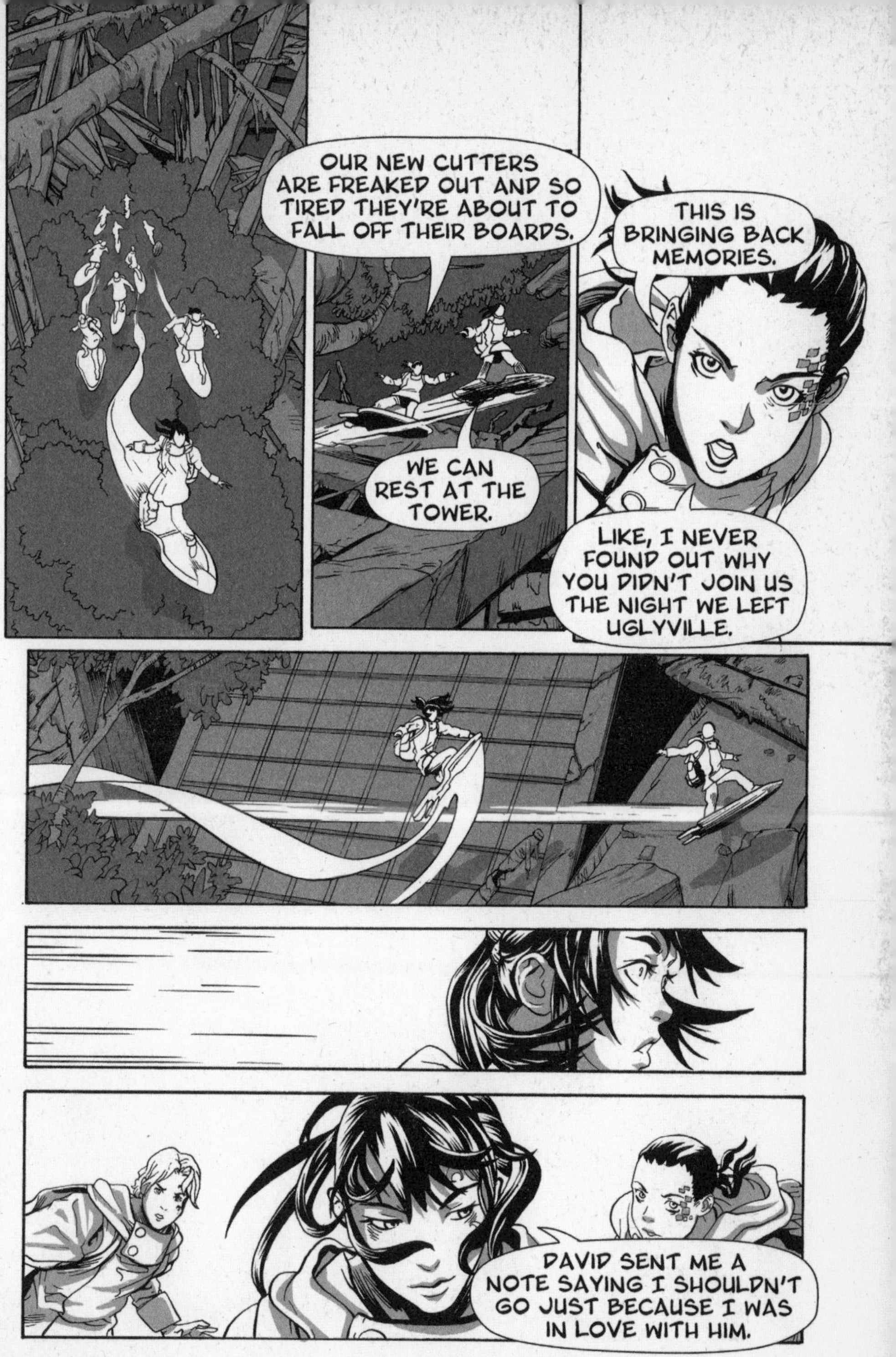
OUR NEW CUTTERS ARE FREAKED OUT AND SO TIRED THEY'RE ABOUT TO FALL OFF THEIR BOARDS.
WE CAN REST AT THE TOWER.
THIS IS BRINGING BACK MEMORIES.
LIKE, I NEVER FOUND OUT WHY YOU DIDN'T JOIN US THE NIGHT WE LEFT UGLYVILLE.
DAVID SENT ME A NOTE SAYING I SHOULDN'T GO JUST BECAUSE I WAS IN LOVE WITH HIM.

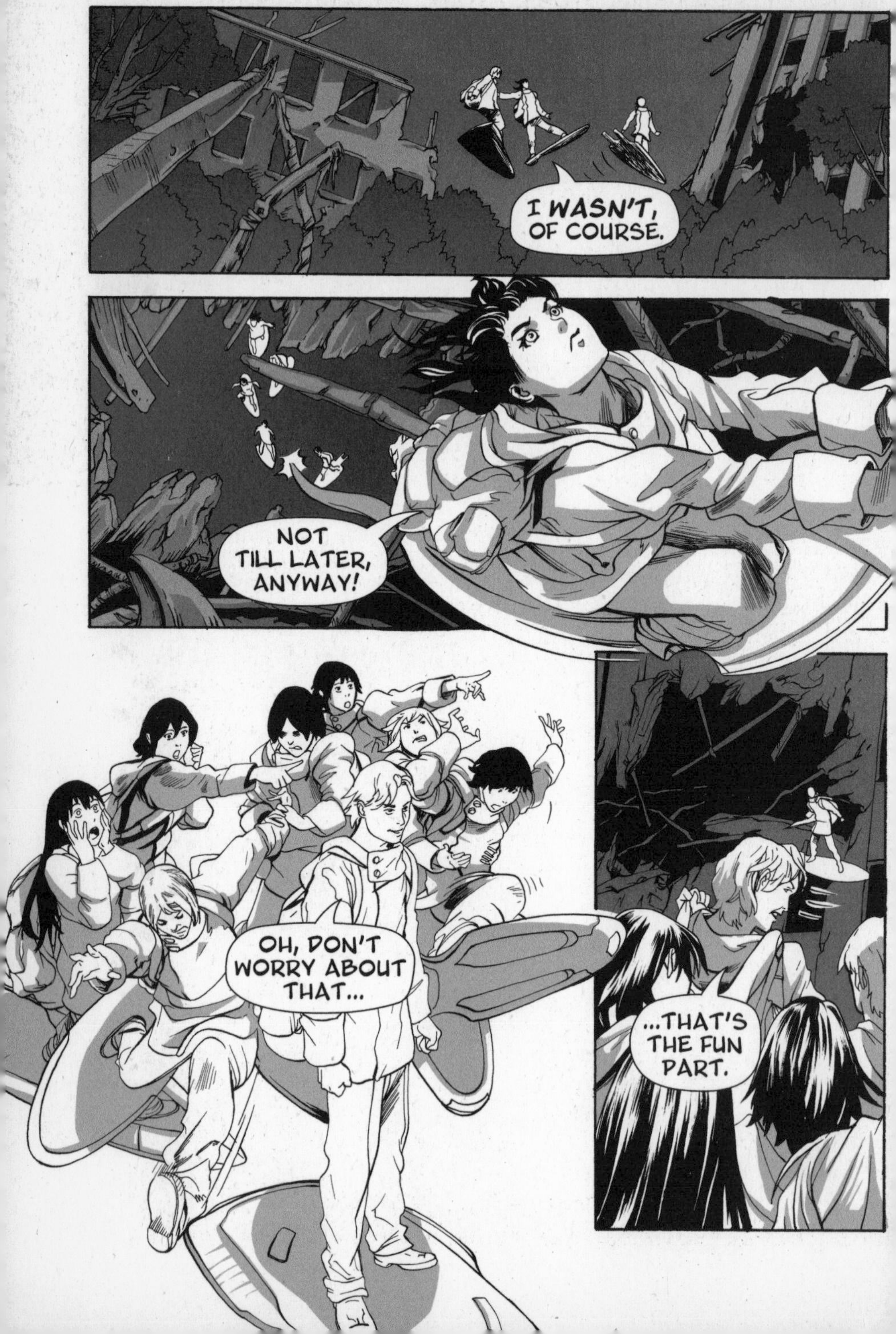
I WASN'T, OF COURSE.
NOT TILL LATER, ANYWAY!
OH, DON'T WORRY ABOUT THAT...
...THAT'S THE FUN PART.

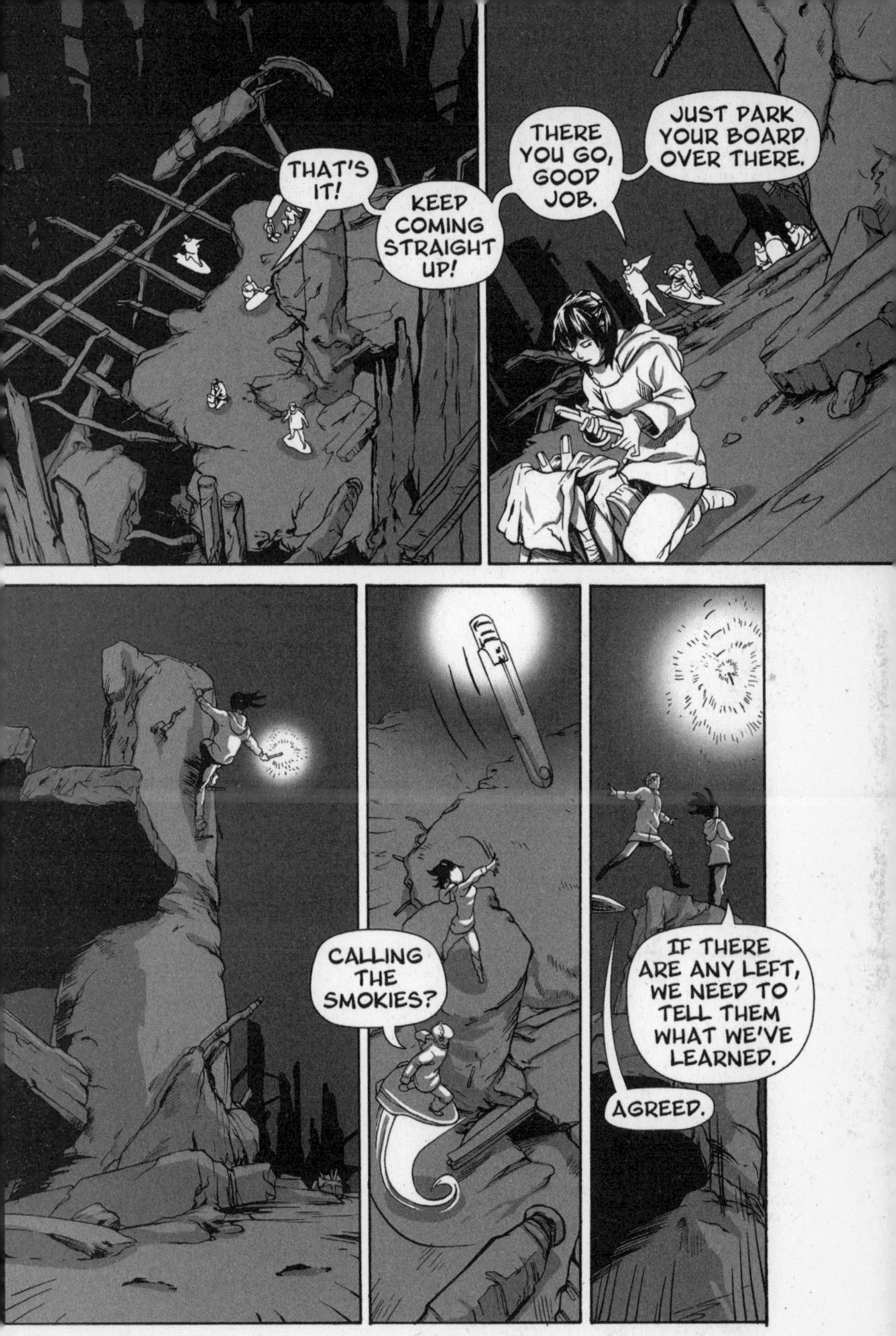
THAT'S IT!
KEEP COMING STRAIGHT UP!
THERE YOU GO, GOOD JOB.
JUST PARK YOUR BOARD OVER THERE.
CALLING THE SMOKIES?
IF THERE ARE ANY LEFT, WE NEED TO TELL THEM WHAT WE'VE LEARNED.
AGREED.

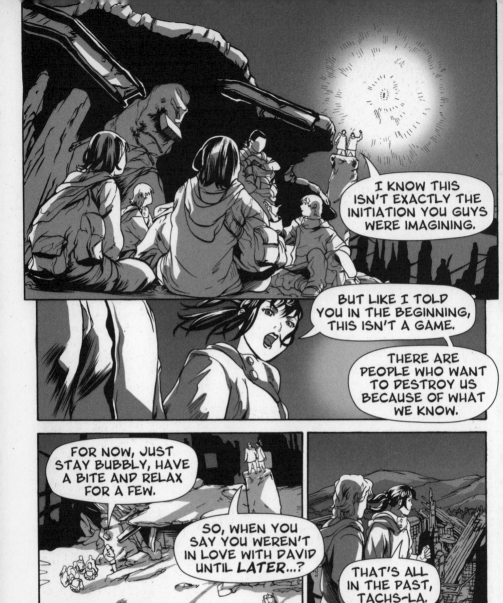

I KNOW THIS ISN'T EXACTLY THE INITIATION YOU GUYS WERE IMAGINING.

BUT LIKE I TOLD YOU IN THE BEGINNING, THIS ISN'T A GAME.

THERE ARE PEOPLE WHO WANT TO DESTROY US BECAUSE OF WHAT WE KNOW.

FOR NOW, JUST STAY BUBBLY, HAVE A BITE AND RELAX FOR A FEW.

SO, WHEN YOU SAY YOU WEREN'T IN LOVE WITH DAVID UNTIL *LATER*...?

THAT'S ALL IN THE PAST, TACHS-LA.

YOU HAVE NOTHING TO WORRY ABOUT.

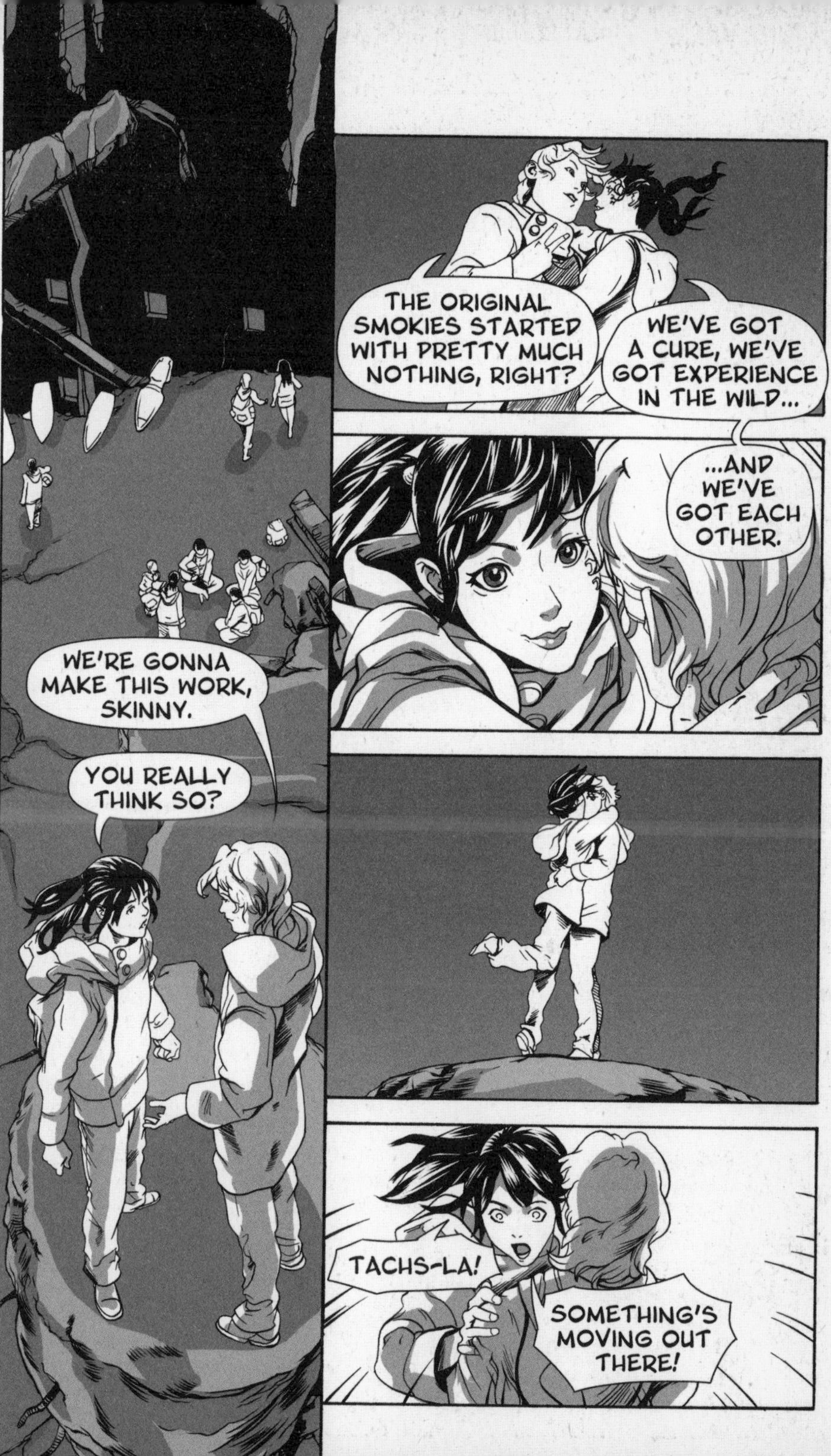
WE'RE GONNA MAKE THIS WORK, SKINNY.
YOU REALLY THINK SO?
THE ORIGINAL SMOKIES STARTED WITH PRETTY MUCH NOTHING, RIGHT?
WE'VE GOT A CURE, WE'VE GOT EXPERIENCE IN THE WILD...
...AND WE'VE GOT EACH OTHER.
TACHS-LA!
SOMETHING'S MOVING OUT THERE!

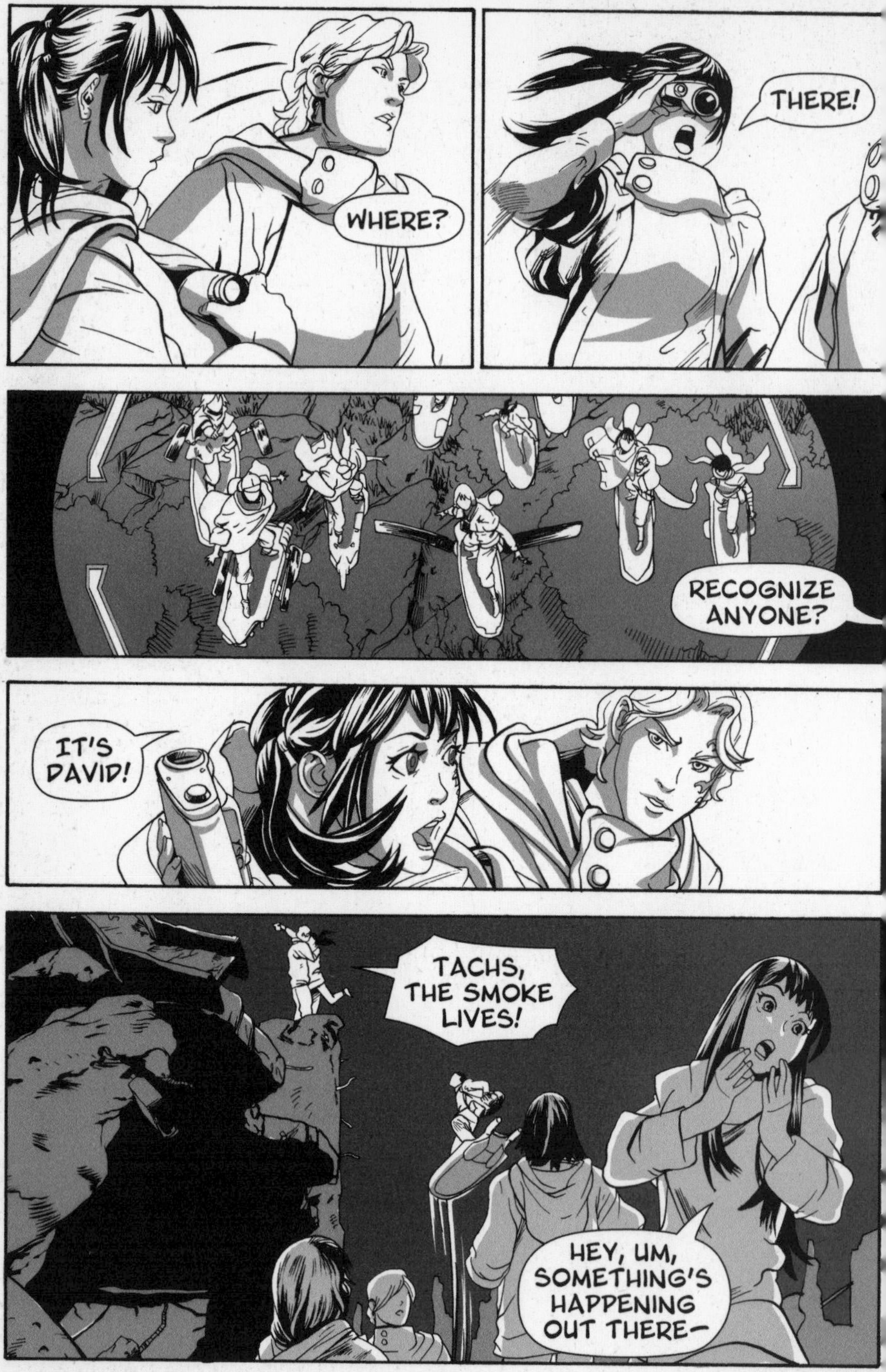
WHERE?
THERE!
RECOGNIZE ANYONE?
IT'S DAVID!
TACHS, THE SMOKE LIVES!
HEY, UM, SOMETHING'S HAPPENING OUT THERE—

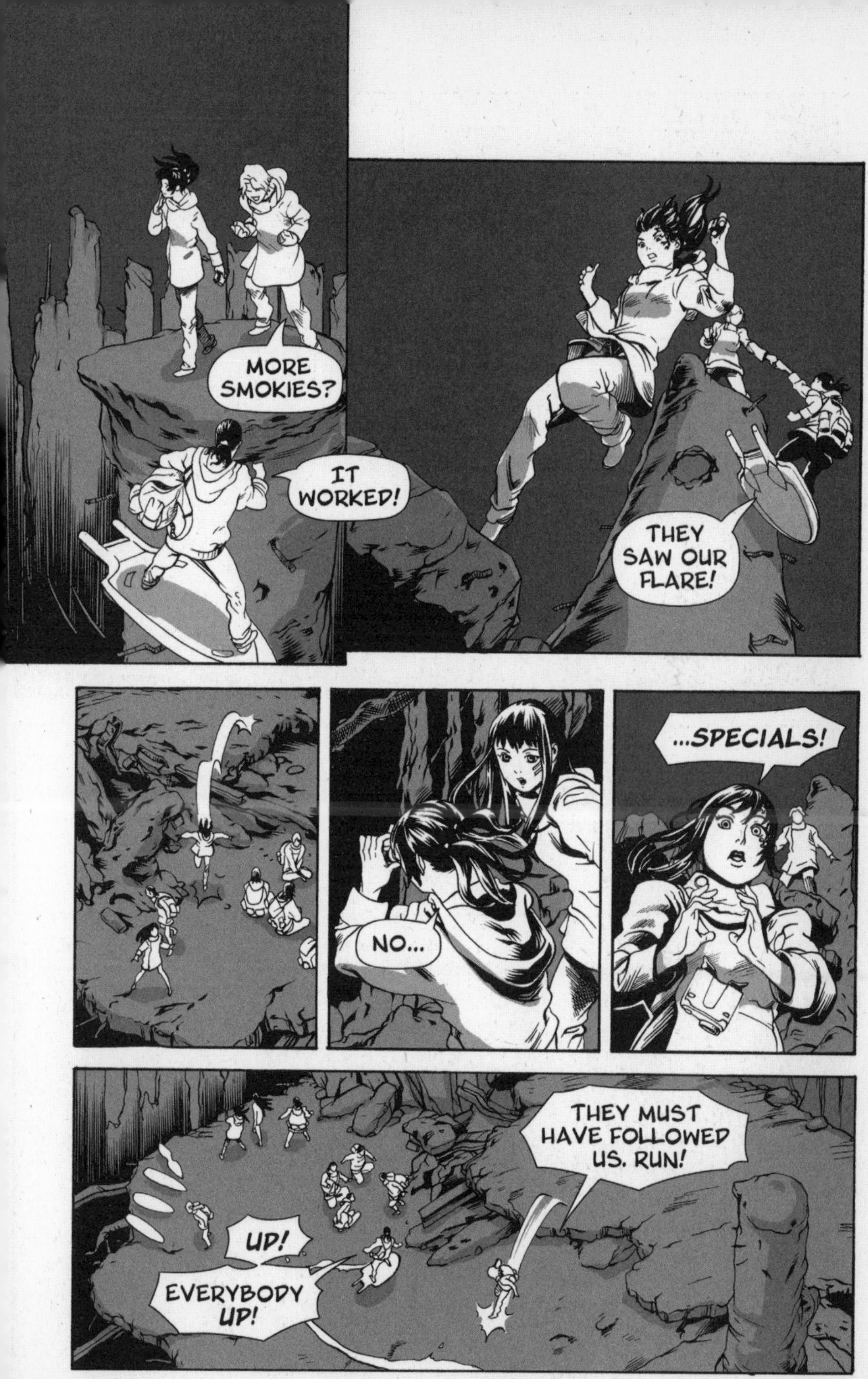
MORE SMOKIES?
IT WORKED!
THEY SAW OUR FLARE!
NO...
...SPECIALS!
THEY MUST HAVE FOLLOWED US. RUN!
UP!
EVERYBODY UP!

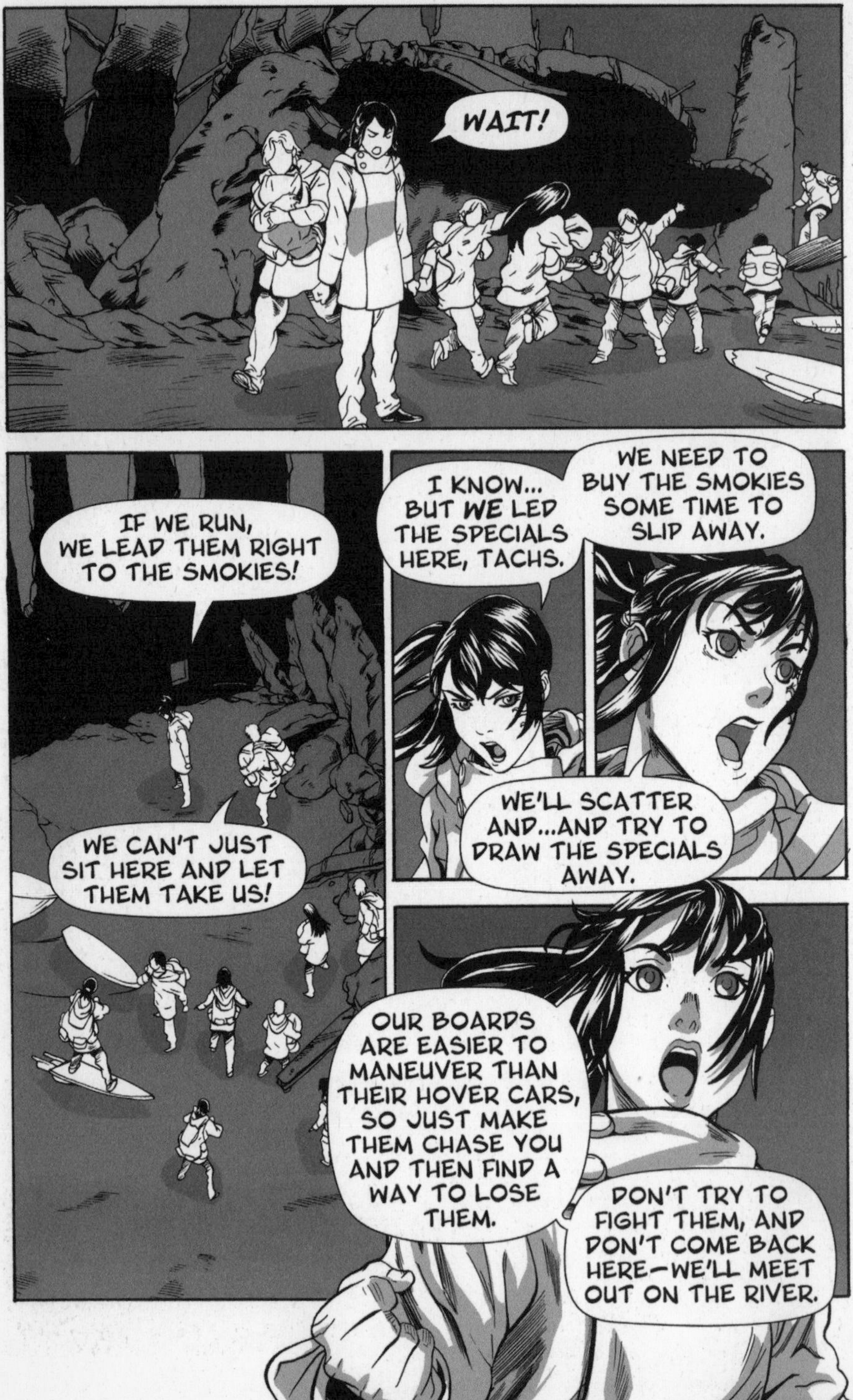
WAIT!
IF WE RUN, WE LEAD THEM RIGHT TO THE SMOKIES!
WE CAN'T JUST SIT HERE AND LET THEM TAKE US!
I KNOW... BUT WE LED THE SPECIALS HERE, TACHS.
WE NEED TO BUY THE SMOKIES SOME TIME TO SLIP AWAY.
WE'LL SCATTER AND...AND TRY TO DRAW THE SPECIALS AWAY.
OUR BOARDS ARE EASIER TO MANEUVER THAN THEIR HOVER CARS, SO JUST MAKE THEM CHASE YOU AND THEN FIND A WAY TO LOSE THEM.
DON'T TRY TO FIGHT THEM, AND DON'T COME BACK HERE—WE'LL MEET OUT ON THE RIVER.

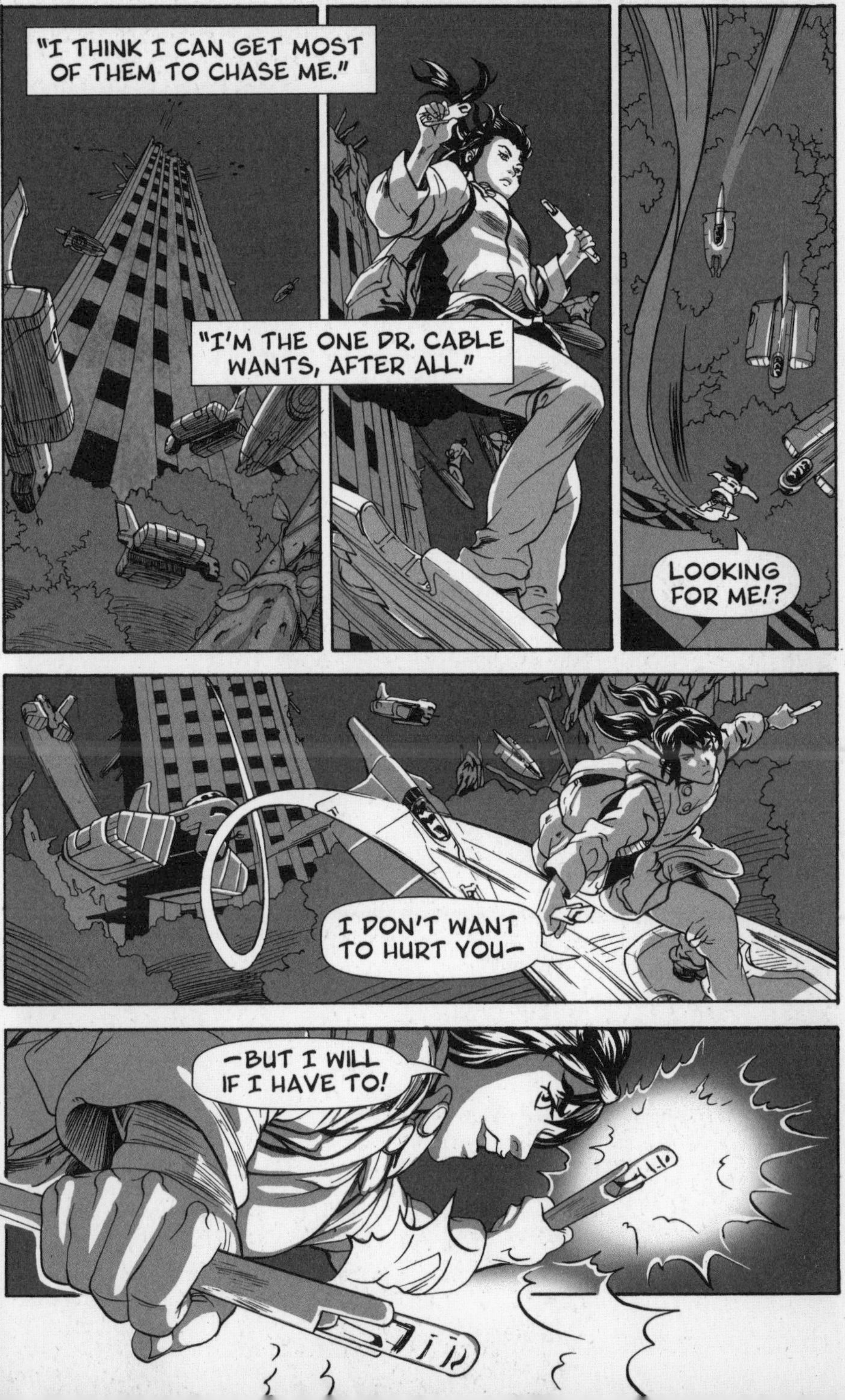
"I THINK I CAN GET MOST OF THEM TO CHASE ME."
"I'M THE ONE DR. CABLE WANTS, AFTER ALL."
LOOKING FOR ME!?
I DON'T WANT TO HURT YOU—
—BUT I WILL IF I HAVE TO!

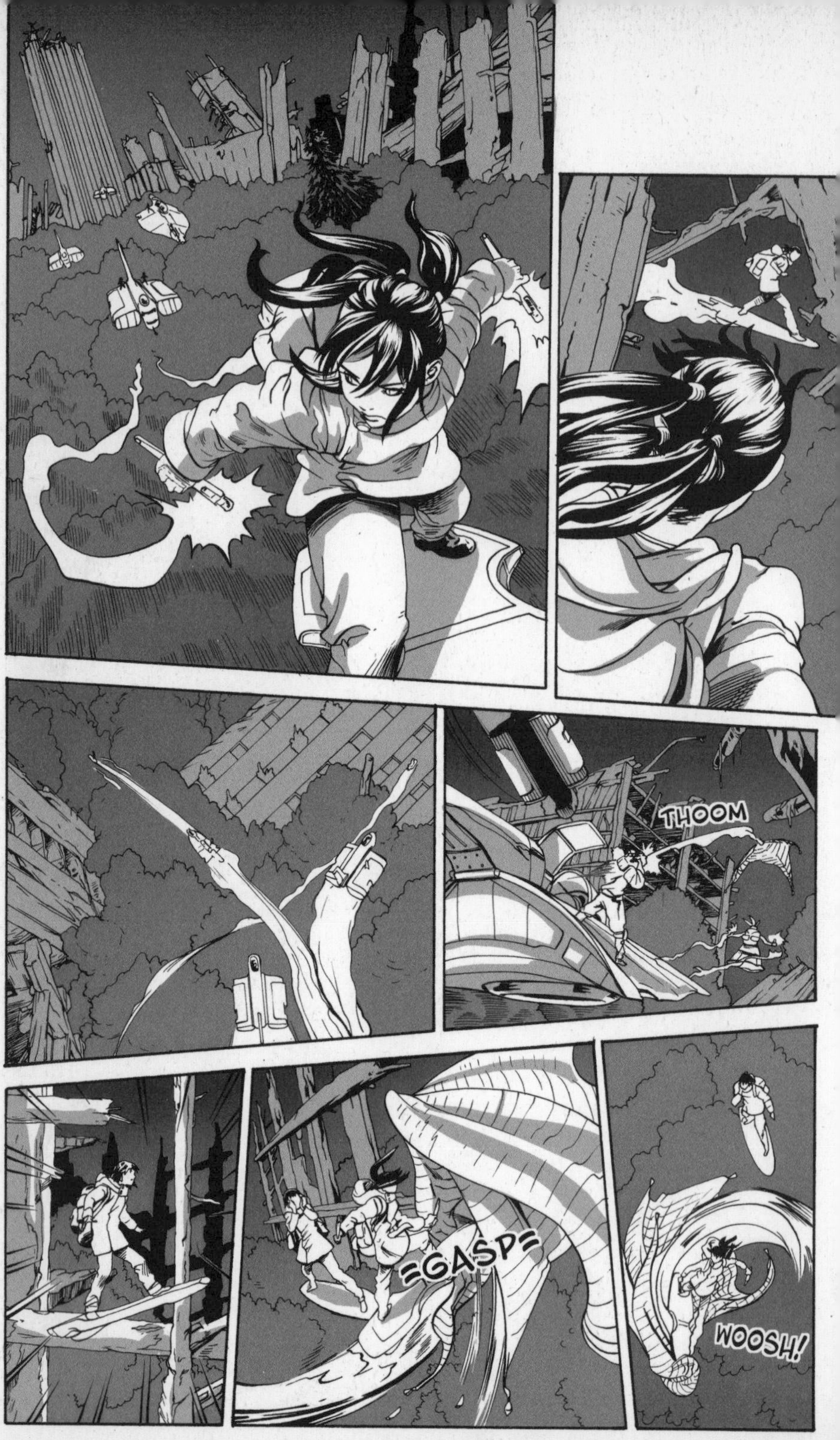
THOOM
=GASP=
WOOSH!

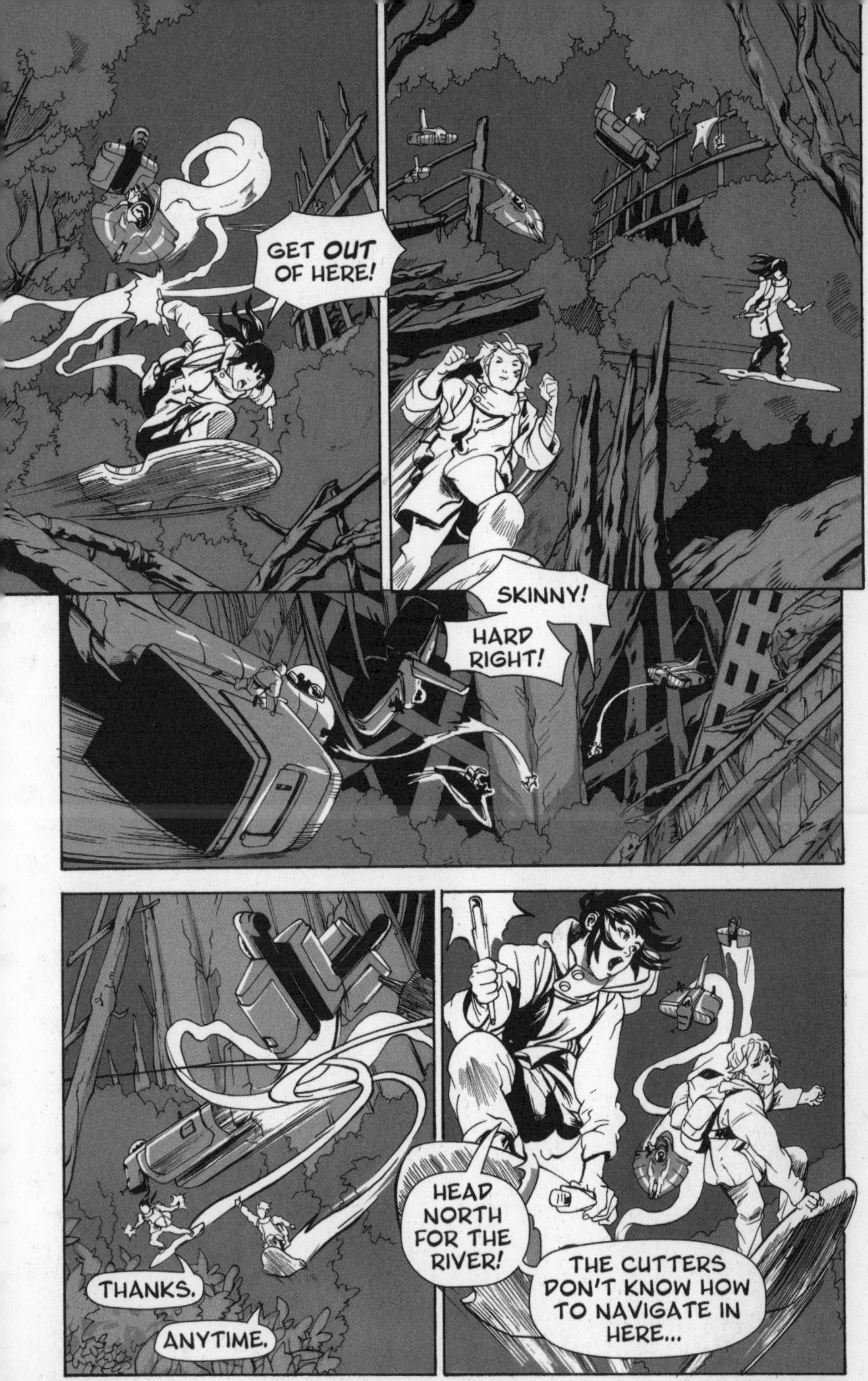
GET OUT OF HERE!
SKINNY!
HARD RIGHT!
THANKS.
ANYTIME.
HEAD NORTH FOR THE RIVER!
THE CUTTERS DON'T KNOW HOW TO NAVIGATE IN HERE...

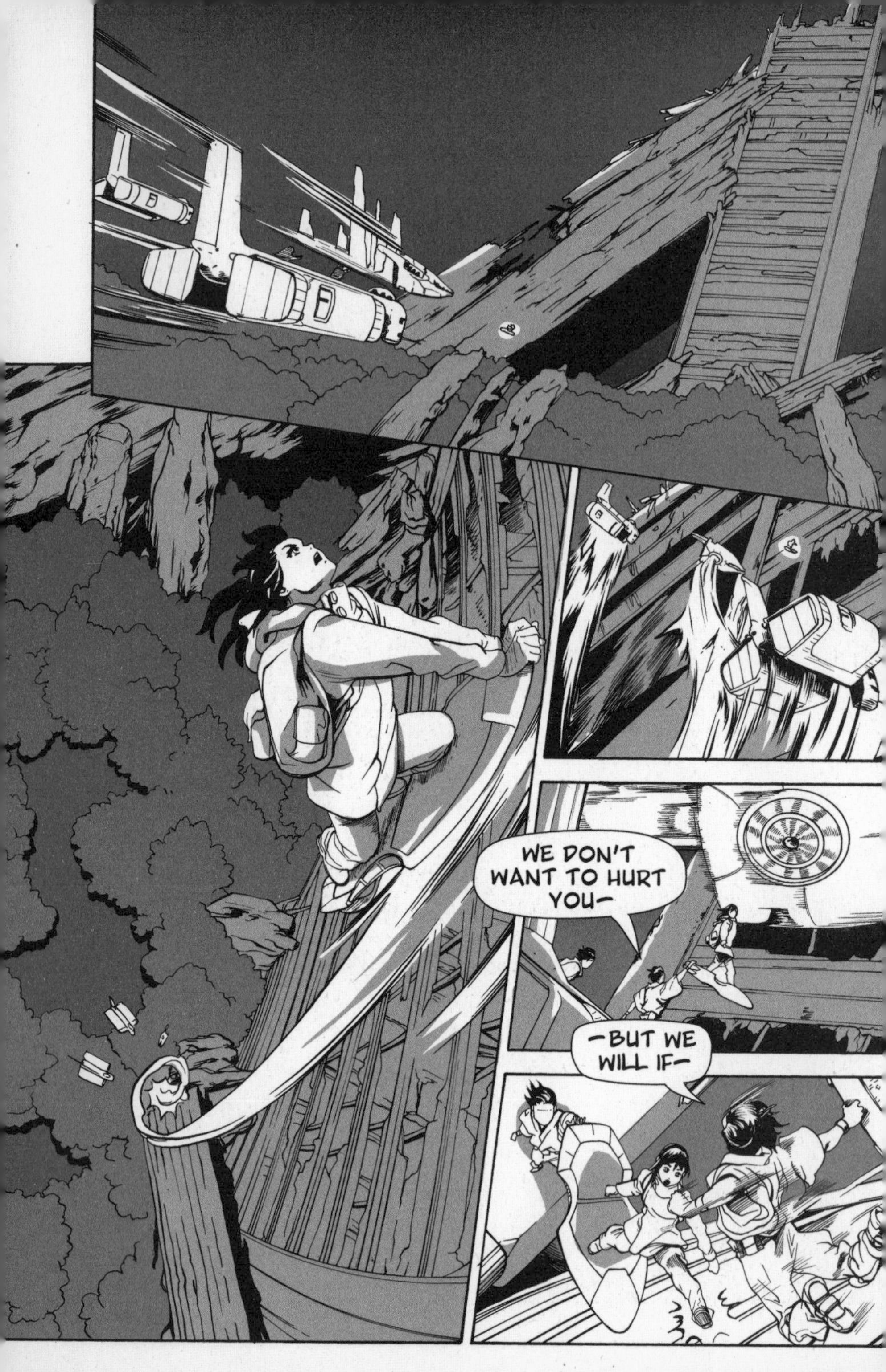
WE DON'T WANT TO HURT YOU–
–BUT WE WILL IF–

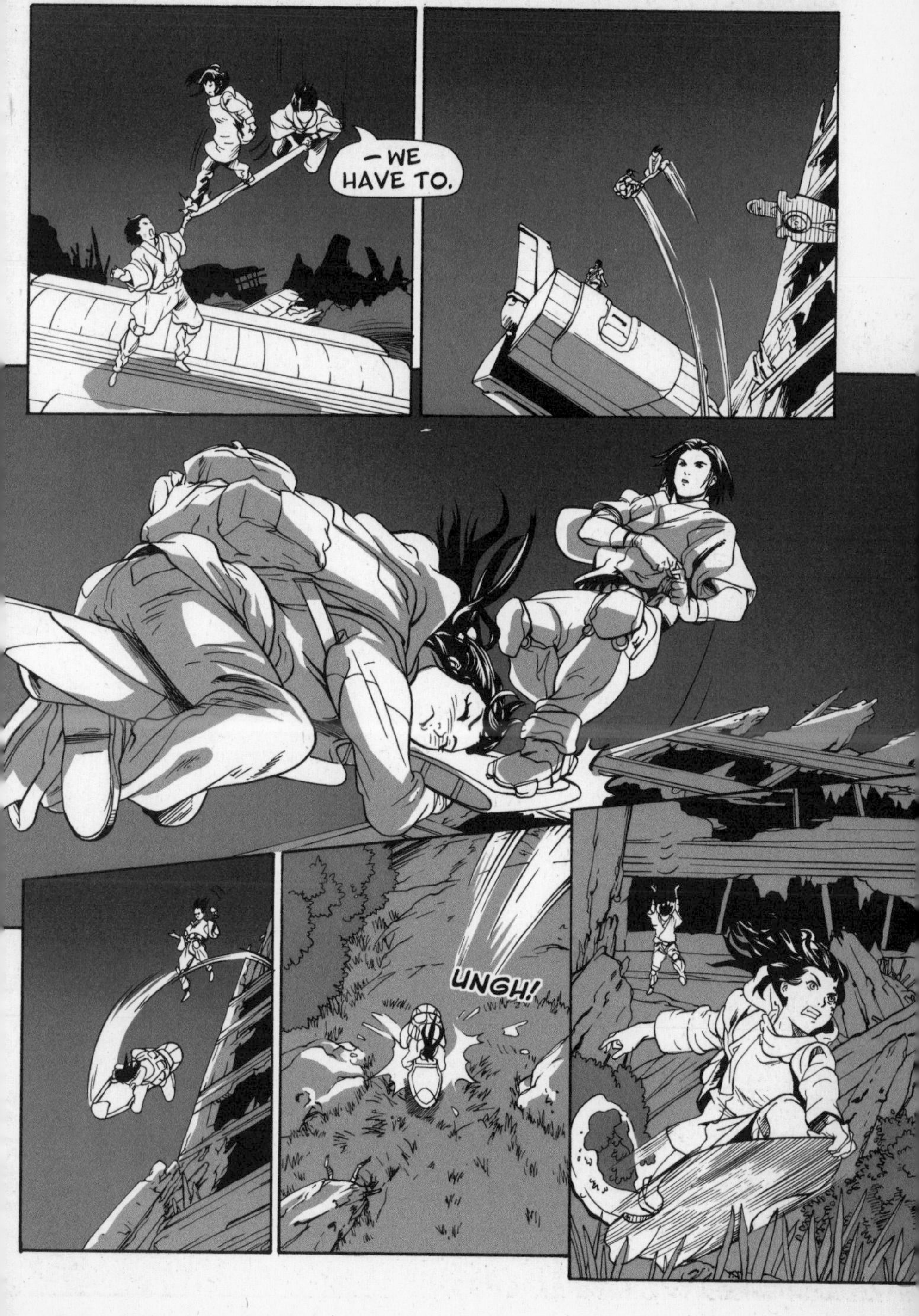
—WE HAVE TO.
UNGH!

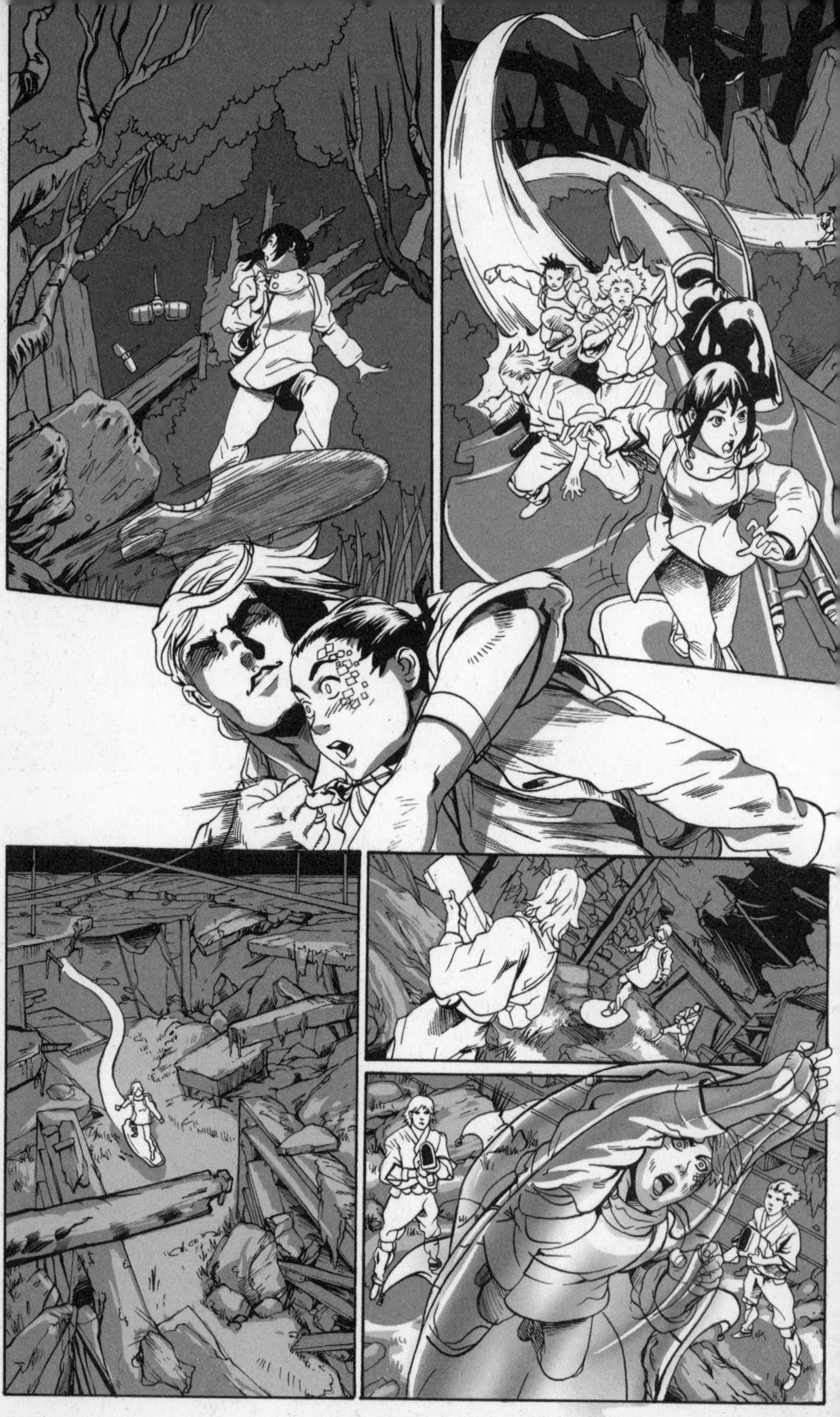

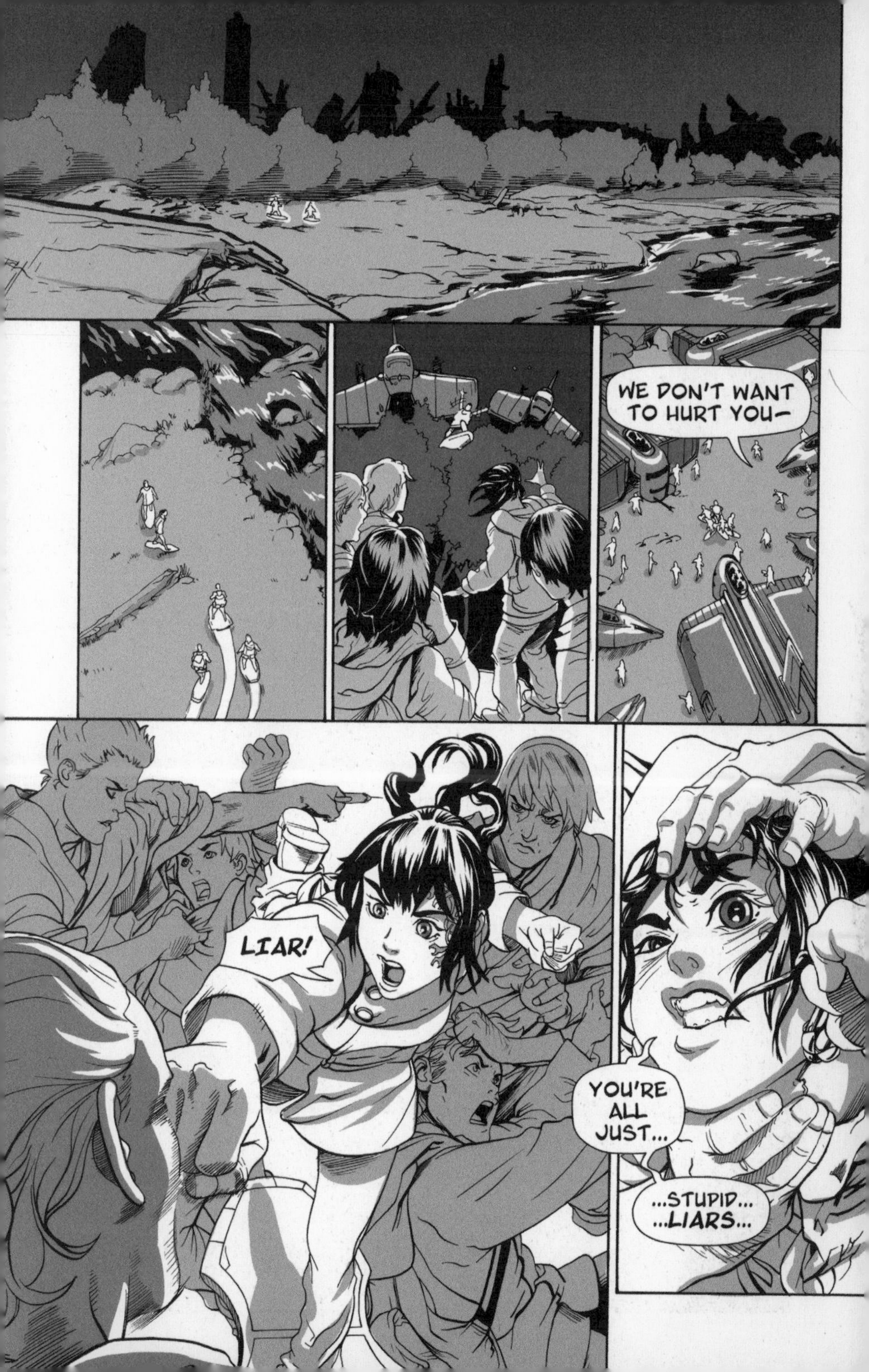
WE DON'T WANT TO HURT YOU—
LIAR!
YOU'RE ALL JUST...
...STUPID... ...LIARS...

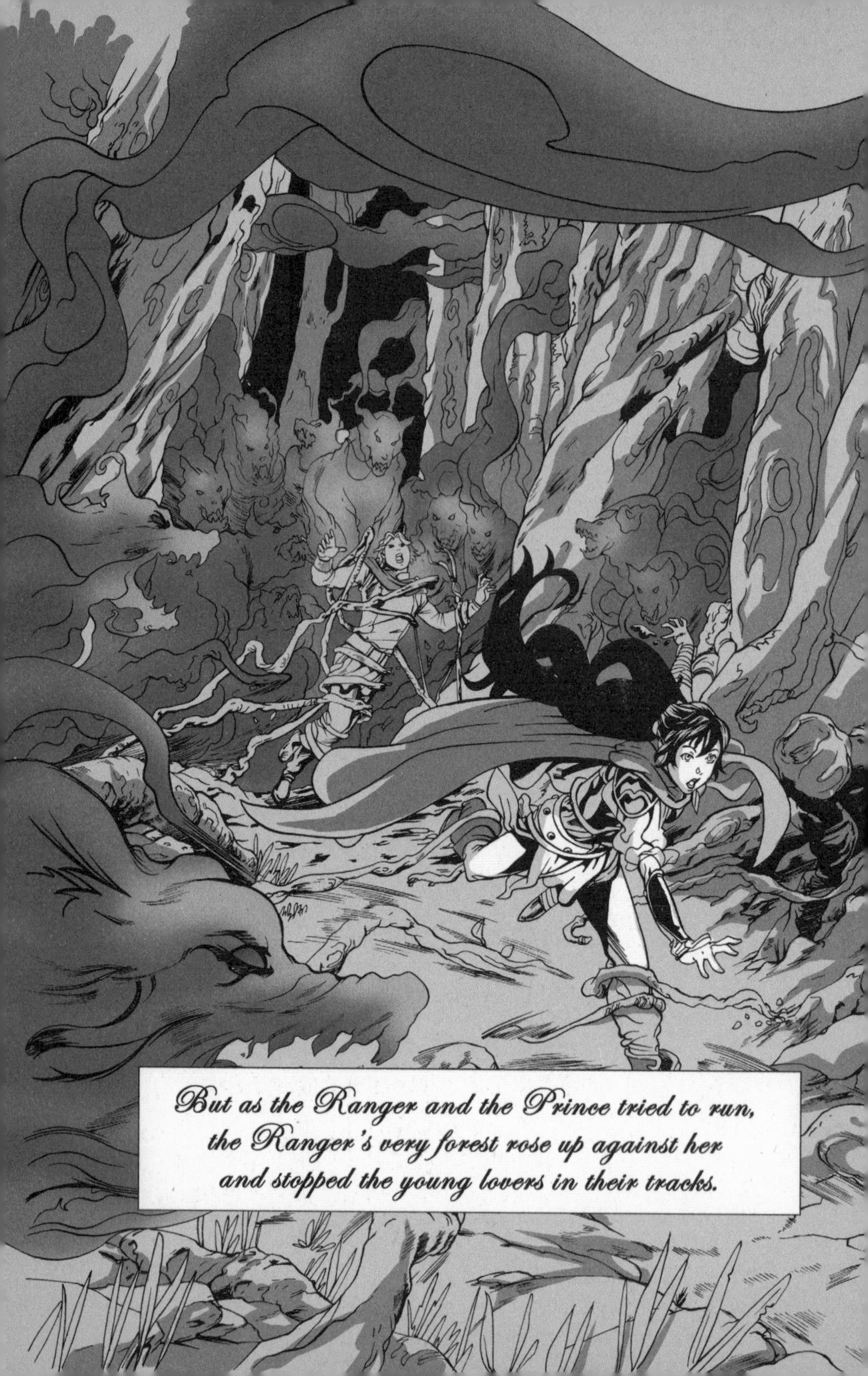
But as the Ranger and the Prince tried to run, the Ranger's very forest rose up against her and stopped the young lovers in their tracks.

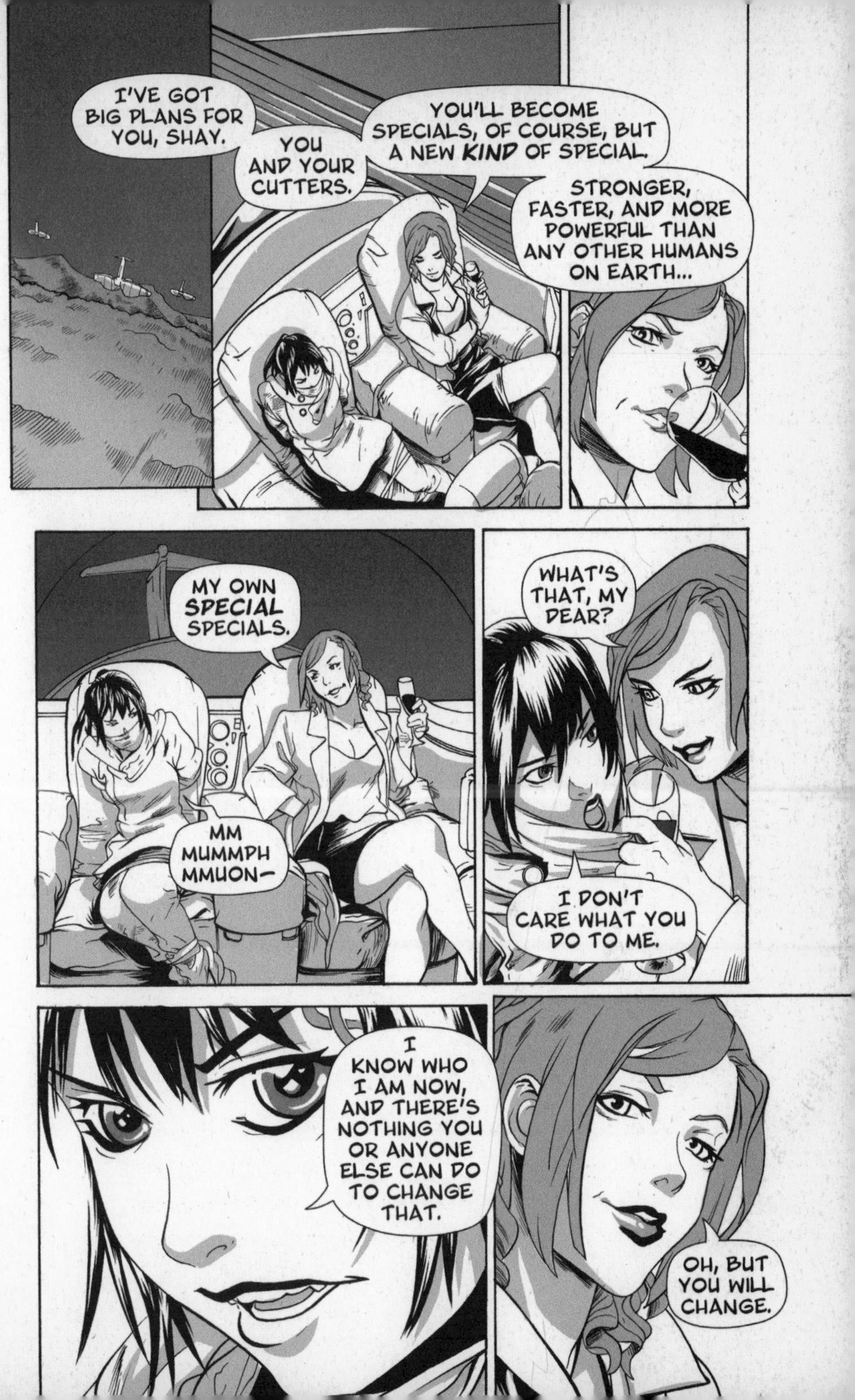

I'VE GOT BIG PLANS FOR YOU, SHAY.
YOU AND YOUR CUTTERS.
YOU'LL BECOME SPECIALS, OF COURSE, BUT A NEW *KIND* OF SPECIAL.
STRONGER, FASTER, AND MORE POWERFUL THAN ANY OTHER HUMANS ON EARTH...
MY OWN *SPECIAL* SPECIALS.
MM MUMMPH MMUON–
WHAT'S THAT, MY DEAR?
I DON'T CARE WHAT YOU DO TO ME.
I KNOW WHO I AM NOW, AND THERE'S NOTHING YOU OR ANYONE ELSE CAN DO TO CHANGE THAT.
OH, BUT YOU WILL CHANGE.

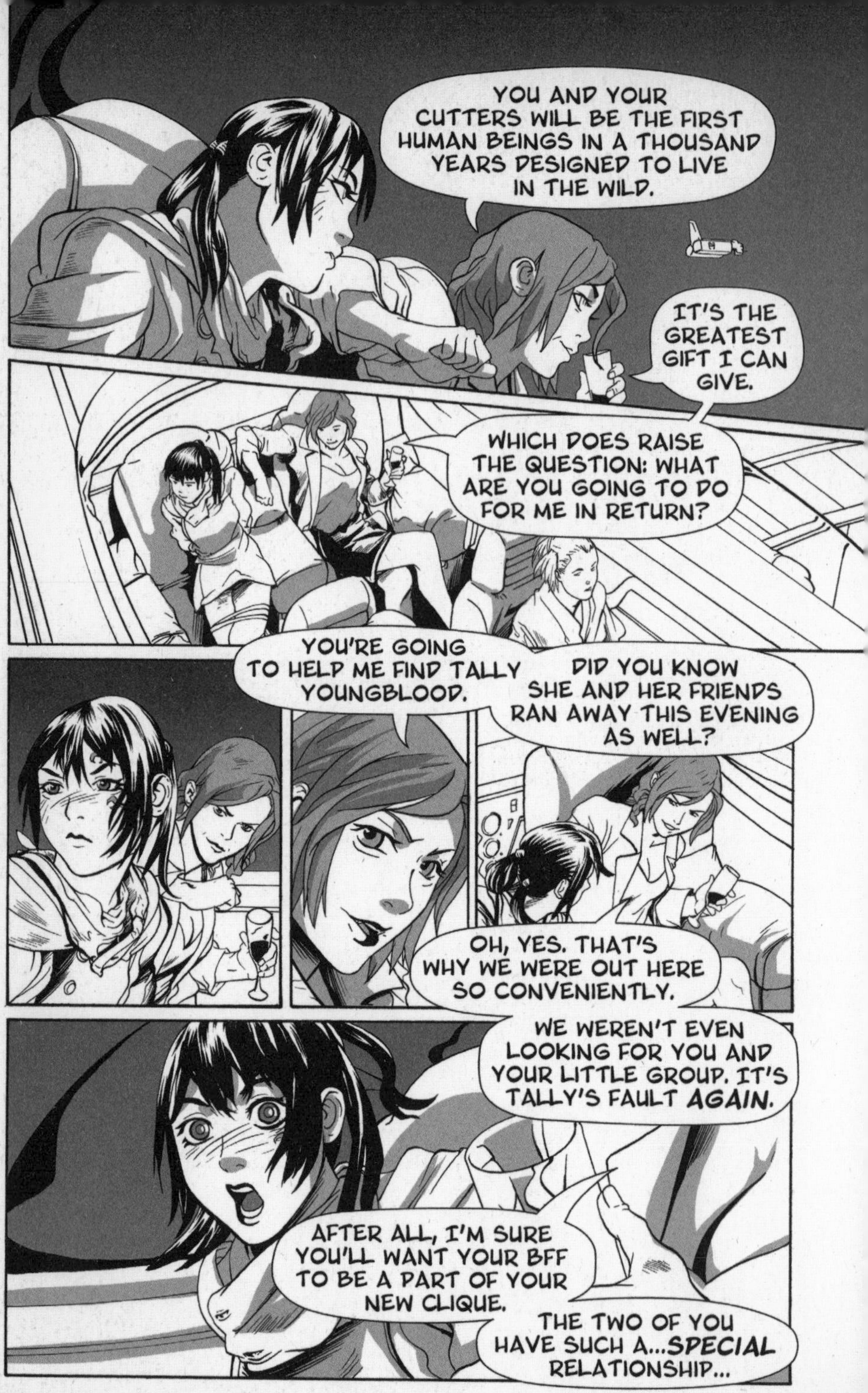

YOU AND YOUR CUTTERS WILL BE THE FIRST HUMAN BEINGS IN A THOUSAND YEARS DESIGNED TO LIVE IN THE WILD.
IT'S THE GREATEST GIFT I CAN GIVE.
WHICH DOES RAISE THE QUESTION: WHAT ARE YOU GOING TO DO FOR ME IN RETURN?
YOU'RE GOING TO HELP ME FIND TALLY YOUNGBLOOD.
DID YOU KNOW SHE AND HER FRIENDS RAN AWAY THIS EVENING AS WELL?
OH, YES. THAT'S WHY WE WERE OUT HERE SO CONVENIENTLY.
WE WEREN'T EVEN LOOKING FOR YOU AND YOUR LITTLE GROUP. IT'S TALLY'S FAULT **AGAIN**.
AFTER ALL, I'M SURE YOU'LL WANT YOUR BFF TO BE A PART OF YOUR NEW CLIQUE.
THE TWO OF YOU HAVE SUCH A...*SPECIAL* RELATIONSHIP...

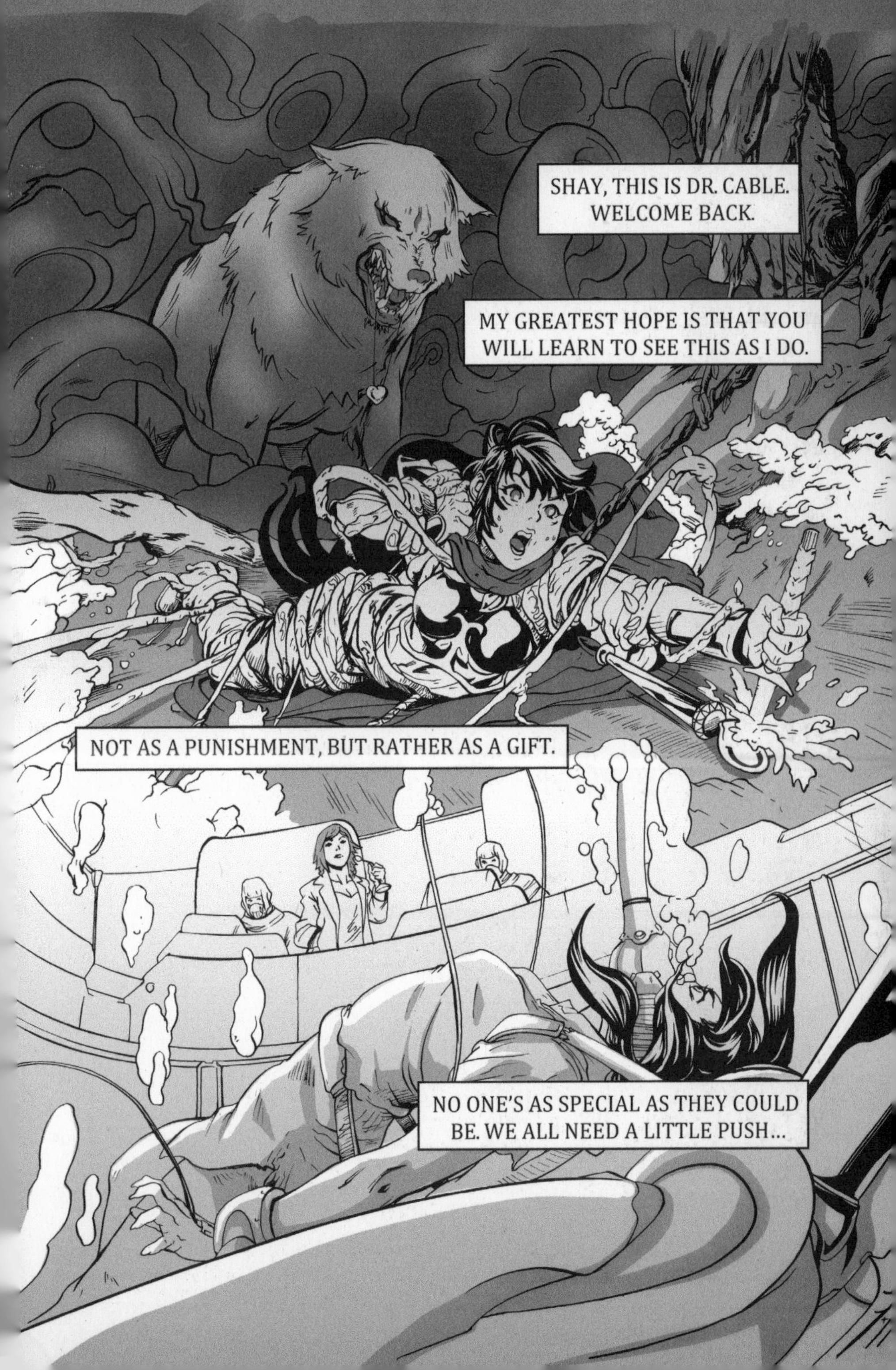
SHAY, THIS IS DR. CABLE. WELCOME BACK.
MY GREATEST HOPE IS THAT YOU WILL LEARN TO SEE THIS AS I DO.
NOT AS A PUNISHMENT, BUT RATHER AS A GIFT.
NO ONE'S AS SPECIAL AS THEY COULD BE. WE ALL NEED A LITTLE PUSH...

ABOUT THE CREATORS

Scott Westerfeld's novels include the Uglies series, the Leviathan trilogy, the Midnighters trilogy, *Peeps, The Last Days,* and more. Scott was born in Texas and alternates summers between Sydney, Australia, and New York City.

Steven Cummings lives with his family in the magical land known as almost-Tokyo. He has worked for a variety of comic and manga publishers, ranging from Marvel and DC to Tokyopop, on titles including *Wolverine: First Class, Elektra, Batman: Legends of the Dark Knight, Deadshot,* and *Pantheon High.* He is also a member of the Canadian art empire known as Udon.

Devin Grayson turned a lifelong obsession with fictional characters into a dynamic writing career. Best known for her work on the Batman titles for DC Comics and the celebrated *X-Men: Evolution* comic for Marvel, she has written in a number of different media and genres, from comic books and novels to videogame scripts and short essays.

ARTIST'S SKETCHBOOK

As with *Uglies: Shay's Story*, artist Steven Cummings worked very closely with Scott Westerfeld to create the unique look of the world of Uglies. Cutters presented a cool new challenge for Steven and Scott: creating Pretty versions of the characters—and designing the gorgeous, outrageous fashions of the Pretty world. Here are Steven's character designs for the Pretty versions of Tachs, Peris, Fausto, and Ho, and some concept art for Pretty fashions.

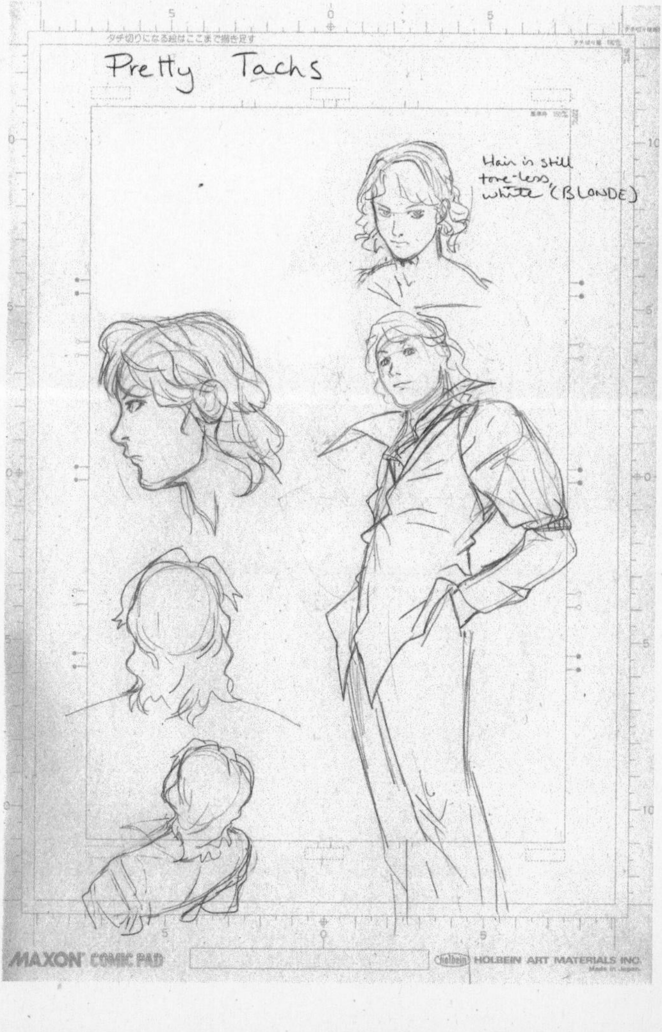
Pretty Tachs
Hair is still tone-less, white (BLONDE)
MAXON COMIC PAD
HOLBEIN ART MATERIALS INC.

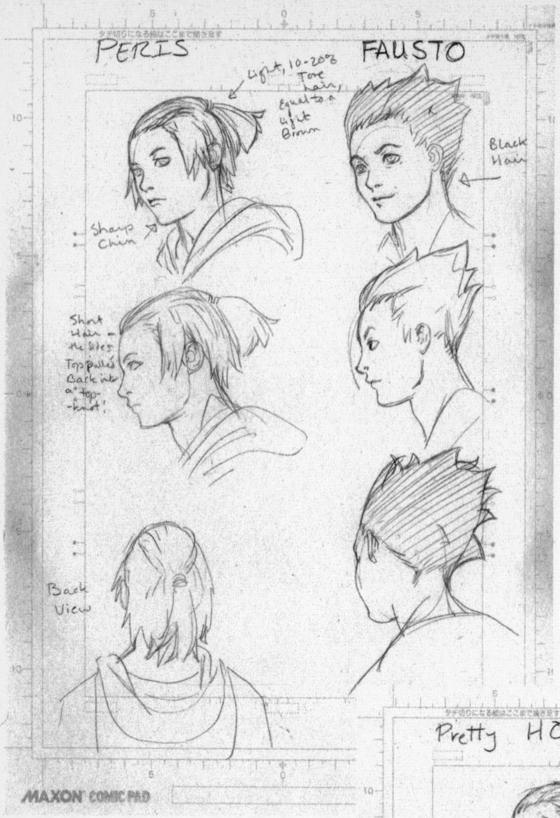
PERIS
FAUSTO
Light, 10-20% Tone hair, Equal to a Light Brown
Black Hair
Sharp Chin
Short Hair on the Sides Top pulled Back into a "top-knot"!
Back View
MAXON COMIC PAD

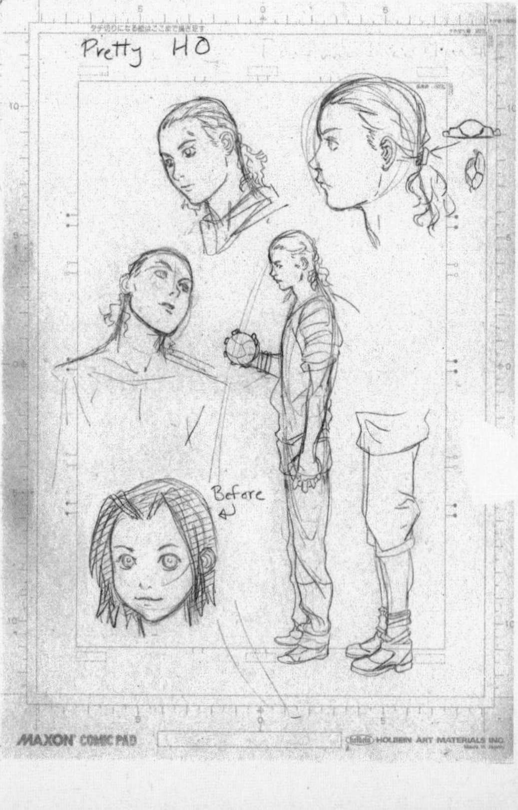
Pretty HO
Before
MAXON COMIC PAD
HOLBEIN ART MATERIALS INC.

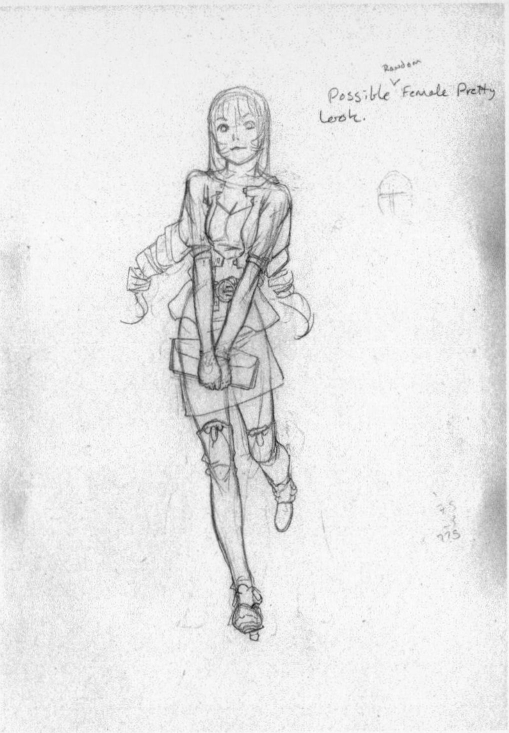
Possible Random Female Pretty Look.

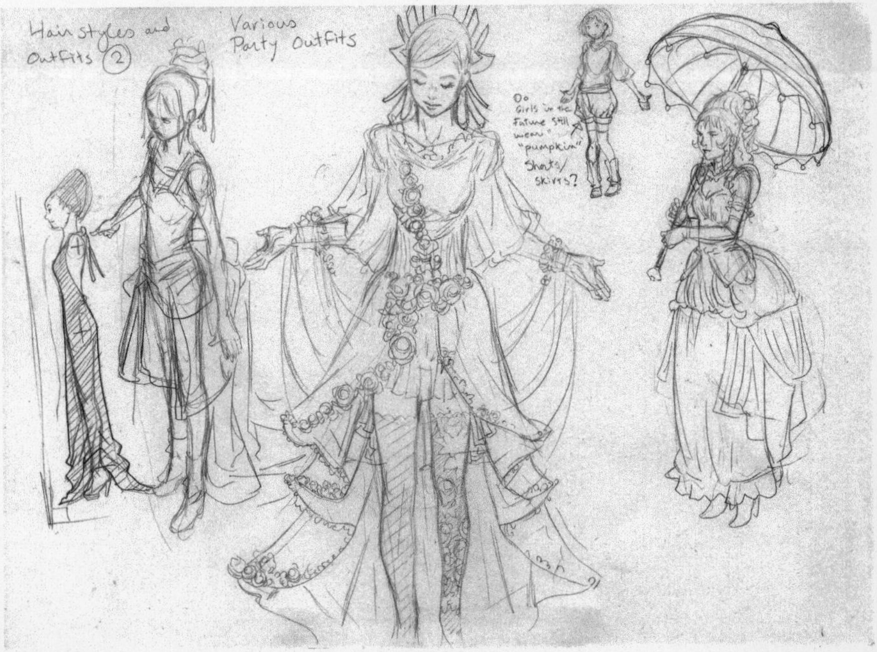
Hairstyles and Outfits 2
Various Party Outfits
Do Girls in the Future still wear "pumpkin" Shorts/ skirts?

Ranger Shay and Princess Tally

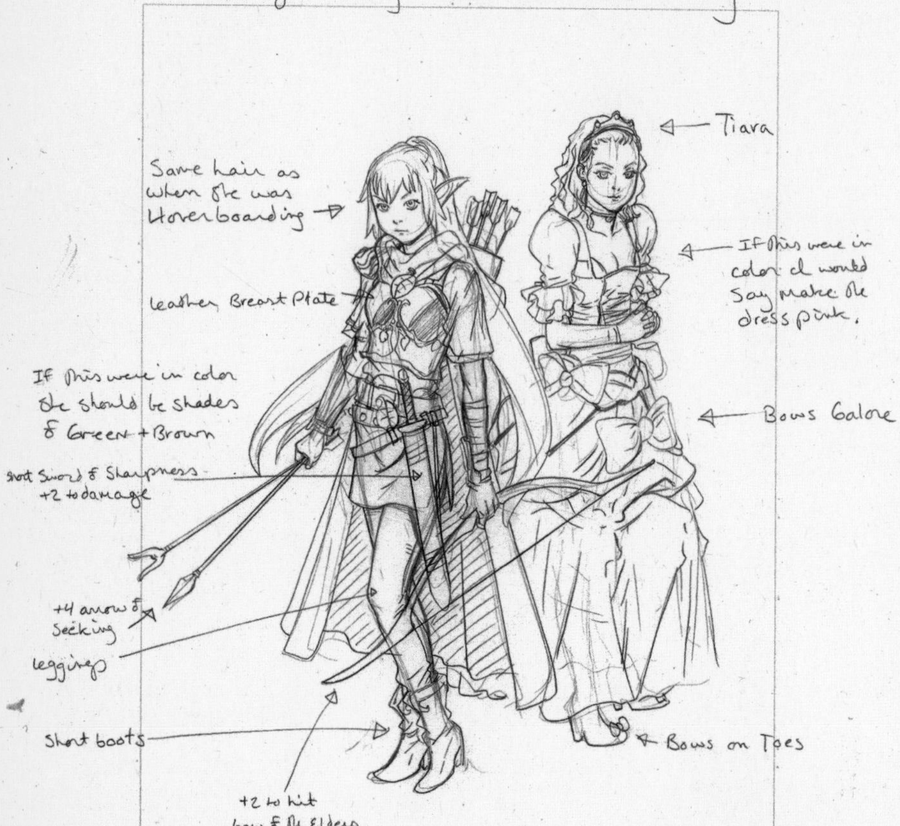

Tiara
Same hair as when she was Hoverboarding
If this were in color I would say make the dress pink.
Leather Breast Plate
If this were in color she should be shades of Green + Brown
Bows Galore
Short Sword of Sharpness +2 to damage
+4 arrow of seeking
leggings
Short boots
Bows on Toes
+2 to hit bow of the Elders.